A THOUSAND PIECES OF YOU

CLAUDIA GRAY

An Imprint of HarperCollinsPublishers

HarperTeen is an imprint of HarperCollins Publishers.

Library of Congress Cataloging-in-Publication Data
Gray, Claudia.
 A thousand pieces of you / Claudia Gray. — First edition.
    pages cm
 Summary: "When eighteen-year-old Marguerite Caine's father
is killed, she must leap into different dimensions and versions
of herself to catch her father's killer and avenge his murder"
—Provided by publisher.
 ISBN 978-0-06-227897-5
 [1. Space and time—Fiction. 2. Adventure and adventurers—
Fiction. 3. Family life—Fiction. 4. Murder—Fiction. 5. Science
fiction.] I. Title.
PZ7.G77625Tho 2014   2014001894
[Fic]—dc23   CIP
                                                              AC

Typography by Torborg Davern

18   19   CG/LSCC   20   19   18   17   16   15   14
                             ❖
First paperback edition, 2015

A
THOUSAND
PIECES
OF
YOU

Also by Claudia Gray

EVERNIGHT
STARGAZER
HOURGLASS
AFTERLIFE
BALTHAZAR

FATEFUL

SPELLCASTER
STEADFAST
SORCERESS

TEN THOUSAND SKIES ABOVE YOU

1

MY HAND SHAKES AS I BRACE MYSELF AGAINST THE BRICK
wall. Rain falls cold and sharp against my skin, from a sky
I've never seen before. It's hard to catch my breath, to get any
sense of where I am. All I know is that the Firebird worked.
It hangs around my neck, still glowing with the heat of the
journey.

There's no time. I don't know whether I have minutes,
or seconds, or even less. Desperately I tug at these unfamiliar clothes—the short dress and shiny jacket I wear have no
pockets, but there's a small bag dangling from my shoulder.
When I fish inside, I can't find a pen, but there's a lipstick.
Fingers trembling, I unscrew it and scrawl on a tattered
poster on the wall of the alley. This is the message I must
pass on, the one goal I have to remember after everything
else I am is gone.

KILL PAUL MARKOV.

Then I can only wait to die.

Die isn't the right word. This body will continue to breathe. The heart will continue to beat. But I won't be the Marguerite Caine living in it anymore.

Instead, this body will return to its rightful owner, the Marguerite who actually belongs in this dimension. The dimension I leaped into, using the Firebird. Her memories will take over again, any second, any moment, and while I know I'll awaken again in time, it's terrifying to think about . . . passing out. Getting lost. Being trapped inside her. Whatever it is that happens to people traveling from another dimension.

It hits me then. The Firebird *really* works. Travel between alternate dimensions is possible. I just proved it. Within my grief and fear, one small ember of pride glows, and it feels like the only heat or hope in the world. Mom's theories are true. My parents' work is vindicated. If only Dad could have known.

Theo. He's not here. It was unrealistic of me to hope he would be, but I hoped anyway.

Please let Theo be all right, I think. It would be a prayer if I still believed in anything, but my faith in God died last night too.

I lean against the brick wall, hands spread like a suspect's on a police car right before the cuffs go on. My heart hammers in my chest. Nobody has ever done this before—which means nobody knows what's about to happen to me. What if the Firebird can't bring me back to my own dimension?

What if this is how I die?

This time yesterday, my dad probably asked himself that same question.

I close my eyes tightly, and the cold rain on my face mingles with hot tears. Although I try not to picture how Dad died, the images force their way into my mind over and over: his car filling with water; brownish river lapping over the windshield; Dad probably dazed from the wreck but scrambling to get the door open, and failing. Gasping for the last inches of air in the car, thinking of me and Mom and Josie—

He must have been so scared.

Dizziness tilts the ground beneath my feet, weakens my limbs. This is it. I'm going under.

So I force my eyes open to stare at the message again. That's the first thing I want the other Marguerite to see. I want that message to stay with her, no matter what. If she sees that, if she keeps running over those words in her mind, that will awaken me within her as surely as the Firebird could. My hate is stronger than the dimensions, stronger than memory, stronger than time. My hate is now the truest part of who I am.

The dizziness builds, and the world turns fuzzy and gray, blackening the words *KILL PAUL MARKOV*—

—and then my vision clears. The word *KILL* sharpens back into focus.

Confused, I step back from the brick wall. I feel wide awake. More so than before, actually.

~~And as I stand there, staring down at~~ my high heels in a puddle, I realize that I'm not going anywhere.

Finally, as I begin to trust my luck, I step farther into the alley. The rain beats down harder on my face as I look up into the storm-drenched sky. A hovercraft looms low over the city like yet another thundercloud. Apparently it's there to fly holographic billboards across the city skyline. Astonished, I gaze at the hovercraft as it soars through this strange new dimension, 3D advertisements flickering through their motions in the sky around it: Nokia. BMW. Coca-Cola.

This is so like my world, and yet not my world at all.

Is Theo as overwhelmed by the journey as I am? He must be. His grief is nearly as deep as mine, even though Dad was only his adviser; more than that, this is what Theo and my parents worked for these past few years. Has he kept his memory as well? If so, we'll be in control throughout the trip, our minds piloting the selves born in this alternate dimension. That means Mom was wrong about one thing—which is kind of staggering, given that every other theory she's ever had has just been proved true. But I'm grateful for it, at least for the moment before my gratitude disintegrates in the hot blaze of anger.

Nothing can stop me now. If Theo made it too and he can find me—and I want so desperately for him to find me—then we'll be able to do this. We can get to Paul. We can take back the Firebird prototype he stole. And we can take our revenge for what he did to my father.

I don't know if I'm the kind of person who can kill a man in cold blood. But I'm going to find out.

2

I'M NOT A PHYSICIST LIKE MOM. NOT EVEN A GRAD STU-
dent in physics like Paul and Theo. I'm the homeschooled
daughter of two scientists who gave me a lot of leeway to
direct my own education. As the only right-brained member
of the family, I wound up pursuing my passion for painting
a whole lot more than I ever studied higher-level science. In
the fall, I'm headed to the Rhode Island School of Design,
where I'm going to major in art restoration. So if you want
to mix oil paints, stretch a canvas, or discuss Kandinsky, I'm
your girl. The science underlying cross-dimensional travel?
No such luck. But here's what I know:

The universe is in fact a multiverse. Countless quantum
realities exist, all layered within one another; we'll call these
dimensions, for short.

Each dimension represents one set of possibilities. Essen-
tially, everything that can happen does happen. There's a

dimension where the Nazis won World War II. A dimension where the Chinese colonized America long before Columbus ever sailed over. And a dimension where Brad Pitt and Jennifer Aniston are still married. Even a dimension just like my own, identical in every way, except on one day in fourth grade, that Marguerite chose to wear a blue shirt while I chose to wear a green one. Every possibility, every time fate flips a coin, splits the dimensions yet again, creating yet more layers of reality. It goes on and on forever, to infinity.

These dimensions aren't off in faraway outer space. They're literally all around us, even within us, but because they exist in another reality, we can't perceive them.

Early in her career, my mom, Dr. Sophia Kovalenka, hypothesized that we should be able not only to detect those dimensions but also to observe them—even interact with them. Everyone laughed. She wrote paper after paper, expanded her theory year after year, and nobody would listen.

Then one day, just when it looked like she was going to get permanently written off as a crackpot, she managed to publish one more paper pointing out parallels between wave theory and her work on dimensional resonance. Possibly only one scientist on earth took that paper seriously— Dr. Henry Caine, an English oceanographer. And physicist. And mathematician. And, obviously, overachiever. When he saw the paper, he was able to grasp potential that nobody else had ever seen before in the theory. This was lucky for Mom, because once they became research partners, her work really started to go somewhere.

This was even luckier for Josie and me, because Dr. Henry Caine would become our dad.

Fast-forward twenty-four years. Their work had reached the point where it was starting to attract notice even outside scientific circles. The experiments in which they'd shown evidence of alternate dimensions had been replicated by other scientists at Stanford and Harvard; nobody was laughing at them anymore. They were ready to try traveling between dimensions—or, at least, to fashion a device that could make it possible.

Mom's theory is that it would be very, very difficult for physical objects to move between dimensions, but energy should be able to move fairly easily. She also says consciousness is a form of energy. This led to all kinds of crazy speculation—but mostly Mom and Dad remained focused on building a device that would turn dimensional travel into more than a dream. Something that would allow people to journey to another dimension at will, and, even trickier, to come back again the same way.

This was daring. Even dangerous. The devices have to be made out of specific materials that move much more easily than other forms of matter; they have to anchor the consciousness of the traveler, which is apparently very difficult; and about a million other technical considerations I'd have to get umpteen physics degrees to even understand. Long story short: the devices are *really* hard to make. Which is why my parents went through several prototypes before even considering a test.

So when they finally had one that seemed like it would work, only a couple of weeks ago, we had to celebrate. Mom and Dad, who usually drink nothing stronger than Darjeeling, opened a bottle of champagne. Theo handed me a glass too, and nobody even cared.

"To the Firebird," Theo said. The final prototype lay on the table around which we stood, its workings gleaming, intricate layers of metal folded in and atop each other like an insect's wings. "Named after the legendary Russian creature that sends heroes on amazing quests and adventures"—here Theo nodded at my mother, before continuing—"and of course after my own muscle car, because yes, it's just that cool." Theo is a guy who says things like "muscle car" ironically. He says almost everything ironically. But there was real admiration in his eyes as he looked at my parents that night. "Here's hoping we have some adventures of our own."

"To the Firebird," Paul said. He must have been plotting what he was going to do right then, even as he lifted his glass and clinked it against Dad's.

Basically, after decades of struggle and ridicule, my parents had finally reached the point where they'd gained real respect—and they were on the brink of a breakthrough that would take them far beyond that. Mom would've been heralded as one of the leading scientists in all history. Dad would have gotten at least Pierre Curie status. We could maybe even have afforded for me to take a summer art tour in Europe, where I could go to the Hermitage and the Prado and every other amazing gallery I'd heard of but never seen before. Everything we'd ever dreamed of was on the horizon.

Then their trusted research assistant, Paul Markov, stole the prototype, killed my father, and ran.

He could have gotten away with it, slipping into another dimension beyond the reach of the law: the perfect crime. He vanished from his dorm room without a trace, leaving his door locked from the inside.

(Apparently when people travel between dimensions, their physical forms are "no longer observable," which is a quantum mechanics thing, and explaining it involves this whole story about a cat that's in a box and is simultaneously alive and dead until you open the box, and it gets seriously complicated. *Never* ask a physicist about that cat.)

Nobody could find Paul; nobody could catch him. But Paul didn't count on Theo.

Theo came to me earlier this evening as I sat on the rickety old deck in our backyard. The only illumination came from the full moon overhead and the lights Josie had strung on the railing last summer, the ones shaped like tropical fish that glowed aquamarine and orange. I had on one of Dad's old cardigans over my ivory lace dress. Even in California, December nights can be cold, and besides—the sweater still smelled like Dad.

I think Theo had watched me for a while before he came out there, waiting for me to pull myself together. My cheeks were flushed and tear streaked. I'd blown my nose so many times that it felt raw every time I inhaled. My head throbbed. But for the moment, I'd cried myself out.

Theo sat on the steps beside me, jittery, on edge, one foot bouncing up and down. "Listen," he said. "I'm about to do something stupid."

"What?"

His dark eyes met mine, so intent that I thought, for one crazy moment, despite everything that was going on, he was about to kiss me.

Instead, he held out his hand. In it were the two other versions of the Firebird. "I'm going after Paul."

"You—" My wavering voice, already strained from crying, broke. I had so many questions that I couldn't even begin at first. "You still have the old prototypes? I thought you broke them down afterward."

"That's what Paul thought too. And—well, technically, always what your parents thought." He hesitated. Even mentioning Dad, only a day after his death, hurt so terribly—for Theo nearly as much as for me. "But I kept the parts we didn't reuse. Tinkered with them, borrowed some equipment from the Triad labs. Used the advances we made on the last Firebird to improve these two. There's a decent shot one of these will work."

A decent shot. Theo was about to take an incredible risk because it gave him a "decent shot" at avenging what Paul had done.

As funny as he'd always been, as flirty as we occasionally got, I'd sometimes wondered whether Theo Beck was full of crap underneath his indie band T-shirts and his hipster hat and the 1981 Pontiac he'd fixed up himself. Now I was ashamed to have ever doubted him.

"When people travel through dimensions," he said, staring down at the prototypes, "they leave traces. Subatomic—okay, I'm gonna cut to the chase. The point is, I can go after Paul. No matter how often he jumps, how many dimensions he tries to move through, he'll always leave a trace. And I know how to set these to follow that trace. Paul can run, but he can't hide."

The Firebirds glinted in his palm. They looked like odd, asymmetrical bronze lockets—maybe jewelry fashioned in the era of Art Nouveau, when organic shapes were all the rage. One of the metals inside was rare enough that it could only be mined in a single valley in the whole world, but anyone who didn't know better would just think they were pretty. Instead the Firebirds were the keys to unlock the universe. No—the *universes*.

"Can you follow him anywhere?"

"Almost anywhere," Theo answered, and he gave me a look. "You know the limits, right? You didn't tune out *every* time we talked about this around the dinner table?"

"I know the limits," I said, stung. "I meant, within those."

"Then yeah."

Living beings can only travel to dimensions where they already exist. A dimension where my parents never met? That's a dimension I can never see. A dimension where I'm already dead? Can't get there from here. Because when a

person travels to another dimension, they actually material-
ize *within* their other self. Wherever that other version of you
might be, whatever they're doing: that's where you are.

"What if Paul jumps somewhere you can't follow?" I
asked.

Theo shrugged. "I'll end up in the next universe over,
I guess. But it's no big. When he jumps again, I'll have a
chance to pick up his trace from there." His gaze was far
away as he turned the Firebirds over in his palm.

To me it sounded like Paul's best bet would be to keep
jumping, as fast as he could, until he found a universe where
none of the rest of us existed. Then he could remain there as
long as he liked, without ever getting caught.

But the thing was, Paul wanted something besides destroying my parents. No matter what a creep he'd turned out to
be, he wasn't stupid. So I knew he wouldn't do this out of
sheer cruelty. If he'd just wanted money, he would have sold
the device to somebody in his own dimension, not fled into
another one.

Whatever he wanted, he couldn't hide forever. Sooner or
later, Paul would have to go after his true, secret goal. When
he did, that was when we could catch him.

We could catch him. Not Theo alone—both of us. Theo
held two prototypes in his hand.

The cool breeze ruffled my hair and made the lights flutter back and forth on the deck railing, like the plastic fish
were trying to swim away. I said, "What happens if the Firebird doesn't actually work?"

He scraped his Doc Martens against the old wood of the deck; a bit of it splintered away. "Well, it might not do anything. I might just stand there feeling stupid."

"That's the worst-case scenario?"

"No, the worst-case scenario involves me getting blended into so much atomic soup."

"Theo—"

"Won't happen," he said, cocky as ever. "At least, I strongly doubt it."

My voice was hardly more than a whisper. "But you'd take that risk. For Dad's sake."

Our eyes met as Theo said, "For all of you."

I could hardly breathe.

But he glanced away after only a second, adding, "Like I said, it won't happen. Probably either of these would work. I mean, I rebuilt them, and as we both know, I'm brilliant."

"When you guys were talking about testing one of these, you said there was no way in hell any of you should even consider it."

"Yeah, well, I exaggerate a lot. You must have realized that by now." Theo may be full of it, but I give him this: at least he *knows* he's full of it. "And besides, that was before I got to work on them. The Firebirds are better now than ever before."

It wasn't like I made a decision at any one moment. When Theo came to sit with me on the deck, I felt powerless against the tragedy that had ripped my family in two; by the time I spoke, I'd known exactly what I intended to do for what seemed like a long time. "If you're that sure, then okay. I'm in."

"Whoa. Hang on. I never said this was a trip for two."

I pointed at the Firebird lockets. "Count 'em."

His fist closed around the Firebirds, and he stared down at his hand like he wished he hadn't brought them both and given me the idea—but too bad, and too late.

Quietly I said, "You're not to blame. But you're also not talking me out of it."

Theo leaned closer to me, and the smirk was gone. "Marguerite, have you thought about the risks you'd be taking?"

"They're no worse than the risks you'd take. My dad is *dead*. Mom deserves some justice. So Paul has to be stopped. I can help you stop him."

"It's dangerous. I'm not even talking about the dimension-jumping stuff right now. I mean—we don't know what kind of worlds we'll find ourselves in. All we know is that, wherever we end up, Paul Markov is there, and he's a volatile son of a bitch."

Paul, volatile. Two days earlier, I would have laughed at that. To me Paul had always seemed as quiet and stolid as the rock cliffs he climbed on weekends.

Now I knew that Paul was a murderer. If he'd do that to my father, he'd do it to Theo or me. None of that mattered anymore.

I said, "I have to do this, Theo. It's important."

"It is important. That's why I'm doing it. Doesn't mean you have to."

"Think about it. You can't jump into any dimensions where you don't exist. There are probably some dimensions I exist in that you don't."

"And vice versa," he retorted.

"Still." I took Theo's free hand then, like I could make him understand how serious I was just by squeezing tightly. "I can follow him to places where you can't. I extend your reach. I make the chances of finding him a lot better. Don't argue with me, because you know it's true."

Theo breathed out, squeezed my hand back, let it go, and ran his fingers through his spiky hair. He was restless and jumpy as always—but I could tell he was considering it.

When his dark eyes next met mine, he sighed. "If your mother had any idea we were talking about this, she'd skin me alive. I'm not being metaphorical about that. I think she could actually, literally skin me. She gets the wild eyes sometimes. There's Cossack blood in her; I'd bet anything."

I hesitated for a moment, thinking of what this meant for my mother. If something went wrong on this trip—if I turned into atomic soup—she would have lost both me and Dad within the space of two days. There weren't even words for what that would do to her.

But if Paul got away with it, that would kill her just as surely—and me, too. I wasn't going to let that happen. "You're already talking about Mom's revenge. That means we're doing this together, doesn't it?"

"Only if you're absolutely sure. Please think about this for a second first."

"I've thought about it," I said, which wasn't exactly true, but it didn't matter. I meant it then as much as I mean it now. "I'm in."

That's how I got here.

But where is here, exactly? As I walk along the street, crowded despite the late hour, I try to study my surroundings. Wherever I am, it's not California.

Picasso could have painted this city with its harsh angles, its rigidity, and the way dark lines of steel seem to slash through buildings like knife strokes. I imagine myself as one of the women he painted—face divided in two, asymmetrical and contradictory, one half appearing to smile while the other is silently screaming.

I stop in my tracks. By now I've found my way to the riverside, and across the dark water, illuminated by spotlights, is a building I recognize: St. Paul's Cathedral.

London. I'm in London.

Okay. All right. That makes sense. Dad is . . . he was English. He didn't move to the United States until he and Mom started working together. In this dimension, I guess she came to his university instead, and we all live here in London.

The thought of my father alive again, somewhere nearby, bubbles up inside me until I can hardly think of anything else. I want to run to him right now, right this second, and hug him tight and apologize for every time I ever talked back to him or made fun of his dorky bow ties.

But this version of my dad won't be my dad. He'll be another version. This Marguerite's father.

I don't care. This is as close as I'm ever going to get to Dad again, and I'm not wasting it.

Okay. Next step: discover where this version of *home* is.

The three trips I've taken to London to visit Aunt Susannah were all fairly quick; Aunt Susannah's all about shopping and gossip, and as much as Dad loved his sister, he could take about six days with her, maximum, before he lost it. But I was there long enough to know that London shouldn't look anything like this.

Even as I walk along the street by the South Bank of the Thames, I can tell computers were invented a little earlier here, because they've advanced further. Several people, despite the drizzling rain, have paused to bring up little glowing squares of light—like computer screens, except they've appeared in thin air in front of their users. One woman is talking to a face; that must be a holographic phone call. As I stand there, one of my wide bangle bracelets is shimmering with light. I lift my wrist closer to my face and read the words, written on the inside in small metallic type:

ConTech Personal Security
DEFENDER Model 2.8
Powered by Verizon

I'm not quite sure what that means, but I don't think this bracelet is just a bracelet.

What other kinds of advanced technology do they have here? To everybody else in this dimension, all this stuff is beyond routine. Both the hoverships above London and the no-rail monorail snaking along overhead are filled with bored passengers, for whom this is just the end of another dull day.

There's no place like home, I think, but the feeble joke falls flat even inside my own head. I look down again at the high heels I wear, so unlike my usual ballet flats. Ruby slippers they're not.

Then I remind myself that I've got the most powerful technology of all—the Firebird—hanging around my neck. I open the locket and look at the device inside.

It's complicated. *Very* complicated. The thing reminds me of our universal remote, which has so many keys and buttons and functions that nobody in my household—which contains multiple physicists, including my mother who is supposed to be the next Einstein—*none* of us can figure out how to switch from the Playstation to the DVR. But just like with the universal remote, I've learned a few functions, the ones that matter most: How to jump into a new dimension. How to jump back from one if I land somewhere immediately dangerous. How to spark a "reminder," if needed.

(The idea was that people who traveled between dimensions wouldn't remain fully conscious throughout—that they'd be more or less asleep within the other versions of themselves. So you can use the Firebird to create a reminder, which would leave your consciousness in control for a while longer. Well, so much for theory. As far as I can tell, the reminders aren't necessary at all.)

As I look down at the glittering Firebird in my palm, I remind myself that if I learned how to work this thing, I can handle anything this dimension has to throw at me. Re-energized, I start observing the people around me more closely. *Watch and learn.*

A woman touches a metal tab clipped to her sleeve, and a holographic computer screen appears in front of her. Quickly I run my hands over my own clothes; this silver jacket doesn't have anything like that on the sleeves, but something similar is pinned to my lapel. I tap it—and jump as a hologram screen appears in front of me. The hologram jumps with me, tethered to the metal tab.

Okay, that's . . . pretty cool. Now what? Voice commands, like Siri on my phone? Can something be "touch-screen" if there's no screen to touch? Experimentally I hold out one hand, and a holographic keyboard appears in front of the screen. So if I pretend to type on it . . .

Sure enough, the words I type appear on the screen, in the search window: *PAUL MARKOV.*

As soon as the eighty zillion results pop up, I feel like a fool. Markov is a fairly common last name in Russia, where Paul's parents emigrated from when he was four; Paul, which has a Russian form too (Pavel), is also popular. So thousands and thousands of people have that name.

So I try again, searching for *Paul Markov* plus *physicist.* There's no guarantee Paul would be a physics student here, too, except that I have to start somewhere, and apparently physics is the only human endeavor he remotely understands.

These results look more promising. Most of them focus on the University of Cambridge, so I pull up the one titled "Faculty Profile." It's for a professor with another name altogether, but the profile lists his research assistants, and sure enough, there's Paul Markov's photo. It's him.

Cambridge. That's in England too. I could get there within a couple of hours—

Which means he could get here within a couple of hours.

We can track Paul, because the Firebirds allow us to know when a dimensional breach occurs. But that means Paul can also track us.

If this is the right dimension—if this is where Paul fled after cutting my dad's brakes and stealing the final Firebird—then Paul already knows I'm here.

Maybe he'll run away, fleeing to the next dimension.

Or maybe he's already coming after me.

3

I HUG MYSELF AS I WALK THROUGH THE MIST. IT FEELS AS though I'm splintering into a dozen directions at once—grief, then rage, then panic. The last thing I need right now is to lose it. Instead I force my mind to go to the place that always calms and centers me: painting.

If I were going to paint the dimension I see in front of me, I'd load my palette up with burnt umber, opaque black, a spectrum of grays—nothing brighter than that. I'd have to grind something into the paint with my thumb, some sort of grit or ash, because the grime here goes deeper than surfaces. Even the air feels dirty against my skin. There's less old stone in this London than I remember, more hard metal. Fewer trees and plants, too. The chill in the air is sharp; this is early December, and yet I'm wearing only a short black dress and a flimsy jacket brighter than tinfoil.

(Yes, it's definitely December. The devices allow dimensional travel, not time travel. "That's another Nobel Prize altogether," Mom once said cheerfully, like she might turn to it whenever she got a spare moment.)

Imagining painting helps a little, but my freak-out only halts when my ring starts blinking.

Startled, I stare down at the silvery band around my right pinky, which is shimmering in loops. My first thought is that it's some kind of LED thing, meant for showing off in nightclubs. But if metal tabs on my jacket create holographic computers, what might this do?

So I reach over and tentatively give the ring a tap. The glow swirls out, a miniature spotlight, and a hologram takes shape in the space in front of me. I'm startled for the one instant it takes me to recognize the face painted in the silver-blue shimmer: "Theo!"

"Marguerite!" He grins, relief shining from him as brilliantly as the hologram beams. "It is you, right?"

"It's me. Oh, my God, you made it. You're alive. I was so scared."

"Hey." His voice can sound so warm, when he wants it to; for all Theo's faux arrogance—and his real arrogance—he sees more about people than he lets on. "Don't waste any more time worrying about me, okay? I always land on the right side. Just like loaded dice."

Even in the middle of all this, Theo is trying to make me laugh. Instead I feel a sudden lump in my throat. After the past twenty-four hours—a day in which my father died, my friend betrayed us, and I leaped out of my home dimension into places unknown—I'm running on empty. I say, "If I'd lost you, I don't think I could have taken it."

"Hey, hey. I'm fine. I'm absolutely fine. See?"

"You sure are." I try to make it flirtatious. Maybe it works, maybe not. I kind of suck at flirting. At any rate, the attempt makes me feel steadier.

He becomes businesslike, or at least as businesslike as someone like Theo can get. His dark eyes—strangely transparent through the hologram—search my face. "Okay, so, you recently had a reminder, because you remember me. That or I'm making one hell of a first impression."

"No, I didn't need a reminder. I remembered everything anyway."

"You said you remembered yourself anyway?" He leans forward intently, temporarily distorting the holographic image. "No periods of confusion?"

"None. Looks like it's that way for you too. Guess Mom was wrong about dimensional travelers forgetting themselves."

But Theo shakes his head. "No. I needed—you know, I used a reminder right when I got here."

"Weird."

Theo seems slightly freaked by the fact that I remember things so easily. That works against all Mom's theories— and, apparently, his own experience—but I guess traveling between dimensions is different for different people. Theories only get refined through experimentation. Mom and Dad taught me that much.

He says only, "Well, about time we caught a lucky break, because we were seriously overdue."

"Where are you?"

"Boston. Looks like I'm at MIT in this dimension. I'm doing my best not to acknowledge all the Red Sox shirts in this closet." Theo doesn't care for sports at all—at least, in our dimension. "I thought I'd gone a long way, but damn, Meg. You landed all the way in London."

Theo started calling me Meg a couple of months ago. I'm still not sure whether it's annoying or cute. But I like how he always smiles when he says it. "How did you track me down so fast? Did you hack my personal information, something like that?"

He raises one eyebrow. "I searched for you online, found your profile, and put through a call request, which the local equivalent of Facebook offers as an option. When I called, you answered. Not exactly rocket science, and I say this as someone who seriously considered rocket science as a career."

"Oh. Okay." Well, that's a relief. Maybe not everything has to be hard. Maybe we can catch the occasional break, and get lucky like we did this time.

Even though our devices are both set to follow in Paul's footsteps, there are no guarantees. We could be separated at any jump. Not this time, though. This time Theo is with me. I look at his face, hazy in the ring's glow, and wish he were here by my side already.

"Have you managed to . . ." Then my voice trails off, because for the first time I'm calm enough to realize I have an English accent now. Just like Dad's.

Which makes sense, of course, because I live here. I guess speaking is a kind of muscle memory that lingers even while the other Marguerite's consciousness is in the passenger seat, so to speak. But it hits me as the weirdest, coolest, funniest thing imaginable.

"Bath," I say, relishing the short *A* of my new accent. "Baaaath. Privacy. Aluminium. Laboratory. Tomato. Schhhhhhedule."

The giggles come over me, and I stop right there, hand against my chest, trying to catch my breath. I know I'm laughing mostly because I refuse to give in and start crying. The grief for my father has nowhere to go and is twisting every other mood I have into knots. And . . . *tomahhhhto.* That's hilarious.

As I wipe away tears of laughter, Theo says, "You're kinda shaky right now, huh?"

My voice is all squeaky as I try to hold it in. "I guess."

"Well, if you were wondering, you sound adorable."

The silly moment passes as soon as it came, replaced by anger and fright. This must be what the brink of hysteria feels like; I have to hold on. "Theo, Paul's very close to London. If he knows we've come to this dimension, he could be on his way here, now."

"What? How do you know that?"

"You're not the only one who's used a computer before, you know. I tracked Paul down at Cambridge."

I look through the night at the harsh cityscape across the

26

river, where the jagged dark outlines of skyscrapers dwarf the dome of the cathedral. Paul might be here already. How long would it take him to reach London?

Fiercely I remind myself that if Paul's chasing me, it saves me the trouble of chasing him. The next time we meet, one of us is going to be sorry, and it won't be me.

I must look murderous, because Theo says, "We have to remember one thing, okay? There's a slim chance I calibrated wrong. We could have jumped into the wrong dimension. The Paul Markov in this dimension might not be our Paul. So we can't overreact until we know the facts."

What he's really saying is, I can't kill an innocent man. I'm not even sure I can kill the guilty one, though I mean to try. My limited skills with the Firebird mean I can't tell the difference between our Paul and any other; it's just one more reason I need Theo with me.

"How fast can you get here?" I ask.

Theo gives me that sly grin of his. "Already bought my ticket, Meg. Couldn't take my pick of flights, traveling last minute—gotta go all the way to Germany and back again, so thanks, Lufthansa—but I should be there by midnight tomorrow. Fast enough for you?"

He's already crossed a dimension to help me; now he's going to cross half the globe, as fast as humanly possible, and the one thing Theo asks is whether he's doing it all fast enough. I whisper, "Thank you."

"We're in this together," Theo says, like it's no big deal. "Listen, if I've figured these ring-phone things out, and I think I have, you can give me tracker access."

"What is that?"

"Hold your ring up to the hologram, okay?" I do it. The ring glitters, and in the holographic screen, I can see his ring light up as well. Theo grins. "Good. Now I can find you any time you've got that ring on, or you can find me. Once you figure out the interface, that is. Okay, where are you headed?"

"Home, I guess. Once I figure out where it is." I laugh. Suddenly Theo looks stricken. Why should he look like that?

"Marguerite—" His voice is very quiet, very serious, not like the usual Theo at all.

Fear flickers stronger within me, and quickly I search for HENRY CAINE AND SOPHIA KOVALENKA. Results pop up instantly: physics papers, a few faculty photos from when they were younger, and video clips.

Video of the hovership accident from years ago, the one that killed three dozen people, including two promising scientists and their older daughter.

I don't have Dad back. He's dead here too. The only difference is that Mom is gone too. And Josie.

My whole family is dead.

I suck in a breath, hard, as if I'd been struck. As though at a great distance, I hear Theo's voice say, "Marguerite? Are you okay?"

I don't answer. I can't.

The holographic screen helpfully starts showing me the video of the wreck, which apparently was a big thing on the news. Right now it feels like that explosion is happening

inside my head, white heat and blinding light and everything I love, everyone who really loved me—Dad and Mom
and Josie—burning to cinders.

It happened above San Francisco. The news articles say
bits and scraps of the wreckage turned up as far away as Las
Vegas, drifting down to earth, sometimes washed down
with the rain.

"Marguerite?" The shimmering of the hologram doesn't
hide the concern on Theo's face. "Your folks—I'm sorry.
I'm so sorry. When I came to in this dimension, I looked
them up first thing—thought they could maybe help us, you
know? I didn't realize you hadn't learned what happened to
them yet."

My heart has been crying out for Dad, over and over,
since the moment the police called our house. I'd even cherished a small hope of seeing him again here, at least a version
of him.

But he's still gone, still dead, and now Mom and Josie are
as lost as he is.

They're fine! I try to tell myself. *That happened in this dimension, but not yours. When you go back home, Mom and Josie will be
there waiting for you—it's not like here, you didn't lose everything,
not absolutely everything—it's going to be okay—*

But it's not. Dad is still gone.

"Why does anybody want to travel through dimensions,
anyway?" I choke out. My fingernails dig into the flesh of
my forearms, which are crossed in front of me like a shield.
The physical pain keeps me from crying; no matter what,

29

I refuse to cry. "They haven't thought enough about what they might find."

"I'm sorry," Theo repeats. He looks like he wants to step forward through the hologram to get to me. "I'm so sorry."

I think, *Is this what you wanted, Paul? Did you hate them so much that you ran to a world where they were already dead? So your work would be done for you?*

Once again I remember Paul's unsmiling face, his gray eyes that seemed to stare through me. I remember the day he watched me painting, his gaze following every stroke my brush made on the canvas. It sickens me now to think that for a little while I almost—

Theo speaks again, his voice firmer this time. "That accident was a long time ago, and a lifetime away. You've gotta think of it like that. All right?"

His words break through my melancholy, bring me back to the now. "All right. Yes. It was just a shock. I won't let it get to me again."

He does me the courtesy of pretending to believe me. "Until tomorrow, hang in there and stay safe. And if you see Paul . . . don't let him see you."

The hologram blinks out. Though I stare down at my ring, hoping against hope that he'll call back, it remains dull metal, silent and dark.

So I go home.

My blinky ring also has a GPS system, and when I ask it to guide me home, it does. I follow its directions without any idea of where I'll end up.

Turns out home is in a particularly posh building—less garish than most of those around, but no less cold. The elevator is one of those glass ones on the outside, which I think are designed specifically to terrify the acrophobic. I expect to feel a little comforted when I walk inside, because her apartment must be, in part, my apartment too. But the minute I see it, I think that I've never seen any place that looked less like home.

It feels like an art gallery, but one of the ones that only shows weird, pop-kitsch art like rhinestone-studded cow skulls. Or maybe it's like a hospital where they do plastic surgery on celebrities. Stark white and brushed metal, no soft seats, nothing comfortable or cozy, and so brightly lit you could see a single speck of dust—which I guess is the idea. I stand there, dripping wet from the rain, aware of myself as grubby, awkward, and misplaced.

Never could I have felt like I belonged here.

"Marguerite?" Aunt Susannah steps out from the hallway in a dressing gown as pristinely white as the decor. I guess I was put into the custody of my Aunt Susannah, of all people.

Her hair is loose, ready for bed, but still falls neatly to her shoulders as if it didn't dare put one wisp astray. She doesn't seem to be that different in this dimension. As she rubs some expensive cream into her face, she says, "You're back awfully early tonight."

It's after one a.m. What time do I normally come home? "I was tired."

"Are you feeling well?"

I shrug.

Aunt Susannah lets that go. "Best get to bed, then. You don't want to make yourself ill."

"Okay. Good night, Aunt Susannah."

She pauses. Do I not say that to her often? I don't sense maternal warmth from her; she's not the maternal type. It's not that I don't love her—I do. And she loves me, too. But I'm guessing parenting didn't come easily to her. Aunt Susannah says simply, "All right. Good night, dear."

As she pads down the hall to her room, I go to the other door, to the room that must be mine.

It's so—*blank*. Not as fancy as the rest of the apartment, but there's nothing about this space that makes me feel like it belongs to me. It might as easily be a room in a luxury hotel.

But that, I realize, must be the point.

The Marguerite who lost her family so young is one who has spent the rest of her life trying not to love anyone or anything that much again.

I haven't decorated a bulletin board with postcards and prints of images I find inspiring. No easel stands in the corner with my latest canvas; do I paint in this dimension at all? No bookshelves. No books. Although I try to hope this dimension's Marguerite has some kind of technologically advanced e-reader in her earrings or something, that's beginning to seem unlikely. She doesn't appear to be the bookish type.

The clothes in my closet include a lot of designer labels I recognize, and some I don't, but I'd wager they're high-end

32

too. None of them are the kinds of things I'd wear at home—instead they're all metallic or leather or plastic, anything hard and shiny. Maybe I ought to be enthused that the Caine family money apparently held out a couple of generations longer in this dimension, but all I can think about is how cold this life is.

Now I have to live in it.

My hand closes around the Firebird locket. I could take it off now if I wanted, since I don't seem to need the reminders. But even the thought of being separated from it terrifies me. Instead I close my eyes and imagine that it could help me fly away to a new place, not this life or my old life, but some newer, shinier reality where everything is okay and nothing can hurt me ever again.

My legs seem to give out, and I flop down on the immaculately made bed. For a long time I lie there, curled in a ball, wishing to be home—my real home—more desperately than I'd known I could ever wish for anything.

4

AS I LIE HERE IN A DIMENSION NOT MY OWN, ON A STARK white bed more forbidding than comforting, I try to paint pictures of home in my mind. I want every face, every corner, every shadow, every beam. I want my reality painted over this one until I can't see the blinding white any longer.

My home—my real home—is in California.

Our house isn't on the beach; it's nestled at the foot of the hills in the shade of tall trees. It's always clean but never neat. Books are piled two deep on the shelves that line nearly every room, Mom's houseplants thrive in every corner and nook, and years ago my parents covered the entire hallway with that chalkboard paint that's meant for little kids' rooms but works perfectly well for physics equations.

When I was little, my friends would get so excited when I told them that my parents did most of their scientific work at home, and they'd come in for the first time looking around for bubbling beakers or dynamos or whatever devices sci-fi shows had taught them to expect. What it mostly means is papers piled on every flat surface. Sure, lately we've had a few gadgets, but only a few. Nobody wants to hear that theoretical physics has less to do with shiny lasery stuff and more to do with numbers.

In the center of the great room is our dinner table, an enormous round wooden one Mom and Dad bought for cheap at a Goodwill back when Josie and I were little. They let us paint it in a rainbow of colors, just goop it on with our hands, because they loved hearing us laugh and also because no two human beings on earth ever cared less about how their furniture looked. Josie thought it was funny to smear swirls on with her fingers. For me, though—that was the first time I noticed how different colors looked when you blended them together, contrasted one next to another. It might have been the moment I fell in love with painting.

"I guess you think painting isn't as important as physics," I said to Paul as I sat at my easel, that one day he watched me work.

"Depends on what you mean by important," he replied.

I could have thrown him out right then. Why didn't I?

My memories become dreams as I fall asleep without knowing it. All night I see Paul's face in front of mine, staring at me, questioning me, planning something I can't guess. The next morning, when I wake up in this cold, foreign bed, I can't remember the dreams. I only know that I tried to go after Paul but never could move.

Surprisingly, there's no disorientation. From the first moment I open my eyes, I know where I am, who I am, and who I'm supposed to be. I remember what Paul did to my father, that I'll never see Dad again. As I lie there amid the rumpled white sheets, I realize how little I want to move. My grief feels like ropes tying me down.

"Come along, sweetie!" Aunt Susannah calls. "Time to make yourself pretty!"

Not unless the technology in this dimension borders on the miraculous. I sit up, catch a glimpse of my crazy bedhead curls reflected in the window, and groan.

Apparently we're going to a "charity luncheon," though my aunt doesn't remotely care about whatever charity it's for; she doesn't even remember what it is. It's a society event—a place to see and be seen—and that's all that matters to Aunt Susannah.

Still, I know I have to stay put and wait for Theo. If I'm going to stop Paul, I'll need all the help I can get—and Theo is the only one who can help me. So, for one whole day, I have to lead this Marguerite's life.

From what I can tell, it's not much fun.

"Come on, dear." Aunt Susannah trips along the cobblestone street in her high-heeled shoes, as nimble as a mountain goat. "We can't be late."

"Can't we?" The idea of navigating a whole social event as another version of myself—it's pretty intimidating.

She gives me a confused glance over her shoulder. "But I wanted you to get to know the duchess. Her niece Romola is at Chanel, you know. If you want to be a fashion designer someday, you've got to make some connections now."

In this reality, I want to be a fashion designer? Well, at least that's creative. "Right. Sure."

"Don't pretend you're too sophisticated to be impressed by a title," Aunt Susannah says. She gets like this—brisk and slightly contemptuous—whenever she's challenged. "You're an even bigger snob than I am, and you know it. Just like your mother."

"What did you say?"

"I know, I know, to you your parents are saints, and they should be. I'm not saying they weren't *absolutely lovely* people. But how your mother used to go on about being descended from Russian nobility! You'd think she personally fled the Red Army with the Romanov jewels in her arms."

"Her family *was* from the nobility. They did flee the Revolution. They were expats in Paris for the next four generations, before her parents finally moved to America. She'd never lie about being something she's not." Then I remember that I'm not supposed to have known my mother very well in this dimension, and that here, she's as lost to me as my father. "I mean, she wouldn't have."

And Mom wouldn't. She only cares about two things: science and the people she loves. The one who wears her crazy-curly hair twisted back with whatever pencil or pen she finds lying around. The one who let me finger paint the table. Nobody on earth is less of a snob than Mom.

We're standing in the middle of the street now, still a block short of the hotel where the duchess and a hundred and forty of her closest friends are taking tea. Aunt Susannah puts one hand to her chest like an actress in a cheesy old movie, and yet I know she's sincere—as sincere as she knows how to be, at least. "I wasn't putting your mum down. You realize that, don't you?"

From Aunt Susannah, "snob" is practically a merit badge. I sigh. "Yeah. I know."

"Now, I'd hate for us to be cross with each other." My aunt comes close and puts her arm around me. "It's always been just us. You and me against the world, hmm?"

I could almost believe we had a good life together, if I hadn't been in that impersonal apartment. Or if I didn't see through the translucent lenses of Aunt Susannah's sunglasses to her bored, impatient gaze.

It's taken me less than a day to discover that Aunt Susannah resents having to play surrogate parent to this dimension's Marguerite. What must it have been like for her to live a whole lifetime knowing that? To feel so rejected by the only family she had left in the world?

"You and me," I repeat, and Aunt Susannah smiles like that's a reason to be happy.

In my real home, it's never been "just us."

As long as I can remember, Mom and Dad's research assistants have spent nearly as much time at my house as I do. When

I was very young, I thought they were as much my siblings as Josie was; I cried so hard the day Swathi gently explained that she was going back to live in New Delhi because she had a job and a family there. Who were these people? How could they be her family when *we* were her family?

My parents started being clearer about their assistants after that, but the fact is, most of them have wound up being more or less informally adopted. Mom and Dad always wanted tons of children, but pregnancy turned out to be difficult for her, so after me they stopped. I guess the grad students have had to fill the empty places where my brothers and sisters should've been. They sleep on our sofas, write their theses on the rainbow table, cry about their love lives, drink our milk straight from the carton. We keep up with every one, and some of them are important people in my life. Diego taught me how to ride a bike. Louis helped me bury my pet goldfish in the backyard even though rain poured down through the entire "funeral." Xiaoting was the only one at home when I started my period for the first time, and she handled it perfectly—explaining how to use everything from our friends at Tampax, then taking me to Cold Stone Creamery.

Still, from the beginning, Paul and Theo were different. Closer to us than any of the others. Special.

And Paul was the most special of all.

Mom joked that she liked him because they were both Russian, that only fellow Russians could ever understand each other's dark humor. Dad made a standing appointment for them to have lunch on campus together, and, once, let

Paul borrow his car. He usually didn't even let *me* borrow the car. Even though Paul was so quiet, so aloof, so apparently invulnerable to laughter—to my parents, he could do no wrong.

("He's weird," I protested to them shortly after his arrival. "He's like some kind of caveman from back before people could even talk."

"That's not very kind," Dad said as he poured milk into his tea. "Marguerite, remember—Paul graduated from high school at age thirteen. He began his PhD studies at seventeen. He never had much of a childhood. Hasn't really had a chance to make friends his own age, and Lord knows he doesn't get a lot of support from home. It makes him a little . . . awkward, but that doesn't mean he's not a good person."

"Besides," Mom interjected, "whether by 'caveman' you mean Cro-Magnons or Neanderthals, there's no reason to assume they lacked human speech.")

Paul was their research assistant for only a year and a half—but they loved him more than any of the others. He practically lived at our house or in their classes, 24/7. They loaned him books, fussed when he didn't have a jacket in winter, even baked him a birthday cake—chocolate with caramel icing, his favorite.

Theo Beck worked just as hard for them. They were never unkind to Theo; I've always felt like he belonged, and he's definitely more fun than strange, watchful Paul. Theo's black hair is always a little bit wild, everything is a joke to him, and okay, he flirts with me some, but I don't think Mom and

Dad ever minded. I'm not even sure they noticed. So Theo should have been equally beloved.

But Paul is smarter. More unique. He's one step over the line that separates "extraordinarily intelligent" from "genius." I could also tell that Mom and Dad thought Paul needed them more. Theo is cocky; Paul is shy. Theo cracks jokes; Paul seems melancholy. So Paul brought out their protective side in a way Theo never could. Sometimes, I knew, when Theo saw how my parents devoted themselves to Paul, he was jealous.

Maybe sometimes I felt jealous myself.

Within twenty minutes of arriving at the luncheon, I've been introduced to the duchess's niece Romola, the one at Chanel. She's not a designer there, merely a publicist, but as Aunt Susannah says, "Every connection helps, right?"

Surprisingly, Romola doesn't treat me like a leech; instead she latches on to me. "We're going to have fun," she whispers. "About time someone interesting showed up."

Ten minutes after that, I'm in the bathroom watching Romola do a line of coke. She offers me some, and I decline, but I suspect this dimension's Marguerite would say yes without a second thought.

So fifteen minutes later, when Romola offers me champagne—at two in the afternoon—I say yes. If I'm going to be convincing as this Marguerite I need to play the part.

Aunt Susannah watches me start drinking, and she doesn't say a word. I guess she's used to it.

This party is the weirdest thing, simultaneously upper-crust and tacky. Cosmetic surgery has warped the faces of every woman over thirty; they don't look younger, just not quite human in a way society has decided to pretend not to see. Half of the people are talking more to the holograms from their rings or badges than they are to the people around them. What conversation I can hear is mostly gossip: who's shagging who, who's making money, who's losing it, who's not invited to the next party like this.

Maybe the technology is different, but the shallowness of the scene is probably universal. So this is the life my father escaped when he chose to go into science, to leave Great Britain and join Mom in California. He was even smarter than I knew.

Here's to you, Dad, I think as I grab another glass of champagne.

Seven hours after the luncheon, I'm behind the wheel of Romola's car—a shiny silver teardrop that actually drives itself, which is good, considering how tipsy I already am. Romola herself is telling me about the amazing clubs we're going to hit tonight. We've hung out all day. She acts like we're friends now, like she's going to get me an internship at Chanel. I know and she knows that we're both just using this as an excuse to get wasted. I don't think she'd let me ditch her if I tried.

I hate this. I'd rather go home, throw up, and pass out, preferably in that order.

But every time I look out at the dark, jagged, futuristic

London in front of me, I remember that Paul is here. I remember that we have to meet again, and what I have to do when that happens. There's no way out—not for him, and not for me.

Paul would say it was our destiny.

"What are you trying to do?" Theo said one time, glaring across the table at Paul. The pieces that would become the very first Firebird prototype were strewn between them, across the rainbow table. "The minute Sophia gets vindicated, you want to turn her into a laughingstock again?"

"What do you mean?" I demanded. I'd come in from piano lessons, and I quickly ditched my sheet music so I'd look less like a kid. Theo is only three and a half years older than me, Paul only two; they were the first of the grad students I'd ever thought of as being more like me than like my parents. I wanted them to think of me the same way. "Why would people be laughing at Mom?"

Paul's gray eyes glanced up to meet mine for only one second before he went back to his work. "It's not her theory. It's mine. I take responsibility."

Theo leaned back in his chair as he gestured toward Paul with his thumb. "This one is ready to risk his scientific credibility—and his adviser's, no matter what he says—by arguing that destiny is real."

"Destiny?" That sounded weirdly . . . romantic from a guy like Paul.

"There are patterns within the dimensions," Paul insisted,

43

never looking up again. "Mathematical parallels. It's plausible to hypothesize that these patterns will be reflected in events and people in each dimension. That people who have met in one quantum reality will be likely to meet in another. Certain things that happen will happen over and over, in different ways, but more often than you could explain by chance alone."

"In other words," I said, "you're trying to prove the existence of fate."

I was joking, but Paul nodded slowly, like I'd said something intelligent. "Yes. That's it exactly."

"You should come to Paris with me next week," Romola shouts over the dance music in the club. I think it's the same one I was standing outside last night, when I arrived in this dimension.

"Sure!" Why not accept? She'll never actually take me; I'll never actually go; and we both know it. "That would be amazing!"

I'm wearing a dress she loaned me: dull pewter leather, skin-tight even on my rail-thin frame. It couldn't be more obvious that my breasts are practically nonexistent, but I'm also showing off a whole lot of leg, and in the opinion of the guys in this club, that makes up for the lack of cleavage. They're all over me, buying me drinks—more drinks I don't need.

And I hate the way they look at me, admiring but appraising, the same kind of hard, greedy assessment they'd give an expensive sports car. Not one of them sees *me*.

"Probably you think it's impractical at least," I said to Paul, that one night he watched me paint. "Art."

"I don't know that practicality is the most important thing."

Which sounded almost like a compliment, for a moment, until I realized that he basically had admitted that he thought it was impractical of me to study painting at college. I was going to take classes in art restoration so I wouldn't wind up living in Mom and Dad's basement when I was thirty, but I didn't feel like defending myself to him. I felt like going on the attack.

It was late November, just after Thanksgiving—only a week and a half ago, and yet already it seems like another lifetime. The evening was surprisingly warm, the last glow of Indian summer—or "Old Ladies' Summer," the Russian phrase my mother prefers. I wore an old camisole smeared with a hundred shades of paint from past evenings of work, and blue jean shorts that I'd cut off myself. Paul stood in the doorway of my bedroom, the only time he'd ever come so close to intruding on my space.

I was so *aware* of him. He's bigger than your average guy, and *way* bigger than your average physics grad student: tall, broad-shouldered, and extremely muscular—from the rock climbing, I guess. Paul's frame seemed to fill the entire door. Although I kept working, rarely looking away from my brush and canvas, it was as if I could sense him behind me. It was like feeling the warmth of a fire even when you're not looking directly at the flame.

"Okay, maybe portraits don't rule the art world anymore," I said. Other students at art shows did collages and mobiles with "found objects," Photoshopped 1960s ads to make postmodern comments on today's society, stuff like that. Sometimes I felt out of step, because all I had to offer were my oil paintings of people's faces. "But plenty of artists earn good money painting portraits. Ten thousand bucks apiece, sometimes, once you have a reputation. I could do that."

"No," Paul said. "I don't think you could."

I turned to him then. My parents might worship the guy, but that didn't mean he could wander into my room and be insulting. "Excuse me?"

"I meant—" He hesitated. Obviously he knew he'd said the wrong thing; just as obviously, he didn't understand why. "The people who get their portraits painted—rich people— they want to look good."

"If you're trying to dig yourself out of a hole, you're doing a crappy job of it. Just FYI."

Paul jammed his hands into the pockets of his threadbare jeans, but his gray eyes met mine evenly. "They want to look perfect. They only want their best side to show. They think a portrait should be—like plastic surgery, but on their image instead of their face. Too beautiful to be real. Your paintings—sometimes they're beautiful, but they're always real."

I couldn't look him in the face any longer. Instead I turned my head toward the gallery of paintings currently hung on my bedroom walls, where my friends and family looked back at me.

"Like your mother," Paul said. His voice was softer. I stared at her portrait as he spoke. I'd tried to make Mom look her best, because I love her, but I didn't only re-create her dark, almond-shaped eyes or her broad smile; I also showed the way her hair always frizzes out wildly in a hundred directions, and how sharply her cheekbones stand out from her thin face. If I hadn't put those things in the painting too, it wouldn't have been *her*. "When I look at that, I see her as she is late at night, when we've been working for ten, fourteen hours. I see her genius. I see her impatience. Her exhaustion. Her kindness. And I'd see all that even if I didn't know her."

"Really?" I glanced back at Paul then, and he nodded, obviously relieved I understood.

"Look at them all. Josie's impatient for her next adventure. Your father is distracted, off on one of his tangents, and there's no telling whether he's wasting time or about to be brilliant. Theo—" He paused as I took in the portrait I was finishing of Theo, complete with black hair gelled into spikiness, brown eyes beneath arched eyebrows, and full lips that would have suited a Renaissance cupid. "Theo's up to no good, as usual."

I started laughing. Paul grinned.

"And then there's your self-portrait."

Although I've participated in various art shows, even had an exhibition of my own in a very small gallery, I've never displayed my self-portrait anywhere besides my bedroom. It's personal in a way that no other painting can ever be.

"Your hair . . ." he said, and his voice trailed off, because even Paul possessed enough tact to know that calling a girl's hair a "disaster zone" was probably unwise. But it is—curlier and thicker and more uncontrollable even than Mom's—and that's how I painted it. "I can see all the ways you're like your mother."

Sure, I thought. *Bony, too tall, too pale.*

"And all the ways you're not like her."

I tried to turn it into a joke. "You mean, you don't see the same incredible genius?"

"No."

It hurt. I wonder if I winced.

Quickly Paul added, "There are perhaps five people born in a century with minds like your mother's. No, you're not as smart as she is. Neither am I. Neither is anyone else either of us is likely to meet in our lifetimes."

That was true. It helped, but my cheeks were still flushed with heat. How could I *feel* him standing near me?

He has a softer voice than you'd think, from the big frame and the hard eyes. "I see . . . the way you're always searching. How much you hate anything fake or phony. How you're older than your years, but still . . . playful, like a little girl. How you're always looking into people, or wondering what they see when they look back at you.

Your eyes. It's all in the eyes."

How could Paul see any of that? How could he know only from the portrait?

But it wasn't only from the portrait. I knew that, too.

Although I ought to have said something, I couldn't have spoken a word. My breath caught in my throat, high and tight. Never once did I look away from my self-portrait and back at Paul.

He said, "You paint the truth, Marguerite. I don't think you could work any other way."

And then he was gone.

After that, I started work on a portrait of Paul. His face is a surprisingly difficult one to capture. The wide forehead— strong, straight eyebrows—the firm jawline—light brown hair with a hint of reddish gold to it that kept me mixing paints for hours in an attempt to get the exact shade—the way he ducks his head slightly, as if he's apologizing for being so tall and so strong—that slightly lost look he has, like he knows he'll never fit in and doesn't even see the point of trying—but it was the eyes that threw me.

Deep-set, intense: I knew what Paul's eyes looked like. But the thing was . . . whenever I painted someone, even myself, I showed them looking slightly away from the viewer. Expressions become more revealing then; it also gives the person in the portrait a hint of mystery—a sense that the real human being inside is beyond anything my work can capture. That's part of painting the truth, too.

But with Paul I couldn't do it. Every time I tried to paint

his gaze, he wouldn't look away from the viewer. From the artist.

He looked at me. He was always, always, looking at me.

The day after my father died, the hour after we learned Paul was responsible, I went to my room, took one of my canvas knives, and slashed his portrait to ribbons.

He made me trust him.

He made me think he saw me.

And it was all just part of Paul's game, one small element of his big plan to destroy us all.

That's just one more reason he has to pay.

Around midnight, my head is whirling, and I feel like I'm going to be sick, but I never stop dancing. The heavy drumbeat of the music reverberates through me and drowns out even the thump of my own pulse. It's like I'm not even alive. Merely a puppet on strings with nothing inside.

A guy's hand closes over my shoulder, and I wonder which one it is. Will he buy me another drink? If he does, I'll pass out. I think I'd like to pass out around now.

But when I turn and see who it is, I gasp, and just like that—I'm alive again.

"Nice dress, Meg." Theo smirks as he glances down my body, then up again. "Where's the rest of it?"

"Theo!" I throw my arms around him, and he hugs me back. For the longest time we're locked together like that, right on the middle of the dance floor.

"Are you drunk?" he murmurs into the curve of my neck.

"Or are they making perfumes that smell like tequila?"

"Get me out of here." Why is it so hard to get the words out? Only then do I realize I'm sobbing.

I've held it together all this time. I've held it together because I had to, carrying the grief and the fear even when I thought the weight would crush me. But now Theo's here, and I can finally let go.

Theo hugs me tighter—so tightly that my feet lift off the ground—and he carries me off the dance floor, away from all the lights. He settles me on one of the long, low couches in the corner. I can't stop crying, so he just holds me, his hands stroking my hair and my back. He rocks me back and forth as gently as he would a child. All around us, the club lights pulse, and the music and dancing roar on.

5

THE SIGHT OF THEO'S FACE, THE WARMTH OF HIS ARMS around me, make me feel as though everything should start getting better right away.

And maybe it would, if I hadn't gotten so drunk that I made myself sick.

"That's right," Theo says, rubbing my back as I lean over the edge of the Millennium Bridge, where I have just vomited into the Thames. "Get that junk out of there."

Shame has painted my face with heat. "I'm so humiliated."

"What, because I saw you puke? Listen, if you saw me on my average Saturday night, you'd know this is nothing. When it comes to this kind of thing—I'm not throwing any stones. Let's leave it at that."

That's more than a joke. Theo's quicksilver mind has never totally concealed how wild he can be. Even though he never brought his problems into our house, I knew Mom and Dad had heard rumors about Theo getting wasted and sometimes going AWOL for hours, even a day at a time. They'd mentioned his "drinking," though really they were worried about substances much, much less legal than his occasional cans of PBR. Even Paul had sometimes quietly suggested that Theo should slow down.

To hell with Paul. Tonight Theo's in control, and he's taking care of me. His hand is warm against my bare back as I stare down at the dark water of the river, trying to regain my composure.

Then I glimpse my fragmented reflection in the river, broken into pieces by the rippling water.

"Do you think this is the last thing Dad saw?" I whisper. My mouth tastes horrible. My body is weak. This is what failure feels like. "The river, right in front of him, like this?"

For a few long moments, Theo doesn't answer. When he does, he sounds even wearier than I feel. "Don't think about that."

"I can't help thinking about it."

"I'm sure it wasn't. Okay? Come on. Let's get you home."

"I hope it was. I hope Dad saw the river rushing up at him, and then—and then it was over." My voice shakes. "Because that would mean he hit his head in the wreck, or when the car struck the water. Then he blacked out, or died right away. He wouldn't have had time to be scared." How long does it take to drown? Three minutes? Five? Long enough to be horrible, I feel sure. Long enough that I hope my dad never had to endure it. "It would be better if he never knew. Don't you think?"

"Stop this." Theo's voice is rough; his hands slide around to my arms, and he grips me as if he's scared I might throw myself over the rail. "Don't do this to yourself. It doesn't help."

Theo's wrong. I need to think about my father's death. I can't start grieving him yet; I need the pain to keep me angry. Sharp. Focused.

When we find Paul, the pain is what will give me the strength to finish him.

I pull one arm away from Theo so I can wipe my mouth. "Okay," I say. "Let's go home."

We walk the rest of the way back to Aunt Susannah's apartment. When the elevator starts moving upward, it makes my knees buckle—there's still a lot of champagne in my system. Theo catches one of my elbows, and I lean my head against his shoulder for the rest of the ride.

As we come to the door, he whispers, "Not too late for me to get a hotel room."

"If we're quiet we won't wake up Aunt Susannah," I say as I press my palm against the electronic lock; it recognizes me, clicks open. "Anyway, I doubt she'd care."

And I need Theo with me now more than I ever have before.

In the darkness, the white-on-white apartment is instead a silvery shade of blue, as if it were made of moonlight.

Everything seems surreal as I silently guide Theo down the hallway and into my bedroom, and shut the door, sealing us in together.

The bedroom isn't that big; the bed itself fills most of the space. There's nowhere else for Theo to sleep but the floor, and nowhere else for him to sit, either. I tell myself I'm being stupid to think this is awkward—to imagine that he's concentrating on anything other than the insane situation we're in, that the flicker of attraction between us could even matter in the middle of all this.

Then our eyes meet, and I know—it's not just me.

"Okay," I say, gesturing toward the en suite. "I'm going to, uh, freshen up."

Theo nods as he walks toward the window. "Sure. Go ahead and take your shower."

I'd only been thinking about brushing my teeth, but a shower sounds nice. My hair and clothes smell like cigarette smoke and stale champagne—like the other Marguerite's life. Right now I need to be myself again.

I step into the white-tiled bathroom and close the door behind me. The leather peels away grudgingly; my skin stings as I tug the dress off. It occurs to me that this is a designer dress worth thousands of pounds; Romola probably meant for me to give this back. Well, I'll mail it to her tomorrow. Right now I let it crumple onto the floor like a skin I've shed. My fist closes over the Firebird, and I lift the locket from around my neck.

Only when I'm standing in the shower, letting the hot

water course over me, do I become aware—vividly aware—that I'm stark naked while Theo is only steps away. I tell myself there's no reason for it to be weird; Theo's practically been living in my home for the past few years, after all. I've bathed and slept and cut my toenails with Theo a room away.

But it feels different now.

Steam wreathes around me as I duck under the shower-head, feel hot water sinking into my curls and trailing down my face. I try to think only about scrubbing away the smell of cigarettes. Instead, my thoughts keep turning to the way Theo took me in his arms at the club, or how, when I leaned against him in the elevator, it felt like the most natural thing in the world.

There's always been . . . *something* between Theo and me. Not because he flirted with me—he flirts with every woman he meets, and even a few guys. He even flirted with Romola, pulling her aside for a moment at the club before he shepherded me out of there. Flirting is just a thing Theo does automatically, without thinking, the way the rest of us breathe. If anything, I knew Theo's feelings toward me were changing because he began flirting with me *less*. When he did, the words had taken on weight; the attention he paid me wasn't meaningless any longer, and we both knew it.

I always told myself nothing was ever going to happen. Theo's older than me. He's snarky and he's selfish and his arrogance would be completely repellent if he didn't have the brilliance to back it up. At times, when he's been awake for two days straight, and he's pacing around our house talking more in math than in English, there's a recklessness to him, like he's determined to push his limits to the brink of self-destruction, and maybe past it. So I told myself I loved Theo as a friend. Okay, a friend who's sort of wickedly hot—yet, still, only a friend.

But the past two days I've seen a whole new side to Theo. Maybe I've finally seen the real Theo. Why did I ever doubt him? Probably the same reason I used to trust Paul. Apparently I don't understand people at all.

Paul is out there. Right now the only thing I can do to get ready to face him is to sleep this off. Theo's with me, and that's enough.

I shut off the water, dry myself, brush my teeth a second time. The Firebird goes back around my neck even before I've toweled my hair. There's a long T-shirt hanging from one of the hooks on the door, so I slide into it. The pale pink color is slightly translucent, and I didn't think to bring in any fresh underwear. But it's darker in the bedroom; it won't matter.

When I step out of the bathroom, Theo's standing at the window, arms braced against the sill. Moonlight has painted his black hair, making it gleam. It takes him a moment to turn and face me; when he does, the same electricity crackles between us, and I feel as though the T-shirt is see-through. But I don't move. I just stand there, facing him.

Theo breaks the silence first. "For what it's worth, I don't see anyone down on the street who seems to be checking this building out. Nobody was following us home from the club, either—at least, as far as I could see."

"Oh, right. Good." Why didn't I think of that? It's at that moment I realize that I've still got way more alcohol in my system than I should. I sink down onto the bed, woozy and whirling. "Do you think Paul knows we're here?"

"If he's thought to check."

Of course he's checking to see if anybody's after him, I want to retort, but then I stop myself. A smile spreads across my face. "Paul doesn't know about the other Firebirds," I say. "You kept it a secret from everyone. Even him."

"Sometimes it pays to be a secretive bastard." Theo grins back. However, I can tell he's not totally confident. "Still, we can't assume Paul doesn't have any more tricks up his sleeve. We underestimated him once. Let's not do it again."

"You're right." My rage at Paul threatens to break through once more, but I force myself to put it aside. My whole body hurts, and my mind is fuzzy and confused and not my own. I need to sleep.

Theo's voice gentles. "Hey. Toss me a pillow, all right? Gonna make myself a dog bed here on the floor."

I throw him one of the pillows; he pulls a spare blanket from the foot of the bed. We're so quiet that I can hear the rustle of fabric on fabric. When I tuck my feet under the bedspread, he flicks off the light so that we're once again in the dark.

Slowly I lie down, but I'm *so aware* of him. My breaths quicken; my heart feels like it might hammer its way out of my chest.

It's stupid to be nervous. I trust Theo. There's no reason

for me to worry about him doing something.

Then I realize—Theo's not the person I'm unsure of. What I don't know is what I might do.

It would be so easy, so good, to forget everything farther away than this bed and my own skin.

And it's Theo. The one person in this world I can rely on, the one I want to keep closer than any other—

My whisper is the only sound in the room. "You don't have to sleep on the floor."

For a moment, the only reply is silence. Then Theo rises from his place at the foot of my bed. His body is silhouetted by the moonlight, and I realize that he's taken off his shirt to sleep.

Without a word he walks around to my side of the bed, then sits down, his hip against my leg. The mattress sinks in beneath him, rolling me slightly closer. Theo braces one hand near my pillow. With the other, he brushes my damp curls away from my face. I want to say something to him, but I can't think of what. All I can do is lie there, breaths coming fast and shallow, staring up at him, both wanting him to touch me again and terrified that he will.

Slowly Theo leans down over me. My T-shirt is slightly off one shoulder, and his lips brush me there—along the line of my collarbone. The kiss lasts only a moment. It crashes through me like lightning.

He whispers, "Ask me again sometime, when we're both ourselves." Then he lifts his head, and his smile is soft. "Next time I won't stop with your shoulder."

With that he rises from the bed and goes back to his own place. Already I know he won't say another word until morning.

Should I feel humiliated or flattered? But my heartbeat is steadying; I feel safe with Theo, safer than I've felt since the moment we heard about Dad. That makes it easy to close my eyes, relax, and surrender to sleep.

I awaken to the sound of laughter.

For one split second, I think I'm back at home. So many days, I've awoken to the sound of my parents and sister laughing in the kitchen, and maybe their research assistants, too, voices floating to me along with the scent of blueberry waffles. But no. I'm still in another Marguerite's bedroom, her body, her world.

No way am I wearing this pink T-shirt in broad daylight, so I fish around in the nightstand, hoping for something to put on. Then my fingers make contact with silk, and I lift a butter-yellow kimono-style dressing gown, elaborately embroidered. It shocks me, weirdly, because this looks more like something I would own. The Marguerite from this dimension saw this silk robe and responded to it like I would . . . because we are the same person, on some level I'm still learning to understand.

I wrap the silk gown around me and hurry to the kitchen. The illusion of my old life must be incredibly strong, because I could still swear I smell blueberry waffles—

"You're a naughty one, you are," Aunt Susannah coos,

and she's still chuckling at her own joke when I walk in to see her sitting at the kitchen island while Theo busies himself at the stove. He's wearing his undershirt and boxers, a serious case of stubble, and a grin.

"We just met, and already you've got my number," Theo says as he pours batter into a frying pan. As he finishes, he looks up and sees me. "Morning, Meg!"

"Uh, hi," I say faintly. "You're . . . making breakfast?"

"Blueberry pancakes. I learned the recipe from the master." By this Theo means my dad. "They were going to be waffles, but Susannah here is shockingly deficient in waffle irons."

"Guilty as charged." Aunt Susannah's hands are folded under her chin in a gesture that would look childish on someone my age, much less hers. I remember from my old London trips that she does this to hide the wrinkles on her neck.

Oh, my God, she's flirting with him. I might feel jealous if it weren't so ludicrous.

Theo is of course flirting back. "Girl, someone needs to take you shopping."

"Don't think I haven't looked for a sugar daddy," she says. "Of course, we're set up all right. Maybe I should try being a sugar momma for a change."

"Intriguing notion." He cocks one of those arched eyebrows of his, then flips the pancake over.

There's only so much of this I can watch. "I'm getting dressed," I announce, and hurry back to my room.

My closet at home is filled with dresses, flowing skirts,

floral patterns and vivid color, crochet and lace. *This* closet looks more like a magazine layout designed to show off the world's most expensive and impractical designer brands. But I find a simple black T and gray slacks that will work, and one pair of shoes that looks like it won't kill my feet.

When I emerge, I cross paths with Aunt Susannah, who's wandering back to her own room with a plate in one hand and a fork in the other; one last wedge of pancake sits on her plate. She beams at me and says, in a stage whisper, "I like that one. He's cleverer than your usual sort."

Who else has the other Marguerite brought home after clubbing? I don't want to think about it.

A plate of pancakes waits for me on the kitchen island, and my stomach grumbles in eager gratitude. Theo is standing by the sink, his hands braced against the counter; he doesn't look up when I walk in.

"Thanks," I say as I sit down to breakfast. "It's good that we're starting early. But you could've woken me."

"Yeah. I guess." He seems distracted—more tired than he was before. Probably he didn't rest well, sleeping on the floor.

"Is pancake batter the same as waffle batter?" When I take a bite, it tastes about right. "Did you eat already?"

"What?"

I look up from my plate to see Theo staring at me. He looks confused—even unnerved—

That's when it hits me. The Firebird isn't hanging around Theo's neck. He must have taken it off last night to sleep, but now his memory has started to fail. Sometime in the past few minutes, my Theo began to lose his hold on this body, this consciousness.

Mom wasn't totally wrong about our consciousness slipping in alternate dimensions after all.

"You need a reminder." I drop my fork, go to him, and grab his hand. Enough of my Theo remains that he doesn't fight me or ask questions as I tow him back toward my bedroom.

I give him a gentle push that makes him sit heavily on the bed. For a moment he looks like himself again, and he smiles. "Didn't we go over this last night?"

"Oh, my God, stop flirting for once in your life." I fish through his clothes on the floor and find his Firebird locket. Quickly I loop it around his neck. "Just wear that, okay?"

"Wear what?"

He's forgotten about it already. He doesn't seem to notice the matching Firebird hanging around my neck, either. Mom explained once that, since the Firebirds belonged to our dimension, they would be very difficult to detect by a native to another dimension. At the moment I call attention to the locket, in theory, Theo could see it—but otherwise it hovers beneath his level of awareness.

It's a good thing that actually works. Otherwise, people would instantly freak out about the Firebirds appearing around their necks and remove them, destabilizing the would-be interdimensional travelers who had just leaped there. As it is, people might wear them for months without noticing. Physics is weird.

"Hang on," I tell him as I take his Firebird in hand and find the sequence that sets a reminder, dropping it in the instant before blue-white light flickers around it.

They told me a reminder would hurt. They didn't tell me how much. Theo bucks against it, almost convulsing, before swearing under his breath as he slumps forward, and for a moment I think he's going to pass out.

("A shock?" I asked my mother when she told me about this. "A reminder is only an electric shock?"

She beamed, like we were talking about butterflies and rainbows. "Not at all. A reminder is a fairly sophisticated resonance shift. It simply *feels* like an electric shock.")

"Theo?" I lean forward and take his shoulders in my hands. "Are you okay again?"

"Yeah. I am." He looks up at me, panting and wide-eyed, then repeats, "I am," as if I'd contradicted him.

"That was close." I put my hand on my chest to remind myself that the Firebird is still there. The curve of hard metal against my palm reassures me, and makes me think. Will I need a reminder too, eventually?

Theo's face is pale, and he's braced himself against the bed like he's expecting an earthquake. At my questioning glance, he says, "I need a few minutes. All right?"

"Sure." That had to have been as terrifying as it was painful. So I gently rumple his already disheveled hair and go back out to the kitchen, where I finish my pancakes while I strategize.

If Paul's not already on his way to us, we'll be on our way to him within the hour. There have to be monorails that would get us to Cambridge quickly, right? Or even a regular train. We find him before he finds us. And then—

—we kill him.

It hasn't escaped my attention that the Paul I need to destroy is currently a passenger in the body of another Paul Markov entirely. Although right now it seems to me that anybody as evil as Paul would be evil in every single dimension, I don't know that for sure. So it's not as simple as finding him and, I don't know, shooting him or something.

But there are things you can do with the Firebird that are dangerous to the traveler inside. Theo told me that much.

In fact, I decide, *we should go over that before we do anything else, even before we leave the house.*

Determined, I put my plate in the sink and return to my bedroom to talk this through with Theo. When I walk inside, though, he's not in the bedroom. His clothes remain on the floor, apart from his thin black jacket, which I don't see.

"Theo?" I walk into the bathroom, and I'm two steps in before it occurs to me how rude it was to do that without knocking first.

At that moment I see him, and I know he wanted to be alone. I also know why.

Because Theo, my guide, is sprawled on the tile floor, shooting up.

6

"THEO?" I TAKE A STEP FORWARD, THEN STOP. FOR SOME stupid reason I feel ashamed to see him like this.

Right after the shame comes anger. Why should *I* be embarrassed? I'm not the one getting high in the middle of something so dangerous, so important—

Then Theo groans as he slumps sideways onto the bathroom floor. He's completely, totally out of it.

"Oh, *shit*." I drop to my knees and roll him onto his back. Theo doesn't even seem to know I'm there. "What are you doing?"

Theo focuses his eyes on me for only a moment and chokes out one word. "Sorry."

"Sorry? You're sorry?"

"Yeah," he says. My anger is very far away from him right now; I can tell. The whole world is far away from Theo at the moment.

I grab the small bottle I see on the bathroom floor; it's still about half full of some liquid that's a brilliant emerald green. What drug looks like that? It must be something from this dimension, because I've never seen anything like it.

I try to adjust him on the bathroom floor so that he's not all crumpled against the vanity; he responds by rolling half-way over to rest his head in my lap. With a sigh, I settle in on the cold bathroom tile, back against the wall, and untie the rubber tube that he'd knotted around his forearm. It can't be good to leave that on for long.

I can feel his breathing, deep and regular, as his chest swells against my thighs.

Leaning my head against the vanity, I try to steady myself. But it's hard. Theo . . . isn't stable. I knew this. We had all begun to realize that about him. His courage and loyalty don't change this one critical fact.

The person I've been relying on to get me through this is someone I can't be sure of relying on at all.

Although I hate to admit it, Paul was the first one who warned me about Theo—the first one who realized how bad he was getting, who tried to say something. And he must have suspected for a while, but kept it to himself. Only the Accident made him speak up.

The Accident was two months ago, and it's the only time I ever saw my parents angry with Theo. They patched it up, and nothing actually happened, but still, it stood out.

That afternoon, I was hanging out with my sister, Josie,

who was home from Scripps for the weekend. She was helping me study for the AP exams, which can be a little tricky when you've been homeschooled with no planning for the standardized tests to come.

I know the stereotypical images people have when they first hear the word *homeschooled*. They assume it's super religious and not very difficult, like we sit around all day learning God made dinosaurs for the cavemen to ride.

In my case, however, my parents took Josie out of public school when the kindergarten teacher said it was impossible for her to already read on a fifth-grade level, so clearly she'd just learned to sound out words without understanding them; I've never so much as stepped into a real school. (From what I hear, I haven't missed out on much.) Instead Mom and Dad lined up a series of tutors—their assistants and grad students from other areas of the university—and made me and Josie work harder than anyone else. Every once in a while they'd bring in other professors' kids, so we'd be "socially well-adjusted." The other kids have become my friends, but mostly it was only my sister and me in it together. So Josie and I learned about modern literature from a would-be PhD who mostly made us study her thesis on Toni Morrison. Our French lessons were taught by a variety of native speakers, though we got a mix of dialects and accents—Parisian, Haitian, Quebecois. And somehow we made it through science as taught by my mother, which was definitely the hardest of all.

It was a Saturday afternoon, gusty and overcast. My parents were at the university, working in their lab; Paul and

Theo were supposed to be going through equations here, but Theo had coaxed Paul outside to see his latest modifications to his beloved muscle car. So Josie and I had the place to ourselves.

And instead of helping me study, Josie was nagging.

"C'mon," Josie said, as she played with one of the long vines of Mom's philodendron. "You'd love the Art Institute."

"Chicago's so cold in winter."

"Whine whine whine. Buy a coat. Besides, it's not like it never gets cold at Ris-lee or Ris-mee—"

"Rizdee." That's how most people shorten the name of the Rhode Island School of Design. "And yeah, I know, but it's still the best place for art restoration in the country, hands down."

Josie gave me a look. We're pretty different, for sisters—she's average height while I'm tall; she's athletic while I'm anything but. She inherited our parents' love of science and is following in Dad's footsteps by becoming an oceanographer; I'm the odd duck of the family, the artsy one. Josie's laid-back while I freak out about every little thing. Yet despite all our differences, sometimes she can see right through me. "Why are you learning how to be an art restorer when you're going to be an artist?"

"I'm going to *try* to be an artist—"

"Do or do not, there is no try," Josie said in her best Yoda impersonation, which is sort of scarily good. "You want to be an artist. A great artist. So be one. The Art Institute of

Chicago would be the place for that, right?"

"Ruskin." The word came out of my mouth before I could stop myself. Josie gave me a look that I knew meant I wasn't going to be able to drop it. "The Ruskin School of Fine Art at Oxford. In England. That would be . . . the ultimate."

"Okay, while I would miss you like crazy if you were in England, don't you think you ought to at least think about getting yourself to your ultimate? Because, trust me, nobody else is going to get you there." But then she got distracted from her lecture. "What is this thing?"

Like I said before, our parents don't usually work with cool sci-fi gizmos. This was one of the exceptions. "It's something Triad Corporation came up with."

Josie frowned. "I haven't seen this before. What is it?"

"It's not a consumer product. You know Triad supplied the funding for Mom and Dad's research, right? Well, this is for measuring . . . dimensional resonance. I think." Sometimes I tune out the technobabble. It's a survival mechanism.

"Is it supposed to be blinking red?"

I don't tune out *everything*. "No."

Quickly I stepped to Josie's side. The Triad device was a fairly plain metal box, like an old-fashioned stereo, but the front panel usually showed various sine waves in shades of blue or green. Now it pulsed in staccato red flashes.

I might not be a scientist, but you don't need advanced degrees to realize that red equals bad.

My first impulse was to open the garage door and yell for Paul and Theo, but Theo sometimes wound up parking way down the road. So I grabbed my cell phone instead. I hit Paul's number, and he answered, short and brusque as ever: "Yes?"

"This—thing from Triad, the one in the corner? Should it be flashing red?"

He paused for less than a second. When he spoke again, the intensity of his words gave me chills. "Get out of there. Now!"

I turned to Josie. "Run!" Instantly she fled; Josie's smart like that. Me? Not quite. I'd kicked off my shoes and so I spent three precious seconds stepping back into them before dashing to the door. Just as I hit the threshold, though—

The light was as brief as a camera flash but a hundred times brighter. I cried out, because it hurt my eyes, and dizziness rushed over me, maybe from moving too fast. Losing my balance, I staggered onto the front steps and tried to suck in a breath, but it was hard to do, as if someone had punched me in the gut.

Then broad, strong hands closed around my shoulders, and when my vision cleared, I was looking up into Paul's eyes.

"Marguerite? Are you all right?"

"Yeah." I leaned forward, trying to find the angle that would allow me to steady myself. Cool rain had begun to fall, but very lightly, almost a mist. My forehead rested against his broad chest; I could feel his heart beating quickly through his damp T-shirt, as if he were the one afraid.

"What happened?" Theo came running across the yard

then, his Doc Martens splashing through the mud. "Marguerite? What happened?" Josie came running up too.

"That damned Triad machine is what happened!" Paul kept holding on to me, but his fury shook me even then—hinting, maybe, at the real Paul inside. "Did you set it to run an overload test?"

"No! Are you crazy? You know I wouldn't do that and leave it unattended."

"Then why did it overload?" Paul demanded.

"What? It *did*?" Theo looked so stricken. "Jesus. How did that happen?"

"What almost happened?" Josie demanded. "Do I even want to know?"

"No, you don't." Paul's fingers tightened around my shoulders; he was gripping me so hard it bruised. I can't explain how that was intimidating and comforting at the same time, but it was. He wasn't looking at me any longer. "Theo, who gave you this? Was it Conley himself? Someone from Triad could have preset a test without our knowing."

Theo huffed, "Stop being so paranoid. Could you do that for once?" His voice gentled as he added, "Deep breaths, Meg. Are you all right?"

"I'm fine," I said, and by then I was. I pulled out of Paul's arms to stand on my own. Josie came to my side, but she was wise enough not to coddle me; she simply stayed close.

Paul walked through the mist to Theo; he's five inches taller and a whole lot broader, but Theo didn't flinch, even when Paul jabbed his finger against his breastbone. "*Someone* set up an overload test. It wasn't you. It wasn't me. Therefore it was Triad. That isn't paranoia. That's fact."

Although Theo clearly wanted to argue, he said, "Okay, all right, maybe they made a mistake."

"A mistake that could have hurt Marguerite! A mistake you should have caught, if you'd been paying attention. But you weren't paying attention, were you?"

"I already admitted I screwed up—"

"It's not enough to admit it! You have to do better than this. You have to keep yourself sharp. If you don't—and you put Marguerite at risk again—there will be consequences." Paul was leaning over Theo, using all his size and anger in an attempt to intimidate him. "Do you understand me?"

Theo's entire body tensed, and for a moment I thought he might push Paul back. But that spark faded as quickly as it had begun. Quietly he said, "I hear you, little brother. I do. You know I feel like shit about this, right?"

They weren't brothers, hadn't even met two years before, but that nickname was something that mattered to them both. Theo, too, had taken Paul under his wing; Paul had seemed to idolize Theo, almost, more awed than envious of Theo's easy humor and crazy social life. It's hard to imagine that Paul didn't mean it that day when his gaze softened and he said, "I know you'd never mean to do anything like that, Theo. But you can't let yourself get distracted. By anything."

"Listen, let me be the one to tell Sophia and Henry about this. I won't hold anything back. It's just—I deserve to hear it from them, you know?" Theo said, looking at all three of us in turn.

"Okay," Paul said, then glanced over at me for confirmation. I nodded. Josie hesitated for a long moment, then finally nodded too. Theo inclined his head, almost as though he were bowing, and then trudged toward his car.

Paul came back to me, guiding me to the house. Apparently it was safe to be inside again. Josie followed us, pointing at the device. "Can we move that thing?"

"Good idea," Paul said. "Get it out of the house. We probably shouldn't have brought it in here to begin with."

Josie hauled it into her arms—that thing was heavy—and headed out, leaving me and Paul alone.

As he pushed my hair back from my face, I felt suddenly shy. So I tried laughing it off. "What, am I radioactive now? Do I get superpowers?"

"No, and I doubt it."

"Did that thing nearly send me into another dimension?"

"It temporarily weakened the boundaries. That's all. Any other effects would be—theoretical." Paul blinked, then took his hands from me. I hugged myself and stepped back. Just when I thought neither of us would be able to think of anything else to say, Paul added, "I think Theo's, ah, extracurricular activities are getting the better of him."

"I don't want to think about it. Nothing went wrong, right?"

"Right."

His gaze met mine, and I remembered how he'd held me

in his arms. Touched my hair. It was the first time we'd been that close . . . and even then, I was thinking of it as the first time. Not the only time.

I was beginning to wonder what else Paul and I might be to each other . . .

Nothing, I tell myself savagely. *No, that's not right. He's your betrayer. And you're going to be his end.*

Back then I told myself the Accident wasn't a sign of any bigger trend in Theo's life, that it was much ado about nothing, but I was wrong.

I know that as I sit here on the bathroom floor, back cramping, a full half hour after I found Theo messed up. Paul might have been lying about everything else, but maybe he really did think of Theo as his "brother," at least a little bit. Maybe he cared enough to wish that Theo would get some help.

Or maybe Paul only wanted me to distrust Theo, so I'd go on trusting him completely.

My hand settles on Theo's head; his hair is thick and silky, wavy against my palm. His arm is slung across my legs. I look for the small tattoo above his wrist, the one he keeps promising to explain but never does . . . but that was stupid. This dimension's Theo apparently doesn't go in for body art.

Slowly he stirs, snuggling into my belly as though I were a pillow, then suddenly pulling himself up to sit beside me. His eyes have a drowsy quality, sensual and unfocused, and yet I know he's mostly himself again. "Mmmph. How long was I out of it?"

"Thirty minutes or so." Theo has caught the last break he's going to get from me. I hold up the bottle of green stuff. "What the hell is this?"

Then I feel sorry for being such a hard-ass, because he looks so desperately ashamed. "Homemade stuff," he says, his voice low. "Something this Theo uses—must've cooked it up with some chemistry guys. It's one hell of a ride."

He's joking about what a great "ride" it is when we're in the middle of something this dangerous? This important? I should've called an ambulance anyway; Theo's going to need one before I'm done with him.

But then he adds, "It also hooks its claws into you, hard. He—we—I needed a hit. I was trying to fight it, but this body belongs to this dimension and, you know, it needs what it needs. While I'm here, I kinda have to play by this world's rules."

"It's not just here, though, is it?" I ask. If it had been, I feel like Theo would have told me about his other self's drug addiction; his secrecy seems to hint at something more. "You use at home, too. Don't you? We all suspected."

Theo runs one hand over his face; his gaze is sharpening back to its usual clarity. "I'm not an addict," he finally says. "Not at home. It's . . . more mental, really. Sometimes I need to step out of my head, to silence all the voices telling me what an asshole I am." The shame shadows his face more harshly. "I hate that I need it. But I do."

"How long have you been using?"

He winces, but his voice is firm as he says, "Only the last

few months, and it never got in the way of the work. Never. I swear that to you."

Has he forgotten the Accident? Mom and Dad lost it when he told them. I rub my tingling arm, which had almost gone to sleep with Theo draped over it. "Okay."

"I'm sorry I checked out on you," Theo continues. He reaches toward my hand, as if to take it, then stops himself. "It's over now, all right? Totally over."

I nod as I push myself to my feet. "Just one thing—"

"Yeah?"

"I'm relying on you." My voice shakes slightly, but I don't attempt to steady it. Let Theo see how badly he hurt me. "We have to stop Paul, no matter what. I can't do that without you, and you can't do that if you're getting high all the time. So get your act together."

He looks stung, but I refuse to feel guilty. Theo always manages to wriggle off the hook with those puppy-dog eyes of his—not this time.

"I need you. I need all of you. Don't you dare check out on me again." I spear Theo with my hardest gaze. "Do you understand?"

He nods as he looks up at me with something that might even be respect.

"Clean yourself up," I say, gesturing toward the shower. "You have fifteen minutes. Then we're out of here. We have a job to do."

7

THEO EMERGES FROM MY ROOM SCRUBBED CLEAN. HE'S put on a fresh T-shirt from his backpack, a gray one with a picture of some rock band I don't know, from the sixties maybe, The Gears. He's freshly shaved and smells of soap; his damp hair is combed back into something that, on another guy, would look almost respectable. When his eyes meet mine, I expect to see lingering embarrassment—but instead Theo seems determined. Focused. Good. I need that more than his regret.

At first, neither of us knows what to say, and he can't hold my gaze very long. I look at his T-shirt because it's less awkward than looking at his face—and then I realize I know a couple of the members of The Gears. "Wait. That's Paul McCartney and George Harrison, but—who are the other guys?"

"No freaking clue." Theo holds his shirt out as he glances

down. "Apparently they never met John Lennon, or even Ringo Starr, so the Beatles never quite happened. These guys seem to have been pretty famous on their own, though."

No Beatles in this universe. It makes me sad, the nonexistence of a band that broke up decades before I was born. I know all their songs word for word, thanks to my father. Dad was the biggest Beatles fan ever. His favorite song was "In My Life," and he'd hum the verses while he washed up after dinner.

The memory stings—and I *hate* that, I hate how all the good memories have turned into things that hurt—but I need the pain.

Aunt Susannah's blow-drying her hair, so we're able to escape from the apartment without any more vomit-worthy flirtation between her and Theo. As the elevator takes us back to ground level, I try to get our plans together. "All right. First we have to figure out whether or not Paul's left Cambridge—"

"Forget it." Theo slips on his jacket. "If he's still in Cambridge, he's not the Paul Markov we're looking for. If Paul leaped into this dimension, if he's in this version of Paul, then he's on the move. Promise."

That seems like a big assumption to make. "Do you know something I don't?"

"I know Paul had been acting borderline paranoid about Triad Corporation the last couple of months," Theo replies. "Like the guys who were funding us would've sabotaged the research they paid for. Makes no sense, right? But I guess now we know Paul wasn't . . . thinking clearly. Let's put it that way."

Maybe that's the secret: Paul spent the past few months slowly going crazy. We thought he was acting normally, but he was always so quiet, so introverted, that there was no telling what might be going on inside. "That makes sense. But how does it help us?"

"Triad Corporation may be one of the world's biggest tech companies, but everybody knows it all boils down to one guy—Wyatt Conley." Triumphant, Theo holds up his wrist and projects a holographic image of a news story in front of us. The newness of the technology fades as I read the headline: CONLEY TO SPEAK AT TECH CONFERENCE IN LONDON.

"He's *here*," I say as I read the date. "Wyatt Conley is in London today."

"Which means we don't have to find Paul. We find Conley—because if our Paul is here, he's going after Conley first."

Stands to reason Conley would be a tech genius here, too. He's only thirty, but he's considered one of the giants— mostly because he developed the core elements of the smartphone when he was only sixteen. Triad is probably the most prestigious corporation in the world, has a glitzy, ultramodern office under construction not far from my home in the Berkeley Hills, and makes the kind of gadgets and gear people stand in line for for two or three days before they're released. Personally I think it's kind of stupid to get that worked up over a phone that's, like, two millimeters thinner than the last one, but I don't knock it, because Triad's R&D money made Mom's work possible.

I guess Paul turned against everyone who ever helped him, all at once.

The elevator doors slide open, and we walk out through the chic mirrored lobby. I smile at the doorman as we go out, cool December air ruffling my hair and Theo's jacket. The doorman seems surprised; I don't think this Marguerite spends a lot of time being nice to people. Once we're alone again, I ask, "How do you know Paul's not coming after us first?"

Theo shrugs. "I don't. But either way, we don't have to waste time looking for him. The fight's coming to us."

The tech conference is being held at a super posh hotel in the center of the city. Theo and I head in on one of the shimmering monorails that slithers over the crowds below.

"How do we get in?" I ask as we sit on the plastic seats. Above our heads, holographic ads glitter and dangle like hallucinogenic Christmas ornaments. "Tech conferences like this don't sell tickets at the door, do they?"

"Hell, no. If Wyatt Conley's the keynote speaker, this thing probably costs a thousand bucks a head."

My eyes widen. I have more money in this dimension, but that's a lot—and anything that expensive probably sells tickets in advance, not in person. "What are we going to do?"

"We're going to sneak in." He gives me a sidelong look,

and he smiles. "Since I'm the one with the criminal instincts on this team, leave that part to me, all right? Once we get past the main entry area, nobody's going to look twice at either of us as long as we play it cool."

The people at this conference are going to be corporate tycoons, millionaires, and so on, but Theo's wearing beat-up jeans, a parka, and a T-shirt. "What about your clothes?"

"*You're* the one who's dressed wrong for a tech conference—not that you don't look as sensational as ever." He's as cocky as he ever was, like I didn't see him stoned and helpless on the bathroom floor an hour ago. Is that infuriating or a relief? Theo gestures to his beat-up jeans. "I'm probably slightly overdressed as it is, but I can get away with it. Just stick close to me, okay?"

"Okay."

Nervous energy is building inside me as we come closer to confronting Paul. Or not—we might have got it wrong. This isn't necessarily our dimension's Paul Markov at all. What if he's fled somewhere else entirely?

Then we'd have to jump into a whole new dimension, with a new set of rules, and maybe an even greater distance to cross to reach each other. The thought of it makes my head hurt.

And yet, a new dimension might be one where I'd be with my parents. Both of them. By now Mom feels almost as lost to me as Dad.

What is Mom doing right now, back home? Theo and I left a message explaining what we were doing; she would have *lost it* when she read that, but without a Firebird of her own, she can't follow us. It's awful to think of her being scared about me and Theo when she's still so raw from losing Dad, but when we decided to go, I didn't stop to think about how long we'd be missing in our own dimensions. We've been gone for a day and a half so far.

I wonder if they've had Dad's memorial service—they couldn't even have a real funeral, couldn't even give him a true resting place—

No. I can't let this get the better of me now. This close to our goal, I have to stay strong.

"Show me how to use the Firebird," I say, pulling mine up from within my shirt.

"You've got the basics, right?"

"I don't mean the basics." This is difficult even to say. "I mean, show me how to use it to kill Paul. Our Paul."

"You want to keep it down?" Theo glances around us; we're surrounded by commuters. But they're too absorbed in their own holoscreens and headphones to have heard a word I've said.

I insist. "Show me."

"Listen. For your safety and my peace of mind, let's leave that part to me, okay?"

"My safety isn't one of our priorities here."

"Speak for yourself," he says, so intense that once again I find myself both thrilled and afraid of what it might mean.

My voice softens, but my resolve doesn't. "You need to show me how to do it, just in case." In my heart I know it's my job to kill Paul—my duty, my right—but I also know that's not an argument Theo wants to hear. If he's worried about safety, fine, we'll talk about safety. "If something happens to you, I have to be able to defend myself."

Theo still looks wary. "You understand that this isn't easy, right? Paul either has to be down for the count before you do this, or you have to have grabbed the Firebird from around his neck—assuming he's got it on him. Which he might not."

Paul might have his locked in a safe somewhere. But I'd bet anything he hasn't. Theo and I are still wearing ours, because this thing is too precious, too valuable, to keep anywhere else but right next to the heart.

"I understand," I say. "Show me."

So Theo leans close and shows me a fairly elaborate set of twists and turns of the Firebird's many layers and gears—by pantomime, of course. There are so many steps to the process that I can hardly even begin to memorize them all. "Why does this take so long? How is anybody supposed to do this in a crisis?"

"Nobody's supposed to do it, period," he answers. His head is so near mine that one of my curls is brushing his cheek, and he doesn't push it away. "We were building ways to travel through dimensions, not killing machines. What I'm showing you is technically a reset—something you should only do in your home dimension, to allow the Firebird to . . . connect to a different person, a different dimensional resonance, you see what I'm saying?"

"Kind of." I'm letting my frustration get the better of me. "I wish it were easier, that's all."

"It has to be difficult, because it's fatal to anyone not in their home dimension. We didn't want anybody doing this accidentally while they were traveling."

As I watch Theo's hands go through the sequence, over and over, I think of it again—the reality that I'm going to kill someone. An actual person, even if he's not in his own body at the time.

He's in someone else's, I remind myself. *You'll be setting this world's Paul free.* But I can't work up much righteous indignation while I'm shanghaiing someone else's body myself.

And it's not some anonymous stranger. It's *Paul.* The one who looked like he'd never received a nicer birthday gift than the lopsided cake Mom baked for him. The one I once teased for buying all his clothes at thrift stores—and then felt so bad when I saw that he was embarrassed, because he didn't shop there to be a hipster, he did it because he was poor. Paul, with his gray eyes and soft laugh and lost look, the one who held me against his chest when I was afraid . . .

Paul was able to look at all the good in my father, all the love Dad had given him, and go on to murder him without blinking an eye. Why can't I do the same? Why can't I be as hard as he is? I'm the one who has a reason, the one with a right to kill. I shouldn't be the one who feels guilty and horrible and sick.

For Dad, I tell myself, but for the first time it rings hollow.

My stomach churns, and the monorail car feels too warm.

I suck in a deep breath, attempting to steady myself, and Theo glances over. "You okay?"

"Yeah," I say shortly. "I think I've got it."

"Be careful when you go through the process," he says, clicking my Firebird back into its proper configuration, all the thin metal layers folding in on one another like an insect's wings. "We built this thing to be easy to repair and customize, so when you have it all spread out like that, it can pop apart. Simple enough to fix if you know how—but that's something I can't teach you in an hour. Or a month."

"Right. It's complicated. You don't have to keep reminding me."

Theo's brown eyes meet mine, warm and knowing. "Somebody's in a mood."

"We're going to kill a man. Should I be perky?"

He holds his hands up, like, *I surrender.* "I know this is hard, all right? It's not easy for me either."

Little brother. Theo used to take Paul out for what he called "Remedial Adolescence"—trying to introduce him to music and clubs and even girls, all the stuff he missed out on when he started doing higher physics at age thirteen. Of course, Theo did that partly to soak up the hero worship, because Paul thought Theo was about eighty times cooler than anyone else on earth.

Or we believed he did, anyway. In the end, Theo was as deeply deceived by Paul as the rest of us. As bitterly betrayed.

"I'm sorry." I lean my head back against the plastic seat and stare upward at the shiny holographic ads squiggling above us, begging me to buy products I've never heard of. "I know I'm acting like a bitch. I'm tired is all."

"It's not easy," he agrees. "We can save 'nice' for later. After."

"Right."

The monorail comes to our stop. Theo and I step out of the car side by side, without saying another word to each other. Maybe he's still thinking that nice comes later. Maybe that's what I should be thinking too. Instead my mind is clouded with uncertainty about what we'll find when we see Paul, whether we'll see him at all, and, worse, with doubts about my resolve.

I can't even look at Theo, lest he see how worked up I am. So I glance around at the crowds rushing by us in this station of metal grids and holographic signs, hoping for a moment's distraction from the dark work ahead.

One figure halts in his tracks. A large man in a long black coat, stopping midstep to check a holographic map of the area floating overhead. As the motion flickers in the corner of my eye, I turn toward it and my first thought is, *He's having a heart attack.*

Then I see who it is.

I've chased Paul Markov across dimensions. Now he's only twenty feet away.

8

I PUT MY HAND OUT, TRYING TO WARN THEO, BUT NO WARN-
ing is needed.

"Son of a bitch," Theo whispers.

He starts forward, but I grab his shirt in my fist. "Don't.
Theo, don't."

"What do you—" At first he's angry I've stopped him—so
angry it shocks me—but then Theo visibly relaxes. "Right.
Not exactly the place for this confrontation. Probably security cameras and transit cops around every corner."

That's not why I stopped Theo. It's because seeing Paul has
taken me back to the first moments after I heard the police
say his name, call him a suspect in Dad's death. Bizarrely, I
didn't get angry right away; I was too dazed for anything as
coherent as anger. I kept thinking that this couldn't be right.
That the horrible things I was hearing couldn't be real.

While the police were standing in our living room, and

Mom cried into her hands as they talked about Paul's "suspicious activity," I kept thinking I should call him, so Paul could explain what was really going on.

And right now, as I look at him, I don't see my father's killer. I see the Paul I used to know.

The one who made me feel like I might finally fall in love.

Thanksgiving at our house is always a little weird. We don't have much family aside from Aunt Susannah, who seems to think Thanksgiving is some barbaric American custom that would give her the cooties. So my parents invite along a motley crew of physics students, other professors, and neighbors. The grad students always contribute a dish, and they come from all over the world, which means we might have kimchi or empanadas along with the turkey. One time Louis—who was from Mississippi—brought something called a turducken; personally I don't think any food should have the word *turd* in its name, but it turned out to be a chicken stuffed inside a duck stuffed inside a turkey, and I have to admit it was delicious. The turducken was one of the better offerings, really. Sometimes they're almost sad, like this year, when Theo brought cupcakes we all pretended hadn't been bought from a store.

Paul asked to borrow our kitchen, because he didn't have access to a stove. So I was there to witness him cooking. "Lasagna?" I boosted myself up to sit on the counter. "Just like the Pilgrims used to make."

"It's the only thing I know how to cook." Paul frowned

down at the tomato sauce in its pot, as though it had done something to offend him. "The only thing worth bringing, anyway."

I resisted the urge to point out that if he was cooking at our house, he wasn't precisely *bringing* it anywhere. We had finally reached the point where I was starting to get comfortable with him—where I was starting to believe I might be able to get beneath all the quiet and awkward to figure Paul Markov out.

Mom and Dad were at the university; Theo was out partying; Josie wouldn't fly in from San Diego until tomorrow morning, apparently because she'd spent the day surfing with her friends. So Paul and I were alone for a change. He wore his usual faded jeans and T-shirt. (I swear it's like he doesn't know people are allowed to wear anything besides black, white, gray, and denim.) Yet somehow he made me feel overdressed in my tunic and leggings.

"Why aren't you going home for Thanksgiving?" I managed not to add, *like a normal person.* "Don't you want to see your parents?"

Paul's lips pressed together in a thin line. "Not particularly."

"Oh." If only I could have grabbed those words back, but I couldn't. Very quietly I added, "Sorry."

"It's all right." After another moment of uneasy silence between us, he added, "My father—he's not a good person. My mother doesn't stand up to him. They don't understand the life I've chosen to lead. They're glad I have scholarships, so I don't cost them any more money. There's not much else to tell."

Which was obviously a big fat lie—how is there not more to tell about *that* story?—but I wasn't going to compound my rudeness by prying. I'd just have to wonder what kind of loser parents would have a problem with their son being a brilliant physicist. Or how much might lie behind the phrase "not a good person."

I tried to figure out how to move the conversation on to a new subject. "So, um, what music is this?"

"Rachmaninoff. The 18th Variation of a Rhapsody on a Theme of Paganini." His gray eyes glanced toward me warily. "Not very current, I realize."

"Theo's the one who teases you about your classical music, not me." Since Theo wasn't around, I finally admitted, "I like it, actually. Classical music."

"You do?"

"I'm not an expert on composers or anything like that. But I learned a little through my piano lessons," I hastened to add. "Just—when I hear it, I think it's pretty." The Rachmaninoff was sort of amazing, actually, piano notes tumbling over and over in endless crescendos.

"You always apologize for things you don't know." Paul didn't even look up from the bowl where he was stirring together mozzarella and cottage cheese. "You should stop."

Stung, I shot back, "Excuse me for not being born already knowing everything."

He stopped, took a deep breath, and looked up at me. "I

meant that you shouldn't feel ashamed of not knowing a subject. We can't begin to learn until we admit how much we don't know. It's all right that you're not familiar with classical music. I'm not familiar with the music you listen to, like Adele and the Machine."

"It's Florence and the Machine. Adele is a solo performer." I gave him a sly glance. "But you knew that, didn't you? You just wanted to make me feel better."

". . . okay," Paul said, and I realized he'd gotten it wrong for real.

Before I could tease him about that, he frowned down at his pan of lasagna like it was a science experiment gone wrong. The noodles he'd layered at the bottom of the dish were curling up, as though trying to escape.

"You bought the no-cook pasta, didn't you?" I said, jumping down from the counter. "It does that sometimes."

"I thought it would be faster!"

"You can put the other noodles in there without cooking them anyway—oh, hang on." I grabbed one of the aprons from its hook and quickly tied it on. "I'll help."

For the next several minutes, we worked side by side: Paul layering in cheese and noodles and sauce, me using wooden spoons to try and hold the curly noodles down flat until we got stuff layered on top of them. Steam frizzed my hair, and Paul swore in Russian, and we both laughed ourselves silly. Before that night, I hadn't known Paul could laugh that much.

Just as we were getting done, we needed to cover the pan

for baking, and we both reached for the tinfoil at the same moment. Our hands touched, only for a second. No big deal.

I'd been with him virtually every day for more than a year, but in that instant, I saw Paul as someone new. It was as though I'd never understood the clarity of his eyes, or the strong lines of his face. As though his body had instantly stopped being large and ungainly and become strong. Masculine.

Attractive.

No. Hot.

And what was he seeing when he looked at me? Whatever it was, it made him part his lips slightly, as if in surprise.

We glanced away from each other right away. Paul tore off the tinfoil, and once the lasagna was in the oven to bake, he said he had some equations he needed to work on. I went to my room to paint, which actually meant me staring down at my tubes of oils for several minutes as I tried to catch my breath.

What just happened? What does it mean? Does it mean anything?

Ever since my father's death, I've wished I could take back that moment with Paul. But I can't.

Paul Markov is dangerous. He killed your father. You know *this. If you can't hate him for that, what kind of weakling are you? Don't waste another chance. The next time you see him, you don't hesitate. You don't think about cooking lasagna together, or listening to Rachmaninoff.*

You act.

★ ★ ★

We manage to follow Paul out of the Tube station without him seeing us.

"That reaction you saw?" Theo mutters. "Probably a reminder. He'll know us now. Stay behind him."

Theo's instinct was right; Paul is headed to the tech conference where Wyatt Conley is going to appear. For an event dedicated to the latest in cutting-edge technology, it's held in an odd venue—a building that has to be a hundred years old, all Edwardian cornices and frills. The people filing in are an odd mix, too: some are sleek professionals in suits the color of gunmetal or ink, talking to multiple holographic screens in front of them the entire time they walk up the steps, while others look like college freshmen who just got out of bed but have even more tech gear on them than the CEO types.

"Told you I was overdressed for this," Theo mutters as Paul vanishes through the door.

"How is he getting in?" I say. "Does he have a badge already, or is he sneaking through security?"

"No point in worrying about how he's getting in until we get in ourselves. Leave this to me, will you, Meg?"

Apparently Theo spent his entire journey over to the UK figuring out exactly how these advanced computer systems work. As we huddle on the steps, pretending we're blasé about going in, he manages to hack into the organizer's database. So when we show up at registration, acting shocked—shocked!—that they don't have our badges ready for us to pick up like we'd arranged, they actually find our names in the system. Two hastily printed temp badges later, and we're in.

Theo offers me his arm; I loop my hand through it as we walk into the conference hall. It's a large space, already slightly darkened, the better to show off the enormous, movie-size screen waiting on the stage. "I have to admit," I whisper to Theo, "that was pretty smooth."

"Smooth is my middle name. Actually, it's Willem, but tell anybody that and, I warn you, I *will* take revenge."

We sit near the back, where we'll have a better chance to survey the whole room and see Paul make his move . . . assuming he's going to make one. He doesn't seem to be in the audience.

If Theo has noticed my dark mood, he gives no sign. "Glad I got to know this dimension the best I could, as soon as I could. It makes a difference." It's obviously as safe to talk here as it was on the Tube; most people are surrounded by tiny holographic screens, having a conversation or two. "We'll have to put that in the guide to interdimensional travel you and I get to coauthor someday: *The Hitchhiker's Guide to the Multiverse.*"

Letting scientists go off on Douglas Adams routines is a bad idea, so I ask a question that's been on my mind since shortly after I got here. "How is this the next dimension over?"

"What do you mean?" Theo frowns.

"I guess I thought—you know, the dimension next door

95

would be a lot closer to our own. With just a couple of differences. Instead it's totally not the same at all."

"First of all, this? This is not 'totally not the same.' National boundaries are the same. Most major brands seem to be the same, present company excepted." He's referring to the "ConTech" logo projected upon the onstage screen; in our universe, Wyatt Conley means Triad. "Trust me, the dimensions can be much more radically altered than this."

"Okay, sure." I can see his point. It's not like the dinosaurs are still around or anything.

Theo—always enamored of any chance to show off what he knows—keeps going. "Second, none of the dimensions are technically any 'closer' or 'farther' from one another. Not in terms of actual distance, anyway. Some dimensions are *mathematically* more similar to each other than others, but that wouldn't necessarily correlate to the dimensions being more similar to each other in any other way."

When the word *correlate* puts in its appearance, I know the conversation is about to go into technobabble mode. So I cut to the chase. "You're saying that if Paul just wanted to run away, 'next door,' *this* could be next door, even though this dimension is different in a lot of ways."

"Exactly." The lights go down, and Theo sits up straighter as the crowd's murmuring dies down and their various hologram calls fade out. "Showtime."

The screen shifts from the ConTech logo to a promotional video, the usual beaming people of various ages and races all using high-tech products to make their already awesome lives even better. Only the products are different—the self-driving cars along tracks like Romola had, the holographic viewscreens, and other stuff that I hadn't seen yet, like medical scanners that diagnose at a touch, and some kind of game like laser tag, except with real lasers. A woman approached by the most clean-cut mugger of all time turns confidently and touches her bracelet; the mugger jolts as if electrocuted, then falls to the ground as she strides away.

I glance down at the bangle around my wrist, the one with the inside label that says *Defender*. Now I get it.

The background music rises to an inspirational high as the images fade out, and the announcer says, "Ladies and gentlemen, the innovator of the age, founder and CEO of ConTech . . . Wyatt Conley."

Applause, a spotlight, and Wyatt Conley walks on stage.

Despite the fact that he's been bankrolling my parents' research for more than a year now, I've never actually met Conley before. But I know what he looks like, as does anyone else who's been online or watched TV during the last decade.

Although he's about thirty, Conley doesn't seem to be much older than Theo or Paul; there's something boyish about him, like he's never been forced to grow up and doesn't intend to start now. His face is long and thin, yet handsome in an eccentric sort of way; Josie's even said she thinks he's hot. He wears the kind of oh-so-casual jeans and long-sleeved T that you just *know* cost a thousand dollars apiece. His hair is as curly and uncontrollable as mine, but lighter, almost red, which matches the freckles across his nose and cheeks. Between that and the famous pranks he's pulled on other celebrities, he's been described as "a Weasley twin set loose in Silicon Valley."

"We're on a journey," Conley says, a small smile on his face. "You, me, everyone on Planet Earth. And that journey is getting faster by the moment—accelerating every second. I'm talking about the journey into the future, specifically, the future we're creating through technology."

As he crosses the stage with a confident swagger, the screen behind him shows an infographic titled "Rates of Technological Change." Throughout most of human history, it's a line moving very slowly upward. Then, in the mid-nineteenth century, it spikes up—and in the most recent three decades, goes almost completely vertical.

Conley says, "For all the differences in their eras, Julius Caesar would have fundamentally understood the world of Napoleon Bonaparte, a warrior who lived nearly two thousand years later. Napoleon *might* have understood Dwight D. Eisenhower, who fought not even a hundred and fifty years after Waterloo. But I don't think Eisenhower could even begin to wrap his mind around drone warfare, spy satellites, or any of the technology that now defines the security of our world."

For a history lesson, this is almost interesting. Maybe it's the way he talks with his hands, like an excited kid. But right when I might actually get drawn in, I see Paul walking swiftly up the side aisle to the exit.

Theo's hand closes over my forearm, tightly, in warning. He whispers, "You see him too?"

I nod. He rises from his seat—crouching low so we don't block anyone's view and create a disturbance—and I do the same as we slip out to the side of the auditorium.

A few people give us annoyed looks, but the only sound in the room remains Conley's voice. "For generations now, people have dreaded World War Three. But they're making a huge mistake. They're expecting war to look the way it looked before."

Nobody much is milling around in the corridors outside, except for a few harried assistants trying to prep for some kind of follow-up reception. So Theo and I go unnoticed as we try to figure out where, exactly, Paul might have gone. In a building this old, nothing is laid out quite like you'd expect.

"Through here, maybe?" Theo opens a door that leads into a darkened room, one empty of chairs or tables.

I follow him inside; as the door swings shut behind us, darkness seals us in, except for the faint glow of the tech we wear—our holoclips, or my security bracelet. We can hear Conley's speech again, but muffled. "The next challenges humanity will face are going to be fundamentally different from any we've faced before. New threats, yes—but new opportunities, too."

Then we hear something else. Footsteps.

Theo's arm catches me across the belly as he pulls us both backward, until we're standing against the wall, hiding in the most absolute darkness. Adrenaline rushes through me; my hair prickles on my scalp, and I can hardly catch my breath.

The steps come closer. Theo and I look over at each other, side by side in the dark, his hand firm against my stomach. It's too dark for me to understand the expression in his eyes.

Then he whispers, "The far corner. Go."

We break apart. I rush into the corner, like he said, while Theo walks straight toward the steps . . . which turn out to belong to a tall man in a uniform who doesn't have a sense of humor.

I *knew* somebody like Wyatt Conley would have security.

"I only wanted to get an autograph afterward," Theo says as he keeps going, leading the guard farther from me. "Do you think he'd sign my arm? I could tattoo the autograph on there forever!"

Probably Theo meant for me to get out of here while he distracts the guard. Instead I creep around closer to the stage, and to Paul.

From onstage, Conley says, "The dangers we have to fear aren't the ones we're used to. They're coming from directions we never imagined."

Theo protests as the guard backs him out of the room, "Oh, come on, no need to overreact—" The door swings shut again, and I can't hear his voice any longer. I glance over my shoulder, as though looking for Theo would bring him back again—

—which is when Paul Markov's hand clamps down over my mouth.

My father's killer whispers, "Don't scream."

9

PAUL PULLS ME BACKWARD. HE HAS ONE HAND AROUND MY waist, the other over my mouth. My legs go watery, and I actually have to tell myself not to pass out.

What do I do? I always envisioned attacking him, not being attacked. How could I let him get the jump on me? How could I have been so stupid?

"What are you doing here?" he whispers. We're just behind the curtain. "How can you even be here?"

I grab at his arm, though I know I'm not strong enough to pull his hand away—and that's when I glimpse the bracelet on my wrist.

Defender.

Quickly I click the bracelet like the woman on the video. Instantly, a blue-white shock jolts into Paul's hand.

Paul yells in pain, and I push myself free of him—and stumble through the curtain onto the stage. For a moment

I stand there in the spotlight, in a state of shock, only a few feet away from Wyatt Conley. We stare at each other while the startled audience murmurs and I try to figure out what I can possibly say.

Then Paul's hand closes on my elbow, and I scream.

"Security!" Conley yells as Paul pulls me offstage and people in the audience start shouting. But security isn't around, because they're busy throwing out Theo. That means it's up to me.

I wrench myself away from Paul as violently as I can; he must still be weakened from the electric shock, because I'm able to get free. Then I run like hell.

How could I have been such a fool? How could I have questioned for one second that Paul was dangerous? He killed my father and I still wanted to give him the benefit of the doubt. Stupid, stupid, stupid. I'm never going to let a guy make me this stupid ever again.

I dash from the building into the rain toward the Tube.

From the footsteps on the pavement, and the shouts of people being pushed out of the way, I know Paul's right behind me.

"Marguerite!" he shouts. "Stop!"

Like that would ever happen.

Raindrops spatter against my face; the sidewalks darken in front of me with every drop. The glowing 3D sign for the Underground spurs me on, giving me the strength to run faster.

I plunge inside, wet hair dripping, and don't even hesitate

before vaulting over the turnstile. If it gets the transit cops' attention, great.

But even as I run I hear Paul jumping the turnstile behind me.

My ring begins to blink; only one person could be calling me. I manage to slap the ring on, and Theo's face appears in front of me, shaking and blurry. "I heard—wait—what's going on?"

"Paul! He's right behind me! We're at the Tube!"

Instantly the screen vanishes. Theo's coming as fast as he can, I know, but I'm not sure he'll be able to reach me in time.

The Tube corridor splits here into different tunnels, different destinations. I run into the nearest one, not caring or thinking which would be better, then curse under my breath as I hear a train pulling in ahead. While the crowds might protect me from Paul, they'll also protect Paul from me.

But I keep running. I'm past the point of turning back.

The passengers swarm toward me, their holographic games and calls swirling around them like electronic fog. How can there be so many this long after rush hour? I angle my shoulders, turning that way and this to avoid crashing into someone—but then Paul's hand grabs my shoulder.

Instantly I turn and slam my fist into Paul's face.

Ow. Oh, *damn.* Nobody tells you that punching someone hurts as badly as getting punched. Paul stumbles back, and a few of the other passengers startle, realizing for the first time what they're seeing.

Paul looks at me, his hand to his reddened jaw, and it's as if . . . as if he doesn't understand. How can he not understand?

Behind me the train slides out of the station with a rush of air and a roar that nearly drowns out his words. "Who brought you here?"

I don't get a chance to answer as Theo shoves through the crowd, launching himself toward Paul and yelling, "Son of a *bitch*!"

Paul's head whips from me to Theo in the split second before they collide. The remainder of the commuting crowd shatters in an instant; people scream and scatter, going in a hundred directions at once. A big guy slams into me hard enough that I bang into one of the metal-grid dividers.

Breathless, I stare through the grid to see Paul and Theo on the ground. Theo has the advantage at first, on his knees while Paul is flat on his back, and his fist makes contact with Paul's jaw so hard that I can hear the crack.

Then Theo tries to hit him again, and in the moment that he blocks Theo's hand with his own, Paul's expression shifts from bewildered hurt to rage.

Red security alert lights begin to pulse. The grids cast strange shadows that seem to carve lines around and through us. Soon the metro police will be here. *Shit.*

Yet none of that matters when I see Paul bodily throw Theo back. Theo tumbles over so far that he actually falls through one of the holographic signs, something about tourism in Italy. As Theo half vanishes behind a translucent version of the Colosseum, Paul leaps after him, kneeling above Theo's crumpled form.

"You," he snarls, clutching Theo's T-shirt. I never knew Paul's face could look like that—soulless with fury. "How did you follow me?"

Theo kicks Paul solidly in the chest, but it only holds him back a moment. Paul recovers within a blink and punches Theo in the jaw. Then again. Then again. It's not like I didn't know Paul was bigger than Theo, but somehow I never realized until now just what a giant he is. How impossible it would be for Theo to take him down alone.

But I've got my breath back. Theo doesn't have to go it alone anymore.

I run toward them, jump through the holographic sign and land on Paul's broad back. He grunts in surprise, and tries to reach for me, but I've got one hand around his neck and another in his hair. So what if hair pulling is a girl move? It hurts, and it *works*.

"What—" Paul tries to twist out of my grip, but as his hand closes around my forearm, he suddenly stills. "Marguerite, stop."

I can hardly hear the words over the rumbling approach of another train.

"Go to hell," I say.

My free hand is the one with the Defender bracelet. When I slam it against his side, it does its job, shocking him again, and he cries out in pain.

Theo's back up, and he goes after Paul's Firebird locket.

That's it, *that's it*, all I have to do is hold Paul while Theo finishes him.

Then Paul angles his head back, and he looks at me. His gray eyes stare upward, searching my face, revealing a depth of betrayal and pain I recognize because it mirrors my own.

For one instant, doubt blots out everything else, and my grip weakens.

One instant is all Paul needs.

He twists free of me and slams his elbow into Theo's face, knocking him back to the floor. I try to regain my hold on Paul, but it's useless; he's up now and using every inch he has on me, every pound, to hold me back.

"What are you doing?" he shouts. The security lights pulse above us, turning the line of blood along his mouth from red to black and back again.

"Stopping you!" I swing at Paul, but his massive hand blocks mine easily.

Theo scrambles to his feet; Paul sees it. Immediately he grabs me—literally picks me up—and shoves his way through the doors of the train car right before they close. I wriggle free of him just in time to see Theo press his hands against the glass door. But it's too late. The train is moving.

For one moment I match my hand to Theo's, separated only by the glass; he looks stricken, but says nothing. What can he say? Nothing can prevent the way the train speeds up, pulling away from him, leaving only his fingerprints.

The train slides into the tunnel, into the darkness. Nobody else is in this car. Paul and I stand there, breathing hard, illuminated only by the holographic ads overhead. He's still wearing his Firebird. We are alone.

"How did Theo bring you here?" Paul says, voice low. "And why?"

I lift my chin. "Theo rebuilt the Firebird prototypes on his own. You didn't think he could, did you?"

"The prototypes. Of course," he whispers, and it's almost like he's glad to hear it. "But . . . but why did he bring you along? Do you not see how dangerous this is?"

"That doesn't matter. If you thought you could kill my father and get away with it, you're—"

"What?" His face pales so suddenly that I think for a moment he might pass out. "What—you said—Henry's dead? He's *dead*?"

The astonishment and pain I see are very real. Some people are good enough actors to feign shock, but shy, uncertain Paul Markov has never had that kind of game. There's no way he could fake this kind of horror, or the tears I can see welling in his eyes.

It hits me then, a blow more stupefying than sharp: *Paul didn't kill my father.*

"Oh, God." Paul wipes hastily at his eyes; he's trying so hard to stay focused. "How can Henry be dead?"

All those moments that have tormented me over the past few days—Paul smiling at his birthday cake, listening to

Rachmaninoff, standing in the doorway of my bedroom. Those were real. Paul is real.

But then what the hell is going on? If Paul didn't kill Dad, who did?

"Wait. You thought *I* killed him?" Paul says it with none of the anger I'd feel in his place. He's just completely confused, like he has no idea how I could ever believe anything so weird. "Marguerite, what happened?"

"His car went into the river. Someone had tampered with Dad's brakes." My voice sounds small, not like my own.

"You have to believe me. I didn't hurt Henry. I would never do that."

"It really looked like it had to be you." And as soon as I realize that, I realize something even worse. "I think someone framed you."

Paul swears under his breath. "Why on earth did Theo bring you along?"

"Why do you keep acting like it's all up to Theo? I chose to come. I have to find out who did this to Dad."

Then it hits me—this wave of anger. I thought I knew who to blame for Dad's death, before; I thought I knew who to hate. Now I don't. For the past few days, my hate has been the only thing keeping me going. I feel naked, unarmed.

The train curves through the tunnel, and the floor beneath us rocks back and forth. All the ads flicker slightly. Paul's face is half in shadow like the album cover of *Rubber Soul*.

"I'll find out who hurt Henry." Paul takes one step toward me. "I swear that to you."

"If it's not all up to Theo, then it's not all up to you either! Okay, so, you didn't kill Dad or trash the data. Then who did? Why did you run?"

He startles me again. "I didn't kill Henry, but I did destroy the data at the lab."

"What? Why?"

Paul puts his hands on my shoulders. I flinch. I can't help it. He jerks away, as though he thinks he might have injured me. "Tell Theo I'm sorry. When I saw him earlier, I thought—I blamed him for something he didn't do. I realize now he was only trying to do something for Henry—" His voice breaks again. Our shared grief pierces us at the same moment, an electrical shock of feeling traveling from him into me, or from me into him. "But tell Theo that he has to take you back home, now. The sooner the better. It's the most important thing he could possibly do."

"No. You have to explain."

He says only: "Go home. I'll fix this."

Then the train rocks on its track hard enough that I stagger. In the second before I can catch my balance, Paul clutches his Firebird in his hand, and—

It's hard to describe exactly what happens next. Although nothing moves, it feels vaguely as if a breeze has stirred the air around us, changing something indefinable about the way Paul looks. He lifts his head, as though startled, and he brings one hand to his torn lip and winces. When he sees the blood on his fingers, he doesn't seem to remember how it got there.

109

Then I realize the Firebird is no longer around his neck. There were no crackling lights, no unearthly sounds, nothing like that; one instant the Firebird was there, and now it's not.

Paul is gone. He's leaped ahead, into yet another dimension.

Which means the guy standing in front of me now is . . . still Paul Markov, but the Paul who belongs in this world.

The train pulls into its next stop. I grab one of the poles to steady myself; Paul does the same, but clumsily, like he hardly understands what's happening. Then I realize he doesn't. He's standing here on this train without any memory of how we got here, or even who I am.

"What's going on?" says Paul/not Paul.

"I—" How am I supposed to explain this? "Let's get off the train, all right?"

Although Paul looks understandably wary, he follows me out, through the station, and onto the street.

We're in an entirely different section of London now, or so it seems; this part looks more like the city I remember, with more old buildings, no hoverships in the sky. It's started to rain again. We duck under a storefront awning, and by now Paul looks less confused, more unnerved. "Where am I?"

"London."

"Yes, of course," he says, and the way his eyes narrow when he's unsure and irritated is so familiar that it's difficult for me to believe this isn't my Paul. "I came in this morning for the tech conference. To hear Wyatt Conley. I'd been planning it for weeks—but I could swear I remember getting off the train. Then it all goes . . . blank."

He was coming to the tech conference anyway. Of course he was. Why wouldn't a physicist be interested in one of the innovators of the age? "Do you not remember anything of the past, I don't know—two days?"

"I remember . . . some things," Paul says. His expressions, the way he moves—it's all slightly different from our Paul, the one I know, the one who just ran away from here. How strange it is to be able to tell the difference in how he tilts his head. "But who are you? Who punched me?"

I did that. Theo and I did that to you, and you're a stranger who never hurt either of us. "There was a fight. It's over. Nothing bad happened."

"But—" He stares down at his broad hands, realizing his knuckles are bruised. His lost expression is suddenly so like Paul's that it makes me suck in a sharp breath.

I find myself wishing I could explain.

So I say, as gently as I can manage, "You wouldn't believe me if I told you. Just—go home. It's all right. You won't see me again."

Although he clearly wants more answers, Paul must want to get the hell away from the crazy stranger even more. He backs away, out from under the awning, until raindrops patter against his long coat and his disheveled hair. Then he turns and walks into the London crowd, lost again in an instant.

Only then do I realize my ring has been vibrating for a while now. I hit it, hoping to get Theo. When his face appears before me in three-dimensional light, I'm hopeful—but then I realize it's a message.

"Marguerite, I hope to God you're okay." His face is stark—afraid for me. Theo continues, "Paul jumped out of this dimension a few seconds ago. I'm guessing you already know that. We have to go after him. Don't worry—I set your Firebird to follow him wherever he leaps, exactly like mine. I feel . . . beyond strange, going on ahead of you, but I know you'd tell me not to let Paul get away, no matter what. Justice for Henry, that's what matters most."

I nod, as though his message could see me. But it's only a hologram talking into the void.

Theo smiles, tense and nervous. "We'll meet in the universe next door, all right, Meg?"

"Yeah," I whisper. "Next door."

Although I take my Firebird in hand, I don't set it for the next jump right away. First I look out at the grimier London in front of me, the one with technological marvels pinned to or floating in front of every person, and each one of them too distracted and careworn to notice. I try to imagine how this Marguerite will feel when she comes to alone in a few seconds, wondering why her heart is pounding.

It seems that she won't remember much. But—I don't need

the reminders the way Theo does, the way Paul appeared to. The experience of traveling is different for me than it is for them. So maybe this Marguerite's experience will be different too. Possibly she'll retain some fragment of this, an image or a sensation that belonged to me and now is shared between us both.

So I flood my mind with thoughts of my parents, the ones she lost so long ago. I think of them laughing while I painted the rainbow table. Of Mom holding me on her shoulders at the natural history museum so that I could look right up into the skull of a triceratops. Of Dad taking me around town on his bike when I was still little enough for the kiddie seat—one of my earliest memories—him laughing with me as we swooped downhill together.

I hope this Marguerite can remember them a little. That it will make some dent in the terrible grief that has walled her into this life . . . and maybe give her enough hope to break free.

Then I begin manipulating my Firebird, turn the final gear, and think, *Oh, God, what's next? What's next?*

I collide with myself—my other self—and this time I lose my balance entirely. In the split second I'm wobbling in midair, I realize I am descending a staircase. Apparently this is a very, very bad moment to have a cross-dimensional traveler hop into your body, because then you miss a step and—

I manage to get my hands in front of me as I fall, which

doesn't keep me from landing on the stairs hard, but at least lets me brace my roll down the next several steps until I catch myself. A necklace around my neck breaks, and I hear beads rolling in a dozen directions. All around me, people cry out and hurry to my side. Dazed, I lift my head.

The first thing I notice is that these stairs are carpeted in red velvet. Which is a good thing, since they seem to be marble beneath; that would've hurt. The second thing I notice is that all the beads clattering and rolling down the steps aren't beads at all. They're pearls.

I put one hand to my aching forehead as I look up. My fingers make contact with something in my hair, the band of this heavy thing atop my head. . . .

Is that a *tiara*?

Finally I see the people crowded around me—one and all in incredibly elegant evening dress: men in unfamiliar military uniforms resplendent with medals and sashes, women in white, floor-length gowns, not unlike the one tangled around my legs.

"Marguerite?" says a kindly man only a few years older than me, one with hair as dark and curly as mine, though his is cut short. From his concern I can see he knows me well, but I've never seen him before. Though—something about his face is oddly familiar—

"I'm all right," I say. I have no idea what else to do, other than reassure them. I put one hand to my chest to steady myself, then gasp as I look down.

The different layers of the Firebird lie scattered in my lap

and on the steps around me. Only its clockwork locket shell
still hangs around my neck.

It's broken.

The Firebird is broken, and I have no idea how to fix it.

Oh, shit.

10

"MARGUERITE?" THE BROWN-HAIRED YOUNG MAN KNEELS next to me and takes my hand; we're both wearing gloves of white leather so thin and soft it's like a second skin. "Margarita? Are you all right?"

"I'm fine. Honestly. Only clumsy." Oh, my God, where am I? What is going on? I thought the last universe was different, but this—is something else altogether.

"You're worrying like an old woman, Vladimir. Again." The largest of the men in our group frowns; his voice is deep and resonant, and from the way he speaks, I can tell he's used to being obeyed without question. His ivory-jacketed uniform bears more medals than anyone else's. He's well over six feet tall.

"I'm a babushka, then," says the young man—Vladimir—as he gives me a reassuring smile. Quickly I gather together all the fragments of the Firebird; a small silk purse dangles from one of my wrists, and I slip the pieces inside.

"Why are you worrying about that trinket?" commands the large man who appears to be in charge of this . . . costume party. Or whatever this is. "The Tarasova pearls are all over the floor, and you simply let them roll away from you."

"We have them, Your Imperial Highness," a woman whispers as she and a few others—dressed less grandly than the rest, including me—begin scrambling to collect every last one of the pearls. I lift my hand to my throat and discover that, besides the Firebird and the now torn, dangling string for the pearls, I'm wearing some sort of enormously heavy choker.

His Imperial Highness?

"Papa, if *I* had such beautiful pearls, I wouldn't fall and break them," says a girl a few years younger than me—even though I've never seen her before, she too looks familiar.

A bit like Vladimir, and a bit like . . .

"If you had such beautiful pearls, Katya, you would lose them long before the ball." The tall man doesn't even look at her as he speaks, and Katya's head droops. "Marguerite, can you still dance tonight? Or must we make excuses for you?"

"I'm fine, really. Please, let me catch my breath." Wait, what am I saying? Dance? What kind of dance? Maybe we're actors, in some sort of performance. That would explain the costumes, right?

But already I know better. The marble steps, the red velvet carpet—they're only part of the enormous space around us, with forty-foot ceilings and molding gilded in what looks like real gold. This is a palace. And we're not tourists being led through roped-off lines and warned about flash photography.

As Vladimir helps me to my feet, the tall man says to him, "Margarita has servants to help her, Vladimir. The son of the tsar should be above . . . nursemaiding."

But Vladimir's eyes flash with fire, and he lifts his chin. "How can it be above any man's dignity to help his sister? Shouldn't the daughter of the tsar be able to expect assistance from anyone, at any moment?"

Sister. My eyes widen in shock as I realize why Vladimir seems so familiar to me. He—and Katya, now that I study her face again—they look a lot like my mom.

Our mom?

No. Absolutely not. They're the children of the tsar—oh, crap, there are still tsars here? What kind of dimension is this?—okay, this guy is the tsar, and these are his kids, but I *can't* be. It's not possible for anyone other than Dr. Henry Caine to be my dad. Like every other individual ever born, my genetic code is unique, incapable of being re-created. The only way I can be born, in any dimension, is to the father and mother I've always known.

Mom? I look around the grandly dressed group, hoping to see her. Whatever version of my mother exists in this dimension, I need her now.

But I don't see her anywhere.

Okay. I know one thing for sure; I can't fake my way through this. Right now I need some time alone to figure out what's going on.

I fall against Vladimir's shoulder in a swoon that's only partly feigned. "I'm so dizzy," I whisper.

"Did you hit your head?" Vladimir cradles me with both arms, his forehead furrowed with worry. He obviously believes he's my older brother; his gentle concern would be incredibly comforting if I'd known him for more than three minutes. "Father, we must fetch the doctor for her."

"I didn't hit my head," I protest. "But I wasn't feeling well earlier today. I—I think I ate something that disagreed with me."

The tsar breathes out in exasperation, seemingly irritated that anything in the world is beyond his control. "You ought to have had the sense to keep to your bed. Return to your rooms. Vladimir and Katya will have to represent the family."

Secure in her spot behind the tsar's crooked arm, Katya sticks her tongue out at me. She seems like a total brat.

"Let me go with her," Vladimir says. I can't get over how much he looks like Mom . . . and like *me*. "I can be back down in minutes."

"Now you push this too far," the tsar growls. "Why does she have ladies in waiting? Why does she have a personal guard? They are the appropriate people to see to her. Even you should understand that."

"I'm all right, Vladimir," I whisper. I don't want to start some kind of family argument, and besides, I need to be alone. "Go."

Vladimir looks reluctant, but he nods and releases me. The hands of my ladies in waiting flutter around me, attempting to support me without actually daring to touch.

The tsar motions to someone else in the group, someone slightly behind me. "You, there. Lieutenant Markov. See her to her room." Then a firm hand clasps my elbow.

I turn to see Paul standing nearby, just outside the circle around me.

In that first instant, I'm afraid of him. But that fear is swiftly followed by hope, because I see the recognition in his eyes. This is my Paul—he's here—and I'm not as alone as I thought.

He is crisp in his infantry uniform, a neatly trimmed beard edging the line of his jaw, with high boots and a sword strapped to his side. Yet at the collar I see the glint of a chain; his Firebird is there.

Paul bows his head, then begins escorting me back up the stairs. The rest of the royal party watches me go: Vladimir with concern, Katya with open glee that she gets to go to the ball while I don't, and the tsar—supposedly my father—with no more than bored contempt.

"Are we doing this right?" I whisper.

"How would I know?" Paul replies in the same hushed tone. "Nobody's saying anything. Keep going."

As we reach the landing at the top of the steps, I catch sight of myself in the long, gilded mirrors that line the wall. The diamond choker around my neck is several rows wide, and each jewel glitters, like the rubies in my tiara. My frilly white gown sparkles slightly too, because the thread looks like pure spun silver. Paul might only be a soldier, but his scarlet-jacketed uniform looks as grand as anything I'm wearing. It feels like we're dressed up for Halloween, or the most over-the-top prom ever.

The moment we're alone, Paul turns to me, furious. "I told you to go home."

"You don't get to give me orders! You think you're in charge just because, what, you're a genius and I'm not?"

"I should be in charge because I'm older than you and I understand what's going on, while you don't," he retorts.

"The only reason I don't understand is because you won't explain."

"Look, Conley is dangerous. You need to go home," he repeats, and there's something about the way he says it that makes me realize what he actually means. Paul's not telling me to get out of his way. He actually means there's some reason I need to be back at home, a reason my presence there is important.

Not that this gets him off the hook. Not by a long shot. But it calms me enough to focus on the most critical problem we have. I palm the little silken purse and show Paul the fragments of the Firebird locket. "I'm not getting home with this."

Most guys would swear. Paul just presses his lips together into a pale line. "This is bad."

"Understatement of the year."

Paul takes the purse from me and begins examining the pieces one by one. I resist the urge to keep arguing with him. If he's fixing the Firebird—i.e., my only shot at not living in this dimension forever—I'm going to let him concentrate.

Finally he says, "It can be repaired."

"Are you sure?"

"Almost sure," Paul answers, like that's just as good when it so is not. He must catch the look on my face, because he adds, "The Firebirds are made to be easily reassembled. We wanted them to snap apart into their components for repair, adjustments, that kind of thing. It looks like that's what happened here."

"So you can pop it back together?" Relief rushes into me, makes me giddy. Talk about dodging a bullet.

"I need better light, and I'll want to double-check it against my own Firebird." Paul hands the silk purse to me and pulls at the chain around his neck; the locket gleams dully against the scarlet of his uniform coat. "Come on. Let's get this done and send you home."

I jerk back. "I'm not going home until you tell me why you're here!"

Paul's not one of those people who gets louder when he gets angry. He gets quieter. Goes still. "This isn't the dimension I was looking for. That much is already obvious. I need to keep moving, but I can't leave here until you—"

"What is the meaning of this?"

We both straighten, startled to see another Russian officer walking toward us. He has gray hair, a beard to rival the tsar's, and a monocle. Paul stands at attention, or at least what looks like attention to me; I don't guess either of us has any idea what proper Russian military protocol would be.

The officer says, "Markov, I'm surprised at you. Pestering Her Imperial Highness like this instead of doing your duty."

Oh, that's me. *I'm* the Imperial Highness. I have to stifle a laugh. "I, uh, I asked him to look at something I broke." I hold out the Firebird locket pieces to show him.

The officer's puffed-out chest falls a little; he seems smaller, robbed of his indignation. But his eyes light up as he finds something else to say. "And what is this? Out of uniform while on duty?"

And he grabs the Firebird from around Paul's neck.

I gasp. Paul's eyes widen. We're both too startled to think, much less move.

"Now that you're finally in appropriate uniform, Lieutenant Markov, you may carry on," the officer says, tucking Paul's Firebird into his pocket as he continues down the long hallway.

We watch him go in mutual horror. I'm the one who finds words first: "Oh, crap."

"We have to get the Firebird back." Paul takes a deep breath. "I have to go after him."

"Surely he's going to give it back to you. Eventually. Right?"

"How would I know? Besides, we don't have much time. My memory—it's already getting cloudy. The Paul Markov from this dimension is going to take over again, any minute."

The rest of it hits me: If Paul can't remember who he really is, he can't fix my Firebird. Meaning unless and until Theo finds us—if Theo even exists in this dimension—we'll be trapped in this dimension. Potentially forever.

"Okay, you'll go after him and—" I put my hands to my head, trying to think, and only when my fingers touch the tiara do I remember who I am here, what I can do. "Wait! No, I go after him, and I *order* him to give back the locket. He has to do it. I'm a *princess*! Or a grand duchess, whatever they call them in Russia—"

"Yes! Good. Right. Go." Paul nods his head, almost comically fast.

I take off down the hallway toward the stairs, running down them as fast as I can—which isn't that fast, because I'm wearing a long dress cut narrow through the skirt, plus high heels that don't even have a strap across the foot to hold them on. My jewelry jangles around my neck; my tiara slides to one side, and I lift one hand to hold it to my head. "Sir!" I shout, wishing I'd thought to ask the guy's name. A name would work better. Could I just yell, *I command you to stop?*

But as I reach the bottom and turn the corner, I see an enormous gathering of people all walking through a broad hallway. This isn't the party itself, but the entrance for most of the guests. Dozens of women in a rainbow of gowns and jewels nearly as fine as mine, from girls my age with feathery fascinators in their hair to elderly dowagers seemingly bent low by the weight of their diamonds—young men in elegant evening suits, brilliant scarves knotted at their throats—

—and military officers. At least fifty of them, all wearing uniforms that look identical to the one on the man who took Paul's Firebird. I strain to catch a glimpse of his face—he had a monocle, they can't all wear those, can they?—but it's impossible to pick him from the crowd. He might already have gone into the ball.

Should I run in there, create a scene? I have a feeling that wouldn't get me very far.

As quickly as I can, I rush back upstairs. Paul is leaning against the wall, as though he were exhausted. "I lost him!" I call out. "He's in the party, but you could recognize him, couldn't you? Help me find him?"

"I—I think so." He winces and puts his fingers to his temple, like he has a headache. His confusion reminds me of Theo, back in London, in the last moments before he would have forgotten himself completely.

"Paul, don't! You have to stay with me." I take his shoulders in my hands and get in his face. "Look at me. *Look at me.*"

"You have to get the Firebird," he says, slow and careful with each word, as if he doesn't trust himself to force them out. "You have to use it to bring me back."

"How do I find that guy again?" How do I do anything in this dimension? My hands are shaking, and the diamond choker around my neck feels like a noose. "Oh God, oh God, he had that big beard, and a monocle—"

"Colonel Azarenko," Paul says absently.

I stare at him. "What?"

He looks at me as though he hadn't seen me before. Then he straightens, pulling out of my hands. "Your Imperial Highness."

This is not my Paul any longer. This is Lieutenant Markov.

He continues, "Forgive me, Your Imperial Highness. I can't think why—I don't remember how I came to be here. Was I taken ill?"

"You . . . became lightheaded." I cover as best I can. "I wasn't feeling well either. So you were to take me to my room, so I could rest."

"Very well, my lady." He bows his head and begins walking briskly through the corridor, his shining boots dark against the red velvet carpet. In something of a daze, I trail along behind.

At least one of us knows where my room is.

Paul and I are trapped here. With no idea how to contact Theo, if I even can. All I have to go on is the name "Colonel Azarenko."

Tomorrow, I tell myself. *I'll be able to ask about him tomorrow, have him brought to me, and get Paul's Firebird back.*

If I can't—

—but no. I can't think about that right now. Instead I straighten the tiara on my head and pretend I know what the hell I'm doing.

11

LATER THAT EVENING, AFTER MY MAIDS (I HAVE THREE) have dressed me in a loose nightgown and settled me into my bed, I lay the pieces of my Firebird on my embroidered coverlet. This enormous bed of carved wood is high above the floor, every blanket and sheet pristinely white, so it feels a bit as though I'm considering my options while resting on a cloud.

With a sigh, I flop onto the soft pillows piled at the head of my bed. The room surrounding me isn't that large, nor is the decor gaudy, and yet there's no mistaking the wealth and elegance that created it. The walls and high ceiling are painted the cool, soft green of aged copper. A writing desk in the corner is scrolled with vines of inlaid wood, as if it were being reclaimed by the forest leaf by leaf. Across from my bed, a broad fireplace set with enameled tiles glows with the fire that warms my room.

My jewels are back in their velvet boxes, along with all the others.

At least this version of me has books, several of which are strewn around me right now. Many of them are in Russian . . . but I can read that here, and speak it too. Apparently that kind of memory is hardwired into the mind differently than emotions and experiences.

From what I can tell from the books I've scanned, just as technology had developed slightly faster in the London dimension, here it has developed far more slowly. My surroundings seem to belong in the year 1900 more than in the twenty-first century. Although some elements of this world are more or less advanced than my dimension was at this point, the overall feel is like stepping back a century in time. In this world, the twenty-first century simply looks very different. People travel by railroad or steamship, or even sometimes on horseback or in sleighs. Telephones exist but are so new we only have a few in the palace, and they're only for official use; nobody has even thought of telephoning a friend merely to chat. The internet hasn't even been dreamed of. Instead, people write letters. I can see a stack of creamy stationery waiting on my desk.

The United States of America exists but is thought of as remote and provincial. (I have no idea whether that's true or not, but everyone here in St. Petersburg would agree.) Royalty still reigns throughout Europe, including of course the House of Romanov. The man everyone thinks is my father is Tsar Alexander V, emperor and autocrat of all the

Russias. So far as I can tell, this dimension doesn't yet contain the equivalent of a Lenin or a Trotsky. This is good, as I have zero interest in pulling an Anastasia—getting shot to death in a basement and then having every crazy woman in Europe pretending to be me for the next fifty years.

A set of leatherbound encyclopedias on a lower shelf has an entry about the House of Romanov. There, in plain text stark on the page, I learn that Tsar Alexander married a young noblewoman named Sophia Kovalenka. With her he had four children: the Tsarevich Vladimir, Grand Duchess Margarita (i.e., yours truly), Grand Duchess Yekaterina (a very fancy name for the brat who stuck her tongue out at me), and finally Grand Duke Piotr.

My mother died giving birth to her fourth child.

Mom and Dad always said pregnancy was "difficult" for her; I never realized that meant "dangerous." They stopped after me and Josie, for the sake of her health. Here, I realize, the Tsar never stopped demanding more children, pressuring her into pregnancy after pregnancy until, finally, she died while in labor with her younger son.

They cut him out of her after she died. I wish I hadn't read that.

My mother is a scientist. She's a genius. She's strong and she's fierce and, okay, she can be a little obtuse about ordinary life, plus she doesn't understand art at all, but still, she's *Mom*. She has more to give the world than almost anyone else I can imagine.

Tsar Alexander thought all she had to offer were heirs to

the throne, so he . . . bred her to death.

I pick up a silver photo frame from my bedside table. The oval portrait there, in slightly fuzzy black and white, shows my mother with younger versions of me, Vladimir, and Katya; she's dressed in an elaborate long-sleeved gown, but the way her arms are curved protectively around me and Vladimir, the way she smiles down at the toddler Katya in her lap—something in her, too, remained the same in this universe.

But not enough. Here, my mother never had the chance to study science. What interested her here? How did she occupy her brilliant, restless mind? Did she ever look at Tsar Alexander with anything like the love and trust she always had with my dad?

And here, Josie was never even born. Dad must have been a fleeting presence in her life, which is almost impossible for me to imagine.

With a shaky hand I put the photograph back where it belongs; even the thought of what happened to my mother is too much to bear right now. I slump back on the piled feather pillows and take slow, deep breaths.

My eyes go to the sliver of light visible beneath my bedroom door. Until a few minutes ago, that light was broken by two dark lines—the shadows of Paul's feet as he stood guard outside. But apparently even the personal guard of one of the grand duchesses is allowed to sleep. The encyclopedia informed me that I live in St. Petersburg, currently in the Winter Palace.

What about Theo? If he exists in this dimension, he probably would be in the United States, or maybe in the Netherlands, where his grandparents were from. My heart sinks as I realize that, in a world where the swiftest travel possible is by train, there's no way Theo could reach me today, or tomorrow, or even within a few weeks. Given the famous savagery of the Russian winters, it's entirely possible he couldn't get here before spring. Even if he did manage to travel to St. Petersburg, how would he ever win an audience with one of the grand duchesses?

It's all right, I tell myself. *You'll find Colonel Azarenko tomorrow. Anyway, Paul's here. You don't need anyone else.*

My mind fills with thoughts of Paul. How could I have completely failed to understand him?

"In other words," I said, "you're trying to prove the existence of fate."

The scene is as vivid for me now as it was on that day: Theo in a faux-weathered RC Cola T-shirt. Paul in one of the heather-gray Ts that I knew he only wore because he had no idea how much they showed off his muscles. Me tucking my hair behind my ears, trying to look and feel as grown up as they were. All of us together in the great room, surrounded by Mom's houseplants and the summer warmth from the open doors to our deck.

I was joking when I spoke about fate, but Paul nodded slowly, like I'd said something intelligent. "Yes. That's it exactly."

Although I knew Theo thought the idea was silly, it intrigued me. Anytime the physics discussions around me shifted from complicated equations to concepts I could connect with, I seized on it. So I sat beside Paul at the rainbow table and said, "How does this work, then? Fate."

He ducked his head, shy with me even after spending more than a year practically living in my house. But like any scientist, he was so fascinated by ideas that he couldn't stay quiet about them for long. He steepled his large hands together, fingertip to fingertip, holding them in front of me, as our illustration of a mirror image. "Patterns reoccur, in dimension after dimension. Those patterns reflect certain resonances—"

"And people each have their own resonance, right?" I thought I'd picked up on that much.

He smiled, encouraged. Paul's smiles were rare—almost out of place on someone so large and brutish and serious. "That's right. So it looks as though the same groups of people find each other, over and over. Not invariably, but far more than mere chance would suggest."

Theo, who was across the room settling back into his own math, made a face. "Listen, little brother, if you write your theory up like that, and you stick the numbers, you're golden. It's when you get into this souls-and-destiny crap that you sink your thesis. Seriously, you're going to get up before the committee and defend that?"

"Stop knocking him," I told Theo. At the time I'd been too enchanted by Paul's idea to listen to even good objections.

"Everybody gets to have wild theories here. Mom's rule."

Theo shrugged, already too absorbed in his work to protest further. Yet Paul looked over at me as though he were grateful for the defense. I realized how close we were sitting—closer than we usually did, so near that my arm nearly brushed against his—but I didn't move away.

Instead I said, "So does destiny create the math, or does math create our destiny?"

"Insufficient data," Paul said, but I could tell, in that moment, how much he wanted to believe in destiny. It was the first time I thought of him as someone who, all appearances to the contrary, might have some poetry in his soul.

Maybe it was the only time I ever understood him at all.

The next day, I discover what it's like to have people get you ready in the morning.

I mean, totally. My maids appear around my bedside as I wake, serving me tea on a silver tray, running me a warm bath in an enormous tub carved of marble, even soaping my back.

(Yes, it's *completely embarrassing* bathing in front of an audience, but it seems this Marguerite does it every day, so I have to roll with it. I guess they already know what I look like naked, which . . . doesn't help that much.)

These women even put the toothpaste on my toothbrush.

They select a dress for me: a soft yellow the color of candlelight, floor length, so formal for everyday that I can hardly keep myself from laughing at it. They braid my hair back and fasten it with pins set with small white enameled roses. I stare at the mirror in disbelief as my uncontrollable, lunatic curls are tamed and settled into a style as complicated as it is beautiful.

I could almost believe that *I'm* beautiful, though really this is a testament to what personal stylists (or their nineteenth-century equivalents) can accomplish.

No makeup is to be seen anywhere, but they rub sweet-smelling creams into the skin of my face and throat, then dust me with lilac-scented powder. By the time they're finished clipping on my pearl earrings, I actually feel like a grand duchess.

"Thank you, ladies," I say. Good manners are expected of royalty, right? Feeling both ridiculous and grand, I open the door and see Paul.

Correction: Lieutenant Markov.

He stands at attention, entirely proper and correct. His clear gray eyes meet mine, almost guiltily, before he glances away. Maybe staring at royalty is forbidden. I seem to remember that megastars like Beyoncé sometimes have riders in their contracts saying that nobody can look them in the eyes; as Beyoncé is to our dimension, a grand duchess is to this one.

Paul—Lieutenant Markov, better think of him that way— doesn't say anything. Of course. It's probably the rule that he can't say anything unless I speak first. "Good morning, Markov."

"Good morning, my lady." His voice is so deep, and yet so gentle. "I hope you feel better today."

"I do, thank you. Tell me, Markov, where might I find Colonel Azarenko?"

He frowns at me. "My commanding officer?"

"Yes. Exactly. Him." Paul might not have been able to retrieve Azarenko from the grand ball last night, but now he can tell me the officers' daily routines, all of that. We'll have his Firebird back by lunchtime, and mine fixed by tonight.

"Colonel Azarenko left for Moscow early this morning, my lady."

Moscow? He's not even in St. Petersburg anymore? "Did he give your—did he give anything back to you before he left?"

By now Lieutenant Markov must think I've gone demented. Although his forehead furrows—the only sign of the frown he's holding back—he politely replies, "No, my lady. What would the Colonel have to give me?"

I'm not even getting into that. Instead I ask, "When is he expected back?"

"After the New Year, my lady."

New Year's Day? That's almost three weeks away.

Three weeks.

How am I supposed to pretend to be a princess for three weeks?

I swallow hard and think, *Guess I'll find out.*

12

STAY CALM. DEEP BREATHS.

I walk through the hallways of the palace in a daze. It's as though my body is too freaked out even to panic. Instead I feel more like I've been drugged. My footsteps weave slightly, and the elaborate brocade pattern of the carpet runner seems dizzying.

"Are you sure you are entirely well, my lady?" Paul—Lieutenant Markov—walks a few respectful steps behind me.

"Quite well, thank you, Markov." *Actually I'm about five seconds from losing it completely, but let's just keep walking, okay?* That's the subtext. Maybe he understands; at any rate, he remains silent as we go on.

It would help if I had any idea where I'm supposed to be going. The Winter Palace is enormous, and I couldn't find my way around it even if I did know what I was meant to be doing next.

Luckily, I'm not alone for long. "There you are!" Vladimir bounds from a side hallway to fall into step with me; despite the late night and all the champagne he must have had, he glows with energy. "Feeling better?"

"Mostly." Smiling at Vladimir turns out to be completely natural. His easy stride and friendly grin charm me, and besides, the affection he feels for his sister is unmistakable. What would an adored little sister say at a moment like this? Let's see. He went to a big party last night, right? Josie's had her share of missed curfews and nights out—more than I have—so I say to him what I might have said to her: "What about you? I'm surprised you're not under the covers whining and holding an ice pack to your head."

Vladimir looks skyward and sighs melodramatically. "You're never going to let me live that one down, are you?"

"Nope, never." This bluffing thing is easier than I thought. I can't help but grin.

He continues, "One night, I drink too many toasts with vodka, and once in my blameless, virtuous life, I wind up getting sick in a decorative urn. The price? My sister's eternal condemnation."

"Not condemnation. But eternal teasing? Definitely."

At that, Vladimir laughs; his laughter is so much like Mom's. So this is what it's like to have a brother. I always wished for one, and Vladimir seems like exactly the brother I'd have wanted—protective, funny, and kind.

Which is the moment I feel a hard pinch on my arm.

"Ow!" I spin around to see Katya, who looks very satisfied

with herself in her pink dress. I'd guess she's about thirteen. Although she resembles the tsar more than the rest of us do, she still has the unruly Kovalenka curls. "What was that for?"

"For thinking I was too little to go to the ball. I showed you. Men danced with me all night!"

I glance at Vladimir for confirmation. He gives Katya a look. "Our little Kathy danced precisely four dances, one of them with me and two with her uncles. But one very nice officer did take her out on the floor, where she danced very well."

Katya lifts her stubborn chin, as though she hadn't been contradicted. With a shake of my head, I say, "They grow up so fast."

"Where does the time go?" Vladimir agrees, joining in the old-and-superior act.

This wins us a scowl from Katya. "You're not so big," she says, and dashes past me—with the end of my sash in her hands. It unties and flutters to the carpet; she drops it as she runs ahead, laughing.

"Oh, honestly." Is she always this irritating? This dimension's Marguerite must hardly be able to stand her.

But something about the way Katya giggles reminds me of a time, several years ago, when I sneaked up behind Josie while she was on the phone and snatched her ponytail clip out of her hair. She had to chase me around the house for at least ten minutes before she caught me. Why did that seem like fun when I was nine? No clue. But it was *awesome*. I even jumped over the sofa at one point, and howled laughing when Josie tried to follow me over and instead wiped out and fell on the floor.

I remember Josie yelling, "Little sisters are the most annoying people on earth!" Chagrined, I realize she was right.

Paul steps in front of me and kneels to collect my sash; when he holds it out to me, he looks into my eyes like—like I'm not merely his responsibility. Like he *knows* me. Has he remembered his real self? My hopes rise for one quickened heartbeat, before I realize this is still Lieutenant Markov. He says only, "My lady."

"Thank you, Markov."

The words come out steadily enough, but it's so strange, looking at Paul and seeing someone who is both him and not him.

Someone very like the man I always daydreamed Paul might be . . .

Vladimir doesn't seem to have noticed anything out of the ordinary between us. "Now that I see you're back to yourself, I shall head down to the barracks," he says as Paul steps behind me once more, and I hastily retie my sash. "Enjoy your lessons."

"See you at supper." Oh, crap, what if they don't eat supper together? Or should I have said dinner? But it doesn't look like I got it wrong, because Vladimir nods. I offer my cheek to him for a quick kiss; his mustache tickles my skin.

At the end of the hallway I discover a library—no, a schoolroom.

"Are you going to let me get a word in edgewise today?" Katya demands as she slides into one of the desks, which are all broad and grand, less like something out of a public school and more like something you'd see in an antiques store. "Or are you going to play teacher's pet again? He's supposed to be tutor to us all, not only you."

"I'll take turns," I promise absently. Footsteps are coming down the hall, small and light.

Then a young boy appears in the doorway, his face open and smiling. "Marguerite!"

The encyclopedia supplied the name I need; the fact that he's *completely adorable* supplies the emotion. "Piotr." I hold out my hands for my younger brother, who dashes into them. He looks even more like Mom than I do—slight, almost fragile, and not nearly big enough for a ten-year-old, but with a sweetness in his face that is only his own. Does the tsar give him anything like the affection he must need? I don't see how. And the way Piotr clings to me reminds me painfully that his mother—my mother, our mother—is gone.

Even Katya softens slightly for him. "Will you dazzle me with your French today, Pierre?"

He nods seriously. "I practiced with Zefirov."

"Zefirov doesn't speak a word of French!" Katya laughs, pointing at the guard standing outside the door, alongside Paul. Zefirov says nothing, just keeps staring straight ahead. "We'll see how you do, Peter."

Pierre, she called him, and then Peter. In the hallway,

Vladimir called her Kathy, and last night he called me Marguerite, even though the encyclopedia confirmed that in this dimension I've been given the Russian form of my name, Margarita. From my history lessons, I know that nineteenth-century nobility often used different forms of their names in all the various languages they spoke, an aristocratic affectation that must have survived here.

I glance over my shoulder at Paul. Here, no doubt, he's Pavel—the Russian form—but I can't bring myself to think of him by a different name.

This classroom is nothing like the dull, institutional places I've seen on television. Instead of plastic desks and bulletin boards, the space has bookshelves that reach from floor to ceiling. The Persian carpet here is a bit more threadbare than those in most of the rooms of the palace, the dark green velvet drapes perhaps slightly shabby. This room isn't for showing off power and wealth. This room feels like home.

I take the seat that must be mine and wonder how in the world I'm going to bluff my way through this part, since I have no idea what they're studying, besides French. Katya can hog the teacher's attention all she likes. I probably wouldn't be able to answer a single question.

Then a familiar-sounding English male voice says, "I see the grand duchesses are none the worse for wear after last night's revels."

I turn and see my father.

He's alive. He's alive, and he's *here*, and more than everything I want to run to him, hug him, tell him I love him, all the things I longed to say just once more. This is the miracle I'd hoped for since the moment this journey began.

But I remain in my seat, hands clasped tightly around the armrests of my chair. What is he doing here? I don't understand—

"Let's begin our lessons then," he says. My father must have come to Russia to teach the sons and daughters of the tsar. Then he met my mother.

I can't jump out of my seat to embrace the "royal tutor." I have to continue to play this role. But it's all I can do to hold back tears of happiness.

He takes his place at the front of the room, papers spilling out of his case. He's no tidier in this dimension than he is at home. Despite the odd formality of the clothes he wears—a full old-fashioned suit complete with waistcoat and wire-rimmed spectacles—he's still completely, utterly my dad. Same narrow but handsome face, same pale blue eyes, same quizzical smile when he's concerned. "Your Imperial Highness, I heard you weren't well. Are you feeling better?"

Oh, right. That means me.

"Much better, thank you, Professor." My voice sounds so strained, as though I can barely get the words out. Dad knows something's up, but he simply studies me for a moment before nodding, allowing me to go on.

"All right, then. I realize you're all wild with anticipation to return to your French, so let's get started."

Peter is learning basic grammar. Katya has translated some text. I'm supposed to be finishing an essay on the works of

Molière. Mercifully, I've studied Molière at home too, so I ought to be able to get through this. Yet all I can do is clutch my book with clammy hands and steal furtive looks at my father, alive and well only steps away.

I never lost anyone before, not like this. My grandparents all died before I was born or when I was so small I hardly remember them. The only funeral I've attended was the one for my pet goldfish. So I had no idea what real grief was.

Now I know grief is a whetstone. It sharpens all your love, all your happiest memories, into blades that tear you apart from within. Something has been torn out from inside me that will never be filled up, not ever, no matter how long I live. They say "time heals," but even now, less than a week after my father's death, I know that's a lie. What people really mean is that eventually you'll get used to the pain. You'll forget who you were without it; you'll forget what you looked like without your scars.

This, I think, is the boundary line of adulthood. Not the crap they claim it is—graduating from high school or losing your virginity or getting your first apartment or whatever. You cross the boundary the first time you're changed forever. You cross it the first time you know you can never go back.

Every time I see Dad's face, or hear his voice, I have to fight the urge to cry. Yet somehow I make it through our classes, French and geography and, finally, current events.

"What changes might we see in the next few decades?" Dad says as we study the most recent issue of *Le Monde* we have (which is from four days ago—everything travels slowly here). He's getting excited, the way he does when his imagination starts going into overdrive. "If this sort of assembly-line manufacturing works for cars, what else might it be applied to? Think of the advances in productivity, and technology!"

"Or war," I say quietly. "They'll make weapons like this too."

Dad gives me a searching look. "I suppose you're right. Automation increases all of humanity's potential, both good and bad."

In the background I can see Peter trying to pay attention, and Katya folding a paper airplane from a page of *Le Monde*. Really I ought to let one of them get a word in edgewise, but I can't pass up any chance to talk with my father.

"However, don't you think, Your Imperial Highness, that the benefits will ultimately outweigh the drawbacks?" Dad pushes his spectacles farther up his nose. I can tell they drive him crazy; this version of Dad doesn't get to wear contacts.

"It's not a simple equation. Not addition and subtraction— more like higher-level calculus." I start to play with my hair before I remember it's actually fixed for once. "Goods will be cheaper and more plentiful, but that leads to people treating them like they're disposable. We'll exchange individuality and craftsmanship for predictability and affordability. Countless jobs will be created, but as industry becomes globalized, those jobs will largely move to developing nations with fewer labor laws to protect . . ."

Everyone else in the room is staring at me. Dad looks admiring; Peter and Katya look unnerved. How many anachronisms did I just use? Maybe this Marguerite doesn't think that much about economics.

". . . so, uh, the effects of the Industrial Revolution are complex. And things. Yes." My smile must look even more awkward than I feel.

"Industrial Revolution," Dad repeats slowly. "What an interesting turn of phrase. You could sum up so much of what's happening in the world today with that. 'Industrial Revolution'—very well said, Your Imperial Highness."

As absurd as the situation is, I can't help basking in the glow of my father's praise. Then that makes me want to cry again, and I have to look away.

Our lessons end, and with regret, I leave the classroom with my siblings. Before I go, I give Dad a smile. It's so much less than I feel, but I can't risk any more. In the hallway, Paul has been waiting for me all this time, Peter and Katya's personal guards at his sides. There's no sign of impatience, though; it's as if he would always wait for me, no matter how long it took.

"Once again, teacher's pet," Katya sniffs as we walk away.

"Oh, hush," I say to her.

Peter laughs. "You're his favorite and you know it. But it's only natural, because you're the cleverest."

My little brother doesn't resent my closeness to our tutor, but my little sister obviously does. "It's hardly even proper, the way you two carry on." Katya tosses her hair, which

145

hangs in a long plait down her back. "Maybe history isn't all he wants to teach you, hmm?"

"Yekaterina!" It comes out hard and cold. Of course she couldn't know how grotesque her joke really is, but that doesn't change the fact that I want to slap her face. "How dare you say anything so unkind? And untrue."

She shrinks back. Even her belligerence only goes so far. "It was only a joke!"

"That's not the sort of thing you can joke about, not even with me. Professor Caine is a good teacher, to all of us, and you should respect that."

"All right, all right," Katya grumbles, clearly ready to let the subject drop. Thank God. The last thing I need is for her to guess the real reason why I'm the favorite.

I discover we're all meant to spend our afternoons in different ways: Katya, embroidering with one of our cousins, which she will hate. Peter, riding lessons and maybe a turn around the soldiers' training camp with Vladimir, which he will love. Me? I'm supposed to spend the rest of the day answering letters from various royal relations throughout Europe.

So many problems with this plan. First of all, I don't actually know who any of these relatives are—sure, I've got a list, but who exactly is Her Serene Highness Princess Dagmar of Denmark? Well, I mean, *obviously* she's a princess named Dagmar, but are we cousins? Friends? Nearly strangers? What do we usually talk about? Second, I'm pretty sure there are protocols for this sort of thing, royal letter formulas to follow, none of which I know.

Still, I'm not sure what else to do at the moment. Until Colonel Azarenko returns, and I can get Paul's Firebird back from him, I have to do my best to pass as the real Grand Duchess Margarita. That means writing letters. In the library, I manage to find a ledger called *The List of Leading Royalty, Nobility, and Officials* that sets out the royal families of each country, with notes that explain how we're related.

I seem to be related to *all of them*.

Paul remains with me throughout this, several feet away. He must notice how bizarre it is for me to need these reference materials, but he says absolutely nothing about it, simply waits patiently. That helps me feel a little more in control, even as I make a mess of the letters. The fountain pen blots every other word, and handwriting takes so long; if you ask me, Skype is a much better way to keep in touch.

Between notes, I search the *List* for any reference to a Theodore Willem Beck. Okay, it would be an extreme long shot for Theo to turn out to be nobility too, but I'm desperate to figure out where he is. In a world without Google, that info is a lot harder to come by. But the book has no mention of him, just like my maids this morning had never heard his name. Theo's whereabouts remain a mystery.

As I work on a letter to a Greek princess who is apparently my aunt, I remain vividly aware of Paul's presence. He stands by the door of the salon where I've chosen to work, the two of us alone in the vast, elegant room, looked upon by oil portraits of my various ancestors, all of whom seem to be disapproving. Finally I can't take the silence any longer.

"You must find this very dull, Markov," I say.

Paul doesn't even turn his head. "Not at all, my lady."

"You wouldn't rather be with your"—Regiment? Is that right?—"fellow soldiers?"

"My duty calls me to remain with you, my lady."

And there's something about the way he says "my lady" that flusters me. I turn back to my letter, but I can only stare down at the page.

Okay, I've learned that Paul Markov isn't a killer. That's a relief, but that truth raises more questions than it answers. Why would Paul destroy my mother's research and data and take off? And if he's entirely innocent, why did he fight Theo so savagely in London?

Well. Theo and I attacked him first, and Paul did say he was suspicious of Theo when he saw him . . .

Wait. My eyes widen. *Theo—it couldn't be.*

No. It actually couldn't be. Theo took an enormous risk to try and help my mother and avenge my father; he leaped through dimensions without any guarantee he wouldn't be turned into "atomic soup." He's as confused about what's going on as I am. The shifting worlds around me have left me unsure of so many things, but Theo's loyalty, at least, has been proved beyond any doubt.

Paul Markov remains a mystery.

Yet he's a mystery I'll have to solve if I'm to have any hope of repairing the Firebird.

I try to concentrate on my letter, but I can't. I drop my

head into one of my hands. Paul takes one step toward me. "My lady? Are you well?"

"I'm . . . overwhelmed. That's all."

"Do you need to walk into the Easter room, my lady?"

Easter room? When I look up, Paul is smiling—but shyly. Even here, in a world where he's a military officer in full uniform, gun and knife in his belt, he remains unsure of saying the right thing.

I rise from my chair and let him lead the way.

Paul takes me through more of the long corridors of the Winter Palace. Gilded ceilings glitter overhead as we walk through columns of green marble, through rooms painted gold or crimson or royal blue; my slippers softly echo the click of his shining boots along the paneled floors. Finally we reach a pair of tall, white doors. Paul pushes them open and steps to one side, allowing me to enter first. I walk inside, and only barely manage to stifle a gasp.

The Easter room turns out to be where our family keeps the Fabergé eggs.

Each egg is a jeweler's masterpiece. Small enough to fit easily in an adult's hand, they are set with porcelain, or gold, or jewels, or most often a combination of the three. Some are modestly pretty, like the pink enamel one latticed with rows of tiny pearls; others are spectacularly inventive, like the egg of lapis lazuli surrounded with silver rings like the planet Saturn, nestled in a "cloud" of milky quartz dotted with platinum stars.

In my dimension, a few dozen Fabergé eggs have survived

from the decades the Romanovs gave them to one another as Easter gifts. In this dimension, that tradition has lasted for well over a century. A couple hundred eggs glint and shine from their places on the long shelves that line the walls. It's like falling into a jewel box, but a thousand times more dazzling, because every single egg is a unique work of art.

Reverently I tiptoe to one of the shelves and pick up an alabaster egg. My inner voice chants, *Don't drop it, don't drop it, don't don't don't.* The silver hinge in the middle opens, and I lift it up to reveal a tiny clockwork dancer inside, a metal marionette who begins to dance while a tune plays. It's so beautiful, so delicate, that it takes my breath away.

"Not your usual favorite, my lady," Paul says softly.

How many times has he brought me here, when I was sad or lonely? I sense this is far from the first afternoon we've found ourselves alone here.

"Which one is my favorite?" I look up into Paul's gray eyes, challenging him to know me.

Without hesitation, he points at an egg the deep, vivid red of wine, decorated with swirls of delicate gold filigree. The beauty of the red alone—I could mix my paints for hours and not capture that depth of color.

I realize why Paul's holding back; surely he's not allowed to touch it.

So I lift my chin and say, "Get it for me, Markov."

He pauses for only the briefest moment, then takes the egg into his broad hands. (And they're so large, so strong. I think he could span my waist with his hands.) As I watch, he lifts the top to reveal the "surprise," the extra layer of finesse or artistry hidden within each egg. Here, it is a small silver charm—a tiny framed portrait of my mother.

"Oh," I whisper. Of course this would be the one I always return to, the one I love best of all. Paul nestles the egg in my waiting palms. His fingers brush against mine for a fraction of a second, and yet I imagine I can feel his touch long after it has ended.

For a few long moments we stand there, so very close, looking down at the delicate, priceless thing in my hands. I am aware of Paul's silence, of the rise and fall of his breath. We are alone in a room that stretches for dozens of feet, with a ceiling that vaults twenty feet above our heads, and yet our nearness feels almost unbearably intimate. The afternoon sunlight slants through the tall window, glinting off his military decorations and the gilding on the egg I hold.

Paul says, "Your mother was very beautiful, my lady."

He's only judging by the portrait. In this dimension, he probably never got the chance to know Mom. I think of how much she loves him, back home, and feel a pang at the loss—this other connection that should have existed, but didn't. "Yes, she was."

"Very like you, my lady."

I can't look up at him. I can't catch my breath.

Why does he get to me like this?

But if I'm being honest, what I'm feeling began a while ago, growing from curiosity to hope to something I can't even name.

"Oh—" I wince as one of the prongs inside the wine-colored egg falls down into the shell. Mom's portrait won't hang in its place any longer. "I broke it."

"Don't worry, my lady. The tutor will be able to fix that, I'm certain. Professor Caine is very adept with his clock-maker's tools."

Of course. At home, every once in a while, Dad tinkers with old clocks, getting them to run again. His fine scientific mind, denied theoretical challenges in this world, has turned to more mechanical ones. Here he must tinker with machinery all the time.

At last I look up at Paul, and I'm beaming with such happiness that I know he's surprised. But I can't help it.

I just thought of another way out.

13

"PROFESSOR CAINE." IT'S SO BIZARRE, CALLING HIM SOME-thing besides Dad.

But what about this isn't bizarre?

Dad walks into the Easter room, escorted by Paul, who went to fetch him at my command. When he sees the wine-colored egg in my hands, Dad nods, anticipating my request. "It's that hook, isn't it? Really, someday soon, you should have the Fabergé jewelers reset that properly, Your Imperial Highness." He reaches into his jacket and withdraws a small leather roll—his packet for his watchmaker's tools. "But I can put it right for now, never fear."

"Of course you can." I smile at him, hoping to butter him up for a favor. Then I realize that's sort of ridiculous. When you're a grand duchess of the House of Romanov, you don't ask for favors; you make commands.

But this is still my father, and more than ever, I want to treat him with respect.

"I had another project for you, if you were willing to take a look at it." Carefully I place the broken egg on a small side table, then reach into my pocket. There, wrapped carefully in my lace handkerchief, are the pieces of the Firebird. "This locket of mine is broken."

Dad glances from the egg over at me, smiling. "I believe you're trying to make a jeweler of me, to avoid any future exams in French."

"No, I promise. This is important to me, and it's complicated—" I stop talking before I begin to sound panicky. If Dad (or Paul, standing guard at the door) realizes how worried I am about the Firebird, there might be questions I won't be able to answer. "The locket's meant to be more than decorative, you see. When all the pieces are put together properly, then it will function again."

"What does it do?" Dad pushes his glasses up his nose as I unwrap the handkerchiefs a little to reveal the bronze-colored pieces within. "Play music?"

"No." But what am I supposed to tell him? He'd hardly believe the truth. "I'm afraid I'm not sure."

"Then I doubt I'd be able to set it right, not knowing how it should work. Of course I want to help you, Your Imperial Highness, but this might be a task best given to a professional."

Oh, no. If Paul and I are going to have any backup plan for getting out of this dimension, I need someone like Dad to work on the Firebird. Okay, he's gotten stuck playing tutor in this lifetime, but that doesn't change the fact that he's a genius. He's my best chance, maybe the only one I have.

There's no guarantee Colonel Azarenko won't have thrown away or sold Paul's Firebird locket by the time he returns from Moscow; if mine doesn't get fixed, Paul and I will both be trapped here forever.

To still my rising panic, I take a few deep breaths and watch as my father works on the red Fabergé egg. He deftly works with a tiny pair of prongs to twist the hook back into shape, but it's what he does next that takes my breath away.

Dad picks up the charm portrait of my mother, the one commissioned by Tsar Alexander V, who probably never looked at it again. But Dad holds the charm for a long moment, his eyes drinking in the image of her face, and within him I glimpse the deepest sadness and longing I've ever seen.

("I had no idea what your father looked like, the first time he came to visit me," Mom said once as we cooked out in the backyard on a hazy summer afternoon. "But I was already half in love with him."

Dad had laughed as she hugged him from behind. "And I'd picked out the wrong faculty photo, so I thought this 'Dr. Kovalenka' was rather elderly." He lifted her hand to his and kissed it. "Still, some very enticing equations had already been exchanged. I was half in love too. So you see it was a very intellectual courtship—at first."

"At first." Mom's smile became positively wicked. "Now,

the other half of falling in love came when we met at the airport and I discovered you were *incredibly sexy*."

"Same here," Dad confessed. "I came near tackling you at baggage claim."

Josie and I had made gag-me faces, because we were younger and still thought it was gross to see our parents cuddling like that. It was before I realized how incredibly rare it is to watch two people actually stay in love their whole lives.)

Maybe it's wrong of me to use his feelings against him, but down deep I know Dad would want to help me, and to comfort the version of Mom back home who's mourning him and desperate for me to return to her. So that makes this all right. At least, I hope so.

"This was my mother's," I say, holding out the lace-wrapped Firebird again.

That does it. Dad turns from the Fabergé egg. "Your mother's?"

"She always used to show it to me, when I was little." The first rule of lying, Theo once explained, is *Keep It Simple, Stupid*. "I can't remember the trick, the thing it did—but I remember loving it. Mom always used to share this with me, so when I found it a few days ago, I was so excited. But you see, it's in pieces. Someone's got to put it together again. You could—I know you could."

Very gently, Dad hangs Mom's tiny enameled portrait back within the wine-colored egg and closes it again. Then he takes the lace handkerchief in his hands and lifts one piece of the Firebird, an oval bit of metal with computer chips inlaid. There's no way he has any idea what the hell a computer chip is, I realize, my heart sinking. Am I fooling myself to believe this is possible?

"Do you have any idea of its basic framework, Your Imperial Highness?" he says.

I tap the locket cover. "It all fits in this locket, folds up until you'd think it was only a piece of jewelry. And I don't think anything's missing or broken, just knocked apart. But—more than that—no."

Dad considers it for another moment, then says, "Most devices have a sort of internal logic. I might be able to work it out, given time."

"Would you try?"

"Why not? I always enjoy a good puzzle."

Hope leaps within me, bright and wild. "Oh, thank you!" My first impulse is to hug him, but I manage to hold back.

Dad smiles as he folds the remnants of the Firebird back in the lace hanky. "My pleasure, Your Imperial Highness. Always a pleasure to help you."

"You'll never know what it means to me." Is it possible I'll actually get out of this?

"I understand," is all he says, but in those two words I hear his love for my mother, and the depth of what he'd do for her memory.

Not even my father is such a genius that he can instantly repair a complicated device he's never seen before. Nor can he create more hours in the day. Christmastime is the heart of the season here in St. Petersburg, which means virtually every night involves another dinner, or a dance, or a social gathering. My dad is exempt from few of these occasions; I am exempt from none. Azarenko is still in Moscow, and without that time machine Mom never got around to inventing, I can't make New Year's come around any faster.

For the time being, I have to make myself at home.

I start with the basics. I memorize as much of that Royal List as I can. A calendar of my appointments turns up in my desk, so I'm able to figure out what I should be doing next, and I find a map of the Winter Palace that helps me learn my way around. (If I get lost in my own house, that's probably going to tip them off that something's up.)

The strangest part is how strange it *isn't*. After a few days, it feels completely ordinary to wear floor-length dresses every day, and wear my hair piled atop my head in a complicated wreath of braids. My palate gets used to the taste of briny caviar, the pickled flavor of borscht, and the strength of Russian tea. I can read and speak English, French, and Russian without any difficulty switching between them— and I make sure to practice a lot, hoping to carry a little of the French and Russian back home with me.

Each morning, the servants prepare me for my day, doing everything I need, from slipping the stockings over each of my legs to polishing my earrings before screwing them tightly upon my earlobes. (No pierced ears for a grand duchess: in this dimension, at least in St. Petersburg, any kind of body piercing is as good as wearing a T-shirt that says, PROSTITUTE HERE, ASK ME ABOUT MY HOURLY RATES.) They even take care of everything when, on my fourth morning here, my period starts. It's a huge hassle, involving this contraption like a garter belt but not one bit sexy, and actual cloth towels folded between my legs. I have to stand there, blushing so hot I must be turning purple, while they change it every few hours and take the towels away to be hand-washed by some unlucky individual. Why couldn't I have had my period in the dimension where I lived in a futuristic London? They probably had, like, miracle space tampons or something. But the servants don't seem to think anything of it, so I try to endure it without giving away how completely freaked out I am.

Each day, I go to the schoolroom and study French, economics, geography, and anything else I can talk Dad into reviewing. He responds to my greater curiosity, introducing more science lessons about the innovations of the day, like the race to develop airplanes. (They've already been invented here, but only just, and planes are still cloth-and-propeller jobs. The longest flight in history, so far, lasted about twenty minutes.) Peter loves it, asking so many questions that I wonder whether he inherited Mom's scientific curiosity; Katya pouts about the additional homework, but I can tell she's intrigued despite herself.

Seeing my father again never gets easier, but I'm glad even for the pain. To have this one last chance to spend time with him is a gift I could never take for granted.

And Paul is always near me. Always with me. If he's not in the room with me, he is outside the door.

At first the reassurance I take from having him near is simple. As long as Paul is nearby, I can make sure he stays safe. I can believe we'll get his Firebird back or my dad will fix mine so that I'll be able to remind Paul of himself—and then I'll be sure that we can get home.

Another grand ball is scheduled, only one of more than a dozen leading up to Christmas. I won't be able to fake another fainting spell to get out of this one. Unfortunately, the kind of dancing they have at grand balls is not the kind I know how to do. Waltzing seems to play a major role.

I have no idea how to waltz. If the tsar's daughter goes out on the dance floor and makes a total fool of herself, people are going to wonder what's wrong with me.

That afternoon, when Paul and I go to the library, I don't even bother sitting at my desk. Instead, as soon as Paul closes the tall doors behind us, I say, "Lieutenant Markov, I would like to learn how to waltz."

He stops. He stares. I don't blame him. After a moment, he ventures, "My lady, you are an excellent dancer. I have seen you waltz on several occasions."

"Be that as it may"—Does that sound regal? Maybe I'm laying it on too thick—"I, um, feel a little rusty. I'd like to practice before tonight. You'll dance with me, won't you?"

Paul straightens, looking as awkward and unsure as he ever did back home. But he says, "As you wish, my lady."

"All right. Good. First we need music." In the corner is an old-timey phonograph machine, complete with one of those fluted trumpet things that used to serve as a speaker. They look easy enough to use in old movies; you drop the record down, crank the handle, and presto.

But when I walk over to it, slippers padding against the thick Persian carpet, I realize this phonograph doesn't use records. I'm familiar enough with those from Dad's vinyl collection, but these are . . . cylinders? Made of wax?

I cover my awkwardness as best I can. "Markov, select some music for us."

He walks smoothly to my side, chooses a cylinder. I watch carefully, so I can do it next time if need be. Then he turns the small crank at the side, and soft, tinny music begins to play, the notes beautiful even through the hiss and crackle of static.

I face Paul, ready to begin, but he says, "The smooth floor would be better, my lady."

Of course. Dance floors are never carpeted.

So I follow him to the part of the room closest to the windows, where no carpet covers the floor. The squares beneath our feet seem to be striped, so rich are the inlays of different woods. Light from the narrow windows falls softly over us, catching the reddish glint in Paul's light brown hair.

"If I may, my lady." He holds his hands out somewhat stiffly—near me but not touching—and I realize that's what he's asking. He needs permission to touch me.

I lift my face to his, and I realize . . . he wants to touch me.

Somehow I say, "You may, Markov."

He takes my right hand in his. My left hand goes to his shoulder—that much I know. His left hand closes around the curve of my waist, warm even through the white silk of my dress.

It's hard to meet his eyes, but I don't look away. I can't.

Then Paul begins to waltz. It's a simple step—ONE two three, ONE two three—and yet for the first few seconds I'm clumsy with it. Dancing is harder to bluff. But I remember something my mother said once about formal dancing; she said you simply had to follow the man's lead. You had to surrender to it completely, let him guide you and move you, every second.

Normally I'm not very good at letting anyone else be in charge. But now I give in to it. I let Paul take over.

Now I feel the subtle pressure of his hand on my back— not shoving me around, but gently, gently hinting at which way he'll turn. Our clasped hands dip together; my posture changes, so that I'm letting him lean me back a little. The leaning and the spinning dizzy me slightly, but that almost helps me. I can surrender to him now. I can stop thinking, stop worrying, and exist only within the dance.

As he recognizes the change, Paul becomes more daring. He whirls me in wider and wider circles. My long skirt spins out around me; I laugh in sheer delight, and am rewarded with his smile. It's as if my entire body knows exactly how he's going to move, and we're dancing with abandon, only for the joy of it. Paul's hand tightens on my back, pulling me closer . . .

. . . which is when the song ends. We jerk to a halt as the music vanishes. Only static is left behind.

For a moment we stand there, in a dancing pose that has become an embrace. Then Paul lets go of me and takes a step backward. "Your dancing remains excellent, Your Imperial Highness."

"Thank you, Markov."

Is that how a princess would behave? Walking away easily from her dancing partner without ever glancing back? I hope so. I sit down at my desk, pretending I can read the letters in front of me, that every part of me isn't completely, utterly aware of Paul going to once again stand guard at the door.

The way he dances with me—looks at me—I have to understand it. What was there between this dimension's Marguerite and Lieutenant Markov?

That evening, as I wait for my maids to appear and make me ready for the ball, I go digging through the Grand Duchess Marguerite's things, looking for . . . love letters, a diary, anything like that. When I see a portfolio case, my heart leaps. She's an artist too! I'd give anything for my oil paints right now.

But this Marguerite doesn't paint with oils. She draws.

Pencils and charcoal: those are her tools, discovered in a small leather case. My own intense interest in color and depth isn't a part of her work in the slightest—instead, she's drawn to details, to precision. And yet I recognize elements in the work that are like my own.

Here's Peter, reading a book, his eyebrows slightly raised in fascination—Katya, trying so hard to look grown up that she instead seems slightly ridiculous—

—and Paul.

Sitting on the embroidered carpet in my bedroom, I flip through the sheets of paper to see two, three, even more sketches of Paul Markov. When I remember my shredded portrait of him, I feel ashamed—not only for destroying my work because I believed something untrue about Paul, but also because I never really captured his personality in the painting. Not compared to this Marguerite: she's *good*.

She's caught something almost intangible about him in this profile, that sense of purpose Paul has that infuses every moment, no matter how casual. This one shows Paul standing at attention, his shoulders sketched with a loving attention to detail that tells me she notices the way his uniform drapes over his body, the way he moves.

Finally I lift a sketch that's set in the Easter room. I can't tell whether Paul willingly posed for the others, but he didn't pose for this; there's something softer about portraits done from memory, both more affectionate and yet more unsure. She's caught that subtle tilt of his head that means he's paying attention, the stormy cast of his eyes. The eggs are sketched in behind him, more as shadows than anything else, though I can see how she's penciled in a few fine details: a hint of enameling on one, the sparkle of gilt on another.

I try to pay attention to those, rather than the way she's drawn Paul here, looking straight at the artist with an expression that is equal parts pain and hope.

(Looking at me. Always, always looking at me.)

Quickly I shuffle together the drawings scattered across the lap of my dress and put them back in their folder. The pencils and charcoals remain out, but—no portraits while I'm here, I think. Maybe it's time to try landscapes for a change.

What the hell, I think. *If I get stuck in this dimension, I can be the one who invents abstract art.*

But I won't get stuck here. I won't. If all else fails, Dad can save me. I have to believe that.

If I don't get stuck here, then I never have to ask myself what emotion made this Marguerite draw Paul over and over again. What she saw in him that allowed her to capture his soul more completely than I ever have.

Or how it is that both Paul's souls seem to be the same.

My maids outdo themselves in preparation for the ball. My dress tonight is pure silver—the silk, the stitching, the beading sewn around the low square neck, the cuffs, and the hem. Once again they nestle the ruby tiara in my hair; they give me diamond earrings so heavy I can't imagine wearing them all night. My reflection in the mirror astonishes me.

Why do I get to look like this in a dimension with no phone cameras? I think in despair, turning that way and this. *I would take selfies for about an hour, and those would be the only pictures I would ever use for the whole rest of my life.*

But when I walk out of my room, I see my truest reflection in Paul's eyes.

He draws in a sharp breath, then says, almost a whisper, "My lady."

"Lieutenant Markov." Even though I know he's supposed to walk me down to the ball, it's all I can do not to hold out my arms and invite him into another dance.

Could we dance tonight? Probably I have to dance with the nobles first—and Vladimir, surely, because if he danced with Katya he'll dance with me—

"Surely you don't mean I'm not invited?"

The masculine voice rings from the hallway as Paul and I descend the stair. From the way everyone around me freezes, I know this is bad news.

Katya comes thumping down the steps behind me, graceless despite her long white dress. "He came," she whispers. "They said he wouldn't."

"It's all right," I say, though I have no idea whether it is or not.

Paul turns to me. "If at any point during the evening you feel yourself to be unsafe—"

"I'll come straight to you," I promise.

Vladimir makes his appearance then, expression grim and at odds with his crisp uniform and shining medals. "Come along, then," he says, offering me his arm. "It looks as though we have to play Happy Family tonight. Let's face the dragon together, hmm?"

By Vladimir's side, with Katya ghosting along behind us, I walk into the main hallway. Once again, dozens of bejeweled and beribboned nobles are milling around, pretending not to notice the thinly veiled confrontation in the center of the hallway. There, Tsar Alexander stands stiffly to receive . . . someone. A man a year or two younger than him, somewhat thinner, but equally tall, wearing a look of prideful disdain and a uniform as resplendent as any of the others in the room.

"Uncle Sergei," Vladimir says, bowing to him. Until this moment, I hadn't realized even a bow could be sarcastic. "How delightful to see you. And just in time for the holidays!"

Grand Duke Sergei. The facts I memorized in the *List* come back to help me. He's the tsar's younger brother, and his rival for power. I hadn't known how seriously to take the newspaper reports about that rivalry, but now that I see the sheer venom in Sergei's glare, I finally understand.

His eyes narrow as he looks at me. "Your flattery deceives no one, Vladimir. But at least you have enough manners to pretend to be glad to see me."

I summon my courage. "Uncle Sergei. Welcome." Then I hold out my hand for him to kiss. Sergei stares at it so long that I wonder if I did something wrong, but then he bows over my hand, takes it in his, and presses his lips to my knuckles.

His lips are cold. I sense that he's imagining what my wrist would feel like without a pulse in it.

Katya offers her hand in turn, her small, stubborn face so unpleasant that I can't help picturing her flipping him off instead. As Sergei gives her the same oily treatment he gave me, I study the faces of those around me—the tsar, my brother, the nobles, Paul. One and all, they look angry, and in several of them I also sense fear.

A rival for power wants that power for himself. He would try to take it away from the tsar, from the man everyone thinks is my father. He would have to eliminate my father's heir—Vladimir. And Piotr. And Katya, And—

Becoming this dimension's Marguerite means taking on all of her life. Not just the dresses and jewels, not just dancing with Paul.

Before, I'd only been afraid of not getting home. Now I'm afraid of not getting out of this dimension in time to escape the danger that I now know is very, very real.

14

with a packet of letters in his hand.

"Are you in charge of the royal correspondence now?" I smile to turn it into a joke, but I honestly want to know why he's doing anything so unusual. After a week and a half in this dimension, I know how weird it is for him to bring the mail instead of a servant.

"There was an odd letter this morning. The head sec-retary asked for my opinion, and I couldn't think what to make of it, so I brought it to you myself." Vladimir thumps the entire packet of envelopes against my desk before hand-ing it to me. "It arrived via the French Embassy. Highly irregular—might simply be the work of some madman—but apparently the cover letter was extremely persuasive. Swore you'd want to see this." He pulls the top envelope from the packet and shows it to me. "Do you?"

Written in fine, elegant English script across the front is *Her Imperial Highness Grand Duchess Margarita of all the Russias.*

Beneath it is another name: *Meg.*

Theo! I grab the envelope from Vladimir's hand so swiftly it makes him laugh in surprise. But he doesn't interrupt as I peel open the wax seal to read the note inside.

> *So, I'm a chemist in Paris, which I thought was pretty freakin' awesome until I read a newspaper and realized what you were up to. How the hell are you the daughter of the tsar? Not sure how that panned out, but—well played, Meg. Well played.*

> *Paul leaped into this dimension, obviously, and you did too; my Firebird tells me that much. Almost a week here, and neither of you has leaped away—I'm going crazy trying to figure out why. I'd be more worried if I didn't know you were surrounded by guards who can protect you if I'm not around to do the job myself. Have you seen Paul? Did you use your princess powers to have him executed in some barbaric Russian fashion?*

It's startling to read Theo's words. It's even worse to remember that, not long ago, I thought Paul was a murderer. I look over the edge of the letter to see Paul standing there at the door. Theo thought I needed guards to protect me from him; instead, Paul is the one protecting me.

In all seriousness, I'm worried about you. I'm not sure why you're sticking around. Are you waiting for me? Please don't. Visas to travel within Russia are hard to come by (I checked), particularly when you don't speak Russian.

The only other possibilities I can think of are that your Firebird got damaged somehow, that you're sick, or that you don't remember your true self right now. If it's the last option—wow, does this letter sound insane. I hope you're not sick; I keep reading the papers every day, trying to learn more about how you are.

If something has happened to your Firebird, get word to me, all right? It's going to be easier for you to write to me than vice versa. You might even be able to wrangle a visa for a promising Parisian chemist. Or hey, you could ask for a trip to Paris to buy all the latest fashions, right? Big damn hats seem to be all the rage. Tell the tsar you need some big damn hats. Do whatever you have to do to get here. Then I can help you out, and just see your face again. I had no idea how much I'd miss seeing that face.

Don't worry about me, by the way. I turned down a job offer to work on radium research, and I live only a couple of Metro stops from the Moulin Rouge. So Paris suits me just fine.

All I need here is you.

I let the letter drop into my lap, overcome with so many emotions I can hardly make sense of them. My joy at hearing from Theo again is coupled with hope (can he fix the

Firebird if Dad can't?), worry (how are we supposed to reach each other?), and guilt . . . because Theo misses me. Worries about me. Cares for me, and I have no idea how I feel about him in return.

Sometimes I think about that night in London, the way he leaned over me in bed and kissed the line of my collarbone. The memory is intoxicating.

And yet it's not as powerful as the memory of Paul standing in the doorway to my bedroom, watching me paint. Or teaching me to waltz, here in this very room.

Once again I look across the room at Paul, just at the moment he looks at me. Our eyes meet, and something within me trembles. Paul straightens, more formal than before, trying to pretend that moment didn't happen.

"You look as though you've been struck by lightning," Vladimir says. Although he's trying to tease me, I can hear the genuine concern in his voice.

"It's personal," I say. When I look up, Vladimir seems almost wounded; probably this dimension's Marguerite tells him almost everything. He seems like a guy you'd confide in. So I hold out one hand, and when Vladimir takes it, I try to smile. "Do you think the tsar would let me travel to Paris to buy some hats?"

"This is about *hats*?"

"In a way."

Vladimir shakes his head. "I shall never understand women."

He leaves us then, so I get to write back to Theo. Then I

try to work my way through the rest of the afternoon letters, but it's impossible to focus. Theo's letter has reminded me how strange my position is here, how difficult it will be to get out of this dimension if I even can, and of all the emotions for him—and for Paul—that I can't afford to explore right now.

I drop my head into my hand, weary and overcome. After a moment, Paul says, "Are you unwell, my lady?"

"No. Not at all, I'm—I guess I'm having trouble getting through it today." I try to come up with something to talk about that isn't a complete emotional minefield. Not easily done, at the moment. "This letter is to a Rumanian princess who's visiting St. Petersburg. Why is a Russian grand duchess writing to a Rumanian princess in English? For that matter, why are we speaking English right now?"

"It has been royal custom for some generations," he says, obviously unsure of where this is going.

Not only is that true in this dimension, but now that I think about my history lessons back home, I realize it was true in mine as well; Nicholas and Alexandra wrote to each other in English. Royal people are weird.

"Would you prefer to speak in Russian, my lady?"

"No, that's all right. Ignore me. I'm just thinking out loud."

"Besides—" Paul's voice hardens, as though he has to work to sound official. "The practice will be of help to you in your future life. My lady."

What is he talking about? I make my question as casual as

possible. "Do you think so? Why in particular?"

Paul straightens. "I was referring to—to your anticipated betrothal to the Prince of Wales. Forgive me for speaking out of turn, my lady."

For one split second, it's hilarious—*I'm going to marry Prince William! I'll get all Kate Middleton's cute coats!* But then I remember from the *List* that the heir to the British Empire in this universe isn't Wills; it's someone a whole lot more inbred, a whole lot less appealing. And even if it were Prince William, it wouldn't be funny for long, because if I'm trapped here I'll actually have to marry some total stranger half a world away.

"My lady?" Paul says, hesitantly.

I'm fine, I want to say—but instead I clap my hand over my mouth, struggling to maintain my composure. I must not break. I must not.

"You mean that I should be fluent in English." My voice shakes; he must know how badly I'm hurting, even if he doesn't fully understand why. "Since I'm to be their queen someday."

Okay, thank God I thought of that, because it makes it a little bit funny—the idea of me waving awkwardly from a carriage, or wearing some huge feathered hat.

But Paul looks nearly as miserable as I feel. He ventures, "My lady, I feel certain His Imperial Majesty would never permit your marriage to any man unworthy of you."

My guess is that Tsar Alexander basically auctioned me off

to the best royal bidder. "I wish I were as certain."

Paul nods, oddly earnest. "Surely, my lady, the Prince of Wales will prove a devoted husband. I cannot imagine that any man would not—would not count himself fortunate to have such a wife. That he could fail to love you at first sight."

We are twenty feet apart and it feels as though we are close enough to touch. I imagine he can hear even the soft catch in my breath.

"Any man would," he says. "My lady."

"Love at first sight." It comes out as hardly more than a whisper, but the quietest words carry in this vast, echoing room. "I've always thought real love could only come later. After you both know each other, trust each other. After days, or weeks, or months spent together—learning to understand everything that isn't spoken out loud."

Paul smiles, which only makes his eyes look sadder. "One can grow into the other, my lady." His words are even quieter than mine. "I have known that to be true."

When we look at each other then, he silently admits something beautiful and dangerous. Does he see the same confession in my eyes?

I know by now that the other Marguerite returned his devotion, without words and without hope.

No regular soldier, regardless of his loyalty and courage, can marry a grand duchess. No grand duchess can dare risk the tsar's wrath with a forbidden love affair.

"Thank you, Lieutenant Markov," I say. I try to make it

sound formal, as though I'm completely unmoved. I fail.

Paul bows his head and goes back to standing at attention like nothing had ever happened. He's better at pretending than I am.

Christmas Day comes. I spend it in church. That alone would be weird enough for me, the daughter of two people who described themselves as "Confuciagnostics." And here, "church" means a Russian Orthodox cathedral, with priests who wear high, embroidered hats and long beards, and choirs singing hymns in minor keys, and the smell of incense so thick in the air that I keep hiding my face behind my hand to cough.

As I kneel in my pew, I think of Mom and Josie back home—spending their first Christmas without Dad, and without me, too. By now they know what Theo and I set out to do, but they must also have given up much hope of us ever returning home.

Does she think we're dead?

I should be with her. Instead I went chasing after Paul because I was too angry to think straight, too upset to slow down and wait until Theo and I were sure of what we were doing. Easy though it would be to blame Theo—he loved Dad nearly as much as I did. He wasn't thinking any more clearly than I was.

No, it's my own fault that I'm not with my mother and sister on what must be the worst Christmas of their lives. My fault that Mom's probably mourning both me and Dad.

Shame chokes me, like the smoke from the incense, and the dark sorrowful eyes of the religious icons seem to condemn me from their gilded frames.

That afternoon, we exchange gifts in the tsar's study. (Thankfully, the Grand Duchess Marguerite is more organized than I am; her gifts were already wrapped and labeled before I got here.) To my surprise, the presents are very ordinary things—Vladimir gave me a fountain pen, I gave Katya lace handkerchiefs, and Tsar Alexander seems perfectly content with a new set of boots from Peter. I would've thought royal families gave one another staggering, epic gifts, like emeralds the size of baseballs. But maybe if you're surrounded by opulence every day, the riches lose their power.

Grand Duke Sergei isn't included in the family Christmas. No shocker there.

Afterward, Paul accompanies me back to my room, like always, but at the door he clears his throat. "My lady?"

"Yes?"

"If you would do me the honor—if it would not be improper for you to accept—I have a gift for you."

He looks so unsure, as awkward as my own universe's Paul ever did. I can't help smiling. "I have one for you, too."

A smile lights up his face. "If I may—"

I nod, excusing him, and he hurries to a nearby room, where he must have stashed it. So I get the final wrapped present I found—in red cloth, not paper, with real white ribbon—and hold it in my hands as I wait. What did she buy him?

Paul returns with a small box, also tied up with ribbon. "For you, my lady."

"And for you." We hand them off to each other at the same moment; it's slightly clumsy, and we both laugh a little. I'm vividly aware that we're doing this at the doorway to my bedroom, where anyone could walk by and see. But the only other option is for me to invite Paul inside, which is about nine hundred kinds of inappropriate. "Here, you go first."

"Very well, my lady." Paul deftly tugs the ribbon and cloth away to reveal a book. His eyes light up—he's thrilled—and I quickly look at the title: *The Laws of Optics, Or, The Refraction of Light.*

Of course. This Paul and my Paul are enough alike that they'd both be fascinated by science, and this dimension's Marguerite must have picked up on that. Standing around all day watching me write letters? That's not enough to occupy Paul's brilliant mind. Now he runs his hand reverently over the leather binding of the book, like I've given him the deepest secrets of the universe.

"Thank you," he says, obviously struggling for the right words. "I was saving my money for this, but now—I will begin reading tonight."

This is a world where books are expensive, and the only sources of information. No wonder he's thrilled. I glow with happiness I don't deserve; I'm not the one who picked it out, after all.

Already Paul is apologizing. "My gift can't compare."

"Don't be silly." I unwrap his present as quickly I can, ribbon fluttering to the floor by my feet. As I pull back the lid of the black box, I see a rainbow of colors, and my face lights up. "Pastels! You bought me pastel chalks."

"I know it is your practice to sketch, my lady. But I had thought—perhaps you might wish to experiment."

Even in my dimension, I always meant to work with pastels someday. I run one fingertip along the pink chalk, tinting my skin rosy. "They're beautiful."

"Not so fine as the gift you gave me—"

"Stop that. Don't you realize we gave each other the same thing?"

Paul tilts his head. "My lady?"

"Every form of art is another way of seeing the world. Another perspective, another window. And science—that's the most spectacular window of all. You can see the entire universe from there." So my parents always said, and as corny as it might be, I believe them. I smile up at Paul. "So it's like we gave each other the whole world, tied up in ribbon."

"You want me to learn the entire universe?" His grin is natural, somewhat abashed; we are no longer guard and grand duchess, just a guy and a girl, standing very close. "For you I will."

"And for you—" I think more about what the pastels mean, artistically. "I spend too much time thinking about . . . lines and shadows. You want me to find subtlety and depth."

Paul's face falls. "It was not a criticism, my lady."

"Oh, no, no. I didn't mean that. I meant that you—you

want to make my world more beautiful. Which is amazing. Thank you."

"And I thank you."

I let my hand rest atop his, for only a moment, but the contact crackles between us. We look into each other's eyes, and I feel something I've only ever felt once before—this dizzying sense like being at the edge of a cliff, both scared to death and yet feeling this inexplicable, insane urge to fling yourself into the sky.

Paul murmurs, "Merry Christmas, my lady."

"Merry Christmas."

Our hands slip apart. He steps away from the door. I shut the door, and back slowly toward the bed. As I clutch the box of pastels, I fall back onto the covers, trying to make sense of what's happening.

That feeling—the one like being at the edge of a cliff—the only other time I felt it was at home, that night Paul and I talked about painting. The night I knew he understood me more deeply than anyone else ever had . . .

I meant it when I said I didn't believe in love at first sight. It takes time to really, truly fall for someone. Yet I believe in a *moment*. A moment when you glimpse the truth within someone, and they glimpse the truth within you. In that moment, you don't belong to yourself any longer, not completely. Part of you belongs to him; part of him belongs to you. After that, you can't take it back, no matter how much you want to, no matter how hard you try.

I tried to take it back when I believed Paul had murdered my father, but I couldn't, not completely. Even when I hated him, I still—I knew I could have loved him. Maybe I was already beginning to.

Yet I can't take back what just happened between me and this universe's Paul, either. Something in me belongs to him now, and I feel, I *know*, that he belongs to me.

You saw this Marguerite's sketches, I tell myself. *She already had deep feelings for him. Maybe it's the other Marguerite . . . bleeding through.*

No. I know better.

I'm in love with Paul Markov. *This* Paul Markov. Totally, unbreakably, passionately in love.

But am I in love with one man or two?

Not long after Christmas, we're to take the royal train to Moscow under the pretext of some official function or other; Tsar Alexander's true plan is to test his nobles and officials, wanting to ensure that they remain loyal to him rather than Grand Duke Sergei. The rest of the family is annoyed. I'm thrilled.

"Will we see Colonel Azarenko there?" I ask Vladimir casually as we prepare to leave.

He frowns. "I suppose so. Why do you care about that stiff old bird?"

I shrug, anticipating the moment when I can stand in front of Azarenko and demand the return of Paul's Firebird.

If he still has it, that is.

Based on my history lessons about Napoleon and a couple of documentaries I half-watched on cable, I had the idea that it was impossible to cross Russia in winter. Not if you're Russian, apparently. The royal train can make the trip to Moscow in a matter of hours. We'll be back for New Year's Eve, and the single biggest ball of the season on January 1.

"I want to meet the engineer!" Peter says as we climb the velvet-cushioned steps into the royal car. "Can't I, this time, please?"

"You will remain with me, like your brother," Tsar Alexander insists. He doesn't even smile at his youngest child. "You're old enough to begin hearing about matters of state."

He's *ten*. But I hold my tongue. By now I know contradicting the tsar can only make things worse. My father, standing slightly to the side and carrying his own valise, tightens his jaw the way he does when he's angry but trying not to show it.

The tsar gives Peter a contemptuous look. "Or would you rather sit in the back with your sisters, embroidering flowers?"

"No, I'll stay with you," Peter says, though he looks petrified. Poor little thing. Once Tsar Alexander has turned away, Dad pats Peter's shoulder and says, "On the way home, you and I will come to the station a little early, so you'll have time to talk to the engineer then. How would that be?"

Peter brightens, and when he and Dad smile at each other,

I wonder—is it possible that Peter is his son too? Somehow I sense not, and yet Dad still devotes himself to the little boy. He takes care of Mom's son for Mom's sake, an act of love she can never see, one that has lasted for nearly a decade after her death.

"My lady?" Paul says quietly.

I blink away my tears. "Ash in my eye. That's all."

While the big manly menfolk go to the next car to talk diplomacy and drink vodka or whatever they do in there, Katya and I remain in the royal car. For once, Katya's not dedicated to annoying me; she's too busy playing some card game with Zefirov.

Paul remains at attention at the front of the train car. I read the latest newspaper, at first in an attempt to settle down, but with more interest as I go on.

It's sort of fascinating: what Paul said about patterns reoccurring in different dimensions is definitely true. Some of the same people who were famous in my universe are famous here, but in unexpected ways. For instance, the "famed songbird Florence Welch" is finishing a concert tour of Europe, where she's been singing librettos from operas. Bill Clinton has recently been elected to his second term as President of the United States; he ran as the candidate of the Bull Moose Party, and his photo shows him with muttonchop whiskers and a mustache any hipster would envy.

And this news item from New York City is accompanied by a photograph of the acclaimed inventor Wyatt Conley.

As the train car sways back and forth, I fold the crinkly newsprint and peer more closely at the picture. Conley's wearing an old-timey suit and has his hair parted in the middle—seriously not a good look, how was that ever popular? Otherwise he seems much the same. His *aw-shucks* grin doesn't conceal his confidence, any more than his boyish face hides his ruthlessness. The story is about his invention of the moving picture, and says he's made films "as long as two minutes," which makes me smirk. Apparently Conley is famous for innovation in any universe.

The brakes squeal against the tracks as the train decelerates; I brace my hand on the velvet seat, frowning. A glance out the window confirms that we're in the middle of nowhere, surrounded by snow-covered fields and pine forests, still far from Moscow. "Why are we stopping?"

"There may be snow covering the tracks," Paul says, but his expression is wary. "Put on your coat, my lady. Just in case."

In case of what? But I do as Paul says, slipping into my long sable coat even as he walks through to one of the other cars to find out what's going on.

"Do I have to put on my coat?" Katya asks Zefirov.

"Not until I win this hand," he says, laughing.

But there's something odd about his laugh.

Slowly I rise to my feet. "Katya?"

"Can't you see I'm busy?" she says.

Zefirov looks up at me, his beefy face smug, and my heart sinks. Something is wrong, desperately wrong. He knows what it is. The rest of us are about to find out.

"Katya!" I put my hand out for her. She turns to me, angry, and would start calling me names. But that's when the gunfire begins.

15

"KATYA!" I GRAB HER BY ONE ARM AND TOW HER TOWARD me. Her cards scatter across the floor of the train car, diamonds and clubs like litter at our feet.

Zefirov doesn't move, only smiles at us, a grin so nasty I want to slap it off his face. "We'll see who's so high and mighty now. Who has to play cards with spoiled brats instead of serving like a real soldier."

Katya starts to cry. I hug her to my chest. Although I want to ask him what's going on, I already know. "Grand Duke Sergei. He's behind this, isn't he?"

"We'll have no more cowards," Zefirov says, rising to his feet. "We'll have a real tsar, with the courage to take us into war."

War? When did war come into this? I thought I was starting to understand this dimension, but I'm not at home, I'm dangerously ignorant of what's going on, and there's no way for me to fully comprehend the trap that's just been sprung.

"You're Peter's guard. You're our friend," Katya protests.

Zefirov laughs as he rises to his feet. His hand goes to the pistol at his belt.

My God. The realization sweeps through me, freezing me in place. *They're going to shoot us all, then do something to the train that makes it look like there was an accident. Then Sergei is rightful heir to the throne. He wins it all as soon as we're dead.*

Screams and shouts echo from the rest of the train along with gunfire. I would run with Katya were there anywhere to run. As it is, I can only stare in horror as Zefirov levels his pistol.

Two shots ring in the train car, so loud my eardrums sting. Katya shrieks. But it's Zefirov who falls.

I whirl around to see Paul standing there, his own weapon outstretched.

As I stand there in shock, my ears ringing, Paul steps forward. "You are unharmed, my lady?"

"We—we're fine. What's happening?"

"Not every soldier on this train is a traitor." Paul looks angrier than I've ever seen him; he just killed a man without hesitation, and he can't even be bothered to glance at the bloody corpse on the floor. "They may have rigged the train with explosives. You must run for the forest."

The forest is a few hundred yards away. Snow has begun to fall, thick and soft, but I think I can get through it. We might be shot—but if we stay here, we'll surely die.

"Go," Paul says, and he takes my hand, squeezing it to

shake me from my shock. "Run as fast as you can, and don't look back. I will find you, my lady. I swear it."

Katya wrestles free from me and grabs her coat; her survival instinct must be stronger than mine. Right behind her, I go for the door, but then I glance back. "Paul, be careful."

"Go!" he shouts as he runs back toward my father's car.

I dash from the train into the snow. It's even higher than I thought—nearly to my knees. Running through it is work, but I do my best.

Wet snow sticks to my coat, my hair, and my eyelashes. Everything is heavy and white, thicker than fog. I can hear gunfire, but less frequent now, and more distant. The fighting is hand-to-hand, loyalist against traitor, and in places the snow is stained red.

"Marguerite!" Peter's high voice carries over the din. I look toward the sound to see him in Dad's arms; Dad is running for the woods as hard and as fast as he can, though he looks back for me, his expression desperate. I change the angle of my escape in an attempt to follow them.

I try to run faster, but only trip myself up. As I stagger, a hand catches me at the elbow; the cruelty of his grip tells me this is an enemy. I yank my arm away, but he has a knife and he's right on me—

"Get off my sister!" Katya literally jumps on the man's back, pounding at him with both fists. It's as stupid and reckless as anything I could imagine, and yet I'd do the same for Josie.

"Katya, no!" I try to pull her from him, to swing her

free so she might escape even if I don't. But another loyalist soldier catches up to us. His knife finds the traitor's gut, and the loyalist grabs Katya in his arms as the dead man falls. He begins running with her back toward the train.

She's safe—as safe as any of us can be right now. Time to run.

I continue in the direction my father ran. At least, I try. The snowfall is thickening moment by moment, obscuring my vision and the tracks of footprints. I'm no longer certain of the right way to go, but I continue on, knowing that even a moment's hesitation might kill me. Every second, I imagine a bullet finding my head, blossoming red within my skull as I fall.

Distant gunfire pops behind me as I finally stagger into the forest. But the tree branches only block a little of the thick snowfall, and I see no one else—not my dad, not Peter, not any member of my family. And no soldiers at all. I am alone.

What do I do? Nothing in my experience, in any dimension, can guide me here. If I call for help, the wrong person may hear me. If I stay put, the soldiers loyal to Sergei might get to me. But if I run, I might get so lost that I can't be found by anyone, not even Paul.

Finally I decide to believe that I've gone in the right direction. Dad and Peter are surely somewhere close by. If they went deeper into the woods, then that's what I should do too.

I start walking, half in a daze. Thank God I have my coat;

without it, I'd surely be hypothermic already. At home, I refuse to wear fur because I think it's disgusting, but I'm grateful for its warmth now. *Sorry, little sables. I swear this time you gave your life for a good cause.*

However, this coat is more decorative than functional. The black toggle closures allow plenty of cold, wet wind to sweep through. I'm wearing slippers, not boots, and by now they're soaked through; my ankles sting from the chill until they begin to go numb. My fur hat is back in the train car, so the snowflakes fall through the pines into my hair, dampening it.

My teeth start to chatter. My steps become clumsier, and my thinking more confused.

You have to keep going, I tell myself. *You have to find Dad. Nothing else matters.*

I stumble and catch myself against a tree. The bark crumbles against my palms, but I can hardly feel it. My hands are red and stiff. The gloves are back in the train car, too.

Keep going, I think, though by now I'm walking so slowly that it's hard to believe I'm making any progress. Keep going.

No Dad. No Firebird. No Theo. No Paul. I don't know where I am any longer. Who I am. I only know that I'm tired. At least I no longer feel so cold; there's a strong, seductive warmth rising up within me, telling me that everything's well, that I can stop now, stop and rest for as long as I want.

Keep going—

I sink to my knees beside one of the larger pines. As I lean my head against the trunk, I tell myself I'm not stopping, not sleeping, only taking a moment to get my strength back.

When I feel myself fall backward, the snow is as soft as a bed beneath me, and I'm not afraid.

I wake to the crackle of fire, cozy and comforting. I'm warm—not the deadly illusion from the forest, but real heat from a real stove.

I feel the softness of a mattress beneath, fur above, and next to me . . .

I open my eyes to see Paul lying by my side.

"My lady?" he whispers, his face alight with sudden hope.

"Where—where are we?"

"A dacha in the woods. A few supplies remained behind, enough for us to use."

Many Russians keep dachas, small cabins in the country-side where they go in summertime to grow vegetables and swim in the lakes; these houses remain vacant throughout the winter, isolated as they are. As I look around, I can see the simple whitewashed walls, an icon of the Holy Mother, and a small woodstove glowing orange with heat. My wet dress, and Paul's uniform, hang on hooks on the wall to dry.

Beneath my fur coat and some blankets, Paul and I lie together, wearing hardly more than our underclothes, in the dacha's simple bed.

He stammers, "I—I meant only to revive you, my lady—"

"Of course." This is what you're supposed to do for people with hypothermia: warm them with another person's body heat. Even if I didn't know that, I'd understand Paul only wanted to help. I roll over to face him. "Where is my father? My brothers and my sister? The tsar?"

If Paul notices that I refer to the tsar and my father as two separate people, he writes it off as grogginess. "The tsar has survived, my lady, and the Tsarevich Vladimir. As for the others—I do not know. Our forces reclaimed the royal train, of that much I am certain. But I could not long remain, as it was my duty to find you."

Have I come all this way only to endure my father's death again? Is he doomed everywhere, a good man destined to be torn apart by the cruelty and greed of others?

If Dad was killed, he died trying to protect Peter. The thought of that little boy lying dead in the snow destroys me almost as much as my fear for my father. And Katya! My little sister turned prizefighter to try to rescue me. Did they cut her down? I can't bear the idea of her dying for me, for an imposter.

And if my father was killed today—if he was lost in the snow, in the woods—the Firebird is probably gone, and I will never go home again.

"My lady," Paul whispers, "don't be afraid."

"You can't tell me whether they're alive or dead. Don't try to comfort me with lies."

"I wouldn't." And it's true; Paul can be harsh, or awkward, or blunt, but he's always honest with me. How could I ever have thought he had deceived us?

I try to smile for him, though I know the expression must look as wrong as it feels. "If you aren't lying, then how can you tell me not to be afraid?"

"I only meant that you are safe, my lady. Once you are warm and rested, tomorrow morning we can set out for the royal train."

My hopes rise. "The others will be there?"

"No, my lady. It is believed that troops loyal to Grand Duke Sergei are just outside St. Petersburg. The tsar and tsarevich have gone forward to establish an encampment in preparation for battle. I am to see you to the train so that you can be conveyed in safety to Moscow, which remains loyal."

If my father and Peter survived, they, too, will go to the encampment. By now I know it is Tsar Alexander's belief that his youngest child should learn to be a soldier; he'll insist that Peter be near the battle, as brutal as that is. My father would never leave Peter alone there. He would insist on being at Peter's side to comfort the little boy, even though it would mean risking his life again. "No. I won't go to Moscow." The only reason I ever had to go there was to look for Azarenko, but he's going to be in the fighting too, isn't he? "You must take me to the encampment."

"My lady, I have orders."

"I can give you orders too, can't I? You have to take me there. I can't go to Moscow."

"You must." Paul's voice takes on more urgency, and unconsciously he shifts closer to me, trying to make me see it as he does. "Otherwise the danger is too great."

"If my father dies, I want to die too."

"Don't say that. You must think of your duty. At least one

member of the next generation of the House of Romanov must remain safe."

"I'll go to the encampment with or without you." All I have to do is follow the railroad tracks back toward St. Petersburg, right? Of course it can't be that simple, but I refuse to admit it. I have to find out whether I still have any hope of going home, or I have to die trying.

Paul says, "You must stay alive, my lady."

"Why?" I clutch at the neck of his shirt. "Why, when I'm trapped in a life that's not my own?"

He can't answer me. He only stares.

My hand begins to shake, as does my voice. "I've failed everyone. I failed my father. My mother, my sister, Theo, you—everyone. I failed at everything. I won't be trapped here. I won't marry a man I don't even know. But I don't see any other way out. If this is all that's left, if this is the only life left to me—I don't want it."

For a few moments Paul can't reply. We lie there, face to face, my hand against his chest, our feet touching. This is the closest we will ever be. We will never have a chance to be truly alone together again.

Paul says, "If not for yourself, my lady, stay alive for me."

Our eyes meet.

His next words are a whisper. "I have no need for a world without you in it."

I don't know if what I feel is for this dimension's Paul, for my own, or for both of them. I can't tell the difference any longer, and in the moment, I don't care.

My fingers trail up his throat to the edge of his jawline, along the line of his close-cropped beard, to find the corner of his mouth. His lips part; his breath catches.

"Paul," I murmur, "call me by my name."

"You know I cannot."

"Just once. Just once I want to hear you say my name."

Paul brings his face close to mine, so close we are nearly touching. "Marguerite."

And we are lost.

I'm the one who breaks the last rule, the final taboo— the one who kisses him. But then he surrenders. He holds nothing back. We tangle together, kissing desperately, clutching at the few clothes we still wear, hardly able to breathe or think or do anything other than lose ourselves in each other.

When I tug at the hem of his shirt, he lifts it up to help me toss it away. Then I shrug the straps of my camisole away from my shoulders; I've never thought of my skinny body as beautiful, not until I've seen Paul's eyes darken at the sight of me, not until he lowers himself over me to kiss me more passionately and hungrily than before.

"Marguerite," Paul pants against my shoulder. "We must not—we *must* not—"

"We must." I arch my body against his, an invitation no man could ever mistake. He kisses me again, our mouths open, and the way we move draws us even closer.

"Are you sure?"

"Yes. Paul, yes, please—"

His mind is fighting it even as his body responds. "Forgive me. Forgive me."

"There's nothing to—oh. *Oh.*"

My fingers dig into his shoulders, and I bite my lower lip. Yet I move my body to meet his, to welcome him completely.

Paul buries his face in the curve of my neck. His entire body shakes with the effort to go slow. He gasps, "You're—are you—"

I kiss his forehead. My hands trace the length of his back, the bend of his hips, reveling in the firmness of muscle and bone. Instead of answering him with words, I move against him. He groans, rakes his teeth along my throat and follows my lead.

"I love you," he whispers. "I've always loved you."

"I love you, too," I say, and I mean it, even if I'm not sure whether I love one of him, or both of him, or all.

When I awaken again, it's the dead of night. The one tiny window reveals a sliver of midnight blue above a sill inches deep in snow. Our stove still glows with warmth, and Paul lies next to me, holding me in his arms, pillowing my head with his shoulder.

The enormity of what I've done is obvious, but I can't regret it. Realizing how the Grand Duchess Marguerite felt about her Paul, I suspect she would have wanted this just as much—made the same choice—but there's no getting past the fact that I made the decision for her. The night she spent with the man she loves belongs to me instead; it's a theft I could never repay.

As for me, well, back home, I'd made out with guys. Way more than made out, really, though I never quite got this far. Yet I'm no less amazed, no less stunned.

Paul's lips brush along my hairline, and I think, *I'll never love anyone else like this. I never could.*

Guiltily, I remember Theo. If he'd been a little more selfish, a little less caring, we would have spent the night together in London.

I also think about my Paul Markov, the one who told me that I could only paint the truth. He's with me now, asleep deep within the man I made love with. I don't know if he'll remember this later, which would be—weird. I don't know him well enough to predict how he's going to react.

But I know *this* Paul in every way it's possible for a woman to know a man. He's proved his loyalty and his devotion time and time again. There's nothing he wouldn't do for me.

"*Golubka*," he whispers. It's a Russian endearment; it means "little dove." That's ordinary enough, in Russian. They're always calling each other little animals of one kind or another.

When Paul says it, though, there's something about the way he holds me—cradling me against his chest, his embrace strong and yet his broad hands cupped so tenderly around my back—it's just the way someone would hold a little bird, something fragile and fluttering, if he were trying to protect it and keep it close.

My mind is made up. I lift my face to his, and Paul smiles softly as his fingers brush through my hair. "Are you well, my lady?"

"'My lady'? Even now?"

"Marguerite." It's obvious he still feels wonder at simply being allowed to speak my name. His gray eyes look searchingly into mine. "You don't regret this?"

"No. I never will. Never could." I kiss him again, and for a while we're lost in each other once more.

When our lips finally part, Paul is slightly breathless. "You must know, I will never betray what has happened here. Not by word or by deed."

What we've done is completely forbidden. If the tsar ever learned we'd had sex . . . well, I doubt he's medieval enough to have Paul killed for it, but he'd demote him and send him off to some remote garrison, perhaps in Siberia. What would happen to me? I'm not sure, but I know it wouldn't be good. "This remains between us," I say gently. "Tonight is ours, and no one else's, forever."

"Forever."

I touch Paul's cheek with one hand. "Now I need to tell you another secret. Do you promise to keep this one, too?"

"Of course, my—Marguerite." Paul frowns, obviously puzzled but willing to follow where I lead. "What is it you need to tell me?"

Deep breath. Here we go. "The truth."

16

MOM AND DAD HAVE TOLD ME HOW INTELLIGENT PAUL IS.
I've seen physics equations flow from his pen while he's talking about something else entirely. Also he helped develop
interdimensional travel. So I know he's smart.

But I never believed in his genius as much as I do now,
when—after less than half an hour of my talking him
through my story—he's pieced together the rough theory of
parallel dimensions.

"You are both the Grand Duchess Marguerite and another
Marguerite," he says. "You are the same individual, living
two separate lifetimes."

"Not so separate, right now."

"And you believe I am both myself and this other Paul,
the one who was privileged to go to university and become
a scientist."

The way Paul phrases this stop me short. Only the sons

of the wealthy can dream about higher education here. No wonder he cherished that book on optics I gave him. "It's true. He's—asleep inside you now. Unaware. But he's a part of you."

He folds his arms across his knees, serious and intent even though we're still in bed together, covers rumpled around us, fur coat draped across our feet. Paul's face wears an expression I've long been familiar with but only recently learned to understand. This is Paul turning a situation over in his mind, weighing every question and permutation, puzzling out its secrets.

Finally he says, "This explains my dreams."

"Dreams?"

"For the past two weeks, my dreams have been—rich and strange." His smile isn't for me; his gaze is on the images that have flickered within his mind. "I dreamed of you painting instead of sketching, your hair wild and loose. And of your mother, alive again, teaching me physics. Professor Caine, acting almost as a father to me. Rooms not so grand as those in the palace, but containing marvels, such as machines that are like a library containing every fact imaginable."

"Those are computers. My mother *is* alive, back home, and she really is your teacher. Your adviser at college. Oh, my God, you remember."

"I also dream of a friend—or a brother, I'm never sure—always making trouble but always meaning well." His eyes narrow as he prepares to test me. "Tell me his name."

"Theo. His name is Theo."

Paul takes a deep breath. "Then what you say is true."

I laugh out loud. "You actually believe me. Most people would think I had gone insane."

"If you ever went mad, you would do so in a more melodramatic manner."

His bluntness catches me off guard.

He notices my reaction. "I only meant—you have a passionate spirit. You crave excitement and create it where you can. If you were unsettled in your mind, your impulses would govern you. Instead you are putting forth a very unorthodox explanation in an entirely reasonable manner. Therefore, you are telling the truth."

Is he right, about my creating excitement where I can? Even being melodramatic?

You went on a half-baked vengeance quest against Paul using a totally untested experimental device, I think. *He might possibly have a point.*

Paul studies my face intently, as if he were the painter, the one who had to know every shadow, every line. Quietly he adds, "I think I would believe you anyway."

Nobody's ever given me that kind of faith. I feel that twist in my heart again, the one that makes me feel peeled open and exposed and yet somehow happier than I've ever been. "You have to help me find the Firebird locket, the one Colonel Azarenko took from you."

"I don't remember it. Then again, according to your description, I wouldn't."

The Firebird has that quality of an object from a foreign

dimension—not intangibility, nor invisibility, but the ability to be easily overlooked. I run my hands through my disheveled hair. "The last we heard, Azarenko was in Moscow. Which side of this fight do you think he's on?"

"He's loyal to Tsar Alexander, to the point of zealotry. He will have led troops from Moscow directly to the fight. I have no doubt he's already on the front lines."

"So, we go to the front lines."

"You should go to Moscow." His eyes meet mine, calm and certain. "You must understand the danger."

"By now you understand that there's more at risk than my life."

"No," he says shortly. "For the Grand Duchess Marguerite this is the only risk, the only real danger."

The wind howls outside, thrashing the windowpanes and tree branches as if in revenge for being locked on the other side of our door.

As a soldier, he might have obeyed my orders despite his protests. Our relationship will never be that simple again. His love for me means he will protect me, even if it means I lose my chance to get back home.

I begin, "For all we know, the Grand Duke Sergei has already been forced to stand down."

Grudgingly, Paul nods. "He would be a fool to rebel with so little support—but I believe him to be a fool."

"Then we should at least look for the encampment. We should find out what's happening before making any other decisions, don't you think?"

"You'll fight me the whole way to Moscow, won't you?"

He says it like he's about to swing me over his shoulder and carry me there himself, even if I kick and scream. Oh, God, he really might. "I have to find out whether my—whether my brothers and sister and Professor Caine survived. Whether the Firebird is still in one piece. If it's been destroyed, and we can't find Colonel Azarenko or he's lost your locket, then I'm trapped here forever."

"And the Grand Duchess Marguerite would be trapped within you forever."

It stops me short—the idea that Paul is still thinking of protecting her first, beyond all things, even beyond me. But would I expect anything else from him?

More gently, Paul adds, "I want freedom for you *both*."

"That makes me the jail cell." It comes out like a joke, which I instantly regret, because it's so, so not. I whisper, "How can you not hate me?"

"You are not my Marguerite. And yet—you are. This essential thing you share—your soul—*that* is what I love." Paul's smile is sadder and more beautiful than I have ever seen before. "I would love you in any shape, in any world, with any past. Never doubt that."

I can hardly bear to look at him; it's like staring into the brightness and the warmth of the sun, knowing that it's burning you while understanding that it makes your whole life possible.

Paul asks, "What will you do if the worst comes to pass? If we cannot retrieve and repair the Firebirds?"

"Then I guess I have to live out this Marguerite's life. Forever." It's enough to make me feel seasick.

"Would it be so terrible?"

"How can you ask me that now?"

His hand closes over mine. "No matter what happens, no matter what becomes of you, if you are here, I'll always be with you."

I capture his fingers in mine. He brings my hand to his lips and kisses it, and we sit there in silence for a few moments.

Finally I say, "I don't want to think about what happens if we fail. Okay? Because we're not going to. We're going to find or repair one of the Firebirds, no matter what it takes. No matter what."

With a sigh, Paul says, "I know what that means. It means I have to take you to the encampment of the tsar's forces." Before I can thank him, he adds, "If combat is under way, or we see evidence of danger, we will turn around, and this time neither of us will stop until we reach Moscow. I will not put you in harm's way."

"Okay. I mean, yes. That's what we'll do."

"In the morning, then."

"In the morning." Which leaves us tonight.

Even though we are naked together in the bed where we made love, neither of us reaches for the other. The truth changes things; I'm not sure exactly how yet, but it does.

"Perhaps we should not . . . we should not," Paul says. "I have endangered you already."

Endangered? Oh. By *danger* he means pregnancy. It's not

like it would be great for me to get pregnant right now in any dimension, but for the Grand Duchess Marguerite—intended to be the virgin bride of the Prince of Wales—it would be personally and politically disastrous. Fear quivers in my belly, but I tell myself it was only once.

Is it wrong of me to want this, given how incredibly complicated this situation is? I don't know. I can't know. The one truth I can hold on to is that we need each other, and that tonight will never come again. So I lift his hand to my lips and kiss each knuckle, the soft pad of each finger, the center of his palm.

Quietly Paul says, "Would she have chosen this? The grand duchess. I would never—if she would not have wanted to be with me, then I—"

"I looked at the drawings she made of you. They told the whole story." At first I feel guilty admitting this, giving away the other Marguerite's secrets. But I know the truth Paul needs to understand too. "She loves you. She dreams about you. If she'd been here, I think she would have made the exact same choice."

How badly he wants to believe me. Written in every tense line of his body is his struggle to hold back. "But which—which part of you chose?"

I lean closer to Paul. "Every part of me," I whisper. "Every Marguerite. We both love you, completely. Body and soul."

"Every Marguerite," he repeats, and the struggle is over. Again we surrender to each other.

★ ★ ★

The next day dawns cold but bright. We set out at breakfast—or what would be breakfast if we had any food. From the dacha I take a brightly patterned scarf to knot around my hair; although it's not as warm as my fur hat, it's better than nothing. Paul insists I wear his gloves. They're too big for me, leather bunching up at the wrist and joints, but I'm grateful for their warmth.

Deep snow means we make poor time until we encounter an old woodcutter and his wife, out seeking firewood. Paul has a few coins and the promise that the tsar will reward them more amply when the time comes; they look dubious, but nonetheless they loan us their sledge and horse, and give us the loaf of bread they had brought along for their day. I insist on taking them to their nearby home before we drive off—a kindness that probably wouldn't have occurred to the privileged Grand Duchess Marguerite, to judge by the reactions I get. The old couple stares at me, and even Paul is taken aback, but we drop them off before heading on.

As we set out toward the railway, I hook my arms around Paul's, but he shakes his head. "You must not, my lady."

"Are you still calling me 'my lady'?" It's kind of hot, actually, but I'd think we'd be on a first-name basis by now.

Paul doesn't even glance at me, simply keeps looking forward as he tugs his arm free. "From now on, at any moment, we may be observed. My behavior toward you must be correct. Beyond reproach. You are the daughter of the tsar. We . . . allowed ourselves to forget that, for a time. We can never forget again."

He's right, but that doesn't make it hurt any less. I fold my hands in my lap; now we are next to each other, but not touching.

Just like before.

When Paul urges the horse forward across the snow, I blink against the brilliance of sunshine on the ice-crusted white ground and tell myself it's the harsh light stinging my eyes, that and nothing else.

It is a long and silent day, broken only by the soggy sound of the horse struggling through the snow, the silvery sound of rails slipping over ice, and my occasional offer of bread or water for Paul. We're both starving, so the loaf goes pretty quickly.

What happens if the tsar's troops have been forced to fall back, or, worse, slaughtered? Only now do I realize that Paul wasn't simply trying to keep us from being shot when he wanted us to go to Moscow; he was trying to keep us fed.

But as the late afternoon sun begins to paint the tops of the pines gold and orange, we see an encampment in the distance—and flying overhead is the red and white Russian flag. The tsar's flag. Paul speeds us the rest of the way, urging the horse on, and even as we approach the outskirts, one of the soldiers is running toward us. I recognize him and stand up, waving my arms. "Vladimir!"

"Margarita!" He holds his arms out to me, and I leap down into them. We embrace so tightly we can scarcely breathe. But Vladimir's mood swiftly changes. "Markov, you were to take her on to Moscow once you'd found her."

"Don't scold him. I ordered Markov to come to you, and he had no choice." I glance back at Paul, but he already stands at attention beside the sledge, once again the proper soldier. So I take Vladimir's hands in mine. "Katya? Peter?"

"Safe in Moscow, where you ought to be. Though I can't blame Markov for that, hmm? You headstrong fool." Vladimir kisses my forehead so soundly that it takes most of the sting from his comment.

Still at attention, Paul says, "Has the insurrection been put down yet, my lord prince?"

"Not entirely, but they're on the run." Vladimir's fingers tighten around mine. "Our father has the loyalty of all but a handful of regiments, and secretly a few of them have already sought leniency if they were to abandon Sergei's cause and lay down their arms. Of course Father's not ready to hear of it, but give him another day or two to simmer down. Once he knows you're well, I daresay he'll be halfway there."

It catches me short—this reminder that, harsh and stern as Tsar Alexander V may be, he truly believes me to be his daughter, and would at least worry if I were hurt. But that doesn't change the fact that I want my real father. "Is Professor Caine all right?"

"Safe and sound. And due for a medal, after the way he rescued Peter. Such nerve under fire! I'd never have believed he wasn't an army man." Vladimir gives Paul a nod, dismissing him; it's a perfectly reasonable thing for him to do, but it feels so slighting, so superior. Really he is only illustrating the gap between the House of Romanov and everyone else in Russia—the gulf between me and Paul, the one we may never be able to cross again.

I look over Vladimir's shoulder at Paul. His gray eyes lock with mine for only an instant before he turns to see to the poor, tired horse.

"Come along," Vladimir says. "We'll get some hot coffee into you, maybe add a few drops of brandy. You can tell me everything about your wild escape."

Not everything, I think.

The tsar is glad I'm alive, or so he says. Mostly he's furious that I'm here instead of Moscow, though he at least directs his ire at me instead of Paul.

"What is it you thought you could do here?" he bellows over dinner in his camp tent, stew served in metal bowls. "Women at the front. Ridiculous!"

"What about nurses?" I protest, and the tsar stares at me as though I'd gone mad. Nobody ever contradicts him. Maybe he should hear differing opinions more often. Very casually, I add, "Where is Colonel Azarenko's regiment? Are they not here?"

"He returned to St. Petersburg to muster additional troops but will be joining us shortly," Vladimir says. "Tomorrow, we expect."

"Worrying about troop movements now, are you?" Tsar Alexander huffs, but I ignore this.

Okay, Colonel Azarenko is on the way. But what are the odds he'll have Paul's Firebird with him? And what if his regiment goes into battle on the way here? He could be killed, which would of course be sad for his family and everything, but I admit, right now I'm mostly freaking out about the thought that if he dies, his knowledge of the Firebird's whereabouts dies with him.

As the group breaks apart after dinner, instead of going back to the small tent that's been prepared for me, I say to Paul, "I want to visit Professor Caine."

He nods. "Very well, my lady." His posture is ramrod straight, his expression so deliberately empty that it has the exact opposite effect from what he intends; anyone paying close attention would realize something between us had changed.

Luckily, none of the officers milling around us notices his behavior. Paul follows a few steps behind as we go to the tent Vladimir said belonged to my father. And even though I've lived in this dimension for weeks now, even though I know to call him Professor Caine—when Paul pulls back the flap of the tent to reveal Dad sitting at a camp table, writing by candlelight—I rush forward and embrace him. Dad laughs, self-consciously. "Your Imperial Highness. They told me you were safe. Thank God."

My voice is muffled against his shoulder. "I'm so glad to see you."

"As I am to see you." He hugs me back, only for a moment. "I hear the heroic Lieutenant Markov is to thank for your safe return."

I smile back at Paul, who just looks even stiffer. "Yes, he

is. You're certain you're well? Shouldn't you have gone on to Moscow too?"

"His Imperial Majesty wishes me to report on these events to my king, to ensure that other nations will hear the true version of the rebellion." Dad's forehead furrows with worry. "But I wish I might have stayed with Peter. He was badly shaken."

"And Katya?" I ask.

Dad smiles. "Katya was ready to aim a cannon at Grand Duke Sergei herself. She had to be dragged from the front. Pity women can't be soldiers. That one has the fighting spirit of ten ordinary men."

"I can believe it." She tackled the soldier who tried to kill me, even though he had a knife and she only had her fists. Then again, no one should underestimate Katya's fists.

"You'll go to Peter soon, won't you? He needs someone." Dad brushes my hair back from my face, then catches himself, realizing he shouldn't show such affection toward the "tsar's daughter."

"Soon," I promise, "but first I need something from you. Do you remember the locket I gave you to work on? Do you still have it?"

Dad blinks, caught off guard. "Yes—it's in my new valise, actually—but surely that doesn't matter now."

"Please let me see it."

His valise sits in one corner of the tent. Dad opens it and draws out the lace handkerchief; my heart sinks as I see that the Firebird remains in several pieces. He's matched up several of the parts, but not nearly enough.

"It's actually rather interesting," Dad says. "The parts do form a mechanism; that much is obvious, even though I don't understand what it's meant to do. But there's a fascinating logic to its construction—complicated, but undeniable. I look forward to puzzling out the rest."

"I need you to hurry. I need this put back together right away." My fingers trail along the locket's chain; it's all I can do not to clutch it in my fist. I never want to be far away from this thing again.

Dad clearly doesn't want to contradict me, but—"Your Imperial Highness, I am under orders from the tsar. Although I fully appreciate the sentimental value of your locket, right now we have more pressing concerns."

"We don't. We really, truly don't." How am I supposed to convince him?

Then I look back at Paul and think, *He believed me. Wouldn't Dad? Especially if Paul backed me up?*

So for the second time in twenty-four hours, I tell someone in this dimension the truth: about who I actually am, where I'm from, what the Firebirds can do.

Dad isn't buying it.

"Your Imperial Highness, stop and consider." His voice is gentle. "Yesterday you suffered a tremendous shock. The fear alone would have confused most people. Combine that with nearly freezing to death—"

"I'm fine! Do I sound hysterical to you?" Wait. I'm ranting about parallel dimensions. Shouldn't have asked that question. So I direct his attention to the steadier dimensional traveler. "What about Lieutenant Markov? His dreams are the memories of my Paul Markov. How could that be possible if none of this were true?"

"What Her Imperial Highness says is accurate," Paul confirms, still standing at attention. "I believe her."

Dad sighs. "Forgive me for saying it out loud, Markov, but I believe you'd back the grand duchess if she claimed to be from the moon."

I keep trying. "I know this talk about parallel dimensions sounds strange, but I'm thinking clearly, and I'm telling you the truth. Which is why I need the Firebird repaired, right away."

He's clearly unconvinced; probably he thinks I'll snap out of this after I've had a good night's rest. "I'll continue to work on it. I promise you that. But your father's orders come first."

And that's when I know how to convince him.

"I know things the Grand Duchess Marguerite never realized on her own," I say. "Things that prove I come from somewhere else. From another reality."

From his place at the flaps of the tent, Paul looks intrigued despite himself. Dad looks more like he's humoring me. "Such as?"

I whisper, "I know the tsar isn't my father. You are."

17

We're sitting together in his tent, my hands in his. The pieces of the Firebird sit on his camp table, glinting in the candlelight. I lean close, eager to hear about how, in this unlikely world, I came to be. "So you weren't sure until now?"

"I was sure." Dad is smiling, but it's the saddest smile I've ever seen. Because he's not looking at me—he's staring into the past, at my mother, whom he will never see again. "We'd already—we weren't together long. It was intensely dangerous for us both. Of course Sophia could not speak of her delicate condition, but I realized after a few months that she was to be a mother again. The tsar might as easily have been the father. I told myself that had to be the truth. Then one day, not long before you were born, she came in to see Vladimir at his lessons. While he was distracted, she . . . she

214

took my hand." Dad's voice breaks. "She placed it on her belly, so I could feel you kick. That was the only acknowledgment she ever made. The only one I ever needed."

"Oh, Dad." I hug him, and he returns the embrace almost convulsively. I realize this is the only time in his life he's ever been able to show his true feelings.

Then Dad stiffens and draws back. "Lieutenant Markov," he says, expression going blank. "Are you going to report this?"

"Of course he isn't!" I look to Paul for confirmation.

Paul bows his head toward me. "The grand duchess's secrets are my secrets. I will speak no word of this to anyone else."

Dad relaxes as he realizes we're safe. I ask, "Katya—she's the tsar's, that much is obvious, but Peter?"

"Your mother and I were never together again. I couldn't endanger her like that. It was a relief that you looked as much like her as you do." Dad's gaze softens as he looks at my face. "I wish she could have seen you grow up."

"She did." I lean forward, hoping to make him understand. "In my dimension, she's alive and well. The two of you fell in love when you began doing scientific research together."

"A scientist? Sophia was able to be a scientist?" There are no words for the joy of his smile. "Her mind was wasted on court etiquette and ballroom dances. She was utterly brilliant."

"I know. Because she invented this." I tap on the Firebird again.

He believes me now, I know, and yet Dad still wants to

hear more about this world in which he and Mom got to be together. "And we're married even now? She and I?"

That catches me short. First of all, Mom and Dad never actually got around to getting married. Apparently they had the license once, but then there was some sort of breakthrough in the lab and by the time they were done working out the ramifications, their license had expired. Mom keeps saying they'll go back to the courthouse eventually, when they have the time, and follow through with an actual ceremony, but honestly I think they've mostly forgotten they aren't already hitched. It never bugged me or Josie; we knew neither of them was going anywhere. I doubt the Henry Caine in this more traditional world would see it the same way, though.

But that's almost irrelevant compared to the fact that my father—the Henry Caine who loved and raised me—is dead.

I can't tell him that. It would be too horrible, to tell him he'd been murdered.

"Nothing would ever keep you and Mom apart," I say. "You study physics side by side, every day. I—I even have an older sister, Josie. I mean, Josephine. She's a scientist, like you."

Dad turns his head sharply, and I realize he has to fight tears at the thought of this other daughter he'll never have the chance to know.

"Please," I whisper. "I know it's selfish of me, but I need to get back home. Mom must be so scared. I have to get back to her."

After a deep breath, Dad looks back at the Firebird. His voice is uneven as he says, "This device is a thousand times more powerful than I'd ever dreamed. You still trust me with it?"

"You helped invent it. That makes you my best chance to get back where I belong. If we're not able to get Paul's Firebird back, you're my *only* chance."

He lifts one of the metal pieces, studying it in the candlelight, and his gaze sharpens. "Then, my darling girl, let's get you home."

My camp cot would be cold and uncomfortable under any circumstances. Now, though, I compare it to the bed I stayed in last night, with Paul wrapped around me, strong and warm.

Tonight Paul is camped with the other soldiers. He is only a few hundred feet away, in a tent not so different from mine. We might as well be on separate planets. Tomorrow he will be sent to join his proper regiment, which is on the way to join our forces.

"We will rendezvous with Colonel Azarenko's regiment on the way," he told me before we parted. "Of course I will ask him about the Firebird as soon as I have a chance—but that doesn't mean I'll get it back."

"What, do you think he might have pawned it or something?"

"No. He wouldn't. But he caught me out of uniform; taking the locket away was punishment. So he won't necessarily give it to me right away."

"He'll give it to *me*," I said. By now I've lived the grand duchess's life long enough to know how to get some royal attitude on. I'm in touch with my inner Beyoncé. I tossed my hair and added, "If he knows what's good for him."

"I look forward to seeing that." Paul smiled, then wiped the expression from his face—afraid we would be seen, and our secret discovered.

I toss and turn on the cot. It seems as though I will never be warm again. As though I can never again know the comfort and safety I felt last night. As though I will never know myself as truly as I did in Paul's arms.

Finally I fall asleep, however fitfully. By the time I awaken, Paul has left with the other soldiers from his regiment. Although my first thought is to spend the day with Dad, I know I need to let him concentrate.

Vladimir provides a completely unexpected distraction.

"Letter for you," he says, frowning down at the envelope in his hand. "We got a mail packet in from St. Petersburg. It looks as if your strange Parisian correspondent is back."

Theo!

I snatch the paper from Vladimir, who chuckles at my impatience. Quickly I unfold the thick paper to see Theo's chicken-scratch handwriting, even worse now that it's in blotchy ink:

Marguerite,
I got your note earlier today—

When was this dated? Days before Christmas. I'd written him almost a week prior to that. Communications crawl here. I'll never bitch about a 3G connection again.

> *—and sat down to write this as soon as I got done freaking out. I don't know what Paul told you in London, and I don't care. We don't have the facts, and until we have the facts, you CANNOT TRUST HIM. Keep your distance. You say he doesn't remember himself, and maybe he doesn't, but the fact that this guy is your guard and is standing right next to you every day, with a gun? This is bad. (Or he has a bayonet or a saber or whatever the hell they carry here. Whatever it is, I don't want it anywhere near you.)*

I shake my head. He doesn't understand yet; he didn't see Paul's face when he learned about Dad's death. And Theo doesn't know "Lieutenant Markov"—doesn't realize that I've never been safer than I am when he's at my side.

> *We're going to leave aside how in the world you managed to fall down and break the Firebird. Yeah, this universe's Henry might be able to fix it, but I'd be a lot happier if I could take a look at the thing. As in, I might someday be able to sleep again.*
> *Here's what's going to happen. You're going to get me a visa to Russia, and I'm going to do whatever it takes to get to you. I don't care if I have to walk the whole way there on*

snowshoes. We have to get you out of this place, safe and sound; nothing's more important than that.

My breath catches, and I struggle to keep my face from betraying emotion. Theo would take on every danger Paul has taken on—he'd fight for me just as fiercely, want to protect me just as much. Everything I've ever felt for him bubbles up, and suddenly I miss him so desperately I can hardly bear it.

There's no CNN in this dimension. Would Theo have heard about the revolt by now? Is he going out of his mind with worry, thinking that I might be wounded or dead?

I'm with the ESPCI here. That's prestigious enough that you ought to be able to sell me as a lecturer, or someone who should be at the university, something like that. I'm going to go to the Russian Embassy again and beg on my own behalf. One way or another, I'm going to be back with you soon.

I got you into this mess, Meg. I swear to you, I'll get you out of it. There's nothing in any universe more important to me than that.

Theo

Slowly I fold the letter and hold the paper against my chest. Vladimir's voice is soft as he says, "I suspect I had better not mention this letter to the tsar."

"Please." As though he'd ever tattle on me. I hold out one hand to him, the only older brother I'll ever know. Vladimir doesn't ask questions, even though he must be wondering what in the world is going on with me. He's by my side no matter what.

I realize I'm going to miss him once I've gone.

Then we hear shouting from outside—not a few men, but dozens of them. Hundreds. Vladimir's hand squeezes mine in shared fear for the moment it takes us to realize that what we're hearing isn't panic. It's celebration.

We dash out of my tent to see the soldiers throwing their hats in the air and pouring vodka out of flasks to toast their happiness. "What is it?" Vladimir shouts. "What is the news?"

Tsar Alexander strides out of the crowd toward us with a broad grin on his face. "Loyal regiments attacked the forces of my traitor brother this afternoon. Sergei is dead. So is his rebellion!"

He joins in the cheers for his brother's death. Given that Sergei tried to kill us too, that might be justifiable. All I can think is that this is the only time I've seen the tsar smile.

Vladimir doesn't start celebrating, but his relief is obvious. "What brave soldiers finished the rebellion?"

The tsar seems to think that's no more than a meaningless detail, but he says, "Azarenko's battalion."

That means Paul was in the battle. "Lieutenant Markov—is he all right? Was he hurt?"

"How should I know?" Tsar Alexander is already bored with talking to his children when there are soldiers ready to cheer him. "Look at the reports, if you want."

Vladimir takes one look at my face and grips my hand. "Come along, Marguerite. I'll get the reports for you."

They turn out to be handwritten sheets of paper, messy because they were sent off before the ink had dried. As I stand in the tsar's tent, clutching the paper and straining to make out the words, I read how the Grand Duke Sergei met his death at the other end of a bayonet. How only nineteen of the tsar's loyal soldiers paid the ultimate price, among them Colonel Azarenko. How eight more of those soldiers are seriously wounded.

And I read that one of the wounded soldiers is Paul.

18

"CAN'T WE GO ANY FASTER?" I FEEL BAD EVEN FOR SAYING it; the horses are doing their best, pulling the sleigh across the snow faster than any motorized vehicle could travel. And yet I feel like I could outrun the horses, like if I gave into the sheer power of my fear for Paul, the bonds of gravity would snap and I'd fly away from here, straight to Paul's side.

"Steady on," Dad says. He's the one who volunteered to take me, which is a mercy. I don't know that I could bear to be with anyone else right now, anyone who didn't know the truth. "We'll be there within the hour, at this rate."

"I know. I'm sorry. It's only that I—" But what can I say?

He says it for me. "It's only that you love him." When I turn to him in astonishment, Dad simply shakes his head ruefully. "I know what forbidden love looks like, Marguerite. I learned to recognize it in your mother's eyes."

I hug his arm. "He has to be all right."

"If Lieutenant Markov doesn't survive, does your Paul die too?"

"Nobody knows for sure. But—probably he would."

Dad glances over at me. "Which one of them are you afraid for?"

"Both of them." The sharp cold air stings my cheeks as we dash forward. "I'm tied to Paul—everywhere, perhaps—the same way you're tied to Mom."

Dad is quiet for a few moments before he says, "We aren't together, in your world. Your mother and I."

"I told you—"

"Yes, you told me, and I've never seen anyone look so sad while she gave supposedly happy news." Dad's words are gentle, as they usually are, but he's always known when, and how, to push me. "It's comfort enough to know that there are infinite worlds. Infinite possibilities. Now I know somewhere, somehow, Sophia and I had our chance. But you mustn't lie to spare my feelings."

"You were together, always. Nothing could have torn you two apart." The truth: Dad deserves it. "Nothing but death."

He breathes in sharply. "I would never have forced her to continue having children."

"Not her," I whisper. "You."

We ride on in silence for a moment after that, with no sound near us but that of the horse's hooves, the sleigh rails in snow, the jingle of the reins. Is Dad freaking out? What would it be like, to hear that you were dead?

Then he puts one arm around me. "My poor darling girl."

My eyes fill with tears as I lean against him. He hugs me closer, comforting me. I realize that this is what being a parent means—facing the most horrible thing that could ever happen to you and yet thinking only of how it will hurt your child.

"Was it very recent?" Dad says quietly.

I nod against his shoulder. "Right before I left."

"It must be difficult for you, seeing me."

"No. It's been wonderful to be with you again. Because you really are the same in more ways than you're different."

"Was I a good father to you? I always wondered how it would have been, if I'd had the chance."

"You were the best." All the little irritations I ever had with my dad—the way he refused to let me borrow the car, or made fun of my addiction to the *Vampire Diaries*, or sometimes just *would not stop* doing the Monty Python Spanish Inquisition bit—none of it mattered, not in the least. "You let me be myself, me and Josie both. Our home was always so weird, not like any of the other kids', and I never cared. Everybody else had to fit in. They had to worry about what other people would think. You and Mom—you never did that. You wanted us to find our own way in the world, but you were always there to help out. You told us you loved us every night before bed. At night, after dinner, you'd wash the dishes and hum Beatles songs. 'In My Life' was your favorite, and I'm never going to be able to hear that song again without thinking of you. I wouldn't want to. I love you so much."

I bury my head back against his shoulder, and his arm tightens around me again. After a very long while, he says, "How do insects come into it?"

"Insects?"

"Beetles?"

"The Beatles were a rock band." That's not going to make any sense to him; I laugh through my tears. "Singers. They were singers you liked."

His hand pats my arm. "And your mother and I were happy?"

"Almost ridiculously happy."

"Sophia has a good life?"

"She's a well-known scientist, working on the research that interests her more than anything else. She has me and Josie, and—she's a pretty great mom, but I guess you got to see that for yourself. I think she would have said her life was nearly perfect, before she lost you."

"Thank you," Dad says. "It will help, remembering that." Then he pauses. "What about the Grand Duchess Marguerite?"

"What do you mean?"

"If and when you leave, what is the effect on the grand duchess? Will she remember any of this? Will she—" His voice catches again. "Will she even know I'm her father?"

My first impulse is to tell him no. I saw how the Paul in the London dimension behaved after my Paul had moved on; he lost memory completely, had no idea what had happened to him.

But Paul and I travel through dimensions very differently, it seems.

So who's to say what the other Marguerites will and won't remember?

"I don't know," I say to Dad. "For her sake, I hope so. She needs you."

"I need her, too."

Remember, I think, trying to sear this moment in my brain so that the traces will be left even after I'm gone. Dad's arm tightens around my shoulder, as if he understands what I'm attempting to do. Maybe he does. *Always remember.*

We finally glimpse the battlefield from atop a high ridge, and at first it looks only like speckles of black and scurries of movement across the vast expanse of white. But as we draw closer, I begin to see the red stains in the snow. The wind shifts, bringing the scent of battle: gunpowder and something I can only call death.

Dad has scarcely stopped the sleigh. A few of the soldiers have rude looks on their faces—a lady sweeping into their midst?—until one of the generals recognizes me. When he calls me "Your Imperial Highness," the others snap to attention. I draw myself up like the grand duchess I am and demand, "Take me to Paul Markov."

I knew medical care in this dimension was far more primitive than in my own, but I'm not prepared for the first sight of the infirmary. Soldiers lie on cots, makeshift bandages binding limbs that have lost a foot or a hand. Metal bowls hold medical instruments and blood. The men are in terrible pain, most of them; morphine exists here, but there's little to go around. I can hear screaming, moaning, prayer, and one boy younger than I am pitifully crying for his mother.

Paul is silent.

I come to his side, looking down at him in horror. He's swaddled in bandages: around his shoulder, both knees, and worst of all, his midsection. I've read enough war novels to know what a gut wound meant in the days before antibiotics.

No. It's not possible. Paul won't die. He can't. I'll see him through it, somehow. I'll write Theo in Paris and tell him to leave the petri dishes out overnight so he can invent penicillin. I'll stay with him every second. Paul will pull through.

When I kneel beside his cot and take his hand, Paul stirs. His head lolls to one side, like it's too heavy for him to move. He opens his eyes, and when he recognizes me, he tries to smile. As badly wounded as he is, he wants to comfort me.

"Everything's going to be all right," I say. The lie is bitter in my mouth. Even if he survives, I know his legs will never be the same. Can he even remain a soldier? It doesn't matter. Nothing matters except saving him. "I'm here now. I won't leave you."

Paul tries to speak, but he can't. His fingers shift around me as if he wants to hold my hand, but he's too weak.

Surely the doctors are nearby; surely other soldiers can hear. To hell with them all. I bend my head to his hand and kiss it. "I love you, Paul. I love you so much. I'll never, ever leave you again."

"Marguerite—" Dad's hand rests on my shoulder, but when I shake my head, he draws away.

Paul takes a deep breath, then closes his eyes. I can't tell if he's awake after that, but in case he is, I keep telling him how much I love him, and I keep holding his hand. Even if he's mostly out of it, even if he can't see or hear, he'll be able to feel that touch and know I'm by his side.

I'm aware that the other soldiers and the doctors are staring at us. What I just said to Paul is something no grand duchess should ever, ever say to a common soldier. But I also know that not one of them will dare to breathe a word of this. Spreading rumors about a member of the royal family is a good way to find yourself transferred to Vladivostok.

With my free hand, I check at his throat, hoping against hope he'll have the Firebird around his neck. I don't care any longer what happens to me. But I could make sure that my Paul traveled onward, that he at least would survive this.

Yet I need this Paul to live too.

It doesn't matter. The Firebird isn't around his neck, and when I command one of the healthy soldiers to search through Paul's trunk, they find nothing even remotely resembling it. Colonel Azarenko died in the fighting, so there is no one else to ask.

The Firebird remains lost, and even now, I am watching two men die in one body.

At nightfall, Paul stirs once more. His eyes flutter open,

and my smile for him is wrecked with my tears. "Paul? I'm here, *golubka*. I'm here."

"Every Marguerite," he says, and then he dies.

For a while after that, nothing is very clear. I think that I stand up very calmly, walk outside, and make sure I am far from the infirmary before I begin to scream. The wounded soldiers need their rest. They shouldn't hear me scream, and scream, until my throat is raw and my eyes water and I fall to my knees in the snow.

When I can scream no longer, I remain outside, alone, for several minutes. My knees and feet are almost numb from the cold; I will my mind and heart to follow suit. Let them freeze. Let them lose feeling. Then the rest of me can stagger on.

Yet every time I think I'm past the point of being able to feel any more pain, a memory comes to me: Paul in the Easter room, cradling one of the Fabergé eggs in his hands; Paul leading me through a waltz, the broad warmth of his hand against the small of my back; Paul kissing me over and over as we fell asleep tangled in each other.

Finally I manage to stumble to my feet. One of the doctors stands not far away. Probably they made him follow me, afraid I was on the verge of collapse. I ask him, "Where is Professor Caine?" My voice is hoarse, more like an old woman's than my own.

I'm led to a tent, apparently designated for me, but Dad is inside. When I walk in, he rises to his feet. "They told me it was over. I thought you needed a few moments to yourself."

"I did. Thank you."

"I'm so sorry, my dear. So incredibly sorry. Markov was a good man."

Hearing his kind words rips the wound open again, but I fight back the tears. Then I see what Dad's been doing all these hours. There, on his camp table, lies my Firebird—apparently back in one piece.

His gaze follows mine. "I dedicated myself to it. Maybe I've got it. But I'm not comfortable letting you do something so dangerous without at least a test."

"I can test it," I say, my voice hollow. I pick up the Firebird and go through the motions to create a reminder—metal layers clicking beneath my fingertips—until the shock jolts through me. Pain, intense and electric and almost unbearable—but it's welcome. That kind of pain is the only thing capable of numbing my heart. I'm grateful for even a few seconds' respite from the grief.

"That looks like it hurt." Dad tries to take the Firebird back from me, but I don't let him.

"It's supposed to hurt—what I just did." I attempt to smile. "You put it together again. See, I knew you were a genius."

Dad runs one hand through his rumpled brown hair. "Are you absolutely certain that's what it's supposed to do?"

He's worried. I can't blame him. Even I feel uneasy at the thought of taking my next trip with this thing. However, my only alternative is to wait for the weeks, or even months, it will take to either summon Theo to Moscow or travel to Paris myself.

I need to get back to Mom. I need to tell her about Conley, and soon. Theo's Firebird will alert him I've moved on, so he'll follow me. The question is where I'll go—my Firebird is still set to follow my version of Paul, who just died in my arms. But it almost doesn't matter where I go, as long as I wind up someplace where Theo can find me. I trust Theo to get me home.

Above all, I trust my father.

"It works," I say, and hopefully it sounds confident. "I'm going to go now."

Dad nods. His eyes are sad. This may be the last time his daughter ever knows him for who he truly is.

It may be the last time I ever see my father's face.

I fling myself into his arms and close my eyes as he wraps me in his embrace. "I love you," Dad whispers. "I have loved you every moment of every hour since you were born. Even before that."

"I love you too, Dad. I told you that almost every day, and I still didn't say it enough. I couldn't have said it enough, no matter what."

It's too much to let him go. So I'm still in his arms as I touch the Firebird; the last thing I feel in this dimension is his kiss on my cheek. Goodbye. Goodbye.

19

already, a nice soft one. *Well, that's a nice change*, I think, before I open my eyes and see—

My gallery of portraits, in my own bedroom.

I realize I'm sitting in my own corner easy chair, looking up at my painting of Josie: same blue eyes, same merry expression. The walls of my room are painted the same soft cream shade. My patterned curtains blow slightly in the breeze, because I've got the window open as usual. I'm even wearing my favorite dress, the red one with yellow birds and cream-colored flowers.

I'm home.

Yet when I glance over at my bed, I realize the bedspread isn't exactly right. It's a sari-silk coverlet Josie gave me for Christmas last year, but the colors and patterns are different. I'd been admiring it in a catalog (I'm not shy about hinting, with gifts), and I remember the description saying *Each item is unique.*

Now that I think of it, Josie's portrait looks the same, but I've got it hanging next to my painting of my friend Angela instead of my painting of Dad. And Mom's portrait shows her in a white cotton button-down shirt, instead of the gray T-shirt I remember choosing.

This dimension is very, very like my own—but it's not home.

At first I feel a terrible pang of homesickness, worse for being surrounded by something that's so like what I remember and yet not mine at all. Then it hits me: If I moved forward to another dimension, and my Firebird was set to follow Paul—does that mean he made it out too?

It must. It has to. He's *alive.* My heart swells with hope at the realization that my Paul has survived, that he's somewhere nearby—

—and I stop short.

Lieutenant Markov of His Imperial Majesty's Own Infantry Battalion—the Paul who saved me, the one I spent a single perfect night with—he's dead, gone, forever.

I curl into a ball in the easy chair, arms wrapped around my legs. The man I loved is dead. Nothing changes that.

I remember his body heavy in my arms, bloody and empty, and I know I've lost something irreplaceable.

It doesn't feel like my room any longer. I might be back in Russia, kneeling in the snow, screaming out my grief without caring who hears. But right now all I can do is cry brokenly.

The possibilities crash into one another; the emotions tie themselves into Gordian knots. A thousand ways for me to love and doubt and lose Paul Markov, and I feel like I'm only starting to discover them all.

Right now all I can do is focus on the fact that Paul, Theo, and I remain in serious danger—and maybe Mom and Josie, too. I must keep going. I have no other choice.

Get it together, I tell myself. I grab a Kleenex—the box is stashed on the exact same shelf—blow my nose, and try to center myself in the here and now.

As I look around my room, the ordinary has become extraordinary. After a couple of weeks in a world where electric lighting was a newfangled innovation, it's dazzling to see my cell phone, my music dock, my tablet. Even the low-tech stuff is beautiful in its familiarity. My paint-splotched work jeans and an old T-shirt lie across my chair; the drop cloth is spread on the floor and my easel is set up. Apparently I was about to settle in for some work.

I pick up my box of paints. Just the sight of their shiny silver tubes fills me with relief to see something familiar again.

I walk out into the hallway, which is covered with chalkboard paint and physics equations, exactly like it should be. In the great room I find Mom's plants, and the rainbow table, and all the piles of paper and books I'd expect. Some of the swirls of paint on the table look a little different, though. I lean down to study its surface—as much of it as is visible under all the paper, anyway—but one of the paperweights catches my eye. It's this thick, round, metallic disc, lying atop a folder with the Triad Corporation logo on the front . . .

Whoa. My eyes get wide. I've never actually seen a Nobel Prize before, but I'm about 95 percent sure that's what they look like.

As I heft the prize into my hands, marveling at how heavy the solid gold is, I realize that Mom and Dad must have made their breakthrough a couple of years earlier in this dimension. I look down at the Nobel Prize and think, *Way to go, Mom.*

What about the rest of us? What about Josie? Yes, she's still studying oceanography at Scripps down in San Diego; she bought us some fridge magnets down there, which are indeed on our refrigerator. In fact, according to the whiteboard calendar in the kitchen, she's coming home tonight to visit for—holy crap, for New Year's Eve. That's today. I sort of lost track of the date while I was in Russia, what with the violent bloody rebellion and everything.

Theo? He's one of Mom and Dad's graduate assistants here, too. That, or they have another hipster wannabe who left his thrift shop fedora on the coatrack. Even now, Theo's probably materializing in this dimension, in his ratty campus apartment. I bet he'll be here within the hour.

And Paul—

The kitchen door swings open, and I hear Mom say, "If

dog cognition is truly closer to human than that of our closest primate relatives, must we then begin to consider dogs
our partners in the evolutionary process?"

"Really we ought to have bought that puppy back when
the girls wanted one." Dad walks into the kitchen after her,
both of them carrying overstuffed cloth shopping bags. "It
would've given us a canine subject to observe, and besides,
we could've named him Ringo."

Mom and Dad. Both alive, both well, both right here
in our kitchen like nothing ever happened—because here,
everything is as it should be.

Mom sees me first. "Hello, sweetheart. I thought you'd be
painting by now."

"Hi," I say. It's completely inadequate, but I can't think of
anything else. So I bound up the two steps that lead to the
kitchen and take both of my parents into my arms.

"What's this for?" Dad laughs.

Somehow I keep my voice steady as I say, "I just—I missed
you guys."

Dad pulls back, looking wary. "Did you spill paint on
something?"

"No! Everything's fine, I swear." I let go of them, but I
can't stop smiling stupidly. Being near them doesn't heal the
wound of Paul's death in Russia—but it helps me feel almost
complete again. "Everything is totally fine."

Mom and Dad exchange glances. She says, "I suppose
eventually a teenage hormone swing had to work in our
favor."

"About time," Dad replies.

I push back at them, but playfully; Mom and Dad could tease me a thousand times worse than this and it wouldn't bother me, not today. "What did you get?"

"The makings for some lasagna. And a little red wine— Josie might want a glass." Mom starts unloading her grocery bags, but I take one of them from her.

"Why don't you let me make dinner? You guys can sit down and relax."

When Mom and Dad look at each other this time, they seem less amused, more worried. Mom says, "Are you feeling all right?"

Dad shakes his head. "You're going to ask to borrow the car."

I laugh out loud; apparently I dodge working in the kitchen as much in this dimension as I do at home. "You guys, stop. Everything's fine. I just feel like it would be fun. That's all."

Although Dad clearly isn't convinced, Mom says, "Henry, don't fight it." She places a package of lasagna noodles in my hands, then turns to my father, pushes him gently by the shoulders and points him toward the sofa. As he walks off, chuckling, Mom pauses at my side. Very softly, she adds, "Thank you for helping out, Marguerite. Right now, it means a lot."

Right now? What does she mean, *right now*?

"Okay," I say. That seems safe.

"I know this—it didn't only happen to us." Mom keeps

238

her voice low; her fingers brush through my curls. She did that when I was little. The last few years, I've found it annoying, but I never will again, not after two worlds without her. "Even if the police find Paul, we may never understand why he did what he did. Your father and I would gladly drop any charges once we got some answers, but Triad never will, so—" Her voice breaks. "I hate what he's done to us, but I can't bear what Paul's done to himself. He's ruined his whole life, and for what?"

I can't answer her. Right now I can hardly breathe.

"Forgive me. You were trying to cheer us up. I'll let you keep trying." Mom pats my shoulder, and goes after Dad.

All I can do is stand there in our kitchen, stupidly clutching a box of pasta, thinking, *What the hell?*

Even without the details, I understand what happened here. Paul betrayed Mom and Dad. Betrayed *us*. Again.

I'd thought I was beginning to understand Paul. Now I think I've never understood him, or anyone, or anything.

Half an hour later. I'm still working in the kitchen, for values of "working" that mean "numbly wandering around in shock." Somehow I managed to get all the ingredients for the tomato sauce into the pot, but it took me five minutes to remember to turn the burner on. My brain is too stunned by Paul's betrayal to concentrate on anything as mundane as dinner.

Should I tell my parents the truth about who I am and where I'm from? I was able to convince my father of cross-dimensional travel in a universe where nobody had even invented radio. Here, they'd believe me instantly. All I'd have to do is pull the Firebird out from under the neckline of my dress.

But I don't need their help now the way I needed Dad's back in Russia. I want to tell them the truth because I want them to comfort me, and listen to me vent about everything I've been through so far. That's not a good enough reason. They're already devastated by what Paul did; how much worse would it be when I told them how much further the betrayal goes?

I still want to believe in Paul, and my heart still aches for the one who died in my arms, but right now—I don't trust my instincts any longer.

The kitchen door opens again, and I turn to see who it is.

"Hey there, Meg." Theo grins at me. "Happy New Year."

I haven't seen him in almost three weeks. It feels like three lifetimes.

"Theo." I throw my arms around his neck. And he can pretend to be blasé all he wants, but he hugs me back even more tightly.

Into my ear he whispers, "Save me that kiss at midnight, huh?"

He's joking. He's also not joking. I blush . . . and yet I can only think of Paul lying on the cot where he died, opening his eyes to see me one last time, and saying, *Every Marguerite.*

I step back from Theo. "We should—uh—I told Mom and Dad I'd cook."

Theo's eyes widen. "It is you, right?"

Realizing what he means, I snag the chain of the Firebird with my thumb and pull it from the neck of my dress. He visibly relaxes, reassured.

From the living room, Dad calls, "Theo! You made it."

"Like I'd miss New Year's Eve," he answers with a grin.

Mom chimes in. "If you're not going to be useful in the kitchen, come here and help me work out these formulae for a thirty-dimensional sphere."

"You know what?" Theo claps his hands together. "Sounds like a good day to learn to cook."

Dad peers around the corner, his face barely visible above Mom's exuberant philodendron. "Have both of you gone mad simultaneously?"

"Yeah," Theo says, "it saves time." That makes Dad laugh; more important, it makes him turn back to what he was doing, so Theo and I have some privacy.

The two of us start layering noodles, sauce, and cheese in the glass baking dish. Everything goes smoothly. No curling pasta, no giggling, no Paul at my side. It's less fun this way.

As we work, I tell Theo in a low voice what I learned during those last moments in London. "If Paul had done it, there's no way he could have looked so surprised. He honestly didn't know."

"My response to that rhymes with shull-bit. Come on. You're too smart to be fooled that easily."

Stung, I whisper, "You didn't see him. I did."

"I don't have to see Paul's face to know what he's done.

You think you're too smart to be lied to? He fooled your parents the geniuses, so I'm pretty sure he could fool you, too."

I can't accept that. I can't. If I know anything about Paul Markov, I know he's not evil enough to murder my dad. And if I owe the Paul from Russia anything for loving me, and saving my life, I owe his other selves the benefit of the doubt.

"He didn't betray us," I say. "And I won't betray him again by doubting him."

Theo sighs as he starts spooning on another layer of ricotta. "You've got a tender heart, Meg. You get angry quick, and you simmer down quick, too. I love that about you, but this is not the time to keep changing directions. The world keeps shifting around us; that means we have to hold on to what we know."

"We don't know anything. We didn't even stick around for the funeral. They might have learned more once they were able to—" *To examine the body. To perform an autopsy.* I can't even say those words aloud while thinking of my father. "Besides, in Russia, Paul died to save me. I don't think he's the villain here."

I remember coming to in the dacha, lying in Paul's arms. His whisper echoes inside my head: *Golubka. Little dove.*

Some flicker of what I'm feeling must show in my face, because Theo gets even more intense. "Okay. So Paul Markov isn't a son of a bitch everywhere. Infinite dimensions equal infinite possibilities. There's probably even a dimension where I'm not instantly desired by every woman I meet." The joke doesn't do much to lighten either of our moods. He continues, "Seriously. Anything can happen. Everything *has* to happen, in one dimension or another. So there has to have been a decent Paul somewhere. You met him. Congrats. But the Paul we're dealing with on this trip? That Paul? He screwed us over, and he wants to do it again. Don't let him. Don't go soft on him now."

It doesn't feel like I'm going soft. It feels like I'm holding firm. "I just don't believe he did it, Theo. He admitted wiping the data, and of course he stole the Firebird, but—"

"So he confessed to everything but the murder, and that's all it takes to get back on your dance card?" Theo runs one hand through his unruly black hair, obviously trying to calm himself. "This is hard for me too, by the way. I loved Paul. I always thought—you know, we'd wind up on the same faculty at Cambridge or Caltech, be mad professors together." His smile is wistful, and fleeting. "In some dimension, I guess we'll get to do that."

"Even you see it," I say, ladling on the final layer of tomato sauce. "You know Paul's not a bad guy. He must have had a good reason for everything he's done."

Theo sighs, and the look on his face is that of a man fighting a lost cause. "Take some time here, while we're safe and things aren't too weird. Think this over. *Really* think. And just remember, the man Paul could be doesn't matter nearly as much as the man he actually is."

I know Theo genuinely wants to protect me—but I know

he's also realized that Paul and I became close in Russia. He doesn't know exactly how close, but he's guessed enough of the truth to be upset.

To be jealous.

When Theo's eyes meet mine, I see that he knows everything I've been thinking. One corner of his mouth curves upward, like he wants to smile but can't quite manage it. "I never claimed to be objective about you, Meg."

"I need you to be objective about Paul."

"One of us is being objective about Paul already," Theo answers. "Guess we have to figure out which one. But it's a high-stakes game. Bet on Paul, get it wrong—and we both might pay with our lives."

20

THE KITCHEN DOOR SWINGS OPEN, AND THEO AND I LOOK up to see Josie standing there wearing a Coronado Island T-shirt and a backpack slung over her shoulders.

She grins wickedly. "Am I interrupting something?"

We were having a serious conversation about a murder in another dimension, that's all, but that's not an explanation my big sister needs to hear. Besides, right now, I'm just too glad to see her.

"Hey, you." I go to Josie and hug her as tightly as I can with the backpack in the way. "Welcome home."

"Thanks." Josie ruffles my hair in the way she knows I hate. Normally that's my cue to scowl at her, but right now I even love her messing with me.

The last time I saw Josie, she was sobbing hysterically in Mom's arms. Now she's her usual laid-back, beach-girl self, complete with flip-flops and a sunburned stripe across her nose. As I study her face, I recognize anew all the ways in which she's similar to my father: the blue eyes, the square jaw, the chestnut color to her hair. I'm the one who looks like Mom, more like Vladimir and Peter—

That stops me short. Only now do I remember I'm in a world where my brothers and little sister never existed.

"Are you okay?" Josie gives me a funny look. Behind us, I can hear Theo putting the lasagna in the oven.

"Yeah. I'm good. It's just—" I make a fluttery gesture with one hand, which is supposed to mean something like, *I haven't got my act together right now.*

But Josie's expression hardens, and I realize she thinks I'm talking about Paul, and the scars his betrayal have left on the family. That's why she's home for New Year's instead of partying with her friends; she's trying to help our parents get through it.

"Mom and Dad are in the great room?" Josie asks, dumping her backpack at the door like she has ever since fourth grade. As she lopes in to see our parents, I lean back against the fridge, disquieted.

When Theo gives me an inquisitive glance, I motion toward the great room. "Go on, hang out for a while. I need a second."

He doesn't look 100 percent satisfied with that response, but he nods, giving me the space I need.

After Theo leaves the kitchen, I stand there staring out the kitchen window. (At home, we have a suncatcher dangling there, a little orange and yellow butterfly. Here, the suncatcher is in the shape of a bird, all blue and green.) My heart aches, and this time, there's no cure for it.

I can see the irony. Throughout this journey, I've longed to be with my family again. Now I'm with them, more or less, but I have another family to miss.

Katya and little Peter—I never even got to see them after the attack on the royal train. Peter must have been utterly terrified. He won't be able to sleep at night; I ought to have a couch brought into my room for him, so he can rest nearby, so I can wake him if he has nightmares. And Katya? Probably she's already arguing that the tsar should allow women in the army. And Vladimir will be urging the tsar to consider more constitutional reforms, so that no other pretender to the throne can rise up to capitalize on the dissent . . .

I should be there, I think, before remembering that, of course, I am. The Marguerite who belongs in that dimension is back in charge of her own life. We are enough alike for me to know that she's taking care of Peter, and that she's adding her voice to Vladimir's, for whatever it will be worth with the obstinate Tsar Alexander.

She's also mourning the loss of Paul Markov, her Paul, dead and gone forever.

Does she even remember her final weeks with him? Does she know that she was able to spend one night with Paul, one night when all the barriers between them came down? If not, then . . . I stole that from her. Something sacred that ought to have been hers alone became mine forever.

I told Theo earlier that I didn't think Paul was the villain here.

Now I realize the villain might be me.

"So, I was wondering about the ethics of traveling through different dimensions," I say at dinner.

Mom and Dad exchange glances, and Theo gives me a look like, *Are you crazy?* I pretend I don't see him.

"We've had these conversations often enough," Mom replies as she helps herself to a piece of the lasagna. "Forgive me, sweetheart, but I never thought you were interested."

I have to admit this is more true than not. If I didn't tune out some of the heavy-duty physics talk from time to time, I'd go crazy. Besides, when was any of this theoretical stuff going to apply to my real life?

Now, of course, I know the answer to that question.

"When you guys were talking about it before, it was always, you know, 'what if.' Abstract, not concrete." Hopefully I sound casual, just interested enough to make conversation. "Things have changed now."

"Yes, they have," Dad says heavily, and I know he's thinking of Paul.

We are gathered around the rainbow table, temporarily cleared of its papers to make room for lasagna, salad, garlic bread, wine, and a ceramic pitcher filled with ice water. (The Nobel Prize is on the floor beside a stack of books, all but forgotten.) In so many ways, this scene is exactly the way it ought to be, cozy and shabby and unmistakably *ours*.

Mom's hair is pinned back into a messy ponytail with two pencils. Dad wears reading glasses with rectangular, tortoiseshell frames. Josie smells like cocoa butter. Theo has his elbows on the table. And I'm kicking the center pedestal of the table, a nervous habit my parents gave up trying to break me of when I was in junior high. There's even a package of shiny hats Josie brought, like she does every year, though we won't put them on until nearly midnight.

Yet there's an empty chair at the table, a place where Paul should be and isn't. The most powerful presence in the room is his absence.

"We thought it would be a chance to glimpse a few small layers of the multiverse though another set of eyes . . . and then we would return home, to share the knowledge." Her gaze turns dark. "But apparently knowledge isn't enough for some people."

"Come on, Sophia." Theo gives her his most charming smile, which is pretty damn charming. "Don't tell me you're turning paranoid too."

Mom shakes her head; one of her curls tumbles loose alongside her face. "I don't condone what Paul has done. He broke faith with us all. But that doesn't mean he was wrong about Triad."

"Wait, Triad's still pushing?" Josie says through a mouthful of salad. "I thought you guys told them to shove it."

Dad sighs. "We tried. Turns out it's rather difficult to get a multinational corporation to shove anything. Particularly when they bankrolled your research."

249

"What exactly is it you're trying to get Triad to shove?"

Theo holds one hand up to my parents, an *I'll-take-this-one* gesture. "Some researchers at Triad wanted to push the boundaries of what we can do. Which theoretically is all good! It's not like we don't want to learn more about the possibilities of traveling between dimensions. But Conley doesn't want to only send energy through dimensions. He wants to send matter."

I shake my head no; this much I understand. "Consciousness is energy and can travel more easily. But matter is incredibly difficult, right? It's kind of a miracle that the Firebird can make the trip."

"That's correct," Mom says, now in full professor mode. "However, the Firebird also proves that matter transfer between dimensions is possible."

"And it's not like that's so bad, on its own," Theo jumps in. "I mean, how awesome would it be if we could bring back some amazing tech from a dimension slightly more advanced than ours? Bring it here, analyze it, figure out how to replicate the effects? That's golden."

I recall the technology from London—holographic viewscreens, smartphone rings, all the rest.

"So far as that goes, I've no objections." Dad looks weary. I decide to pour him a little more wine; normally he'd never have more than one glass even on New Year's Eve, but tonight maybe he needs it. "But Conley's pushing a more aggressive agenda. It sounds less like he wants to study other dimensions, more like he wants to, well, *spy* on them."

"Can you imagine it?" Mom says. "He wants to find ways to let the travelers fully take over the bodies of their other selves. For long periods of time, if not permanently. That's not what we envisioned. We never wanted to harm anyone, and what Conley's talking about goes beyond harm. The Firebirds would be used to . . . to steal people from themselves."

Dad shakes his head as though he's just had a chill. "You could be talking to your best friend and have no idea they'd been replaced by a spy from another dimension. It's bloody well terrifying."

Theo and I glance sideways at each other and sit very, very still.

Mom takes a deep breath. "Anyway. As I said, Paul went too far. It's too late to keep Triad from developing the technology further. Much too late." She says this with obvious regret. "They've only been set back a few months. He would have done better to work with us; I still think we might be able to convince Conley that the risks outweigh the benefits."

"Exactly," Theo says. "Change comes from within, right?"

"Which is why we let you take on that Triad internship, but we shouldn't have," Dad says. "They've overworked you these past few months; we weren't even sure we'd get to see you tonight. You're aware you're running dangerously behind on your dissertation, aren't you?"

Theo groans. "Please, can we not invoke the name of the

251

dissertation on a holiday? It's like saying 'Bloody Mary' three times in front of a mirror at midnight."

Dad holds up his hands, like, *I surrender.* I remember him making that exact same gesture when I argued that I should get to paint in my room, because any stains would be my own problem. The memory makes me smile, and yet want to cry at the same time.

"Anyway, I didn't mind being at Triad," Theo continues. "It gave me a chance to defend our work. And, you know, I get that Conley wants some return on his investment. We simply have to make him understand the limits, ethical and literal. Because, seriously, there's only so much we're ever going to be able to bring across dimensions."

"Let us pray. Now can we discuss something else? I confess, I can't yet think of Paul without—" Dad's voice trails off, and I know he wants to say something about being angry, but that's not right. He's not angry; he's heartbroken.

Quietly Mom says, "I made him a birthday cake."

"Don't do this to yourself." Theo takes Mom's hand and squeezes it tightly, a gesture as loving as any I've ever given her. "Okay, Sophia?" She nods sadly.

Then Dad straightens in his chair. "Marguerite, we're distracted, but we're not *that* distracted."

What is he talking about? Then I realize that, after pouring wine for everyone else at the table, I had helped myself to some. We drank wine in the Winter Palace; I'd honestly forgotten there was such a thing as an age limit. "Sorry," I mutter.

"Go ahead," Mom says. "It's New Year's Eve." She raises one eyebrow. "But don't go making a habit of it."

"All my fault, I'm sure." Theo grins. "Everybody knows I'm a bad influence."

Josie shoots him a look. "You'd better not be *too* bad an influence." She's talking about what she thinks she saw in the kitchen, which brings up the whole question of what I do or don't feel for Theo, on top of every other confusing thing that's happened . . .

I take a sip of the wine. It doesn't help.

After dinner, Dad does the dishes. When he starts humming "In My Life," at first it's the most beautiful thing I've ever heard. Then I remember that this is the last time I'll ever hear him humming his beloved Beatles—and I have to bite my lip to hold back the tears.

Or I could just stay here, in this dimension, forever.

It's tempting. Dad's alive. Our family is together. Whatever happened with Paul, we can get to the bottom of it, put things right.

But back home, Mom is mourning Dad, worried about Paul, and scared to death for me and Theo. I have to get back to her. This dimension may look like home, but it's not, and never will be.

I stay right outside the kitchen, listening, until Dad finishes. Then I slip out to the back deck, needing a few minutes alone to steady myself before we start watching the festivities in Times Square on TV.

It's the same deck, the same weird sloping backyard that's not even flat enough for a folding chair. Even the electric lights are identical, Josie's plastic tropical fish glowing along the rail. The tall trees that ring our yard obscure the houses near us; even though we're in the heart of the Berkeley Hills, it's possible to imagine that we're isolated, alone. When I was a little kid, I used to pretend the trees were a stone wall around our castle. I wish that were true.

The sliding door behind me opens. I don't turn my head as I remain sitting on the steps of the deck.

Theo drapes Mom's apple-green cardigan around my shoulders before he sits down next to me. "And here we are again."

I laugh despite myself. "This is where this whole crazy trip began."

"You must wish I'd never even told you about the Fire-birds."

"No, I'm glad you did." I think of everything I've seen, every aspect I've discovered of the people I love. Especially Paul—always, always Paul.

Where is he right now? If he were here, maybe I'd know whether what I love in him is the same, whether it lives on. All I know is I want him here with me so desperately it almost hurts.

"You've got that faraway look in your eyes." Theo rests his forearms on his knees, leaning forward to study my face. "How are you doing?"

"I think I could try to figure that out for most of the next year and still not know."

"Is it hard, being around your dad? I keep wanting to hug the guy. At least you can do that without Henry wondering if you're high."

Coming from Theo, that's not just a joke.

But Theo has held it together, at least as far as I can tell. Probably I shouldn't ask what he got up to in Paris. I bet it involved absinthe.

"Listen," he says. "It's obvious that you want to pin the blame on Triad instead of Paul. Right?"

"Even you admitted Triad had gone too far," I say. "Who knows what else they're up to?"

"Wyatt Conley, that's who." Theo runs one hand through his hair. "So why don't we ask him?"

I stare at him. "Just walk up to one of the biggest tech tycoons in the world, any world, and ask him what he's doing?"

"Don't be so literal. In this dimension, we've worked with Triad a lot more closely. Remember, I've been interning there for months. That means I have access to their HQ—the mega-cool modern one, which is complete here, so we'll see it first when we walk right through the front doors tomorrow." From a front pocket of his shirt he pulls a laminated security pass bearing the triangular Triad logo.

"We can get into the building," I whisper, starting to smile. "You have access to their computers."

Theo holds up a warning hand. "My security clearance won't be all-knowing, all-seeing. But it might be a bit more comprehensive than they meant for it to be. Besides, on New Year's Day, the place will be all but deserted. Gives us a chance to stick our noses where they don't belong."

By now, I'm very curious to find out more about what kind of man Wyatt Conley might be. Because I'm beginning to believe he's played a bigger role in my life, and my father's death, than anyone ever suspected.

Theo adds, "While we're there, we might even be able to figure out how to track down this dimension's Paul. Right now, he's on the run, and we'll never find him on our own. But Triad? These are the guys who developed the software the NSA uses; they're not easy to hide from."

I fist my hands in my curls. "Why are you still so sure he hurt Dad?"

"Why are you suddenly so sure he didn't? And don't give me the 'he looked innocent' thing again. That is not valid evidence."

"These journeys—the other dimensions we've seen— haven't they taught you anything?" No, I don't want to get defensive. I especially don't want to be short with Theo, not after everything he's done for my sake, and for Dad's. So I turn to him as I struggle for the right words. "Each Marguerite I've been was her own individual, with her own strengths and weaknesses. But they were all *me*, Theo. I'm not sure there's anything in those Marguerites that isn't in me, too. And I haven't only learned more about myself. I've learned more about Paul." If I think about Paul in Russia again, I won't be able to bear it. So I force myself to concentrate on the here and now. "All those versions of Paul *are* Paul. I know him better now than I ever did before. He's not a murderer. I'd stake my life on it."

"You *are* staking your life on it. Don't you see?" Theo groans, scuffing his tennis shoe against the deck. "I never should have let you come along on this trip."

"If it's anyone's job to avenge Dad, it's mine. Yes, even more than yours. You know that."

"Do you think I've spent one second of this trip not kicking myself for putting you in danger? That I haven't hated myself for putting you through this?" Theo's dark eyes search mine. "Now I hear you getting confused, watch you letting your guard down, and all I can think is, *Marguerite's gonna get hurt.* If you get hurt, it's going to be my fault, and I will never, ever get over that."

I shake my head no, but I can't answer him. The raw emotion in his voice has stolen my own.

He comes even closer to me, so close our faces are nearly touching. "You say you've seen these different versions of Paul. You've learned who he really was. Well, what did you learn about me, Marguerite?"

"Theo . . ."

His hand grips the curve of my neck, his touch hard and possessive, and then he kisses me.

I gasp, and Theo's tongue slips into my open mouth. My skin flushes hot; my limbs go weak. My body knows what this is even if my mind doesn't. Theo puts his arms around me, and for one instant all I want is to kiss him back.

Then I remember Paul, and the dacha in the snow, and making love to him in the glow of the fire. I remember loving Paul more than my own life.

Turning my face away, I say, "Stop. Theo, please, don't."

He remains completely still for a second, then lets me go. For a while we sit next to each other, breathing hard, unable to speak.

Finally Theo says, "He's gotten to you."

I want to argue with him, but it would only make this moment worse.

With a sigh, Theo stands. When I look up at him, I'm surprised, and heartened, to see that he's trying to smile. "Let's just . . . start over tomorrow. Okay?"

"Okay. Tomorrow." When we walk into Triad Corporation headquarters, side by side. Even now—always—Theo is my ally. As he fishes his keys out of his pocket, I say, "You won't even stay until midnight?"

"And the traditional kiss?" Theo arches one eyebrow. He's trying to turn this into a joke, but it doesn't quite work. "Doubt my luck would improve."

He deserves better than this. But "deserves" doesn't have a lot to do with falling in love.

21

MY OWN ROOM. MY OWN BED. YET I CAN'T SLEEP.

I keep taking my tPhone from its charging dock and staring at my contacts list. Paul Markov is there, exactly like at home. I even assigned him the same ringtone.

Rachmaninoff.

For an instant it's as though I'm back at home, cooking by Paul's side while we both pretend our arms aren't brushing against each other—

Apparently my feelings about Paul are confused in this dimension, too.

(I found his sliced-up portrait in the downstairs storage room, torn canvas hanging limply from its frame.)

Mathematics or fate: Whatever that force is that keeps bringing us together in world after world, it's powerful. Undeniable. But I still don't know whether that force means my salvation or my destruction.

Around 2 a.m., I give in to temptation and text Paul. I compose then delete at least a dozen messages before I settle on simply: **We need to talk.**

Although I lie awake for another couple of hours, no answer ever comes. I fall asleep thinking of his dead body in my arms.

"You doing okay?" Theo asks for about the tenth time in a thirty-minute drive.

"Yeah. I'm good. It's just—this morning was hard."

This morning was like countless others in my life: Dad making blueberry waffles (albeit in his green foil party hat from last night); Josie rambling on about the crazy-complicated dreams she always has; Mom wearing her yoga outfit while the rest of us are still in the stuff we slept in, because even on New Year's Day she was up at dawn doing her sun salutations. But this time I was both living it and watching it from the viewpoint of someone who knows what it's like to lose such moments. Before now I never understood how beautiful the ordinary can be.

"I can imagine." Theo looks over at me, his gaze gentle, but only for a moment; his attention is reserved for the road. Currently we're doing at least twenty miles over the speed limit, Theo threading his muscle car through every break in the traffic to get us to Triad faster. "Hang in there, Meg."

I fiddle with the Firebird's chain, dangling beneath my T-shirt. Theo and I have been careful in this dimension to keep our Firebirds concealed beneath clothes that won't show their outlines; in this world, my parents would recognize them in an instant and realize what's up.

My phone is in the pocket of my skirt, set to vibrate, so it's not like I could miss a call or a text. Still, I take it out and check it again. Nothing.

As Theo's car comes over the crest of a hill, far enough into the burbs that we're now surrounded by more trees than buildings, I see a brilliant silver curve rising high on the horizon. When I realize what it is, my jaw drops. Theo laughs. "Pretty spectacular, huh?"

At home, Triad's ultramodern HQ is still more theoretical than real—airbrushed artwork on billboards in front of construction sites. Here, the construction is complete, and it shimmers like some sort of fantastic mirage—surreal and yet so substantial that it dominates the landscape. The mirrored cube of the main building is surrounded by a shining ring structure: the world's largest and most efficient generator of solar energy. Triad Corporation's building follows the same design aesthetic as their products, the marriage of beauty and power.

Theo has a badge on his license plate that allows us to drive through the security gate at the boundary of their grounds. The grass seems to have been manicured to a uniform length, like on a golf course. Long rows of oleander bushes line the straight, smooth path into Triad's parking lot.

"C'mon," Theo says. He's grinning, like this is no big deal. Probably he's psyched just to get a look at the place. "Let's get you a guest pass."

I fall into step at his side, but I can't help staring upward at the sheer enormity of the building as we walk toward the entrance. The sunlight reflects so brilliantly from the glass that it's hard to focus on it for long.

If Paul is right—if Triad's plots go beyond Mom and Dad's worst fears—I'm walking straight into the lion's den.

The glass doors part for us as we walk into a lobby even more dazzling than the building's exterior. While Theo flirts with the female security guard to hurry along my pass, I indulge the impulse to stare. This space would be spectacular no matter what, but it's sort of surreal to have it all to ourselves, my footsteps echoing slightly in the silence. The lobby ceiling is at least ten stories high, lined with viewscreens showing different demos of Triad products both real and theoretical. Always, at least one of the screens is glowing Triad's trademark emerald green, with white letters spelling out the corporate motto: "Everyplace, Everytime, Everyone."

A tug at the hem of my cardigan makes me look around to see that Theo has clipped my security pass right there, at my hip. He winks at me. "Relax. Remember—no matter how impressive all this looks, your parents are still the biggest thing that ever happened to this place."

Hardly. This is the house that Wyatt Conley built, and everyone knows it. Still, Theo's smile helps quiet the butterflies in my stomach. With him, I feel safer.

He holds out his hand. It's a casual gesture, or he wants it to seem that way—but I can tell he's nervous. Last night's kiss flickers through me, a reminder of everything I feel for Theo, and everything I don't. We can't meet each other's eyes.

But I take Theo's hand.

Of course this building also has those awful glass elevators. We step inside, and Theo says, "Lab Eleven."

"Certainly, Mr. Beck," the elevator replies. Okay, that computer is maybe a bit too smart. Smoothly it lifts us through the lobby, viewscreens shining brilliantly all around us.

"We ought to have the place pretty much to ourselves," Theo says. His thumb brushes across my knuckles. "Jordyn at the security desk says only five other people have signed in all day."

Just as he says it, though, the elevator gently glides to a stop at a floor I can tell isn't our destination, from the way Theo frowns. The doors open—and Wyatt Conley steps inside.

Wyatt Conley. *Himself.* Yes, he's the founder and CEO of Triad, which means obviously he'd show up at headquarters sometimes, but actually running into him in the elevator . . . it's like taking the Universal Studios tour only to be personally greeted by Leonardo DiCaprio.

Except how it's not like that at all, because I'm beginning to believe this might be the man responsible for my father's death.

"Theo." Conley says that name so easily you could imagine he doesn't have a couple thousand employees, and that it isn't kind of weird that he apparently knows every single one of their names. "Are you here to work or to show off for your girlfriend? I wouldn't blame you if it were the latter."

"This isn't—I mean, this is Marguerite Caine." Theo's hand tightens slightly around mine. "Dr. Kovalenka and Professor Caine's daughter."

Conley's smile widens. "Well, well, well. About time I met you."

Technically we met back in London, if my running onstage during his presentation counts as "met." But that was a different universe's version of Wyatt Conley. This one dresses pretty much the same, though: careless rich, faux casual, more like a kid than a tycoon. He seems . . . not homicidal. Whatever that is. I mean, Conley definitely seems to be full of himself, but what do you expect from a thirty-year-old internet mogul?

"Pleased to meet you," I lie, hoping Conley believes I'm being awkward only because it's soooo awesome to meet someone famous.

Apparently Theo thinks I'm being awkward, period, because he quickly says, "Thought Marguerite ought to have a chance to look around."

"Absolutely." Conley's smile is so easy, so natural, that despite everything, I could believe he's actually being sincere—at least, at the moment. "I see the resemblance to Dr. Kovalenka. Your parents are remarkable people, Marguerite. You should be proud of them."

"Yeah, I am." *And I don't need you to remind me.*

The elevator glides to a stop on the tenth floor. Theo leads me out, but Conley comes with us; either he was headed this way to start with, or he has way too much time on his hands. Even though Theo must be unnerved too, he acts like it's completely normal for Conley to tag along. Our path takes us along a corridor with one glass wall looking down on the lobby below, so the brilliant colors from the screens shine through. Conley grins as he says, "The daughter of two geniuses. Who knows what we might expect out of you one day?"

"I'm not one of the family geniuses," I say hastily. "At all."

"Marguerite's selling herself short." Theo smiles sideways at me, an expression gentler than usual. Sometimes I forget how kind he can be beneath all the attitude. "She's not a scientist, but she's incredibly talented. An artist, in more ways than one."

Conley nods. "That's right. Portraits, isn't it? Maybe I should get you to paint me someday."

Two months ago, that suggestion would have been the most exciting idea possible. A painting of Wyatt Conley? That would turn me into a nationally recognized portraitist overnight. Now I have different priorities.

Then again—I've always believed that a portrait shows the truth. (I hear in my mind, *You always, always paint the truth.*) If Conley sat for me for a few hours, and I painted what I truly saw there, maybe I'd learn exactly what kind of man he is.

"That would be amazing." I smile when I say it, bright and girlish. That's what he expects from me, right?

Conley chuckles. "I like a young woman who knows a golden opportunity when she sees it. Now, Theo, are you set up for the final-level Mercury tests?"

"Absolutely," Theo says, doing a great job of acting like he knows what that is. Or maybe he read about it on this Theo's computer and is about to bluff his way through a whole lot of tech jargon.

At that moment, my phone buzzes inside the pocket of my skirt. I step away from Theo and Conley with the usual apologetic *text message—what can you do?* shrug. They keep talking while I take up my phone, hoping desperately to hear from Paul but knowing it's probably Angela wanting to tell me about her big New Year's date, or Mom telling me to pick up some milk on the way home.

It's Paul.

His message says, in its entirety: **Don't go in there.**

Quickly I type back: **Go in where?**

Lab Eleven. You have to get out of there NOW.

A chill sweeps through me as I realize: Paul is watching us, even at this moment.

I look around, half expecting him to peer out from behind a corner, though that can't be right. Then I notice the small mirrored semispheres up by the ceiling, evenly spaced, serving no obvious function. They're not merely part of the ultrafuturistic decor; some of them must conceal security cameras.

Paul worked here alongside Theo for most of the past few months. He didn't only sabotage my parents' data—he also hacked into Triad's internal security system, which must be one of the best in the world.

My phone buzzes in my palm again. **You two didn't run into Conley by accident. Theo's not in danger, but you are.**

When I glance at Conley and Theo, I can tell that Theo suspects nothing. He's grinning as they talk, and Conley nods as he listens to Theo's ideas. So far as I can tell, everything is as it should be.

I glance at the door only a few feet away, the one marked LABORATORY 11.

You have to get out now.

I type back, **How else am I going to get any answers?** Not from Paul, obviously. **How else can I find out what Conley's after?**

Theo looks toward me, more relaxed than he's been since we walked in. Clearly he doesn't feel like anything has gone wrong. "Ready?"

Then my phone vibrates with one more text. I look down and read Paul's next message:

Conley is after YOU.

"Marguerite?" Theo now looks puzzled. "You okay?"

I don't know what to say; I don't even know what to think. It all comes down to this: Do I trust Paul or not?

As soon as I put it that way, I know I am *not* walking through that door.

"Yeah, I, um, ah—" *Think fast, think fast!* "It's my friend Angela. Sorry. I borrowed a bracelet of hers that she wants back for a big date tonight."

Conley gets this look on his face, like I'm *so cute*, like a GIF of baby puppies or something. I wish I could slap him. "Ah, to be eighteen again."

"The thing is, I put it on this morning, but I don't have it on now." I hold up my wrist, trusting that Theo didn't notice I wasn't wearing a bracelet this morning. With my other hand, I drop my phone back into the pocket of my skirt. "I feel sure I had it on in the car. Can I just—I want to run down and check the lobby, maybe the car, too? Sorry, but if I've lost this bracelet, oh, my God, Angela will *totally* kill me."

Okay, I laid on the silly-teen-girl routine a little thick at the end, but right now I need Conley to think that's all I am. I need him to be one more of those assholes who thinks my brain couldn't hold anything other than gossip and favorite colors of nail polish. If he believes that, he'll let me go in the confidence that I'll be right back.

Theo exchanges a glance with Conley and says, "Women. What are you gonna do?" I'm going to give him hell for that later, but maybe he's realized I need to walk away. He takes his car keys from his pocket and tosses them to me. "Hurry back, all right? Oh, hey, there's a Starbucks in the caf that delivers to the labs. They're open today, I think. You want a latte?"

"Sounds great." I smile at him, but the smile can't be very convincing. Here's hoping it only looks like I'm worried about a lost bracelet.

Even turning my back to them as I wait for the elevator is

excruciating. Every second I keep expecting Conley to call me back, or to feel his hand on my shoulder. Yet when the chime sounds and the doors slide open, I'm able to step in without any problems.

As soon as the elevator begins its drop, I grab my phone to see that Paul has texted again. **Good job. Now get out of the building. Go somewhere safe.**

I type back, **Tell me where you are. I won't take no for an answer.**

Answers—that's what I need, and I'm not waiting for them any longer. But my phone remains silent as I keep sliding down, the screens projecting green light at me with the message "Everyplace, Everytime, Everywhere."

So I send one more message. **Tell me or I swear I'll go back up there.**

I mean it, too. Because if Paul isn't ready to tell me the truth even now, maybe I've been wrong to believe in him. Maybe I was right to want him dead.

My phone buzzes. **San Francisco, the Tenderloin. Meet me in Union Square Park.**

The elevator deposits me in the lobby and politely says, "Have a nice day, Miss Caine." That thing is creepy.

In case Conley's watching from above, I pretend to look around in the lobby for my bracelet, then apologize to the security guard as I turn in my badge and head outside. Then I run for Theo's car so fast my flats nearly fly off my feet.

As I unlock the door, Paul texts, **You know you need to steal the car.**

"Borrow," I say out loud, knowing he can't hear me. "I'm *borrowing* Theo's car. He'll understand. Eventually."

I punch the key into the ignition and hurriedly send, **What do you mean, Conley is after me?**

The answer comes even before I can put the car in reverse: **This is all about you, Marguerite.**

You're the one Conley has wanted all along.

22

THEO ALWAYS SAID HE'D TEACH ME TO DRIVE A MANUAL transmission someday, but he never seemed to have the time. So really this is all his fault.

The clutch grinds, or the motor grinds—I don't know *what* it is making that sound in Theo's car, but I know it's not right. As soon as I get near a BART station, I stash Theo's car in a garage and hop onto a train that will take me into the city.

Now, though, as I sit there on the train—so plain in dull pale blue, so unlike the holographic Tube cars in London—I can feel my heart beating so hard that it seems to be drumming against my locket.

I've run straight to the guy who seems to have betrayed everyone I love, the man no one believes in but me.

Once upon a time, the Tenderloin was a seedy part of town, or so Mom and Dad tell me. But Union Square Park is now bordered by Saks Fifth Avenue, Macy's, Nordstrom. Most people are bundled up in coats; to me, after weeks in St. Petersburg, the day doesn't feel so cold. Everyone seems busy and cheerful, especially the crowds on the ice-skating rink, the one they always set up during the holidays. For a moment, the whirling, giggling figures on the ice take me back to St. Petersburg—and then I see one still, silent person in the background.

Paul stands near the foot of the Victoria Monument, wearing his one good winter coat, the one Mom gave him. He must have seen me before I saw him, because he doesn't flinch. Instead he squares his shoulders, like he's preparing for a fight.

Paul. My heart is equal parts joy, pain, and fear. Joy to see him alive again. Pain because this isn't the same Paul who died in Russia—because his very presence is a reminder that a Paul I loved, a Paul who loved me, is gone forever.

Fear because I still don't know what's going on. I don't know whether Paul's saving me or leading me even deeper into danger than I already am.

I can't make myself keep walking forward. It's as though I'm pinned to the spot. But Paul is already coming to me, closing the rest of the distance. Every step he takes toward me brings him into sharper focus, and I find myself noticing each detail that reminds me of Paul in Russia, and each one that makes them different.

He speaks first. "Thank you for coming here. For trusting me."

I still can't get over seeing him alive again. "How—how did you get out of Russia?"

"Azarenko returned the Firebird to me before the battle. I leaped out not long after the fighting started."

Paul looks worried, and I realize he wants to ask about his other self. Whether he lived. I can't bring myself to talk about Lieutenant Markov. I'd break down, and I can't afford that, not now. "What's going on?"

"I've taken a room in a nearby hostel. Theo got me a fake ID last year, so I used it to check in, and hostels take cash. Even Conley can't trace me here. Tomorrow morning, early, I'm taking the train to the airport. I've got a flight to Quito."

That's nice, but so not what I was asking.

He adds, "Quito is in Ecuador."

"I know where Quito is!" I snap, which is technically true because he just told me. "I meant, what's going on? With you and with Conley and all of it. Don't tell me to go back home like a good girl. If you do that again, I swear—"

"I won't do that again." But Paul says it less like a promise, more like . . . admitting defeat. "You should have gone home when I told you to, but now it's too late."

"So are you going to explain? Finally?"

"Yes." Paul looks up at the sky, as though he's afraid we're being watched. Then again, Triad owns satellites. Conley could watch us from space if he wanted to.

I think Paul's paranoia is infecting me.

"Come on," Paul says. "Let's go back to the hostel."

We walk there together, side by side, without saying a

word. Lieutenant Markov in Russia might have offered me his arm; if he knew nobody was watching, he would have held my hand. Paul doesn't.

Most of what I know about hostels comes from Josie, who backpacked around Europe one summer and around Australia and Southeast Asia the next. According to her, they're for people who want all the discomfort of camping out but none of the peace and quiet. She likes them anyway, though, because you get to meet people from all over the world. Sure enough, the lobby is filled with a group of Swedish college students trying to figure out the best time to visit Alcatraz. Paul pays the extra $10 to have a second guest, introducing me as his "girlfriend" so awkwardly that I wonder if the lady at the desk thinks I'm a hooker. But she signs me in, under my own fake ID.

"Hostels have private rooms?" I say, as Paul shuts the door behind us.

"Sometimes. I took one here because I knew I needed some privacy to work."

The room looks like a split-open supercomputer. He's hooked together five different laptops and a couple of devices I don't recognize. The screens scroll on and on with lines of glowing code. Although the room is shadowy, almost devoid of natural light, Paul doesn't turn on the lamp, maybe to avoid glare on the screens, which flicker with every new line of data. "What are you doing?"

"Tapping into Triad's servers."

"I thought you already did that." Sure enough, a tablet

computer propped against the wall flips through various security camera images from within Triad headquarters.

"Some data is more heavily protected. If I can break into that before I leave the country, great. If not, I'll have to make some educated guesses."

"About what?"

Paul doesn't answer me directly, just takes off his coat. The Firebird gleams dully against his black sweater. "You wanted answers. So let's begin."

I sit down on the side of the bed that isn't heaped with computers. Paul sits cross-legged on the floor, not even a foot away—there's no room in here for us to give each other personal space. My phone buzzes in the pocket of my skirt—which, I realize, it's been doing almost this whole time. I didn't even notice. When I pick it up, there are a couple dozen text messages from Theo in varying states of panic. **Where are What did you This isn't Did Paul My car Why did you Meg Are you okay?**

With a wince, I set my phone to Do Not Disturb. "Theo's going to kill me," I say, then I think more about what Theo might be doing at this moment. "Conley wouldn't hurt him, would he?" When I dashed out of Triad, I never even wondered whether I might be putting Theo at risk.

"Probably not," he says.

"Probably?"

"The odds are better than fifty-fifty." Paul seems to think this is much more reassuring than it is. "Today, he's safe. I didn't see anything unexpected on the security cameras after you left. Theo's confused, and Conley's angry."

I remember how Conley acted as though he'd run into us at random, but then fell into step with us as if the CEO of a massive global corporation had nothing else to do on New Year's Day. He was trying to be casual while following us into Lab Eleven, where he would have done . . . what?

"Theo idolizes Wyatt Conley," Paul says. "He's begun to realize the situation with Triad is mixed-up, but he refuses to see the extent of it."

"What do you mean, refuses?"

Paul shakes his head, but fondly. "Theo is—ambitious, in the best sense. He believes in the real-world applications of our work, and he wants everyone to benefit and profit from what we've discovered. Working with big companies, convincing people like Conley to give us more funding—I can't do that kind of thing. I try and it's ridiculous. Like a dog walking on its hind legs."

"You pitched Mom and Dad's research to Triad?"

"Basically, I stood there while Theo did," Paul says. "He talks to them, and hundreds of thousands of dollars in R&D fall down on us like rain. But Theo's not just making use of Conley and Triad; he's dazzled by them. He believes in Conley because he wants to believe."

Although I want to defend Theo, I know him well enough to see the truth of what Paul's saying.

Paul continues, "Theo would never have brought you anywhere near Triad if he'd realized Conley's real agenda. It goes beyond spying, into coercion—perhaps kidnapping between dimensions—and Conley's only getting started."

"Are we to the part where this is somehow all about me? Because that makes no sense whatsoever. Or is it only something you said to get me out of Triad?"

There's laughter on the staircase, loud voices speaking Italian or Portuguese, some language I can almost recognize, but not quite. We both wait for their footsteps to thump downstairs and away from us, as though any overheard word could be dangerous.

Finally, silence. Paul meets my gaze and holds it. "It's not just something I said. It's the truth."

"Still not making sense. What do I have to do with any of this? Mom and Dad are the geniuses behind the technology. You and Theo come next. I'm the one sitting around the rainbow table asking stupid questions."

"Stop calling yourself stupid. You're not." Paul takes a deep breath. "You have your own intelligence. Your own value. But that's not what Conley wanted from you."

"Conley doesn't even know me."

"No. But he knows us—your parents, Theo and me. He needs to manipulate us; he needs to control us. And there's only one way. Don't you see, Marguerite? You're the only person all four of us love."

I feel my cheeks flush with heat. "That's—it's—why would Conley care about that?"

The angles of Paul's face are carved more deeply by the flickering lights of code around us—his strong jawline, the searching quality of his gaze. "By now you've traveled to three parallel dimensions. What have you noticed about traveling? About your reaction to it—yours, specifically?"

"I remember things better than you guys," I say. "I haven't needed a single reminder."

"Exactly. Theo and I need the reminders to know who we are. You don't. In every dimension you can enter, you remain in total control throughout. Do you realize how valuable that is?"

I remember what Mom and Dad were talking about last night, and all their amorphous fears suddenly take shape, forming a wall around me.

Paul tilts his head, as if he's studying me. "In this dimension, I learned—or this Paul learned—that Conley's already sending spies into other dimensions. They've found ways to stabilize their spies for longer periods of time than the reminder shocks, for a day or two at a time, but their methods are still imperfect. Anyone who travels to another dimension remains vulnerable. Anyone except you."

"There must be others," I protest. "If I can do this, other people can too."

"No. In our dimension, it's only you."

"You can't know that! Think about it, will you?" Maybe Paul is paranoid after all. I brace my hands against the bed, trying to control my frustration as I ask, "What are the odds that the one and only person in our dimension who can travel like that would just happen to be the daughter of the people who invented the technology?"

Paul shakes his head. "It's not random. It's deliberate. Conley did this to you."

"*Did* this?"

"The Accident. That day with the 'overload test.' You remember, don't you?"

It comes back to me, more vivid than it was even when it was happening. That weird device Triad gave us, the way both Paul and Theo freaked out about it, the sense that I'd been in serious danger . . . the way Paul held me in his arms as though he'd nearly lost me . . .

He must see the realization in my face, because he nods. "You can only create a disruption like that once in a dimension. You can only use it to alter one person. Conley set it up so that the device would alter you."

"Josie was there too."

"She would have been the backup. Conley's alternate target, someone else he could use to manipulate your parents. But I think he wanted you all along."

"Why me?" But I haven't forgotten what Paul said earlier, about being the only person all of them love. "He wants to use me against you. Doesn't he?"

Paul nods.

Fate and mathematics. I can reach so many different versions of my parents—the people who discover interdimensional travel, the ones Conley will have to control in universe after universe if he wants to keep the technology for himself. Even though I want to think Conley could never force me to do his bidding, I know he could. All he'd have to do is threaten someone I love.

I ask, "Which Conley is doing this? The one from this dimension, or ours?"

"I think this Conley has been visiting our dimension for a while now. Months, probably. I'd say he was using our version, except I wonder if they aren't actually working together." Paul's smile is thin and mirthless. "A conspiracy of one."

Mom and Dad told me the spying might have already begun in this dimension, but I never realized Triad was spying on *us*. I shudder, and Paul looks pained, as though he hates himself for scaring me. He tried so hard to keep this secret, so I wouldn't be scared.

And finally, finally, I understand.

"That's why you ruined the data," I whisper. "Why you stole the Firebird. You knew the faster we had the technology, the faster Conley would come after me."

Paul nods. "When I realized what had been done to you, I knew they would test you soon. I thought—if I took our only good Firebird, and I made it difficult to build another—then that would put the test off for months. That was time I could use to try to reach this dimension and find out more about their plans, maybe learn something we could use."

"Then why did we go to the other dimensions at all?"

He looks almost defeated, his broad shoulders slumping as he leans forward. His head is near my knee. "They were . . . wrong turns. Dimensions mathematically similar to this one.

The universes next door. At first I thought London might be the right place, and I went to confront Conley there, but then you showed up and he didn't recognize you. As for Russia, I would've left immediately if Azarenko hadn't taken my Firebird."

"Then you got here, and this is the world you've been looking for."

Paul looks so tired. "I thought I'd have a chance to sabotage them from within. But this Paul had realized what was going on, and had already gone after Triad on his own. I guess he—he wanted to protect every version of you. Everywhere."

Which is what Paul was trying to do when all this began: he was trying to keep them from finding out that they'd turned me into their perfect spy. Instead, I went chasing after him, because I was angry and ignorant and overwhelmed, and wound up proving the very thing he was trying to hide. "I messed it all up when I came after you, didn't I?"

"Theo kept the other Firebirds." Paul's hands clench into fists, then relax, as though he still has to force himself to accept that his plan went wrong. "I should have guessed he wouldn't let them go. When I first saw you two in London, I suspected Theo—but then I realized he was trying to take care of you too, without knowing what the consequences would be. I had no idea about Henry."

I understand it all now, except what happened to Dad, and there I can guess. Probably he'd begun to realize what Conley was up to. He knew too much, and Conley had him murdered. Dad has been dead less than a month, and a couple of hours ago, Conley walked onto the elevator and gave me a smile. It sickens me.

"Why didn't you tell us?" I ask.

"I didn't want to say anything beforehand, because I wanted everyone else to act normally. That way, Conley would suspect nothing. But I set up an encoded note for Sophia to be delivered forty-eight hours after I left."

If Theo and I had waited for one more day, we'd have understood everything. "You could have been killed. You still might be."

"I intend to survive if at all possible," Paul says, very seriously.

"But you risked everything."

He glances away, then, with a clear effort of will, makes himself look me straight in the face as he says, "You were in danger—I had to protect you if I could." His gaze searches mine. "The risks don't matter. You're the only one who matters."

Neither of us can speak. We sit there, all alone in the dim light, sealed in together away from the rest of the world.

Then my phone rings.

We both startle, and Paul laughs slightly, trying to cover the awkward moment. But my skin prickles with fear as I remember—I had set my phone to Do Not Disturb. Nobody should be able to call me.

I take the phone from my pocket. The call is from an "unknown number."

Like about 75 percent of America, I use a Triad cell phone. I say, "Can Conley hack into tPhones?"

Paul's face falls as he realizes what's going on. "Theoretically."

"I don't think it's just theory." The phone keeps ringing; voice mail should have picked up by now, but he has a way around that too. "I can't answer. If I answer, he'll know where I am."

"The cell phone tower will already have pinged your location." Paul glances toward the door, like the police might burst through at any moment. Maybe they will. "Go ahead. Answer it."

My father's murderer is on the phone. What does he want? But I already know. He only wants me.

23

I SLIDE THE BAR ACROSS MY PHONE SCREEN AND SAY, "Hello, Mr. Conley."

"Marguerite," he says, as chummy as he was back at Triad headquarters. His voice is even younger than his face; he sounds like another one of Mom and Dad's grad students who's come by to hang out at the rainbow table. The volume is down on my phone, but both Paul and I lean close to hear him over the hum of the computers. "What a relief to finally hear from you. I take it you found your friend's bracelet?"

It infuriates me. If Conley were here, I'd smash my fist right into his freckled face. "Oh, please. You think you have the right to call *me* out on being dishonest? I'm not the epic liar here. So cut the crap and say what you have to say."

Paul gives me a look like, *Damn*. I think he's impressed.

"Cutting the crap, then," Conley says, as amiable as before. "You're a talented young woman. I think we need to discuss

284

how best to use those talents, going forward."

"I'm not your traveler. I'm not your spy. That's all there is to it."

"I see you've spoken with Mr. Markov. Is he there with you now?" I don't answer, but that's probably as good as a yes. Paul says nothing, only narrows his eyes. Conley continues, "If only things were that simple. You've become a very important person in a very important place. That means acquiring your talents is one of Triad Corporation's top priorities."

"Your priorities don't interest me," I shoot back.

"The people who help me achieve my goals are rewarded, Marguerite. I could reward you more richly than you can imagine."

"Money doesn't make up for what you've done." My throat tightens as I think of my father, dead in a river a universe away.

"I can make up for a lot."

Paul stands, slowly. I realize he's getting ready to move. Of course—if Conley is already tracking our location, he could have people here any second. I stand up too, edging out of the way so that Paul can start unplugging the computers and stuffing them into his duffel bag.

To cover the sound of his packing, I start talking again, "Is this the part where you start threatening everyone else I love?"

"Do you mean Mr. Beck? He's absolutely fine, at the moment. Slightly annoyed that you stole his car. He's back in his own office, waiting for the company car to take him home. Eventually."

The subtle threat to Theo chills me. Paul pauses in his work, as frightened for Theo as I am. But he doesn't stop packing for long. Time is already running out.

Conley continues, "We need to meet, Marguerite. There are certain tests I need to run to determine the full extent of your potential. Nothing painful, I promise."

"Your promises aren't worth much," I say.

"You're underestimating me. People don't do that often." He sounds almost amused by the novelty. "Just meet with me. Choose a neutral location. Paul can come along, if you'd find that comforting. Let me figure out how much you have to bargain with, and then we'll bargain."

How can he not be getting the message? "You don't have anything I want!"

Conley's voice gets very quiet. "Yes, I do. I have something you want very much."

And there's something about the way he says it that makes me believe him.

Is he talking about Theo? I glance at Paul, whose eyes are wide. He knows what Conley's referring to—and whatever it is, it's important. It's real.

"The Chinatown Dragon Gate," I say. It's the first land-mark that comes to mind. "Meet me there in one hour. It has to be you, and you have to come alone. Got it? One hour from—now." With that I hang up the call, and shut off the phone. Even Conley's hackers can't undo the plain old off switch.

Paul stares at me. "You can't meet with Conley."

"No shit. But I bought us one hour. While he's in Chinatown, we can get you to the airport."

"You're good at this." A smile spreads across Paul's face. "Being on the run."

"I'm getting a lot of practice."

Paul and I sit next to each other on the BART train, his enormous duffel bag like a third person crammed in with us. It's about half an hour to the airport, which gives us more time to talk.

And yet there's so much to ask, so much to say, that I find it hard to find any words at all.

Finally I ask the simplest question I can think of. "Why Ecuador?"

"The other Paul made these plans, not me. I assume it's because Ecuador has no extradition treaty with the United States."

Of course. Erasing Mom and Dad's data was one thing, but when Paul attacked Triad as well, he committed a crime that won't be forgiven. The Paul from this dimension needs to make his own escape, so this Paul is seeing it through. "You always leave yourself a back door, don't you?"

"Before you get into trouble, it pays to ask yourself how you'll get out again." He looks back at me now, gray eyes darkened by their intensity. "You need to get out of this too, Marguerite."

"Whoa. You want me to run off with you to Ecuador?"

"You're not coming with me," he says flatly. Even though I had exactly zero intention of dashing away to South America, his blunt refusal stings. Paul pauses, then adds, "I meant—you need to go home."

"We're both going home now. Right?" I assume Paul's waiting to jump until he's taken this version safely to the airport.

But Paul hesitates before answering, one second too long.

"Where are you going now?"

"I can't tell you that yet."

I could strangle him. "Has keeping secrets done any good at any point on this journey? Why can't you trust me?"

He shuts his eyes, like I'm making his head hurt. "It's not about distrusting you."

"Then what is it about? I've tried to trust you—even when everyone else told me not to—"

"You believed I killed Henry," Paul shoots back. Which is a good point.

"That doesn't count. Conley framed you. Made it look like you cut Dad's brakes."

Paul shrugs. He thinks I should've known better, and maybe he's right.

Quietly, I say, "I'm sorry."

"No. Don't apologize. I understand that you weren't

yourself. And Conley can be convincing, when he wants to be." But Paul's entire body remains tense. If he's not angry, then why . . . ?

Oh.

"In Russia—" I don't know what to say, where to begin. "You and me—I don't know if you remember everything, or anything—"

"I remember having sex."

I want to turn my head away, but how ridiculous would it be to get bashful now?

Paul seems to realize he's once again been too blunt. "I, ah, I also remember getting wounded. Did he survive?"

"No. You—he—died in my arms."

Paul's head ducks, as if he feels the loss as deeply as I do. Maybe he does. "I'm sorry."

Tears well in my eyes, but I try to fight them back.

Quietly he adds, "I know you loved him. Not me."

"Maybe. I don't know," I whisper.

He takes a deep breath, almost in wonder. I realize that even *maybe* is more than Paul had dared to dream of. Everything he's done, everything he gave up and risked for me: Paul did all that without the slightest idea of being loved in return.

"Marguerite—"

"I don't know where he stops and you begin."

The train slows as it pulls into its next stop, and apparently half the population of this neighborhood is headed to the airport today. As dozens of people crowd on, hauling their bags with them, Paul and I fall silent, unable to look each other in the eye.

I think about the Rachmaninoff ringtone on my phone. What are Paul and I to each other, in this dimension? We must be very nearly the same, if that one song still reminds me of him. If he was willing to once again give up everything—wreck his own life—trying to protect my parents' work, and to protect me—

The train slides back into motion, and everyone starts talking or listening to music; the chatter surrounds us, giving us privacy again. Finally Paul says, "What about you and Theo? I thought he was the one who—well. I thought he was the one."

I care about Theo. There's no denying that, no setting it aside easily. But whatever it is I feel for him—it's not what I feel for Paul. "No. Not Theo."

I fell in love with one Paul. I fell in love with his unchanging soul. Does that mean I fell in love with every Paul, everywhere?

Paul rushes to fill the silence, words tumbling over one another, as if he'd held them back for so long that he can't last one second more. "I know I'm not—I've never been—" He stares down at his own broad hands on his duffel bag. "I'm not good with words. I never know the right thing to say, because with you—every time we talk I seem to get it wrong."

"You don't always get it wrong."

He shakes his head slightly, the smile on his face rueful. "I'm not the Paul from Russia. I can't speak the way he did. I wish I could."

"That's not what I mean." Everything would be so much simpler if I were sure that I only cared for Lieutenant Markov. But since when did love become simple? "That time you watched me paint, and you told me I always painted the truth—you got that right. Really right."

Paul's smile softens, like he's starting to believe. "You said you don't know where Lieutenant Markov stops and I begin."

I nod as I hug myself, and curl down into my seat.

"I remember being a part of him." His voice is low, and soft. I lift my eyes to his. It feels both like it's hard to meet his gaze and like I could never look away. "I know we both liked the way you look for beauty in every person. Every moment. He wished he could be funny like you, sure of your words, and I do too. We both daydreamed about kissing you against a wall. Neither of us thought we ever had a chance with anyone as amazing as you. We would both do anything, give up anything, to keep you safe."

By now my vision has blurred with tears. Paul must see that in my eyes, and he hesitates—like he feels guilty for upsetting me. But he keeps going.

"Lieutenant Markov and I are not the same man," he says. "Nobody knows that better than I do. But we're not completely different, either. The one way we were most alike was—was how we felt about you."

The train rattles into its last stop, at the airport. Everyone starts hauling their bags out, and I wipe my cheeks, then help Paul maneuver his duffel through the doors. Instead of following the crowd forward, though, he lingers on the dimly lit platform, and I know it's because he wants to tell me goodbye while we're alone.

As soon as everyone else is farther ahead, I say, "Paul—"

"I love you."

It makes me gasp. Not in surprise—by now I knew, I knew that as surely as I knew anything in the world. But it still feels like going through the rapids, over a waterfall, falling into the roar.

He keeps going, as if afraid to trust my reaction. "I told myself it didn't matter if I never got to be with you. It was enough just to love you. When you were in danger, I needed you to be safe. You don't owe me anything for that. You don't have to say—to pretend—"

I reach out and press two fingers to his mouth. As overwhelmed as I am right now, I have to touch him. I have to *know*.

Paul breathes out sharply, like a man struck. He pulls me close, his enormous hands cradling my face as though I were fragile and delicate. Like a little dove. Slowly Paul lowers his face to mine, nuzzling my temple, my cheeks, the corner of my mouth. I breathe in the scent of his skin as I wrap my fingers around his forearms, guiding him gently, gently down.

Of course I've always known Paul was a big man, so much taller than me, and yet I never realized how he could wrap himself around me. How he could enclose me here in the darkness and become my whole world.

He brushes the first kiss against my cheekbone. The touch is so soft, even tentative—but the power of the emotion behind it overcomes me, bears me down more surely than force ever could. I tilt my head back, and Paul responds to the invitation by kissing the hollow of my throat, then finding the place on my neck where my pulse is pounding hardest. When he pulls me against his chest, I can feel his heart beating equally fast. We're both so scared, yet neither of us wants to pull away.

Paul scrapes his teeth along my throat. The sharp edge between pain and pleasure makes me cry out in the instant before he silences me with his kiss.

Our lips part. I feel his tongue brush against mine as we breathe each other in. The world is turning upside down. I clutch at his T-shirt as my hands become fists. His broad hands cradle me at the waist, and all I can think is that this is perfect, absolutely perfect, just like . . .

Just like the way the other Paul kissed me in Russia.

It ought to reassure me. Instead it horrifies me. The man I loved died two days ago, and now I'm in someone else's arms—except I don't even know if this counts as someone else—

I turn my head from Paul, breaking the kiss. "Stop," I whisper. "Please, stop."

Paul stops immediately, though his arms remain around me. "Marguerite? What did I do wrong?"

"Nothing." My voice trembles. "I feel like I'm being unfaithful. Which is completely crazy, but I don't—I can't."

"Okay. It's okay." Paul pulls me closer, but not in passion. Instead he rubs my back, slow and gentle, comforting me as I struggle against tears and think of the Paul I lost.

Am I betraying him now? Or am I being a fool, because the man I loved has basically come back to life but I can't love him again?

"You're not crazy," Paul murmurs. "This situation—it's hard to know what to think. What to feel."

I nod. His lips brush my hairline, almost too gently to even be called a kiss, as he keeps stroking my back.

Then we hear the crackle of a walkie-talkie—which means the police.

We both go tense at the same moment, hanging on to each other as the officer wanders along the platform. If she even saw us kissing, she gives no sign. This is just a standard patrol . . . I hope. "They're not coming after us. Why would they be?"

"Conley could have made Theo call the car in as stolen. He might even have argued that I abducted you. Whatever it took to get you back under his control. By now he probably realizes you're not going to the Dragon Gate."

Paul has a point. We have no more time to lose. I say, "This Paul needs to get away. You have to go."

"Right. Okay." He hesitates one moment longer. I know he wants to kiss me; I can't tell whether I want him to or not. He doesn't.

For a moment we both straighten ourselves—me smoothing my curls back from my face, Paul untucking his T-shirt. A smudge of lipstick is deep pink against his cheek, and I reach out to wipe it off with my thumb. He looks at me, smiling at the touch.

But the smile fades quickly. "Go home," he says. "Tell Sophia what's going on, and wait for me there."

I've been so overwhelmed I almost forgot that he's still keeping secrets from me. "I'll tell Mom what's going on as soon as I know. Tell me where you're going."

"Not yet."

"But you found the right dimension! You got all this background information on Triad and Conley! What else is there to do?"

"When I went through Triad's information here, I found—something I need to check out. Let's leave it at that."

I didn't know it was possible to go from making out with someone to wanting to smack them upside the head, hard, in less than a minute—but here we are. "You're still keeping secrets from me. *Still.*"

"Marguerite—"

"No more secrets! I don't know how much more screwed up things have to get before you finally see that."

"Please listen." Paul takes my hand and leans close; the way he looks at me isn't like a guy making an excuse—he's steady, and strong, and almost maddeningly sure of himself. "I know I've made mistakes, keeping so much from you, but this is different. If I tell you what I'm thinking now, and I'm wrong, it would be terrible. No, beyond even that. It would be the most hurtful thing I could ever do to you."

What is he talking about? I can't begin to imagine. How much deeper do Triad's crimes go?

Paul's fingers tighten around mine. "I know you've had to take a lot on faith. You'll never realize what it means, that you regained your trust in me. That you can still believe. But I need you to keep believing a little while longer."

I can't even begin to tell him how sick I am of being in the dark. And yet—despite everything—I believe him.

"Okay. All right. Fine." Believing Paul isn't the same thing as doing whatever he says. "You don't have to explain if it's that important, but I'm coming with you."

Paul turns my hand over in his, brushes against my palm with his thumb. "I'd feel much better if I knew you were safe."

This isn't about your feelings, I want to say, but I know Paul's been through as much as I have these past few weeks. We're both at the brink; that's why we need each other to keep ourselves strong, to make ourselves see clearly. "Wyatt Conley is chasing me through different dimensions, right? That means I'm safest when I'm with you."

"You're extremely stubborn."

"Guess you'd better get used to that."

He smiles despite himself. That expression—it's nothing like the Paul from Russia. It belongs to my Paul alone, and yet it seems to light me up inside.

"Let's go," Paul says. I reach for my Firebird, but he stops me. "Not yet. I'm going to walk into the airport and get my boarding pass before I leap out. Otherwise the other Paul might not realize what's going on in time."

"Okay. Wait fifteen minutes?"

"Fifteen minutes, then follow me."

Guess I might as well stay in the BART station. After hauling this version of Marguerite all the way to the far side of San Francisco, I ought to at least make it easier for her to get home again. For a moment I think about messaging Theo to let him know what's going on, but that's not necessary; his Firebird will signal that Paul and I have jumped ahead, and Theo will surely follow.

So we're done. Yet for a moment longer Paul and I stand there in the darkness, overcome with our new knowledge of each other, and the realization that in five minutes we might be half a world apart again.

Paul adjusts his duffel bag, his gray eyes searching mine. "You're all right?"

"As all right as I'm going to be for a while. Just—be careful."

He nods. Even that one small thing—my telling him to be careful—for him, it's like a beacon. A reason to hope. I wish I could tell him he was right to hope; I wish I knew.

Then Paul turns and walks away from me, heading straight toward the passageway to the airport. But right before he passes out of sight, he looks over his shoulder at me one last time.

We'll find each other, I tell myself as he disappears. *We always do.*

I take the Firebird in hand, counting off the seconds before I can follow Paul.

24

THIS TIME, WHEN I SLAM INTO THE NEXT VERSION OF ME, I wake myself up; I feel like I just got thrown into bed. Groggily I shift onto my elbows to look around. Although this bedroom is much smaller than the one I have at home, it's recognizably mine—artwork hangs on the nearest wall, and there's a brightly patterned scarf on the bedside table that looks like something I'd own.

It must be the dead of night, to judge by the darkness in my room. That makes me wonder where I am. The Firebirds allow me to travel through dimensions, but not through time. Since I left my home in California sometime after lunch, I must be halfway across the globe, someplace where it's either very late or very early.

Three of the portraits on my wall are more than familiar: Mom, Dad, and Josie each look out from their canvases. As long as we're together, this dimension is probably okay.

Yet the portraits are different here—Mom's hair is shorter, and Josie's is tied back. Dad seems more driven, less distracted. And my technique isn't quite the same, either: I'm layering paint much more thickly, going for a more impressionistic take. It's different from both my usual photorealistic style and the delicate, detailed sketches by Grand Duchess Margarita. I run my finger along Josie's picture, feeling the thick ridges and swirls of dried paint against my skin.

From my bedside table, my alarm goes off, cuing up some pop music I don't recognize. As I shut it off, I frown down at the time: 7 a.m. Even in winter, I'd expect some light outside at this hour. Then I remember Russia, and how St. Petersburg only received a few hours of daylight per day in December. Do we live in the far north here, too?

I swing my feet out of bed and walk toward one of the dark, oddly curved windows, hoping to get a sense of my new surroundings. When I look out, at first I see nothing—

—and then a school of tropical fish swims by.

It's dark outside because we're underwater.

Well, this is new.

My home turns out to be the oceanographic station *Salacia*, located in the heart of the Coral Sea. *Salacia* is one of the most sophisticated stations of its kind in the world, which is why the man in charge is the illustrious oceanographer Dr. Henry Caine.

A quick review of the internet reveals that, in this dimension, global water levels have risen much farther and faster than at home—more like the worst-case projections for climate change a century from now. Is this because of greater pollution? Some other phenomenon? Believe it or not, politicians are *still* arguing about this on a planet with continents now shaped completely differently than the ones I recognize. While people bicker about the cause, humanity has had to find new ways to live. The vast majority of the world's population continues to dwell on land, though sometimes in new cities that don't exist in my dimension, or in semi-aquatic versions of the old ones. (New York City looks more like Venice now.) But increasing numbers of people are casting themselves onto the water in vast ships that function as towns, or on science stations like this one.

Here, oceanography is the most important subject for scientific study. What's happening with marine life; iron, oxygen, and contaminant levels in the water; the behavior of newly unpredictable tides and rogue waves—this is the information people need in order to create a new society that has to be at least partially aquatic. So Dad never left oceanography to devote himself to Mom's research; here, Mom went into oceanography too, and the two of them met while crewing on a science vessel. (At least, according to their Wikipedia entries—my parents aren't quite as well known here as they are at home, but they still rate bios online.) We've been on the *Salacia* for five years now. For me, this is home.

But on an oceanographic station, nobody gets to just hang out, not even kids. Everyone who lives here works hard to keep it going, as I discover when my computer lights up with DAILY ASSIGNMENT ROSTER.

This is why I find myself climbing through one of the maintenance tubes before breakfast, going out to manually check the wind sensors (whatever that means). I ascend through water that shifts from nearly black to translucent blue, and then into daylight. The sight of the ocean stretching out to the horizon in every direction takes my breath away. The quality of the light on the waves changes in brilliance and depth each second, and the effect is dazzling.

Does the other Marguerite still see how amazing this is, even though it surrounds her every day? I smile as I realize she must, if we have anything in common at all.

In my jeans and T-shirt, I walk out onto the surface platform—metal ridged to add traction when it's wet, which must be always. Everything smells like salt and sunshine. The sea breeze catches at my curls, and immediately I see why Josie and Mom wear their hair differently here. As I hurriedly tuck mine back into a sloppy ponytail, I hear a call from the other edge of the platform: "Took you long enough!"

I glance over to see Josie, who's scrubbing algae off something right at the surface of the water. She must have been out here a while already, but in any universe, I know how to handle Josie's teasing. I grin as I flip her off, then start climbing the metal ladder up to the wind sensors.

Heights aren't my favorite. I'm not phobic or anything, but when Paul talks about rock climbing, I can never believe anyone does that for *fun*. So as I make my way up the ladder, I remind myself that, for this Marguerite, clambering forty feet up is no big deal.

You have steel-toed boots with treads so deep you can dig into the rungs on the ladder! I remind myself, trying to be cheerful as I go higher and higher. *You have a safety belt, which you're nearly 85 percent sure you attached correctly! Nothing to worry about!*

At least my view of the seascape around us only gets better with every few steps. The surface section of the *Salacia* looks like an overgrown hamster maze: huge metal pipes and tubes connected by various platforms. Yet for this Marguerite, this is home.

As I go through each sensor in turn, I have to concentrate hard on the instructions I read back in my room; basically I'm checking to make sure everything looks right, and . . . I guess it does?

Even all that isn't enough to silence the fear deep inside, the words that keep repeating:

Me. Triad is after me.

Although families eat dinner in their own quarters, breakfast and lunch are apparently served cafeteria-style. This cafeteria is nothing like any other one I've seen, though. It's underwater but close to surface level, with enormous arched windows that reveal lots of shimmering light through blue water. People say hello to friends as they gather at various round tables, and families are all together, including little kids and even some elderly people. While this is a working scientific station, it's obviously meant to include regular people as well—half laboratory, half small town.

When Dad walks in, people don't come to attention or anything so formal; they notice the boss, but they smile. He keeps stopping by each table to check on people and see how they're doing. It's weird to see him in charge, and yet not surprising to see that he's great at it. I watch him from across the room, my tray in my hands. By now I've learned to endure the strange, poignant feeling of missing my father while he's not quite gone.

"Good morning, Marguerite." Mom kisses my cheek as she takes her seat. "Are you all right?"

I realize I've been standing in place with my tray for a few minutes now. "Oh. Yeah. Sure."

As we take our seats, Josie joins us and asks Mom, "What's the latest from the weather service?"

"We'll start seeing some chop tonight, but the worst of the storm front shouldn't blow in until lunchtime tomorrow." Mom sips her tea, completely oblivious to the enormous stingray swimming by behind her head. "Probably we can expect some communication blackouts as well."

Josie makes a face. "Good thing I already downloaded the surfing competition."

Why wouldn't we go back to shore, if a dangerous storm is coming in? But I remember what I read about *Salacia* in my room—in particular, where we are. The closest land masses (New Zealand and Papua New Guinea) are both hours away by air. So we have to ride out storms as they come. *Salacia* is built to take that kind of punishment, I assume—I *hope*. But based on what Mom said, we might have hours or even days of communications silence.

Wait. I only have a little while to contact the outside world?

"You know, I'm not hungry," I say, even as I stuff down a couple of bites of toast. "I'm going to run back to our cabin for a while, okay?"

Mom gives me one of her looks—the one that means *Clearly something is up and I know it and you know I know but I won't call you on it yet.* "Hurry up. Don't forget, you've got that big test today."

Big test? Crap. Apparently the holidays don't cut you much time off from school on a science station. But that's the least of my concerns.

With one final glance at Dad, I leave the cafeteria and head back down to the residence levels of the station. I'm pretty sure I remember where we live. Even though my father's in charge here, our suite of rooms seems to be exactly like everybody else's—tiny bedrooms, and one combination kitchen/den that is just big enough to be comfortable but not one square inch bigger. Honestly, besides the fact that it's underwater, our home here looks totally ordinary; we have cans of Coke in the fridge, and Josie's flip-flops are by the front door, like always.

I take up my tablet computer to start my searches, then stop and stare at it. The logo reads ConTech . . . which was Wyatt Conley's company in the London dimension. And, apparently, in this dimension too. How far does his influence reach?

Surely not to the Coral Sea. The tension in my chest relaxes slightly as I realize Conley can't get at me easily, not here.

Is that why Paul chose this dimension? Because it's safe from Conley? Here, scientists have directed all their energies toward adapting humanity to life in and on water. That means Mom hasn't invented the Firebird technology—so Conley wouldn't have much reason to travel here himself.

Yet that answer doesn't feel quite right.

Paul's purpose remains maddeningly opaque. Whatever brought him here, to this dimension—that, apparently, is too big for him to speak about.

I've chosen to trust Paul, but that doesn't make it any easier to do without the answers.

So far the station's Wi-Fi is still working perfectly. I type in a search for "Paul Markov, physicist" . . . then backspace and replace it with, "Paul Markov, oceanographer." That's the subject all the best and brightest will study in this world.

Paul turns out to be doing his doctoral research on a vessel taking deepwater samples in the Pacific, though I can't find out exactly where. He could be only a couple of hours away, or across half the planet. I ping his account on his ship, but he must not be in front of his computer. So I tap the screen to record a video message.

"Hi, Paul. It's me. I mean, it's really me." I hook one thumb under the chain of my Firebird, so he can see it. "I'm safe here, and I'm with my family, so—you don't have to worry on my account. Looks like you're doing all right too. I might not have internet access for long, though. When you get this, call, okay?"

I hope Paul's just had a reminder when he sees that. Otherwise, he's going to be incredibly confused.

Theo turns out to be studying in Australia, in a harbor city called New Perth that's about two hundred miles inland from where Perth used to be. I ping him, too, and even though it must be the wee hours of the morning where he is, he answers almost instantly. His face takes shape on the screen—hair rumpled, plenty of stubble—and he immediately says, "You *stole my car.*"

"Hi to you, too." I can't resist a grin.

"What the hell was that about? One minute I'm telling Conley how great you are, the next minute you're peeling out of the parking lot." Theo looks pissed off, and I know it's not the car he's angry about. "Tell me you didn't go to meet Paul."

"I went to meet Paul."

"Jesus *Christ.*"

"You were wrong about him, Theo. He finally explained what's really been happening, with Conley and with—" I can't bring myself to say, *with me.* Saying that I'm Conley's true target makes it all too real. "It's complicated. It would be better if I could tell you all this in person. Do you think you could get here? It's not so far."

"It's thousands of miles, Meg. You need to brush up

307

on your geography." Theo leans backward, thumping his head against the wall. His wrinkled T-shirt is, once again, the Gears; the Beatles must have not quite made it to this dimension either. "But yeah. I can get there. Looks like science stations and oceanography institutes all work together pretty tightly in this dimension. If I radio in, say I've been on an observation flight or cruise, and I need a berth, they'll take me in. Now all I have to do is find one of those."

If anybody is resourceful enough to pull that off, it's Theo. I grin at him. "Fantastic."

"Is Paul there with you?" Theo says shortly.

"No. He's on a research vessel." This is the first time I've had more information than Theo, and I can tell he doesn't like being in the dark. Still, I can't blame him for being impatient for answers. Even though I agreed to take Paul on faith a while longer, I'm past ready to find out what else is going on.

More gently, Theo says, "If he calls you, or shows up— listen, I know you feel like Paul's innocent, but will you please exercise some basic caution until I get there? A healthy skepticism?"

"What exactly is it you think Paul's going to do now? If he were going to hurt me, he's already had his chance."

"He already hurt us all." The way Theo says it awakens all my grief for my father, which is somehow stronger for being shared. I reach out to touch my tablet, and he touches his, too; our fingertips seem to meet through the screen. "I'm only looking out for you. Trying to take care of you.

Why can't you see that? I wish I could make you see that, just once."

"Theo—"

He doesn't let me finish. "All right, Meg. See you soon."

His image goes to black, and for a while I remain there, fingertips on the screen, wondering if I've broken Theo's heart.

I go through this Marguerite's day, which fortunately is pleasant enough. Here, I attend school—but instead of one of the enormous, dull, cliquish schools I see on TV, it's a group of about fifty kids from my age all the way down to preschool, and everything's pretty low-key and free-form. The "big test" turns out to be French; lucky thing I just spent nearly three weeks in Russia studying Molière. As I breezily write out a paragraph on *Tartuffe*, I think, *I'm borrowing this Marguerite's body, but at least this time I'm paying her back for the favor.*

I think about Paul. My need to know how he is, what he's doing, why he's here—it burns inside me, as constant as a torch. Whenever I get a moment, I check my account to see if he's called back. But communications cloud out before lunchtime. My only responses are black screens and static.

Dinner is some chicken thing that comes wrapped in an airtight pouch, and vegetables that emerge from deep freeze with a bad case of soggy. Out here, probably, nothing is fresh except seafood; that would be fine with me, but I'm guessing the rest of my family, after a few years on the *Salacia*, is sick and tired of it.

But I don't care about the crappy meal. We're all together, me and Josie, Mom and Dad. I took that for granted in my own dimension until it was ripped away. So I'm not making that mistake again. From now on, I'm very aware that every moment I'm with my dad might be the last.

"We only got half the data packet out before the comms went down," Mom says to Dad as she pours herself some tea. "And the forecasts are only getting worse."

"Swaying like a hammock already," Dad says cheerfully.

"That's why you're the boss here." Josie shakes her head. "Only you are weird enough to love storms at sea."

He smiles with genuine pride. "As to the count of weirdness, I plead guilty."

Now that he mentions it, the floor *is* swaying slightly; I realize the *Salacia* must have been built with a certain amount of give, so that it can work with the tides and currents instead of constantly being battered by them. Normally I'd be wretched with motion sickness, but this Marguerite must have gotten her sea legs years ago.

"You're awfully quiet tonight," Mom says to me. "Are you sure you're all right? You've been a little off all day." The back of her hand finds my forehead, checking for fever as if I were still five years old.

"Just thinking. That's all." I miss my real Mom, back home. A lump rises in my throat, but I manage to keep it together. I don't want to spoil the evening.

After we eat, Josie asks me if I want to watch the surfing competition with her. I find it hard to believe I care about surfing a whole lot more in this dimension than I do at home—which is to say, at all—but any distraction seems like a good idea. So I sit beside her on the sofa while Dad starts on the dishes, but when he starts to hum, I once again have to struggle against the urge to cry.

Josie squints at me. "Mom's right. You're weirder than usual today."

"Ha ha." I brush my hair back and try to act casual. And then I remember the T-shirt Theo wore: The Gears.

My mind is working fast, comparing the knowledge of different dimensions.

The Beatles never existed here. The Gears were a band featuring Paul McCartney and George Harrison—not John Lennon. But John Lennon is the one who wrote "In My Life" for the Beatles. I'm sure of it. That song doesn't exist in this dimension.

So how is Dad humming it?

I think back to what Paul told me in San Francisco. He'd found the dimension that was spying on our own, and proved what Conley was up to. Yet he wouldn't come back with me because now he had learned something else, something important. Something he couldn't tell me, because it would be too horrible if he were wrong . . .

When we travel into a new dimension, our bodies are "no longer observable." At the time I left home, the authorities hadn't yet pulled Dad's body from the river. They were dredging for him then—dipping nets into the water, sending divers down into the muck. I was hardly able to think about it, because the images were so horrible. Worse was the idea of Mom having to go identify the body after it had been in the river for a few days, after it no longer looked like Dad, or like anything human.

But what if he wasn't lost in the current? What if his body was simply not observable, because he was kidnapped into another dimension?

What if Dad isn't dead? What if he's *right here*?

"Marguerite?" Josie copies Mom's hand-to-the-forehead move. "You're seriously zoned out."

I can't even bother with an excuse. "Be right back."

Heart pounding, I walk into the kitchen area where Dad is finishing up. He gives me a pleasant, somewhat distracted smile. "Don't tell me you're still hungry."

"Can we talk?"

"Of course."

"Not here. In the corridor, maybe."

Despite his evident confusion, he says, "All right."

Nobody pays any attention to our stepping outside our quarters; Mom is in the bedroom she shares with Dad, and Josie is already concentrating on her computer again. The corridors of the *Salacia* aren't necessarily private, but most people seem to be eating dinner now, which means my father and I are alone. Our only witnesses are the fish swimming by the porthole window.

Dad's not wearing a Firebird. Then again, if he's been

312

kidnapped, someone brought him here and then stranded him. Without his own Firebird, Dad not only wouldn't be able to get back home; he wouldn't be able to receive any reminders. He would have no idea who he is. My father would be only a glimmer within this version of Dr. Henry Caine—a part of his subconscious.

The part that would still hum a song by the Beatles.

"Is everything okay, sweetheart?" Dad folds his arms in front of his chest. "What's this about?"

"I need you to trust me for a minute." My voice has begun to shake. "Okay?"

By now Dad looks deeply worried, but he nods.

I take the Firebird from around my neck and put it around Dad's. He raises an eyebrow, but I ignore him, instead going through the motions that will set a reminder. I drop it against his chest, realizing I'm holding my breath—

"Gahhh—dammit!" Dad says, staggering backward as he grabs the Firebird. But then he freezes. First he slowly looks down at the Firebird in his hand, recognizing it, then lifts his face to mine. "Marguerite?" he gasps. "Oh, my God."

It's the same face, the same eyes, but I see the difference. I know *my dad*.

Then I'm laughing and crying at the same time, but it doesn't matter, because Dad's hugging me, and we're together, and he's alive.

And now I know why Paul brought us here.

25

"DEAR LORD." DAD RUNS HIS HANDS THROUGH HIS HAIR, AS absolutely bewildered as anyone would be to wake up in another dimension. "How long has it been?"

"Almost a month. It'll be a month on January fifth, so, three days from now."

"A month gone. No, not gone. I remember it—I was aware—but it was the strangest state of being, Marguerite. The way it is in dreams sometimes, when you're both watching the events around you and living them at the same time. It never occurred to me to wonder where I was, or why."

Maybe this fugue state is what it's like for most people traveling between dimensions. "You remember now," I say, taking Dad's hand. "And I've got the Firebird, so I can remind you as much as you need."

By now we're sitting together in the cafeteria. This late, no one else is here, and the illumination comes mostly from external lamps filtering through the windows. In the dark waters beyond, the occasional fish swims by, but the currents have become choppy as the storm front starts to come in. Even the fish are looking for safe coves now. Mom and Josie must realize Dad and I are having a heart-to-heart about something—though nobody could blame them for not guessing exactly what.

"My poor darling Sophie." Dad closes his eyes, as though in pain. "And Josephine. My God."

"They'll be okay as soon as you're home." A broad smile spreads across my face. *Home*. I get to take Dad home.

"I don't know whether to strangle Paul and Theo or thank them. Both, I think."

"Don't be angry, Dad. They've been so strong, and loyal to you, and protective of me. I never knew how amazing they were before this. Paul and Theo both love you a lot." I want to tell my father how Paul and I feel about each other, but that can wait until we're all back where we should be. "Was it Conley who kidnapped you?"

"No. It was someone else, someone I'd never seen before. A woman . . ." His voice trails off, and then he shakes his head. "It's all rather murky, I'm afraid. I'd driven to the university, to find out what the devil had happened to our data, and as I got out of the car, she came toward me. I remember thinking she must be a new graduate student, or a prospective faculty member. Something about her was a little too polished, I suppose, for the average undergrad." Dad sighs. "The next thing I knew, I was twenty thousand leagues under the sea. I had my memories for a few minutes, but no Firebird. So I knew I was stranded in this dimension, possibly forever. That was . . . difficult."

His face shifts in a way I haven't seen since Gran died years ago, and I realize the memory of that powerless fear has brought him close to tears. Hatred for Wyatt Conley blazes through me, and I tell myself we'll deal with him when we get back. He has the power right now, but all his power is built on my mother's genius and my parents' hard work. We have Paul. We have Theo. And if I'm the ultimate weapon— they have me.

Against all of us, together? Conley doesn't stand a chance.

Dad says, "It was like being stunned. Or drugged. I was a part of this person who was both myself and not myself, and not even aware enough to fight it. Locked in the perfect prison." He takes a deep breath, and when he looks at me, he smiles. "Until my brave girl came and found me."

I had thought I'd never feel this happy again. "Now we just have to get you back home."

Although my dad is still smiling, I can sense his sadness. "Marguerite, you must have done the math by now. There are two of us, and you only have one Firebird."

"For now," I say. "You made one, so you can make another. When Paul and Theo get here, they can help."

"Constructing a Firebird takes months . . . wait. Did you say Paul and Theo were coming here?"

"Theo's already on his way. Paul might be too, but communications have been down so long, I don't know."

"Heading out here with a storm like this coming in? That's madness." Dad sighs. "Then again, jumping through dimensions to chase a dead man is madness too. I had long suspected their lunacy but this confirmation is nonetheless disquieting."

"See? Everything's going to be fine."

Dad brushes my hair back from my face, the way he used to when I was a little girl who got messy playing in the backyard. "The resources to make a Firebird were difficult enough to come by. In this dimension, obtaining them might be impossible."

"Impossible?" Then I realize what he means. One of the metals used in the Firebirds is found in only one valley in the world, and other components are rare and valuable, too. This is a world where even desalinated water is a hot commodity; nations aren't as free with their resources any longer. Getting the materials we need will be a considerable challenge.

"If you have to go back without me," he says quietly, "you're to tell your mother how very much I love her. Josie too. And you must warn them about Triad. If Conley would do this, he's capable of anything."

"Stop it. We're going to figure it out, okay? We will."

Dad's only reply is to take me back into his arms.

As I hug him tightly, looking out at the churning sea, I know I'm going to get my father back home, no matter what it takes.

Even if I have to give him my Firebird. Even if I'm the one who stays here forever.

Once we're back in our family quarters, the night becomes a pleasant one like almost any other. Mom doesn't pry about the father/daughter chat, and Josie's so engrossed in watching surfing that I'm not sure she even noticed we left. I curl next to Dad on the couch the way I did when I was little, still reveling in having him back.

Yet I'm turning the situation over and over in my head.

Triad kidnapped Dad. But why? For leverage over my mother? No, because then they would have told Mom what they'd done, rather than let her think her husband was dead.

Was it—for leverage over *me*? If Theo and I hadn't taken off when we did, would Wyatt Conley or someone else from Triad have come to me and made it clear that if I didn't travel for them, do whatever they said, my father would never get to come home?

Yes. They would have.

This was all about getting to me. All the anguish Mom and Josie felt, the pain they put Theo and me through . . . it was all so Triad could control me.

My mind still can't wrap itself around the fact that I'm at the center of all this, after years of half listening across the room while Mom, Dad, Theo, and Paul brainstormed their phenomenal technology. Yet that's where I seem to be. I also have no idea how I'm going to stop Triad from hurting the people I love, or trying to control me.

But if I have a power Triad wants—that means *I have power*. And I intend to use it.

By the time I stagger to bed, I'm utterly exhausted. Yet I'm not so tired that I don't notice the blinking light that means I've received a message. I dive for it, instantly rejuvenated. Communications must have cleared for a few minutes, long enough for Paul to get something through.

The message is from Paul, but it's not video, not even audio. Probably I should have known not to expect a love letter from a guy who expresses himself through actions rather than words. He sent only three words, but they're the only words I need: **On my way.**

"Put on your waterproofs," Mom calls to me as I grope for my alarm the next morning. "There's a break in the storm, but not much."

Yes, even in hellacious weather conditions, the morning maintenance has to get done. My waterproofs turn out to be a neon orange parka and pants made out of plastic, so I look *super hot.* As I head out through our kitchen, Dad walks right past me in the front room with only a groggy smile, no acknowledgment of the night before. He's this Henry Caine again, and my dad is merely a flicker inside him, watching without knowing.

I can get him back, I remind myself as I touch the outline of the Firebird against my chest. *Anytime I want, and soon, for good.*

"*This* is what she calls a break in the storm?" I call to Josie as we walk out onto the platform.

"C'mon, you've seen it worse than this!" Josie laughs.

Seriously, have I? Because this weather is dire. Gusts of wind, sharpened by salt and sea, beat against me. My baggy waterproofs flap and snap in the gales, and my hood blows back almost instantly. A little wet hair never hurt anybody, but the wind and water have made it cold, even though it's midsummer here. Overhead the sky is low and gray with clouds in a specific rippled pattern that must mean trouble.

So I whip through the maintenance, doubly glad for my safety harness. Within minutes I'm back down and headed for the door, when I hear Josie shout, "We've got refugees!"

I look in her direction and see the helicopter approaching from a distance.

Josie joins a handful of other people to ready the helipad. I don't. This is one situation I don't intend to bluff my way through; those people need help, not me screwing things up. But I watch the others prepare to tether the chopper to the deck as soon as it lands.

The rotor blades churn the air up even more as I stand there, squinting against the rain. All around us the ocean has darkened to the color of steel. As soon as the helicopter has landed, people spring into action, attaching cables even before the rotor stops spinning. I go for the pilot's side door to help him out. The moment I open it, the pilot holds up his hands and says, "Don't blame me, all right? This guy insisted he'd pay me triple. Which he'd better."

"I'm good for it, buddy. Relax." Theo leans across him and smiles at me. "You know, we really have to stop meeting like this."

★ ★ ★

Ten minutes later, even though my belly is growling for breakfast, I'm still in the landing bay with Theo, bubbling over with everything I've learned. Theo, meanwhile, is still arguing.

"You're imagining things. Anybody would, by this point. It's been the craziest month of your life," he says as we sit on one of the low plastic benches that stretches between the equipment lockers. "I would know, because it's been the craziest month of my life, too, and as much as I loved Henry, he wasn't my father."

"Love." I can't stop grinning. "Present tense love. Dad's right here."

Theo sighs into the towel he's using to mop his damp hair and face. "Do you not see that everything Paul's told you is exactly what you want to hear?"

I cock my head as I study him. "I never realized before just how cynical you are."

He'd like to argue with me, but that's the moment when my father walks in, fixing Theo with his most piercing stare. "I hear we have some refugees from the storm," Dad says. "But I'm most interested in exactly how it is that one of these refugees knows my daughter."

"Sorry about this," I say to Dad as I rise to my feet and slip the Firebird over his neck. A few clicks, one reminder that makes Dad curse in pain, and—

"Theo!" Dad laughs out loud, then immediately touches the chain of Theo's Firebird, visible beneath his flight suit.

"My God, Theo. I'm going to bloody well kill you for bringing Marguerite along. Whatever were you thinking? But first, come here, son."

As Dad wraps his arms around Theo, Theo's eyes go wide. "Holy crap," he mutters. "Whoa. *Whoa.*"

"I told you." I can't help laughing.

Theo hugs Dad back, fierce and hard. "Henry. I'm glad you're all right. You don't know—you can't know how much."

Dad slaps him once on the shoulder, I guess so they can both feel like the hug is all manly. "I meant what I said. You're in serious trouble for pulling Marguerite into this. But it looks like my daughter's a bolder traveler than I ever realized."

I want to protest that Theo didn't pull me into this; given what I now understand about Triad's real agenda, and my abilities, I know I would have been involved sooner or later. Still, first things first. "Now all Theo has to do is figure out how to make another Firebird. You rebuilt the others, so you should be able to build one from scratch, right, Theo?"

"Probably. Maybe. Wow. I gotta think." Theo's expression looks completely dazed, like he got hit by a truck. I can't blame him. "It's going to be a while before I can say anything more coherent than *wow.*"

"Take a few moments. Catch your breath." Dad squints at the double-reinforced window in the landing bay door. "This is shaping up to be a decent break in the storm. We've had reports of another couple of refugees, via ships—looks like we'll be able to land them. Who knows? Maybe one of them is Paul. It would be nice to all be together again." He smiles softly, and I know the happiness within Dad's heart is a mirror of my own.

Once Dad has gone back to running the station, Theo and I are alone again. I can't resist. "Told you."

"You did. You did tell me. But I had to see it for myself." He shakes his head slowly. "I can't believe Paul—that he figured all this out."

"Me neither. When we get home, we have to go back to the beginning with Triad." Then I think about how ruthless Conley is, what a risk I'm asking Theo to take. "I know it's dangerous, taking them on. I'd never want you to get hurt. You don't have to—"

"You're worried about *me*?" Theo's voice breaks on the final word. "You just found out they're hunting you in multiple dimensions, and you're trying to take care of me."

We all have to take care of each other, I want to say, but Theo has risen to his feet, and he takes me in his arms.

"Stop it, okay?" he says as he hugs me tightly. "You're the one who needs taking care of. Don't waste your time worrying about me."

We break apart, and Theo smiles as if he's embarrassed, which coming from him is practically a first. Before I can speak, though, someone else walks into the room. I don't remember who this guy is, if I even met him yesterday, but his coverall looks a lot like my dad's, and he acts like he has some authority. "Ms. Caine, we need you on submersible duty. Someone's got to go out and retrieve that fallen winch."

Mom was talking about that this morning: a winch fell off one of the high cranes last night, buffeted by the winds. Now it's on the ocean floor, on the not-horribly-deep shelf the *Salacia* occupies, but the stronger currents whipped up by the storm might push it into a deeper trench nearby.

So what exactly am I supposed to be doing? Submersible duty? What does that mean?

Then my eyes widen as I realize a submersible is an underwater craft. A submarine.

I'm on submarine duty?

"It's a two-man vessel," the guy says to Theo. "Your bio says you're licensed as a pilot as well. Want to go out there with her? Make yourself useful as long as you're here?"

"Yeah," Theo says slowly. "Sure. Yes. I'm—very good— at, uh, at piloting submarines."

The guy kind of stares at us, but says only, "Berth four," before walking off, which is when Theo turns to me and mouths, *Oh, shit.*

"We're supposed to be piloting a submarine? No. No way."

"I actually ran some simulations on the way out here. This dimension's Theo had them queued up on his computer anyway . . ."

"Theo, no."

He gives me his best puppy-dog eyes—and believe me, his are really, really good—but finally says, "You're no fun."

"We *can't.*"

"So what do we do?"

I run one hand through my wet hair. "We—we go to berth four, and—" And what? Say something is wrong with the sub? They'll figure out that it's fine and know we're lying. "Then we call my father from there. He'll send someone else down."

We find berth four easily enough. The sub is not some huge, nuclear, *Hunt for Red October* sub; instead it's tiny and curved, with bright white walls and smooth black touchscreen controls like a tPhone. Beyond the curved transparent dome in front is an endless expanse of dark blue water.

"Look at this," Theo says as he studies the controls. "It's just like the simulator. I mean, *exactly* like it."

"Theo . . ."

He shrugs, but his face is lighting up in that wicked-boy way he has. "I played with it for hours on the way out here. It's better than any video game ever." Then Theo drums his hand on the back of one of the seats. "You don't often get a chance to play a video game for real . . ."

"No. Uh-uh. No way."

"Come on! I know what I'm doing!"

"Because you played a simulator game?"

"Because I logged about seven hours of practice time, and because we're only supposed to go about half a mile before turning back around. And because this would be totally, legitimately, eternally awesome. You know in your heart I'm telling the truth."

Eternal awesome, however elusive, is no reason to take

325

off in a submarine. But there's something underlying Theo's enthusiasm, a wistfulness that betrays the sorrow inside.

He's done so much for me on the trip. Risked his life to help my father. All he's asking for in return is a few moments of fun. It's not so much to ask, is it?

"If at any moment you have the slightest doubt about what you're doing, we turn around immediately," I say in the strictest tone I can manage. But I can't help smiling when Theo begins drumming a hard rhythm against the seat, in celebration.

So five minutes later, we're ready to go—and I have to admit, he actually seems to know how to handle this thing. "About to release the clamps," he says. "Ready?"

I nod. So he flips the control panel toggle that releases this submersible from the *Salacia*. For a moment, we drift free, and then he turns the props on low, just enough to get us out of the underwater dock.

The front of the submersible is made of superthick glass, which means we have a perfect, panoramic view of the ocean before us. Right now it's chalky white sand, a few fronds of fan coral jutting up from the rocks here and there, and the endless blue. Theo and I sit side by side in the front compartment, though the watertight doors to the back aren't closed; he explained that since nobody's going diving on this trip, we don't have to seal it off.

That's good, because otherwise this might feel a little too intimate. In a submersible there's no room to spare, so Theo and I are practically thigh to thigh. I only wore a black tank top and leggings beneath my waterproofs this morning, so that's all I've got on now. While Theo has on a normal white T-shirt, it's still slightly damp from the rain. He's not as big a guy as Paul, so sometimes I forget Theo's pretty buff. There's no forgetting it at the moment.

All I say is, "Uh, how do we look for the winch we're supposed to be finding?"

"Activating sonar." Theo's hands move deftly on the control panel, as though he'd been doing this for a hundred years.

The green sweep of the sonar begins, and I squint down at the screen, trying to figure out which of the shapes are merely rocks, and which might be the equipment we're looking for. "There, you think?"

I point at the shape I mean. Theo does the same. Our hands brush against each other, and I don't think it was an accident.

"Yeah," Theo says. He doesn't look at me; his profile is silhouetted against the blueness. "Worth a shot."

So he moves the submersible forward, taking us to medium speed. As we sweep forward through the dark, our spotlights illuminating the water around us, I keep glancing over at Theo, who seems to be struggling for words. Is he going to apologize for doubting Paul? Or is he going to try to kiss me again?

"You must be—" My words falter, because I don't know

what to say. "It's good to know Paul was on the level all along. Right?"

"Yeah. Of course." Theo opens his mouth to say something else, then closes it. He looks more tormented by this than I ever thought he would be.

Just then, Dad breaks in over the comm. "What the *devil* are you two doing in a submersible?"

"We're handling it fine," Theo insists. "And having a blast. Admit it; you're jealous."

"I'm worried. Also jealous, yes, but that's about fifteen percent to worried's eighty-five percent. How's it going out there?"

"Fine so far," I say, glancing up at the speaker in the roof. "We think we see the winch."

"Brilliant. I'll take the worried down to about fifty percent, then. Listen, one of the refugee vessels just signaled. I thought I'd patch you in." I can hear the smile in his voice. "Talk to you later."

Then there's a moment of static as the original call is replaced by the new one, and I hear a deep voice say, "Marguerite?"

It's like fireworks going off. "*Paul*. You made it."

"Almost. I should dock within the next ten minutes."

"And you talked to Dad?"

"Yes. Thank God he was here. From Triad's files I thought he would be—but I wasn't sure, not until we spoke."

"Now we build another Firebird and go home." I'm grinning up at the speaker as if I could see Paul there, yet all my

328

happiness can't blind me to the fact that we're not alone. "Theo's here too."

"Hey, little brother," Theo says. His expression is rueful. "Looks like you've been one step ahead of us the whole way."

"I should have come to you at the beginning." It's impossible not to envision Paul's face as he says this—grave and repentant. "I had no idea what they would do to Henry, or I would have."

"Water under the bridge." Then Theo looks up at the distant glitter of the ocean surface above us and adds, "Pun not intended."

I still can't believe Paul made it here. "Where were you?" I ask. "Did you set out immediately, or did you need a reminder?"

"I started toward you as soon as I got here. I don't need the reminders any longer," Paul says.

"Don't need them?" I frown. Next to me, Theo sits up straighter.

"In the last dimension we visited, Triad has developed a way for its spies to remain in control throughout their trips. It's this drug—damaging, and sometimes hard to get, so it's not a permanent solution—but it works in short doses," Paul says. "You can make it out of ordinary chemicals, easily found in almost any dimension you'd go to. They call it Nightthief. An injectable liquid, this brilliant green color—"

Paul keeps talking. I don't hear a word.

Slowly I look down at Theo, who is looking directly at

me. He doesn't say anything; he knows I know.

Nightthief. The green liquid I saw Theo injecting in London. They're one and the same.

Theo would never—

No. My Theo wouldn't.

But this is not my Theo.

26

"NIGHTTHIEF CAUSES HALLUCINATIONS—INTENSE PAIN—
but it buys you days of controlled consciousness. I knew I'd
need to use it to reach you." Paul continues speaking over
the intercom, unaware that we can hear but are not listening.

I stare at Theo; he meets my gaze evenly, and in his face
I see shame, but also relief. Like he's thinking, *At last she
knows.*

Everything in me rejects this. *Theo wouldn't. He'd never spy
for Triad; he'd never hurt my family. He'd never hurt me.*

My Theo really wouldn't. But this isn't my Theo, and it
hasn't been for a very long time.

Since before this journey began . . .

I scream even as Theo vaults toward me. "Paul, it's Theo!
Theo's the spy!" But Theo snaps off the comm with one
elbow as he pushes me back against the wall. I try to shove
him off, but the sub is so small that I'm crumpled beneath

him, unable to brace myself or get any leverage.

"Will you—just—will you listen? Okay?" Theo scrambles to keep me down, his forearms holding mine down. His brown eyes beseech me even as his weight bears down hard. "Please. I don't want to hurt you."

"It was you the whole time. That's why you had the Firebirds." Of course—he didn't keep the extras and "repair" them; this other Theo, from the dimension where Triad is one step ahead of us—he was able to use those materials to re-create their own superior technology. "You doctored Dad's car and framed Paul for murder."

"Guilty as charged, Meg."

In his face I hiss, *"Stop calling me that!"*

Theo shoves me out of my seat, and we collapse onto the floor of the sub. I can feel the sub tilting downward—we're going to run into the sand—but I can't get him off me. His knees pin my legs down; his hands hold mine to the metal floor.

"Are you going to keep fighting me or are you going to listen?" He breathes out sharply, as if he's the one who's upset. "I can explain."

"The hell you can."

Theo presses down harder. His face is just above mine. "I came to your dimension three months ago. We knew your parents were on the verge of their breakthrough; as far as we know, you're only the second dimension remotely comparable to ours to develop the tech. That meant we needed to form a strategic alliance."

Three months ago is when he started using drugs, going AWOL for hours at a time, calling me Meg—acting different in every way. How could I not have seen it? Although I try to twist beneath him, I can hardly move. "Is this your idea—of—making friends?"

"Every alliance has a leader." Theo's expression truly looks more sad than angry. "Like every war has a general."

"War? Are you even listening to yourself? Two dimensions can't—go to war with each other! It's insane."

"Back in the day, they thought the invention of the airplane would make war impossible. You know, who could move troops in secret once people could look down from the air? But then someone thought of putting bombs in the planes, and everything changed. Every technology mankind invents, human beings turn against one another. It's only a matter of time. If we don't start the battle, another dimension will, and they might be a hell of a lot worse."

I remember Conley's speech in the Londonverse, about how warfare evolves along with us. That stops me short for a moment. I'm no less furious at Theo, but the idea of what could be out there—watching, waiting, looking for a moment to strike—

Theo nods, suddenly hopeful. "You see now, right? We have to band together. We have to take the power for ourselves, before it's taken away from us."

"Nobody's threatening you." My wrists hurt; his grip around them is harder than handcuffs. "You're the ones who went on the attack. Don't pretend you're not."

He keeps talking like I hadn't said anything at all. "When I came over, at first I was supposed to slow your parents down a little bit—let us get a little farther ahead—but it was already too late for that. What I could do was create a traveler. A perfect traveler. You only get one chance per dimension, you know. Conley is ours. For your dimension, out of everyone else in the world, he chose you."

"Wow. I feel really special," I spit back at him. Literally—our faces are that close. The sub is rocking now, rudderless, the white crescent of sand tilting through the window. "So you let them kidnap Dad?"

"Paul was screwing everything up. They took Henry, and I—you know, I drove his car to the river, messed with the brakes, made sure it went over the side. If the car went into the water, you guys wouldn't expect to find a body right away, if ever. It was just about buying Triad time."

Of course. Theo's always been the one working on cars. Why didn't I realize he'd be the one to cut somebody's brakes? "You let me think Dad was dead. Mom still thinks that, and Josie too. Did you even ask yourself what you were doing to us?"

"Come on, come on, listen to me, will you? Do you understand how much power this gives you? This is a huge opportunity, if you'll just take it." Theo shakes his head; there are actually tears in his eyes. "I've *hated* lying to you. To all of you. What I feel for you, it's not only what your Theo felt, you know? It looked like I didn't have a chance with you in my own dimension, and when I realized I might get another shot, I wasn't going to waste it. But I didn't take advantage. You know I didn't. In London, I held back. I wanted you to make your own decision. I said, *when we were both ourselves*, remember?"

"Yeah, you deserve a medal."

"I swear to God, if I could get you out of this whole mess, I would. But I can't, Marguerite. I can't. The only way I can save you is by getting you to see how you have to play this."

"'Play this'? It's not a game, Theo! You would've killed Paul." By now I'm as close to crying as Theo is, though mine are tears of rage.

"I was always going to come clean eventually. What do you think was going to happen in Lab Eleven? What Conley was going to tell you if you'd made the meet at the Dragon Gate? We were going to tell you the truth, the whole truth, make you see that you could get Henry home safe and sound. Conley was bringing you on board! Don't you get it? The smart move here is to join him. Join *us*. If you join us, you'll never be hurt again. Not ever. I'd spend the rest of my life making sure of that, Meg. I promise you."

You mean, you were going to blackmail me by holding Dad hostage. I'm on the verge of shouting that back at Theo, trying to snap him out of his delusions about Conley—but then the sub shifts more violently beneath us, and I see the entire view turn white with sand. I scream just before we crash.

The sub grounds out, with the grinding of propellers breaking against stone. We tumble over and over, Theo and me bouncing away from and into each other, a dozen small collisions that all seem to draw blood. I manage to grab onto my seat as the submersible skids over the lip of the trench, and we begin to tumble down into the infinite deep.

Theo told me earlier—this submersible will only hold to about 1,500 feet. After that, the underwater pressure will crush us like a fist around a soda can.

"Shit." Theo braces himself against one wall, then pushes forward to the control panel. He tries to restart our propellers, but the terrible grinding sound they make tells us they aren't working. The gauge reads 650 feet—700—750—

I swing into my seat, trying to ignore the terrible bobbing and scraping that's taking us farther down into blackness. "What do we do?"

"We try to hang on." With shaking, bruised hands Theo activates the retrieval clamp; it swings out, trying to find purchase.

Theo and I sit side by side, wordless, listening to metal thud against stone. Our fall never slows. Just as I feel fear rising to the point of panic, the clamp finds some spur or jutting stone and locks on. We jerk to a stop, then swing there, suspended. For the moment, we're safe—but as we both know, the clamp may only have hooked onto something very fragile. Any moment, the weight of the sub could break it and send us hurtling down again, to our deaths.

"Okay," Theo says, taking a deep breath. He flips the comm switch back to on. "*Salacia? Salacia,* this is—what, Submersible One? It's Theo and Marguerite. Over."

No response, not even static: We're too deep for our

communications system to work.

He runs one hand through his hair. "So, we have to stay calm and figure out—"

I slam Theo's head into the console, as hard as I can.

In the split second he's stunned, I claw at his throat, forcing him down the way he forced me. "We're not partners." The words grind out through my gritted teeth. "We never will be. Tell Conley that."

Theo's stronger than I am—he throws me off, and I stagger backward. Before he can follow, though, I get myself on the other side of the divide and hit the button that separates the sub compartments. The watertight doors slam shut, separating me from Theo—him in the front with the now useless control panel, and me in the back with the diving gear.

Fortunately the lock is clearly labeled. I make sure it's activated, keeping us apart.

"Marguerite?" Theo's face appears in the door's thin sliver of superthick glass. "What the hell do you think you're doing?"

"Getting out of here."

Because one of the other very clearly labeled things in the back is the ESCAPE POD.

The small, circular passageway is something I can slide through easily; what waits on the other side is a tiny dark sphere that will require me to curl into a ball. What about air? What about getting back to the surface? I'd assume something like this is pretty much automated—but I don't like making assumptions almost a thousand feet underwater.

Still, my only alternative is hanging around here. Theo's going to figure out how to get through that lock sooner or later. Probably sooner. So I have to go.

"You can't make it up on your own from this depth," Theo calls through the thick glass. "Don't kill yourself trying to get away from me, all right? I'm not going to hurt you."

"I'm getting out of here and going home," I repeat, stepping closer to the door where he stands. "And I'm taking my dad with me."

Then I slam my hand against the glass and watch Theo's eyes widen as he sees what I've been holding in my palm—his Firebird.

The one I snatched from his neck during our fight. The one he was counting on to get him out of this—and the one that's going to bring my father back where he belongs.

"Come on. Don't do this." Theo's face is white. Good.

"You thought this dimension was good enough to strand Dad in," I say as I go to the escape pod's opening. "Hope you like being stranded here too."

"Marguerite!"

Then I slide into the pod, and Theo's words are muffled so that I can't exactly hear him any longer.

Right now, I'm in a lot more danger than he is. This submarine seems to be intact; even if it can't move right now, it's watertight and pressurized. Sure, Theo is stuck, but a crew from the *Salacia* will be down as soon as possible. As angry as Dad's going to be when he realizes the truth about

Theo, he'd never leave anyone to die.

Me? I'm launching myself into the hostile world beyond the sub—into the cold, crushing dark.

But if I stay here, eventually Theo's going to get through that door. He'll get the Firebird back from me, and then Dad and I will once again be at the mercy of Wyatt Conley's schemes.

That's not going to happen.

Shaking, I hit the yellow panel that says Launch Prep.

Metal discs pinwheel out from the sides of the door to seal me in completely. There's a distant pounding, probably Theo throwing himself against the doors in a last, desperate bid to get my attention, but I refuse to look.

No expansive large windows here—just a slim transparent sliver that lets me see just how forbidding it is outside. Nothing is near us, nothing at all except the depth of the crevasse. But this is my only chance. I suck in a deep breath, put my hand to the red panel that says Final Launch—and hit it.

Instantly metal clamps click and thud, and then the pod falls into the ocean.

At first I'm terrified. *I'm falling! I'm going to fall all the way down*—but then some sort of motor kicks in and propels me upward. Then it feels like liberation. As unbelievably dark and cramped as it is in here, I'm free.

Down this far, it's too dark to see the surface of the water. Maybe I could on a brighter day, but the storm overhead is blocking what little light might penetrate this deep. The only illumination comes from the glow-in-the-dark paint within the pod . . . but that's not much, just a few lines within the panels. Probably I was supposed to bring some kind of flashlight in here with me. *I'll have to remember that next time*, I think, but it's not funny.

Surely there's some sort of heat, or insulating safety blankets I haven't found. All I know is this chill can't be safe. I'm surrounded by metal, and by water that's only a few degrees above freezing, which means it's already so cold in here I'm shaking. Every moment I get clumsier as my limbs start to go numb.

Another factor I hadn't counted on was my exhaustion. Theo and I just took turns beating the crap out of each other—and that's after a morning that began with me climbing weather stations in storm-force gales. It's important to stay awake, to figure out how to contact help once I get to the surface, but the cold and the weariness are dragging me down. Adrenaline can only take me so far, but I'm determined that it's going to take me far enough.

You can make it, I think, but it sounds desperate and unrealistic, even to me. *I bet it's safe. You'll be to the surface soon; it can't be much farther.*

Oh, God, how much farther is it? How far?

And then, brilliant as a sunrise, light breaks underwater, streaming through the one slim window I have to the ocean beyond.

The spotlights bathe me in their glow, so bright I have to turn my head away and squint. As they come closer, the form behind them takes shape—it's a sub, but not one of the ones from *Salacia*.

Which means there's only one person it could be.

Slowly my murky view of the world above takes the shape of the sub's white belly as it lowers itself over the escape pod; it's like looking up into the sky. A crescent-shaped opening waxes above me like a moon the color of night. The pod bobs up through that opening, into the diving bay of the sub. The door shuts again, and water begins to be pumped out, the levels falling moment by moment as the pod settles onto the diving bay's floor.

I feel so heavy. So tired. But I manage to stay awake, even to stay mostly calm, despite the dizziness and nausea I recognize as potential signs of pressure sickness.

Water ebbs from the escape pod; only trickles remain on the floor. From where I sit curled within the pod, I watch the pressure indicator on the wall glow red—still red—and then green.

I hit the green panel that says Door Release; the metal spirals open again, and I'm able to push open the pod's door. I flop onto the wet metal mesh of the floor like a hooked fish, weak and shaking. As I gulp in a deep breath, I hear the doors near me slide open. I turn to see Paul running toward me, something silvery in his hands.

"Marguerite," he whispers as he fastens a breathing mask over my nose and mouth. "You're safe, all right? You're safe. Just breathe in and out, as deeply as you can." All I can do is nod, and breathe.

Within two inhalations, I feel slightly better. Which is to say—I feel like crap, but no longer like I might be on the verge of passing out. "What is this stuff?"

"Don't talk," Paul says as he unfolds a shiny insulating blanket and covers me with it, tucking it around my shoulders, my legs. "You're breathing a special gas designed to counteract pressure sickness. Very advanced. Invented by the brilliant oceanographer Dr. Sophia Kovalenka."

Of course Mom turned out to be as much of a genius in oceanography as she was in physics. Of *course*. I can't help smiling beneath the mask.

Paul sits on the wet floor by me, close enough to lift my head so that it rests against his knee. His hands warm me, rubbing my cold arms and legs, even as he bends and kisses my forehead.

"I wasn't sure it was you," he murmurs. "It could have been Theo in the pod—and I thought, if he left her down there, if he hurt her, stranded her—"

"No. He's the one who's stranded." I look up at him as best I can with the silver mask over my face. "I took Theo's Firebird. That means Dad can go home."

"My God." Then Paul bends over me, cradles me in his arms, as if he's sheltering me from the whole world. I close my eyes, and despite everything, I think I've never felt so safe.

We rise through the water until it once again turns blue around us, and the breathing mask is no longer necessary. Paul only stops looking after me to dock his sub—one of the bigger, long-distance models that only travel with the largest science vessels.

"We get to go home," I whisper. Moments ago I was exhausted and terrified; now I'm warm and safe in Paul's arms. I could almost fall asleep right here in his lap, pillowing my head against his strong chest. His muscles flex as he works the directional controls; I love that he's piloting the sub without letting go of me. "We won."

"The battle. Not the war."

"I know Triad will come after me again. I realize that. And they think I'm theirs to manipulate." I'm vulnerable to them; as long as there are people in the world I love, that will be true. But vulnerable isn't the same as helpless. "They're going to learn better."

Paul smiles. "When they went after you—Triad didn't know what they were getting into."

He turns his attention back to the controls as we complete docking. The clamps settle around his sub with a solid, metallic clang, and I hear the whirring sound of the station's airlock coupling with ours. Paul puts one hand under my knees and stands with me in his arms, carrying me to the portal.

When the door swooshes open, Josie is standing on the other side to check in the latest refugees. She startles as she sees me. "Marguerite?"

"We wrecked," I say. "Theo's still out there. I swam up the first couple hundred feet; Paul picked me up from there."

"Holy crap. *You crashed the submersible?*" Josie puts her hands on her hips. "And exactly how many guys are showing up to visit you today?"

"I think she's a little out of it," Paul says to Josie, as he gently settles me back on my feet. "At any rate, she could use something warm to drink and a lot of rest. And I know Marguerite wants to see her father."

I say, "I can hear you, you know." But Paul might not be wrong about my being out of it. I'm overwhelmed physically, emotionally, you name it. Right now I only want to curl back into Paul's arms.

I take Josie's hand and let her help me over the step. She guides me to one of the benches as she says, "Aren't you coming?"

"No," Paul replies.

"Paul?" I look back at him. He stands there in his own sub, his T-shirt and slacks striped with water, the Firebird hanging around his neck. He looks at me as if he's drinking me in, as if he's trying to memorize me. "What are you doing?"

"The storm's blowing in hard. Theo's in a broken submersible hanging over the edge of the trench. I can't leave him out there."

Josie turns on me. "Wait, what? You wrecked in the trench?"

I ignore this. "If it's dangerous for him, it's dangerous for you. And he's the one who started it."

"The Theo who spied on us started it," Paul agrees. "But the Theo from this dimension never hurt us. He doesn't deserve to die for someone else's sins. And . . . he's *Theo*."

344

He's right—so right it shames me. "I shouldn't have stranded him down there."

"You stranded that guy? On *purpose*?" By now Josie is beside herself.

Paul takes one step toward me, his gray eyes intense. "You did what you had to do, to save your father and yourself. Don't blame yourself for a situation someone else put you in. But I have to rescue Theo if I can."

"You just had to ditch me one more time on this trip, huh?"

"Marguerite—"

But I can't even deal any longer. "Go, and come back in one piece, or I swear to God I will kick your ass."

Paul touches my face—his thumb against my still-wet lips, like a kiss—then steps back into his sub. His hand thumps a panel on the wall, and the doors slide shut again.

When I turn to Josie, she's staring at me like I grew a second head. Very quietly she says, "Do I even want to know what's going on?"

"No."

She exhales, puffing out her cheeks in frustration—but instantly she's back to business. "We need the airlock. Let's go."

Within minutes, I'm standing at one of the lower windows, watching Paul's white sub vanish into the murky waters. I press my palm against the cold glass.

"Marguerite?" I turn my head to see Dad walking toward me, concern etched into every line of his face. "Josie's in a state. She's told me what happened, or what she thinks happened, but the story doesn't make a lot of sense. Are you all right?"

I can't tell whether he remembers himself right now or not. It doesn't matter.

"I'm all right." I fish out the other Firebird and put it in his hand. "We're going home."

27

I OPEN MY EYES.

This time, there's no sensation of force, no moment of disorientation. Instead it's almost as if I nodded off for a moment, then gently woke. Slowly, I look around. Night has fallen here, but only just—the western edge of the sky is still a paler blue, tinted faintly pink at the horizon. I'm sitting on the steps of our deck, wearing my lace dress with my father's cardigan over it, both hands clasping the Firebird around my neck. In other words, I'm in the exact same position I was when I left a month ago.

"I'm home," I whisper. "I'm *home*."

Quickly I scramble up the back steps and to the sliding glass doors. As usual, Mom hasn't locked them, so I run inside. The sight of my own house fills me with almost delirious happiness: Piles of paper! Physics equations on the walls! Mom's potted plants! Even the rainbow table—

—and, sitting on the sofa, Mom.

She gasps, "Marguerite!"

"Mom!" I run to her, but she meets me halfway. Her arms go around me so tightly that I realize anew how badly I must have scared her these past few weeks. "I'm so sorry, Mom, but I made it. We made it."

"You're safe? You're well?" Tears spill down my mother's face as she brushes my hair back from my face. "But you didn't hurt Paul, did you? We decoded his note hours after we got yours—"

"Oh, my God, you're back!" Josie comes barreling out of the kitchen to tackle me onto the sofa. "I'm going to *kill* you for scaring us like that. But first I have to tell you I love you, you crazy little brat."

"I love you, too," I say as I hug her close. "But there's so much we have to talk about."

"Triad," Mom says, and her smile dims, but only slightly. "We know. That doesn't matter now, sweetheart, as long as you're home and safe."

"You know? But how . . ." My voice trails off as a third person steps out of the hallway.

Theo.

He tries to grin at me, but it doesn't quite work. "Welcome back."

At first all I can feel is panic. *He followed me here, somehow he got out of the sub and followed me here*—and then I realize what this actually means. The guy standing here in his Mumford & Sons shirt and cargo pants is *my* Theo, the one

Triad took over months ago so that their spy could act in his place. This Theo would never have done any of this to me or to anybody in my family.

I know that. I believe it. And yet it's hard to make my heart accept it.

"You know the truth, then. I can see it in your face." Theo grimaces. "You never used to be scared of me."

Quickly I say, "I'm not scared. It's just—it's a lot to take in. And, yeah. I know."

"Did he hurt you?" Theo's voice breaks. "If that son of a bitch hurt you—"

"No," I say, which almost isn't a lie.

"And Paul? Is Paul okay?" At that moment, when I see that Theo's as frightened for Paul as he was for me, I remember the love between them, and that even now, a dimension away, Paul is risking his life to save a Theo he doesn't even know—and a Theo who tried to kill him.

"Paul's all right. He'll come back soon," I say. Josie breathes out a sigh of relief, and I can see the tension in Theo's shoulders relax the tiniest amount.

Mom interjects, "Theo came to us the moment Triad's spy left. He told us everything. But by then it was too late—you were gone, and we knew Triad could get to you and we couldn't, so there was nothing we could do or even say without endangering you. We've been working on our own Firebirds, hoping to follow you, but that work doesn't go quickly. The last month has been hell." She sounds more than four weeks older as she says it. "But now you're here. You've come home."

I wrest myself from Josie's embrace, my smile returning to my face. "And now we have to go. All of us, right this second."

"Go where?" Mom asks, frowning.

She doesn't understand. None of them do. None of them know yet, the best news of all.

"To the university." I take my mother's hands to ease the shock, and look into all of their faces in turn before saying, "We have to pick up Dad."

Despite everything that's happened to me in the past couple of hours, I'm the only one calm enough to drive. So I steer Josie's silver Volkswagen through the hilly streets. In the back seat, Mom and Josie are alternating between sobs of joy and horrible moments of doubt. They're still overwhelmed, still afraid to believe.

Theo rides in the seat next to me, his expression stark as he stares straight ahead. Neither of us has spoken to the other since we got in the car. I don't think we have any idea what to say.

Then I realize the first thing I need to know. "What was it like when you were, you know—taken over?"

Although he still doesn't look at me, he relaxes a little. "At first it was like I was just losing time. Blacking out or something. I thought I was working too hard on the Firebird project, skipping too much sleep, something like that. Didn't mention it to Henry or Sophia, because I thought they'd tell me to take it easy and I might miss out." Theo sighs. "If I had, maybe one of them would've realized what was going on. So, that was pretty stupid."

"You couldn't have known." Inside I find myself thinking of every other Marguerite I inhabited. At the time, I felt as though I was making responsible choices—or that if I made mistakes, they were the mistakes those Marguerites would have made in my place. But now that I see Theo's profound sense of violation, I wonder if that's how they feel, too.

"After he started using that green stuff, everything changed. I was aware of what was going on, but it was—distant. Foggy. It reminded me of twilight sleep at the dentist. Then he'd leave. Go back to his own dimension to, I don't know, report in or whatever. By the time I could feel myself sobering up, he'd be back."

I remember now, back in the Triadverse, the talk about Theo's time-consuming "internship" with Conley. Really Theo was traveling between dimensions as Conley's spy— going back only often enough to maintain his cover story.

Finally Theo looks at me, though his gaze is hesitant. "Once the son of a bitch moved on for good, I could only remember the big details—that they'd done something awful to Henry, that I'd framed Paul for it, and that they were after you. They'd been after you the whole time, and I couldn't even warn you. We had to wait here, not knowing if we'd ever see you again."

As much as I sympathize with the pain I hear in his voice, I can't let Theo keep beating himself up about this. "I made it back. Okay? You have to stop worrying about the past. Worry about the future, because Triad's definitely going to keep trying."

"Oh, I've been thinking about Triad. Trust me, I've been thinking a lot. They had their chance to surprise us, and now they're going to get a few surprises in return." Theo actually smiles, but it's the scariest-looking smile I've ever seen. I wouldn't want to be Wyatt Conley right now.

We reach the university campus. It's a still place between semesters, almost abandoned, with only a handful of the usual cars in the parking lots and a few forlorn international students wandering around. With a stomp on the gas pedal, I speed us toward the lab and pull into the closest spot.

Josie's Volkswagen is so tiny that we must look like clowns spilling out of a circus car. As I peer through the darkness on the grounds, I don't see anyone close by.

Mom steps in front of me. "Henry?" Her voice shakes as she calls his name again. *"Henry?"*

Then I see what she's seen—the shape running out of the shadows.

"Sophie!" Dad shouts as he dashes straight into Mom's arms.

Somehow we all wind up on the ground in a group hug, and everyone's crying and everyone's laughing and we probably look like crazy people, but I don't care one bit.

And yet, down deep, I'm still afraid.

What about Paul?

As we disentangle ourselves and get to our feet again, Mom kisses Dad—and I don't mean, like, a normal kiss; I mean, she *lays one on him*. I've always been glad my parents loved each other so much, but I never felt like I was watching anything quite this intimate. As I turn my head to give them a little privacy, Josie giggles. "That's right," she says, wiping tears from her cheeks. "You weren't with me that time I walked in on them doing the deed. Seriously Freudian horror."

"You saw your parents at their best," Mom murmurs, before Dad sweeps her into another kiss.

"Go ahead," Josie calls. "Mate in public. Tonight we won't even mind. You deserve to break a few decency laws."

I can't bear it any longer. "I have to go. I have to find Paul."

Slowly Theo nods. "Come on. I'll take you there."

Together we run across the dark campus, past enormous, empty buildings and then into a block of dormitories. They look nicer than I thought dorms would be—more like apartment buildings. The lock on the door is ultramodern: a huge black access-card reader that stops me in my tracks.

"ID reader," Theo says as he fishes his student ID out of his wallet. One swipe, and the lock clicks, letting us in the building.

Together Theo and I walk up two flights of stairs and along the hallway until we reach Paul's door. Hoping against hope, I knock and call out, "Paul?"

No reply.

So we stand there in the hallway, with nothing to do but wait.

"You say Paul's in danger because he's saving my evil twin?" Theo leans against one wall, folding his arms in front of his chest.

"And the other you, the oceanographer from that dimension. The one who got pulled into this against his will, like you did."

"Little brother," Theo says softly.

"You know he'd never leave you when you were in trouble."

"Yeah. I know. But even evil me?"

I take a moment to word this correctly, because it's a hard thing to accept, and probably even harder if you've been through what Theo has. "Evil you is still you," I say as gently as I can. "He actually thought he was helping me. The guy's not a monster. He's just a . . . slightly inferior version."

Theo sighs. "If you say so."

Silence falls between us. I keep staring at the door, willing Paul to suddenly appear on the other side and open it for me. Nothing happens.

The storm was getting worse. What if Paul's sub wasn't able to dock? What if he crashed like Theo and I did? Maybe they're both drowning, even now, or being crushed by the impossible pressure—

"Tell me one thing," Theo says.

I never stop staring at Paul's door. "Sure, okay. What?"

"This other Theo—he cost me my chance with you, didn't he?"

Stricken, I turn back toward Theo, who smiles at me unevenly.

"Because I did have a chance, didn't I? For a little while there? Could've sworn I did." He shrugs. "But now you're standing here looking at Paul's freakin' door the way I always used to wish you'd look at me."

A few months ago, if Theo had said something—would it have changed who I fell for? I don't know; I'll never know.

So I say only, "I'm sorry."

"Me too. But if I have to let somebody else have you, at least it's him." Theo nods toward the door.

And within that room, something moves.

I suck in a breath. Theo and I exchange glances, and then I call out, "Paul? Paul, are you in there?" Quickly I knock. "It's me. It's—"

The door opens, and my fist makes contact with Paul's chest.

In that first instant, I can't speak. I can only stare up at him as he slowly smiles. I launch myself into his arms. Paul hugs me back fiercely, like he never wants to let me go.

"Happy endings all around, almost," Theo says as he takes a couple of steps backward. "I'm going to head out, you guys."

"Theo?" Paul never lets go of me, but he looks over my shoulder, only slightly less happy about this second reunion. "It's really you?"

"The one and only," Theo says. "Accept no substitutes. Which I realize is easier said than done, these days." He sounds like his old self, and I have to grin.

Paul reaches one hand out to Theo, who clasps it in something that's more than a handshake—it looks like old paintings of Romans swearing allegiance to each other, swearing to die by each other's side. Their bond is too powerful to be destroyed by their feelings for me, or their rivalry.

But Theo can't keep up the pretense that it doesn't bother him, seeing us wrapped together like this. As he lets go of Paul and takes a few steps back, his smile is strained. "I'm gonna—I'm grabbing the good Dr. Kovalenka and the resurrected Dr. Caine and the soon-to-be-doctor Josephine and bringing them over this way. Soon we'll have the band back together."

I whisper, "Thank you, Theo."

"You crazy kids have fun," he says, and then he turns around to go.

For a moment we watch him leave—but then Paul pulls me into his room and closes the door.

As soon as he does, though, reality intrudes. Everything I know about Paul, everything I feel for him, is swallowed up in uncertainty. In the love I felt for Lieutenant Markov, who lies dead a universe away.

I don't say a word, but Paul understands. He takes a deep

breath as he steps slightly closer. "I'm not the one you loved. I know that."

"How can you know when I don't?"

He shakes his head, not denying what I'm saying but moving past it. "Something in us has to be the same, Marguerite. I know we both feel the same way about you. After the way you lost him, I don't expect you to—to rush into anything, to know your own heart right away. But I'd like for us to find out if what you felt . . . if it wasn't for him alone. If anything you felt was for me."

Some of it was. Is. I know that; I always have.

Paul says, "Will you give me a chance, Marguerite?"

I feel the smile spreading over my face, lighting me up inside. "Yeah," I whisper as I take his hand. "Oh, yeah."

ACKNOWLEDGMENTS

THIS BOOK COULD NOT HAVE BEEN WRITTEN WITHOUT Jordan Weaver (formerly my publicist in Australia); Dan Wells and Lauren Oliver (my partners on the book tour where I first thought of this concept); Diana Fox (my agent and destroyer of plot holes); Ruth Hanna, Edy Moulton, and Amy Garvey (beta readers and cheerleaders extraordinaire); Sarah Landis (my former editor at HarperTeen, whose input on the first draft was invaluable); Rodney Crouther, Jesse Holland, Whitney Swindoll Raju, and Eric O'Neill (for constant encouragement); Walter Wolf and Alexandra Mora (who recommended a book that wound up being inspirational); my parents and the rest of my family (for all their enthusiasm and encouragement); Kiersten White (for providing constant support); Florence Welch (of the Machine fame); and last but not least, Marina Frants (when you are writing a book that involves both Russia and oceanography, it is very helpful to have a friend who is both Russian and an oceanographer). Not all of the above people knew they were contributing—I feel sure Florence Welch is oblivious to her part in this— but each of them provided some critical element that went into *A Thousand Pieces of You*.

READ ON FOR A
SNEAK PREVIEW OF

NEW YORK TIMES BESTSELLING AUTHOR

CLAUDIA GRAY

1

THE FIRST TIME I TRAVELED TO ANOTHER DIMENSION, I intended to take a life. Now I'm trying to save one.

But I can't do that unless I save myself. At the moment, I'm running through the winding streets of a near-medieval Rome, trying not to get burned at the stake.

Welcome to the nonstop fun of traveling through alternate universes.

"She is the sorcerers' daughter!" someone from the mob shouts. "She bears the tools of their witchcraft!" Her voice echoes off the cobblestones, just like the jeers from the crowd around her. A few of them hold burning torches, the better to chase me through the night.

My parents are scientists, not sorcerers. In this universe, looks like nobody knows the difference.

What I'm carrying in the pockets of my robe or cloak or whatever you'd call this shapeless red thing—it's not witchcraft. It's a spyglass, a.k.a. a primitive handheld tele-scope. This six-inch-long gadget looks like a prop for steampunk cosplay: tortoiseshell sides, brass fittings, lenses ground by hand. But this might just be the tool that brings this dimension out of the Dark Ages—assuming it doesn't get my entire family killed first.

Panting, I dodge around every corner I come to, pay-ing no attention to where I'm going. It's not like I have any idea where I am anyway. When I leap into one of my other selves—the other Marguerites, who live in these parallel dimensions—I don't get to access their memories. Some of their knowledge and ability carries over, but those are only the deeper, no-longer-wholly-conscious things. Knowing where the hell I am in this version of Rome? No such luck.

All I know is that I have to get away. Finding the Castel Sant'Angelo—and Paul, who should be there—well, that has to wait until I'm safe.

Of course, I could escape this dimension at any moment, thanks to the heavy weight on a chain around my neck. To anyone in this dimension, and virtually anyone in ours, it would look like nothing more than a large, fairly elab-orate locket—if they even noticed it, which they probably wouldn't.

This isn't any old necklace. This doesn't belong in their reality. This is the Firebird.

The Firebird—the one and only device that allows human consciousness to travel through alternate dimensions. The invention of my mother, Dr. Sophia Kovalenka, with the help of my father, Dr. Henry Caine. The thing that can instantly transport my mind out of this universe completely and send me back to my own body, my own home, and safety. Even as I run through an alternate Rome in an ankle-length woolen dress and cloak, my stiff boots sliding against the rain-wet cobblestones on the road, I keep the Firebird clutched in one hand; if I lose this thing, I'm screwed.

But I won't go. I can't leave this dimension until I do what I came here to do.

I must save Paul Markov.

A couple more twists and turns through dark alleyways, and I finally manage to lose the mob. Although I can still hear murmuring and shouting in the distance, I have a moment to catch my breath. The frantic thumping of my heart begins to slow. My back is to a wall the color of terra-cotta; the only illumination comes from a few lanterns and candles visible through windows that have no glass. And, of course, the stars. I look upward, momentarily dazzled by how many more stars you can see in a sky unclouded by artificial light.

The view around me could have been taken from any one of a hundred early Italian paintings I've studied. This is a world without electricity, where only fire shows the way after dark. A cart pulled by a donkey rattles along in the distance, stacked high with bags of something, probably grain. Forget Wi-Fi, tablet computers, or airplanes—here, even steam engines are centuries away. It's not that I've traveled back in time, though; the Firebirds don't do that. But some dimensions develop faster, some slower. I've already been to futuristic worlds where everyone communicates by hologram and travels by hovership. It was only a matter of time before I reached one where the Renaissance is still in full swing.

Not that this is exactly the same as our Renaissance: The clothing looks more like tenth or eleventh century to me, and yet the telescope my parents have invented didn't come into being in our world until long after that. Also, somehow, there doesn't seem to be any old-fashioned gender roles in place, or any gender roles at all. The priest who condemned me to the mob was a woman. I'll cheer for equality later.

The man I spoke to told me I could find Paolo Markov of Russia at the Castel Sant'Angelo. I imagine Paul chained in a castle dungeon, being beaten or even tortured, and I want to cry.

This is no time for tears. Paul needs me. Crying can happen later.

And once I've handled everything else, I'll deal with Wyatt Conley.

The angry buzz of the crowd has faded. Where do I go now? I'm surrounded by dark, twisting alleys and a jumble of buildings filled with people I can't trust. They said the Castel Sant'Angelo was to the west, but which way is west? Without the sun in the sky for me to judge by, I can't guess what direction to go in. Still, I have to begin somewhere. One more deep breath, and I start toward a narrow street that leads down a seemingly quiet road—

—then gasp as a hand closes over my shoulder.

"Not that way," a woman whispers. A noblewoman, I realize, her face all but hidden under her blue velvet cloak. "They may gather near the Pantheon."

I don't know what that is, but if the mob is going to be there, I'll head in another direction. "Thanks."

(The above conversation? Not verbatim. Both my new friend and I are speaking what I have to assume is either late-stage Latin or early Italian. I don't know what it is exactly, but thanks to the deeply ingrained knowledge of this world's Marguerite, I speak it.)

"Your parents are leading us to wisdom," the noblewoman says gently. "The others fear what they do not understand."

She steps forward, just enough for some of the dim lighting to illuminate her face—thick golden hair, strong square jaw—and it's all I can do not to gape at her.

We've met before.

Her name is Romola. If I ever knew her last name, I've forgotten it. I encountered her in the very first alternate universe I ever visited: a futuristic London where she was the daughter of a duchess. Spoiled, rich, high on drugs, and drunk on champagne—Romola dragged me from nightclub to nightclub while I drank as much as she did. I was exhausted, afraid, and heartsick; it was only two days after the police told my family that my father had died. Dad turned out to be fine—well, if "fine" includes "kidnapped into an alternate dimension." But I didn't know that at the time. So those surreal, sick, miserable hours with Romola loom larger in my mind than they should. It seems like I

5

knew her forever, not just for one weird day.

I shouldn't be surprised to see her again. We've learned that people usually cross paths in many dimensions—that no matter how different the worlds may be, fate draws us together.

"Are you well?" Romola puts one hand to my forehead, like my mom did when I was little. "You seem dazed. No one could blame you, after what they've put you through."

"I'm fine. Really." I pull myself together for the rest of my escape. "I need to get to the Castel Sant'Angelo. Which way should I go?"

Romola gives me directions. Most of the landmarks she names are unknown to me (Via Flaminia?), but she points along the road. I thank her and wave as I start running again.

At home, I think I could run a few miles without getting winded. This Marguerite doesn't seem to get as much exercise. A stitch makes my gut clench; my breaths are coming too fast. Despite the cool air of early April, sweat slicks my skin. These thick woolen clothes feel as if they're loaded with weights. And my boots—let's just say shoemaking technology is a whole lot better at home. The blisters already swell at my heel and toes.

But I have to reach Paul as fast as I can. He could be in terrible danger—

Or he could be fine. Maybe he's one of the castle guards. He could even be a prince! You'll probably interrupt him at a banquet or something.

How long has he been here? We tried not to panic when

he hadn't returned to our dimension after twenty-four hours; after forty-eight hours, we all knew something was wrong. We got really afraid when we searched for him in the Triadverse and realized he'd left but hadn't come back home. Mom and Theo outdid themselves, coming up with a way to trace Paul's next leap, which was into this dimension.

Paul had no reason to come here. If he'd found what he was looking for—the cure for Theo—he would have come straight home. That was how we knew he'd been kidnapped. I haven't been able to sleep since.

Just get him back. We'll figure the rest out later—how to save Theo, how to defeat Triad. That can all wait until you bring Paul home.

I know the Castel Sant'Angelo as soon as I see it: an enormous stone structure at the top of a hill, lit by blazing torches. The firelight reveals the dull black gleam of cannons jutting from slots in the masonry. As I walk up, I see that the palace guards wear outfits simultaneously hilarious and intimidating: full striped breeches, brilliant yellow coats with puffy sleeves, metal breastplates and helmets, and swords that look like they could run through a human being in an instant. Although the soldiers come to attention as I step closer, obviously a winded teenage girl isn't their idea of a threat.

What if Paul's a prisoner here? I have no idea how the guards are going to react, but there's only one way to find out. A couple of deep breaths, and then I say as firmly as I can manage, "I've come to speak to Paul Markov of Russia."

The guards look at each other and say nothing. Crap. Should I have called him Paolo, the Italian version of the name? Or Pavel, the Russian version? Or maybe he is a prisoner—or he isn't actually here at all—

"Follow me," says one of the guards. "You can wait in the usual room."

The usual room? I have to stifle a smile as I follow them to a small, stone-walled chamber. Of course Paul and I know each other in this world too.

Always, we find each other.

In my world, Paul is one of my parents' research assistants as he works on his doctorate at Berkeley. For the first year and a half I knew him, I mostly thought he was strange: silent, awkward, too big for any room he was in. When he did speak, he was blunt. Most of the time he didn't speak at all. But as time went on, I began to realize that his bluntness wasn't him being rude or unkind—that instead it was a rough kind of honesty, sometimes hard to hear but always true. His awkwardness was only shyness, Paul's belief that he had never fit in anywhere and never would. And the way he hung around my parents' house wasn't because he had no life and nowhere else to go. It was because nobody had ever accepted him before. He'd never been around a family who cared about each other, never had a real friend before he met my parents' other assistant, Theo.

And he had never fallen in love before he knew me. He just didn't know how to say it.

I've visited a few dozen dimensions by now. Paul and I

have known each other in most of them; in many, we're already together. Fate and mathematics bring us to each other time after time. Paul's doctoral thesis presents a series of equations that prove destiny is real . . . but I don't need the math to convince me. I've seen it for myself so many times, beginning in a Russia where the tsars never fell.

For a moment I think of Lieutenant Markov, the Paul I knew there, and my throat tightens. But that's when a figure in a dark cloak appears in the stone archway of the room.

Paul steps forward, looking at me so sadly that I ache for him without even knowing why. "You know you should not have come," he says softly.

"I had to."

Bluffing your way through alternate dimensions can sometimes be tricky. When in doubt, remain silent as long as you can, and let the natives do the talking.

And right now I'm only speaking to this world's Paul. A few cues tip me off to the differences—subtle things anyone else might miss, like the way he walks, or his ease in this medieval chamber. My Paul's consciousness—his soul—must be within this body, but semiconscious, unable to act, unable to think, hardly even able to remember. For the time being, he's forgotten himself. That's what happens to most people when they travel through the dimensions: they become absorbed into their other selves, unable to escape, or even think that they should escape.

It's like a fairy tale in reverse. The prince is the one asleep in a glass coffin. I'm the one who'll awaken him.

If only a kiss would work.

Paul steps closer to me, and the flickering lanterns paint his face in golden light. He's a big man, almost intimidatingly so—six foot two and broad-shouldered. This version isn't as powerfully muscled, or maybe I just can't tell beneath the black robes he wears.

Wait. Are these *priest's robes*?

"I have prayed and prayed," Paul whispers. His gray eyes search mine, and I wish I didn't recognize how lost he looks. How alone. "Surely I cannot abandon the vows I made to God. And yet if he did not want me to marry as other men do—to feel desire, and love—why would he have brought me to you?"

Even without knowing any more of the story, this is enough to make me melt. This world's Marguerite must be as in love with him as he is with her, or else they wouldn't have had this conversation before. That makes it okay for me to say, "We're brought together by a power greater than either of us. Something bigger than our own world."

It's not just a romantic saying; it's scientific fact.

Paul breathes out heavily like a man struggling. I wonder what his life has been like here—born in Russia, surely. Back in the Middle Ages, lots of children were more or less given to the church when they were small, so they had no real choice about whether to enter the priesthood or convent or whatever; if Paul's already taken vows one month after his twentieth birthday, that must be what happened to him. Perhaps he traveled to Rome to serve the pope. Then he met the inventors' daughter, and everything changed.

I hope this world's Paul and Marguerite will get their chance to be together. At any other time, I'd be tempted to stay here longer and help if I could. For now, though, nothing matters as much as rescuing my Paul and bringing him home.

"Paul?" I step closer to him. The firelight catches the faint reddish tint in his pale brown hair. "Come here."

"We shouldn't," he says, like a man who desperately wishes we would.

"Not for that. It's all right." I lift my eyes to his and smile as gently as I can. "Trust me."

At that Paul straightens, nods, and closes the distance between us. It would be so easy to hold him, for him to put his arms around me—

—but instead, when my hand brushes against his chest, I feel metal under the cloth. I reach beneath the collar of his robes and pull out his Firebird.

He still has it? I'd brought a second one with me, believing Conley would have stolen Paul's. Maybe it's broken. That would explain a lot.

Paul stares at the necklace he just discovered hanging against his chest. To him it must have seemed to appear by magic. Obviously he can't imagine what I'm up to, but he remains silent, trusting me completely. That makes it a little harder to manipulate the Firebird controls into the combination for a reminder. Because reminders *hurt*.

Paul shouts in pain and jerks backward. But this is the part where my Paul wakes up inside him, when we're together again and we can go back home.

Except that the reminder doesn't work.

"Why did you do that?" Father Paul lifts the Firebird and frowns. "What manner of device hangs around my neck?"

He doesn't know. He really has no idea. Nothing like this has ever happened before. How could a reminder just . . . not work?

I run one hand through my curly hair, thinking fast. "It's my parents' latest invention. It wasn't supposed to hurt you—probably it's broken. Here, let me have it."

Paul hands it back, still trusting me, but now wary of the Firebird itself. I don't blame him. If only I were another science geek instead of the artist in the family, because then maybe I could fix this on my own. As it is, I might have to go home without Paul. Even though I know I could come back for him, maybe in only a few minutes, I can't bear the thought of losing him again.

You're the scientific wonder of the twenty-first century! I think as I look down at the Firebird. *How can you go dead on me now?* Maybe Conley broke it. But why bother breaking the Firebird when he could have stolen it for his own use?

The Firebird hasn't gone dead. It isn't broken. Every control reads normal. Yet when I double-check, I see that the Firebird is showing a reading I've never seen before.

Another man steps into the room, and my eyes go wide.

"Allow me to interpret it for you," he says with a smirk. "That's what splintering looks like."

His red robes look as if they belong in this strange medieval world, but his face is familiar. Too familiar.

Fate and mathematics don't only bring you back to the people you love. They can also bring you to the people you hate.

In this world, they brought me back to Wyatt Conley.

MARGUERITE'S STORY
CONTINUES IN . . .

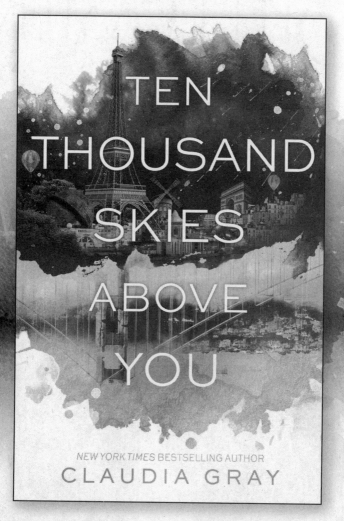

TEN
THOUSAND
SKIES
ABOVE
YOU

NEW YORK TIMES BESTSELLING AUTHOR
CLAUDIA GRAY

After Paul's soul is splintered into pieces—
pieces that are trapped within Pauls in other dimensions—
Marguerite and Theo must travel to the most
dangerous universes yet to save him.

DON'T MISS A SINGLE PAGE OF THE

SPELLCASTER

SERIES

JOIN THE

Epic Reads
COMMUNITY

THE ULTIMATE YA DESTINATION

◄ DISCOVER ►
your next favorite read

◄ MEET ►
new authors to love

◄ WIN ►
free books

◄ SHARE ►
infographics, playlists, quizzes, and more

◄ WATCH ►
the latest videos

◄ TUNE IN ►
to Tea Time with Team Epic Reads